SHE COULDN'T DISGUISE HER PASSION

"You did a good job, Casey," Dru said. "That's good cookin'. Glad you're aboard, son."

Taking the plate a little shakily, Cassandra dipped it into the sudsy water. Dru's proximity was unnerving and her heart began to beat rapidly. She had never known a man so handsome, so virile.

She went to the chuck wagon and hurried inside. Going to her pallet, she sat down and sighed despairingly. Pretending to be a boy was becoming more and more difficult. She was falling so deeply in love that she literally ached to be held in his arms.

She picked up her hand mirror and studied her reflection. If Dru were to see her unclothed, would he find her desirable? Or would he be so furious with her for deceiving him that he wouldn't care if she was attractive or not?

Cassandra wiped away a tear at the corner of her eye. Dru could never be hers, except in her dreams.

Good Did read Finished 9/16/95

ELUSIVE ENCHANTMENT
ROCHELLE WAYNE

ZEBRA BOOKS
KENSINGTON PUBLISHING CORP.

ZEBRA BOOKS

are published by

Kensington Publishing Corp.
850 Third Avenue
New York, NY 10022

Second Printing: May, 1995

Printed in the United States of America

For Lynn and Impressive

Chapter One

Cassandra Stevenson heaved a weary sigh, sat down on the porch step and gazed vacantly at the radiant sunset. The western sky was a brilliant red streaked with gold, but Cassandra was too deep in thought to notice nature's colorful painting. A small frown creased her brow as she wondered why her brother was so late returning from town. Surely he wasn't gambling! He had promised her faithfully that he would go straight to the general store, purchase the items on the list she had given him, then come back home.

Cassandra's frown deepened. She knew her brother's promise was worthless. Oh, when he'd made the promise, he had been sincere, but when it came to gambling, he was weak. He couldn't resist a game of poker any more than a man dying of thirst could turn down a drink of water.

She groaned inwardly as her vision flitted briefly over the fields that stretched as far as the eye could see . . . fields that even in the best of times had never been fully cultivated. But now even a smaller portion of the land was tilled, for she and her brother didn't have the financial means to plant more crops. Cassandra knew, depressingly, that even if they had the money to improve their land, her brother Russ lacked the initiative to make their farm flourish. He hated farming and all the work it entailed.

The Stevensons' home was falling apart, and there was nothing Cassandra could do about it. She wasn't sure just why she wanted to hold on to the run-down farm; she supposed it was because it was the only home she had ever known. She had been born here and during her twenty years of life had never lived anywhere else. Although the farm only produced a marginal living, it was still home and afforded a certain amount of security. However, taxes were due, and barring a miracle, there was no feasible way that she and Russ could come up with the amount needed.

Cassandra placed her elbows on her knees and cupped her chin in her hands. They were undoubtedly going to lose the farm; it was inevitable. That was a bitter pill to swallow, but she might as well accept it and go on from there. She considered her circumstances. She'd soon be homeless. The thought was gloomy, and she turned her musings to Russ. His dream was to go to San Francisco, and she knew if it wasn't for her, he'd have left for California a long time ago. But she was his unmarried sister, and he felt responsible for her. Well, if she married Silas Taylor, she'd not only free her brother but guarantee herself a home. Silas's farm was prosperous and his house was large and in good condition. She supposed she could do a lot worse. As Silas's wife, she'd have security and a comfortable place to live. Six months had passed since Silas had asked her to marry him, and, so far, she hadn't given him a definite answer. He had dropped by last night and had made it quite apparent that he was growing impatient. So she had promised that she'd have an answer for him soon.

She sighed despairingly. When she saw Silas again. she'd tell him that she'd marry him. What other logical choice did she have? Losing her home was unavoidable, and Russ had his heart set on San Francisco. Marrying Silas Taylor would solve everything.

Now that she had secured her future as well as her brothers', she wished she could feel somewhat elated. But Cassandra didn't foolishly try to delude herself. How could she possibly be ecstatic about marrying Silas when she wasn't in love with him? She respected him and was fond of him, but that was as far as her feelings went.

Sometimes love comes after marriage, she reminded herself, trying to bolster her spirits. So Silas Taylor wasn't the man of her dreams! Her dream lover, who had been created out of her romantic fantasies, probably didn't even exist. How could any man possibly be the perfect replica of the lover she had conjured up in her mind?

Cassandra's eyes took on a dreamy haze as the image of her fantasy lover flashed before her. His tall frame was lissome but discernibly strong, and his hair was jet black. Although his movements were graceful, he was so blatantly male that his mere presence could melt a woman's defenses. But it wasn't just his physical appearance that fascinated Cassandra, it was also his strong character. In her dream lover's embrace, she'd feel safe, passionately loved, and a woman in every sense of the word.

Suddenly, remembering she was heating bathwater, Cassandra banished the image of her make-believe lover from her thoughts. It was time to return to reality. She'd take a bath and go to bed; tomorrow she'd ride to Silas's home and give him her answer.

9

She rose slowly from the porch step, for marrying a man she didn't truly love was depressing. However, she swore solemnly that she'd make Silas a good wife and never give him cause to regret their union.

As Cassandra opened the screen door, it squeaked in protest and swung in its lopsided frame. She had told Russ weeks ago to put new hinges on the door, but he had neglected to do so. Well, she thought ill-temperedly, I don't care if it does fall off! Whoever buys this place can worry about it! Repairing the screen door will be the least of their problems!

She walked into the parlor and averted her eyes from its shabby appearance. The furniture was old and the upholstery was tearing in places; the draperies and rugs were also in poor condition. Although Cassandra kept the room immaculately clean, it was depressing nonetheless and she had no wish to view it as she headed for the kitchen.

The huge iron kettle, filled with steaming water, was on the wood stove. She moved quickly to the walk-in pantry, pulled out a round tub and dragged it to the center of the room.

It was early summer, and the temperature inside the kitchen was very warm. Summers in Arkansas were unbearably hot, and she was dreading the next few months. She wondered if Silas's house was as uncomfortably warm as this one. She doubted it, for it was newer and had been built with hot summers in mind. Unlike her own home, Silas's faced north and south, avoiding the sun's direct rays.

The Stevensons' house had been built by Cassandra's maternal grandfather, who had moved to Arkansas from Indiana and was unfamiliar with scorching southern summers. His wife had died when Cassandra's mother had been a baby, and he never remarried. He lived to be sixty, and when he passed away, the farm had gone to his daughter. She was a schoolteacher when she met and married Cassandra's father. Her husband, city-bred, was a poor farmer, and the Stevensons' homestead slowly deteriorated. When the War Between the States was declared, he left his wife and children to fight for the Confederacy. He was killed early in the war, and after hearing of his father's death, Russ joined the army, leaving his sister and mother alone on the farm. With hard work and a strong resilience, Cassandra and her mother survived the war-ravaged years. Six months after the war had been over, Cassandra and Russ's mother died of scarlet fever.

Now, wiping a hand across her perspiring forehead, Cassandra considered taking a cold bath, for it would be cooling. But she decided quickly to take a warm one, for she planned to wash her hair and it would come cleaner in heated water.

Her golden blond hair was bound into a tight bun, and as she removed the pins, the long tresses cascaded gracefully past her shoulders in their full, silky radiance.

Cassandra Stevenson was strikingly beautiful, her tall, supple frame softly curvaceous. Her large eyes, a perfect jade green, were accentuated by naturally arched brows and long lashes.

She reached behind her back to release the buttons on her plain gingham gown, but at the sound of footsteps crossing the parlor, she called out, "Russ, is that you?"

"It's me," he replied, reaching the closed door to the kitchen. "Are you in the tub?"

"No, not yet. You can come in."

He was smiling broadly as he entered the kitchen.

11

"Sis, I have fantastic news!"

Unaffected by his apparent elation, she asked sharply, "Russ, why are you so late? Were you gambling again?"

He brushed his fingers through his thick blond hair, a gesture he always used when he was excited about something. His hazel eyes shone brightly as he remarked, "Yes, I was gambling! I played poker with Jubal Thurston, and I won three hundred dollars!" Slipping a hand into his pocket, he withdrew a folded stack of bills. Waving them through the air, he exclaimed. "Just look at all this money!"

Cassandra was apprehensive. "You played poker with Jubal Thurston?"

Shoving the money back into his pocket, he asked her, "Why do you look so worried? I should think you'd be estatic."

"Well, I'm pleased that you won," she stammered. "But . . . but Jubal and his brothers are mean and dangerous. I don't trust the Thurstons. I'm afraid Jubal will try to get even with you."

Cassandra despised the Thurston brothers, and when in town, she always tried to avoid them. They were ex-Union soldiers, and although the war had been over for two years, they still flaunted their victory and their hate for Southerners.

"What can Thurston do?" Russ asked archly. "I won his money fair and square."

She was about to answer when she heard the screen door squeak. "Someone's here," she said, feeling a little frightened.

Russ was unarmed, for he'd left his rifle on his horse. But he wasn't unduly alarmed. "It's probably Silas."

"What if it's Jubal Thurston?" Cassandra gasped,

12

and the words had barely passed her lips when the man's strong frame filled the doorway.

Furious, Russ demanded, "What the hell do you want, Thurston?"

Inching his way into the room, he answered in a hard tone, "I want my money back."

"I won your money honestly!" Russ remarked, enraged. "Get out of my home, and don't come back!"

Listening, Cassandra's frightened eyes went to Thurston. He was an attractive man, his frame tall and muscular. His chestnut hair was curly with soft ringlets falling boyishly about his forehead, and his clean-shaven face was handsome. Thurston, conceited, relished his good looks.

Jubal drew his holstered pistol and aimed it at Russ. "Hand over the money."

Moving with incredible speed, Russ's arm shot out, knocking the gun from Thurston's hand. Lunging, Stevenson's body collided with Jubal's, sending them both crashing to the floor.

Thurston was the stronger, and with relative ease, he managed to escape Russ's hold, knock him to the side and leap to his feet. The gun was within his reach, but it was also within Cassandra's, and they grabbed for it simultaneously; however, he was quicker.

Grasping the pistol, Jubal once again pointed it at Russ. His expression furious, his eyes radiating hate, he said with deadly intent, "You goddamned Johnny Rebel, I'm gonna blow you to hell!"

"If you kill him, you'll hang!" Cassandra cried desperately.

Jubal laughed gruffly. "Who's gonna hang me? The town's run by Yankees; even the sheriff fought for the Union. Hang? Hell, I'll be rewarded for getting rid of a damned murdering rebel!"

Cassandra's heart sank. She knew Thurston was right. Following the war, the small town of Clarksville had been taken over by Yankees. It was close to the Texas border, which enhanced its appeal.

"Please!" Cassandra pleaded. "Don't kill him!" Her gaze flew to her brother, who was getting slowly to his feet. "Russ, for God's sake, give him his money!"

Stevenson was too angry to take heed. "Thurston, you son of a bitch!"

A cold, murderous grin came to Jubal's face. "Stevenson, you just signed your death warrant. No man calls me a son of a bitch and lives to talk about it!"

Meanwhile, Cassandra, knowing that the man would carry out his threat, looked frantically about the room, hoping to spot something she could use for a weapon. As her frenzied gaze centered on the steaming kettle, she stepped furtively to the stove.

Jubal, unaware of Cassandra's maneuver, was saying to Russ, "After I kill you, I'm gonna rape your sister. She's the prettiest little Southern bitch in these parts, and I'm sure gonna enjoy getting between her legs."

Now, blinded by rage, Russ started to leap at Thurston, but reading his intent, Jubal drew back the hammer on his Colt revolver.

Thurston was about to pull the trigger when Cassandra, having removed the kettle from the stove, rushed to his side and doused him with the hot, scalding water. Most of the liquid splashed on the left side of his face, and screaming with pain, Thurston dropped his pistol.

Retrieving the gun, Russ stepped quickly to the

14

injured man, who was now on his knees, his hands covering his face. Deep, agonized moans shook his body as he rocked back and forth.

Helping him to his feet, Russ said anxiously, "God! I need to get you to a doctor!"

Pulling away, Thurston kept his hands over his face as he muttered viciously, "So help me God, you and your sister are gonna die!" He stumbled to the doorway, turned about and, letting his hands drop to his sides, glared at Cassandra. The horrible sight of his red, blistering face caused her to gasp.

"You damned bitch!" Jubal thundered furiously. "If I'm scarred, when I'm finished with you you're gonna be beggin' me to kill you and get you out of your misery!"

Suffering excruciating pain, Thurston swayed unsteadily for a moment; then, regaining his balance, he left the kitchen and tottered through the parlor and outside. Mounting his horse clumsily, he spurred the steed into a fast canter and headed for town. He'd get even with Stevenson and his goddamned sister! He'd make that bitch pay, if it was the last thing he ever did in his life!

Cassandra felt numb, but as Thurston was riding away from the house, she was suddenly struck with what she had done. "Oh, God, Russ!" she cried. "I didn't want to scald him, but he was going to kill you!"

Taking her into his arms, Russ held her close. "It's all right, honey."

"He'll be back!" she sobbed. "And he'll have his five brothers with him! Russ, they'll kill us!"

"No, they won't," he answered crisply, releasing her. "When they get here, we'll be gone. Hurry and pack clothes for both of us and add some provisions.

15

I'll hitch up the wagon."

"Where are we going?" she asked with a gasp.

"We'll head into Texas."

"And then what?"

"We'll keep headin' westward until we reach San Francisco. Maybe we'll come upon a wagon train and can join up with it." He patted the bills in his pocket. "At least we aren't broke."

"Oh, Russ!" she said uncertainly. "It sounds awfully dangerous!"

"Not as dangerous as staying here and waiting for the Thurstons."

She conceded to reason. "I'll pack our clothes and provisions."

An hour later, Cassandra was sitting on the wagon seat beside her brother. Russ had attached the old canvas covering, and their belongings were packed safely beneath, away from the elements. Russ's horse, young and spirited, was tied to the backboard, but the two mules pulling the wagon were getting on in years, and Russ knew he'd have to buy another team as soon as they had traveled a safe distance from the Arkansas-Texas border. He also planned to purchase a sturdy wagon, for this one was in poor condition. However, first things first: He had to put a good distance between them and the Thurston brothers.

As Russ slapped the reins against the mules, setting the rickety wagon into motion, Cassandra scooted to the far side of the seat and looked back at the old homestead. She had a feeling that she was seeing it for the last time. Although it had never been a grand home, it was nonetheless her haven, and as

16

she looked at it for the last time, tears filled her eyes.

Sensing her mood, Russ said cheerfully, "Sis, don't feel sad about leaving this damned farm. I have a feeling that this will all prove to be a blessing in disguise. Honey, we're about to embark on a better and more prosperous life."

Despite Jubal's threat, Russ's spirits were high. He would have made this move to San Francisco a long time ago if he'd had three hundred dollars and Cassandra's approval.

By now the house had faded into the dark shadows of night, and wiping away the last trace of tears, Cassandra turned about in the seat. She sighed deeply, but said with a undertone of humor, "Russ, you're such an optimist. We have exactly three hundred and twenty dollars to our name, a wagon that is about to fall apart, a pair of old mules, and the Thurston brothers hot on our heels, and you say we're about to embark on a better life."

"What do you mean, three hundred and twenty dollars?"

She smiled. "Well, I had twenty saved from the household expenses."

He patted her hand. "See? Things are already looking up. We're richer than I thought we were." His hazel eyes twinkled mischievously.

Caught up in his enthusiasm, she said with an inward smile, "Well, I guess Silas will have to marry someone else."

He became serious. "I'm sorry, Cassandra. Do you love him a lot?"

She shrugged. "No, not really."

He quirked a brow. "Will you take some good advice from your older brother?"

She nodded.

"Don't marry a man unless you're head over heels in love with him."

"How will I know if I'm head over heels in love?"

He chuckled. "You'll know! Believe me, you'll know!"

She moved closer to Russ and tucked her arm into his. Their flight was perilous, and she couldn't help but feel frightened. She looked around at the familiar countryside. It would soon be gone, and then they'd be surrounded by strange terrain. What unknown dangers awaited them? How many hardships were they destined to encounter? What if they didn't meet up with a wagon train and were forced to travel across hostile lands alone? Envisioning a band of Indian warriors chasing their wagon across a desolate plain made her shudder inwardly.

Although Cassandra could only imagine what lay ahead, she knew what lay behind. Jubal Thurston and his brothers!

18

Chapter Two

"The damned axle is broken!" Russ, his temper getting the better of him, kicked the wagon's cracked wheel.

"Can it be fixed?" Cassandra asked hopefully.

Still furious, Russ snapped, "Yeah, if I could get it to a blacksmith's!" He had no idea how far they were from the nearest town but was sure that it was probably several miles away.

The sun was dipping into the west, and Cassandra suggested, "I guess we may as well camp here for the night; then in the morning . . ." Her voice faded. What would they do tomorrow? Leave the wagon? What other choice did they have? They had been traveling for more than two weeks, and due to the rickety wagon, the arduous journey had been agonizingly slow. By now Jubal and his brothers were probably dangerously close.

Russ began unhitching the team. "I wish we had another horse," he muttered grumpily. "But at least we have these two mules. We can use one to carry provisions, and you can ride the other one. When we reach the next town, we'll buy another wagon, a fresh team, and an extra horse." He silently cursed himself for not taking care of the matter sooner. But he had thought it wiser to bypass towns in case the Thurstons might be stopping along the way and asking questions.

Cassandra didn't say anything, but she knew such a purchase would take a large part of their money. She went to the wagon, climbed inside and gathered up what she'd need to cook supper.

She was wearing a pair of Russ's trousers and one of his shirts, so she moved with ease as she left the wagon. She was also wearing an old wide-brimmed hat, and her long blond hair was tucked up beneath it. Because the setting sun was still shining brightly, she left the hat on as she hunted for firewood. They were in a fertile area and kindling was plentiful.

As she built the campfire, Russ, watching her, began to chuckle.

"What's so funny?" she asked.

Walking over to sit beside her, he said, "With my clothes on, and your hair hidden under that hat, you look like a boy."

Cassandra let his remark pass. She didn't care if she did look like a boy. Traveling in a long dress had not only been uncomfortable, but also a hindrance, and this morning she had discarded her own clothes for her brother's.

Russ continued to watch his sister. He was very proud of her, for she was holding up remarkably well. In his opinion, she was a real trooper. He was about to voice his thoughts when the sound of a horse approaching sent him bounding to his feet. He hurried to the wagon and grabbed his rifle.

He had the weapon cocked and ready to fire as the lone horseman rode into camp. Eyeing the rifle, the stranger said cordially, "I'm not lookin' for trouble, mister. I spotted your campfire and thought maybe you'd offer me a cup of coffee. My name's Virgil

Jensen."

Cautiously, Russ lowered the rifle.

"Mind if I get down?" the man asked.

"You're welcome to a cup of coffee, but I'll have to ask you to leave your gun belt on your horse."

Virgil smiled, unbuckled his holster and swung it about the saddle horn. Dismounting, he remarked, "You're kind of distrustful of strangers, aren't you?" He didn't give Russ a chance to reply. "Well, I don't blame you. In these parts, a man can't be too careful."

Cassandra, pulling the brim of her hat low on her forehead, studied the stranger as he ambled over toward her and the campfire. He appeared to be in his late fifties, but his strong, tight-muscled build belied his years. He was a nice-looking man, and his dark beard was well groomed. Cassandra looked into his blue eyes and saw a twinkling warmth in them that made her take an instant liking to him.

Reaching the campfire, Virgil sat down, and his gaze met Cassandra's. Nodding at the simmering coffeepot, he asked, "Is it all right, son, if I help myself?"

Son! Cassandra inhaled sharply. My goodness, he had mistaken her for a boy!

Russ, joining them, had heard Jensen. Deciding it might be best if the man didn't know that Cassandra was really a beautiful young woman, he said quickly, "Help yourself, sir." He sat down beside Virgil. "By the way, my name is Russ Stevenson." He gestured across the fire at Cassandra. "And this is my younger brother." His eyes looked pointedly into Cassandra's.

"What's you name, son?" Virgil asked, pouring a cup of coffee.

"Cas . . ." Catching her near blunder, she paused

21

abruptly. Then, thinking quickly and lowering her voice, she muttered, "Casey. My name's Casey."

Jensen glanced at the broken axle. "Looks like you've got a serious problem. Where are you two headed?"

"Westward," Russ answered. "We had a farm outside of Clarksville, but lost it to back taxes. So we decided to head west."

Virgil laughed good-naturedly. "Seems to me that you and your brother should've made better plans before takin' off. Don't you realize there's dangerous terrain ahead? The farther west you travel, the more hostile it becomes."

"We didn't have much choice," Russ answered. "We were homeless."

Virgil studied Russ thoughtfully for a moment. "I've got a trail drive a little ways back. My nephew and I are takin' a herd of horses to Fort Laramie. We're shorthanded and could use another wrangler. I'll give you a job if you want one, and then when we reach the fort, you and Casey can join up with a wagon train. If you're determined to go west, it's a lot safer to travel with a large group. Your brother can work on the chuck wagon. Our cook could use the extra help."

Russ knew this was a great opportunity. They'd not only get to Fort Laramie, where they could join a wagon train, but, more importantly, Thurston would never look for them on a trail drive. A worried frown furrowed his brow. But what about Cassandra? Jensen had mistaken her for a boy, but that didn't mean he wouldn't eventually catch on to her disguise. And then there were the other wranglers to consider. If they were to learn that Cassandra was a woman, would she be in danger? No, he decided quickly. Like

22

his sister, he had taken an immediate liking to Virgil, and he was sure the man wouldn't let any harm come to a woman. Their dismissal was the worst that could happen.

Meanwhile, Cassandra's thoughts were coinciding with Russ's. She felt that Virgil Jensen was a godsend. On a trail drive they would be safe from Jubal and his brothers.

Growing impatient with their silence, Virgil insisted, "Well? Do you two want work or not?"

"Yes, sir!" Cassandra spoke up at once, remembering to keep her voice an octave lower.

Virgil finished his coffee, put down his cup and looked at Russ. "How do you feel about it?"

"I accept the job gratefully, Mr. Jensen."

"Good," he remarked, standing. "About two hours after sunrise, the herd will pass right by here. Be ready. You can join up with us then. You'll have to leave your wagon and belongings. We travel light on a trail drive, so don't bother to pack anything except for a change of clothes. I need to get back. I left hours ago to scout around, and if I don't get back before too much longer, Dru will be out searchin' for me. Dru's my nephew. We have a ranch farther south. The horses we're takin' to the army were rounded up in Mexico." He eyed Russ directly. "These are wild horses, young fellow. So keep that in mind when you're herdin' 'em."

"I will, Mr. Jensen." Russ stood and offered the man his hand.

"Call me Virgil," he said, grasping Stevenson's hand and shaking it firmly. He glanced at Cassandra. "See you in the mornin', son."

He walked swiftly to his horse, mounted, tipped his weatherworn hat and said, "Thanks for the coffee. Get a good night's sleep. Herdin' horses is a full day's work."

With that, he slapped the reins against his steed and rode away, disappearing quickly into the surrounding vegetation.

Russ was suddenly plagued with second thoughts. "Cassandra, maybe we shouldn't go through with this. Passing you off as a boy isn't going to be easy."

Going to her brother's side, she clutched his arm. "Joining this trail drive is the best choice we have. You know as well as I do that we can't outrun the Thurstons."

"If they're following us, they'll find our wagon and signs of a herd passing through."

"Yes, but they'll never dream that we're with the trail drive. They'll think that we simply abandoned the wagon and are riding to the nearest town."

"But I'm sure the Thurstons know how to read tracks."

"After that herd passes through, there'll be no distinguishable tracks."

"I suppose you're right."

"You know I'm right!" she said strongly. "Tonight I'll practice lowering my voice and moving more like a boy. My disguise is important. If Mr. Jensen knew I was a woman, he certainly wouldn't have offered us a job. I'm sure women aren't welcome on a trail drive."

Russ warned a little hesitantly, "Sis, those cowboys are going to think you're a boy, so they aren't going to curb their language or their manners. You're liable to hear and see things that—"

"I understand, Russ," she interrupted. "But I'm not a shrinking violet, nor am I fainthearted. I'll survive."

His eyes filled with pride, he murmured, "You're

one helluva woman. And I'm glad you didn't marry Silas. He isn't the kind of man who would appreciate your qualities."

"And what kind of man would?" she asked pertly.

"One with the same strong qualities." He reached over and removed her hat. As her golden tresses fell softly past her shoulders, he said with concern, "When we join the trail drive, remember to keep this hat on snugly, for if it were to fall off . . ."

Russ was surprised when Cassandra suddenly rushed to the wagon and climbed inside. Returning after a moment, she handed him a pair of scissors. "I packed my sewing kit, and these were inside it."

He looked at the scissors resting in the palm of his hand. "Surely you don't want me to—to cut your hair?"

"You must," she replied.

He shook his head. "But, Cassandra, your hair is so beautiful."

"It'll grow back," she remarked brightly, although she hated having her hair cut.

She took a seat at the fire, and Russ knelt behind her. For a moment he admired his sister's blond tresses. Then, dreading his task, he sighed heavily as he clipped a radiant strand.

As her golden curls fell to the ground with feathery softness, Cassandra wondered sullenly how she'd look with a boy's haircut.

Cassandra spent the night inside the wagon, and waking early, she sat up, reached for her hand mirror and looked at her reflection. She had hoped that this morning she'd find her haircut a little less shocking.

A deep frown creased her brow as she continued to

study herself. She ran her fingers through her short-cropped locks, sighed heavily and placed the mirror aside. I look dreadful! she thought glumly. Oh, well, cutting my hair was necessary, she reminded herself, lifting her spirits. If Jubal Thurston were to find me, I wouldn't have to worry about my hair, but my life!

She dressed quickly, slipping into her trousers, shirt and an old pair of Russ's boots. For a man, Russ had small feet and hands, and by wadding a sock in the toe of each boot, Cassandra was able to make them fit fairly well. She knew her neck looked too feminine, so she tied a bandanna about it loosely, concealing her smooth alabaster flesh. She also put on a pair of gloves, for her long slender hands certainly didn't look like a boy's. She realized she couldn't wear the gloves all the time, but surely if she rubbed a little dirt in her hands, they'd seem less like a woman's.

Grabbing her hat, she climbed down from the wagon and looked about the grassy area; spotting a patch of bare earth, she hurried over. Kneeling, she removed her gloves and smeared her hands with dirt, remembering to rub a little of it over her face.

She was so busy that she didn't hear Russ walking up behind her. "What are you doing?" he asked.

Startled, Cassandra leapt to her feet. "My skin's too feminine, and I'm trying to camouflage it."

Russ laughed lightly. "Virgil won't want you working in the chuck wagon with dirt all over you."

"I don't look that dirty, do I?"

He perused her thoughtfully. "No, the dirt's pretty well rubbed in."

"But do I look like a boy?" she asked intensely.

"You know, you just might get by with it if it weren't for . . ." His eyes were centered on her

26

bosom.

Cassandra blushed. How could she have overlooked something so obvious?

"I have an idea," Russ suggested. "Tear up a sheet and bind yourself."

She moved away quickly and returned to the wagon. Minutes later, when she emerged and joined Russ for coffee, the fullness of her breasts was completely hidden.

They were on their second cups of coffee when they heard the thundering of horses hooves. The herd was soon in sight, and Cassandra was amazed by its size. She had never seen so many horses at one time. She supposed there must be hundreds of them.

Cutting away from the herd, Virgil rode into their camp. Remaining mounted, he asked, "Are you two ready?"

They had packed their clothes last night and had the bags tied on one of the mules. "We're ready," Russ answered. He gestured toward the two mules. "I'll have to bring them along. I can't just leave them here."

Virgil agreed. "Mount up and take your mules to the chuck wagon." He looked at Cassandra and offered her his hand. "Casey, mount up behind me."

Remembering to look somewhat ungainly, she grasped Virgil's hand and swung up onto his horse. She was about to wrap her arms about his waist, but then reconsidered. A boy wouldn't hold on to another man, would he?

Virgil's horse took off with a bolt, and Cassandra came close to falling. She hoped it wouldn't take too long to reach the chuck wagon, for the horse's gait was jolting and her balance was precarious.

She had thought that Virgil would circle the herd,

and when he headed his horse straight into their midst, Cassandra forgot about behaving as a boy and laced her arms securely about the man's waist.

Chuckling, Virgil asked, "Are you scared, son?"

"No, sir," she managed to reply in a voice that didn't tremble. "Just cautious."

Glancing over her shoulder, Cassandra was relieved to see that Russ was wisely circling the herd. She watched, wide-eyed, as Virgil expertly guided his steed through the mass of wild horses. She envisioned herself falling and being trampled to death. Finding the possibility horrifying, she quickly banished the picture from her mind, held on dearly and shut her eyes.

It took only a few minutes for them to make their way through the herd and to the chuck wagon, but to Cassandra it seemed interminably long.

Reining in, Virgil told Cassandra to jump down. Doing so, she hoped she wouldn't fall flat on her rear. Luck was with her, and she landed solidly on her feet.

A short, bristly-bearded man was standing beside the wagon, and Cassandra looked at him briefly, then turned back to her new boss.

Remaining on his horse, Virgil said, "Casey, I've got some disturbin' news. Last night when I returned to camp, I found out that our cook quit. Without any warnin', he packed up his bag and took off for Mexico. Which means you and I are gonna have to do the cookin'. I'm not much of a cook, and I kinda doubt if you are. But, somehow, I'm sure we'll manage." He waved a hand tersely toward the man beside the wagon. "This is Pete. He's gonna teach you how to handle a team. This wagon is drawn by six horses, and you're gonna have to learn how to control 'em.

Driving the chuck wagon will be one of your duties."

Cassandra, keeping her face impassive, swallowed nervously. Drive a six-horse team? Her only experience along these lines consisted of handling two old mules. She cast a quick glance at the six horses and was slightly unnerved to see that they were a far cry from sluggish mules.

Virgil continued. "I won't see you again until we set up camp for the night. Then, together, we'll see if we can't conjure up something fittin' to eat."

"What about lunch?" she inquired.

"We don't stop for lunch. That's why the men always eat a large breakfast and an even larger supper."

No lunch! Cassandra cringed inwardly. This morning she had been too apprehensive to eat breakfast, and she knew that by dinnertime she'd be starved.

Virgil turned his attention to Pete. "When Casey's brother gets here, have him tie his mules to the wagon. Then tell him to ride out and find me so I can put him to work."

Without further ado, Virgil slapped the reins against his horse's neck and took off.

Shortly thereafter, Russ arrived, carried out his instructions and left.

Cassandra followed Pete up onto the wagon seat. He didn't seem to be in a hurry to teach her how to handle the team, for he took up the reins.

The chuck wagon always trailed the herd at a distance and as Pete guided the wagon to its place, Cassandra watched him thoughtfully, paying close attention to the way in which he controlled the team.

Pete, totally relaxed, allowed the multiple reins to rest loosely in his hands. They rode in silence for a while; then the man asked good-naturedly, "You don't talk much, do you?"

"I'm usually kinda quiet," she mumbled.

"Ever worked on a trail drive before?"

"No," she replied.

"It's hard work, but the Jensens pay good wages."

"Jensens?" She questioned the plural.

"Virgil's nephew is his partner."

Now Cassandra remembered Virgil's mentioning a nephew. He had said that his name was Dru.

"What's the nephew like?" She hoped he was as nice as his uncle.

"Dru's a fair man and a good boss. All the hands like 'im. You do right by 'im, and he'll do right by you. But Dru ain't no man to cross. Can be as mean as a rattlesnake when he's riled."

She wondered apprehensively what this man would do if he were to learn that she was a woman. He's as mean as a rattlesnake, Pete had said. Cassandra could feel sudden nervous perspiration beading on her brow.

"Well, kid," Pete drawled, "I reckon it's 'bout time to start teachin' you how to handle the team. It ain't too hard, you just got to let 'em know who's boss."

Cassandra had a sinking feeling that it wasn't as simple as Pete made it sound. Nonetheless, girding herself for action, she reached over and took the reins.

Chapter Three

Cassandra was fatigued; she had never felt so completely drained. Learning to handle the spirited team had been tiring, but the work that followed proved to be even more exhausting. As soon as they had set up camp, Virgil had informed her that they had to cook supper for twenty-five hungry men. When her new boss had told her that he wasn't much of a cook, he hadn't been putting it mildly. It didn't take Cassandra long to realize that if the meal was going to be worth eating, she'd have to prepare it herself.

Virgil, pleased to learn that Casey was an adequate cook, gladly withdrew his assistance and gave his young employee full charge.

Later, when the hands came in from tending to the herd, they were delighted to find that the new cook was a lot better than the one that had quit. They ate with gusto, and between mouthfuls of food, complimented the lad on a job well done.

Behaving like a boy, Cassandra accepted their exultant praises reluctantly, giving the impression that she'd rather be doing a man's work. Inwardly, however, she was pleased that they liked her cooking. During the meal she and Russ shared several secret, amused glances.

Everyone had finished eating when Virgil's nephew

31

came into camp. Cassandra was busy washing dishes and was unaware of the man's arrival until she heard him ask his uncle if supper was worth eating.

Smiling broadly, Virgil assured him that the meal was delicious. Knowing his uncle wasn't much of a cook, Dru voiced his skepticism.

Meanwhile, as the two men were bantering, Cassandra had turned away from her chore to get a good look at her other boss. Her eyes widened incredulously. She felt as though she were seeing her dream lover! The man's likeness was uncanny! His tall, lissome frame was blatantly strong, and although he was wearing a hat, it was pushed back from his brow and she could see that his hair was jet black. He sported a trim mustache the same color as his hair, and when he suddenly glanced in her direction, she looked into a pair of eyes that were brilliantly blue.

Dru, thinking her a lad, merely gave her a cursory glance, nodded tersely and returned his attention to his uncle. "So the boy's a good cook, eh?"

"Find out for yourself," Virgil replied. Taking a plate, he filled it with savory stew and handed it to him.

Sitting down at the fire, Dru began to eat. Finding the fare tasty, he quickly cleaned his plate and helped himself to seconds.

Pleased, Cassandra went back to her chore, giving it her full concentration. She was about through when, unexpectedly, Dru was at her side, handing her his plate.

"You did a good job, kid. How did you learn to cook like this?"

Taking the plate a little shakily, Cassandra dipped it into the sudsy water. Dru's proximity was unnerving, and her heart began to beat rapidly. Turning away from his piercing blue eyes, she muttered in her boyish voice, "When Ma died, I had to do all the cookin' for myself and my brother."

Dru grinned warmly, offered Cassandra his hand and said, "Glad to have you aboard, son."

She wiped her soapy hand on her pants leg, then received his friendly shake.

Entranced, Cassandra watched him closely as he walked back to the campfire. She had never seen a man so ruggedly handsome, so obtrusively virile!

Trying unsuccessfully to clear Dru from her mind, she returned to her work. She was soon finished and was looking forward to retiring when Virgil told her to gather up some firewood for the morning.

She accepted the added chore somewhat gratefully for it would give her the opportunity to go off alone. She needed the privacy afforded by bushes.

They were camped close to a shallow river, and she slipped into the dense foliage that grew along the water's edge. Then, noticing ample kindling spread about, she began gathering it. Her arms loaded, she was about to head back for camp when, to her dismay, Dru seemed to appear out of nowhere.

She was grateful that the darkness of night shadowed her face, for his mere presence had brought a blush to her cheeks. When she saw that he carried a towel, a bar of soap and a change of clothes, her blush deepened. My goodness, he was planning to take a bath! She had to get away, and fast!

Holding the kindling precariously, she made a move to brush past him, but he detained her. "What's your hurry, kid? Stick around; I want to talk to you."

"I . . . I need to get back to camp."

He placed his belongings on the grassy bank. "I plan to take a bath." Cassandra had washed her

33

hands thoroughly before starting dinner, but a thin layer of dirt still coated her face. Noticing this, Dru added, "You could use a bath yourself."

She swallowed nervously. "I might take one later, but I still got work to do."

"What's your name, son?" Dru began unbuttoning his shirt.

"Casey," she mumbled. She lowered her eyes and stared down at the ground. Oh, Lord, she must get out of here! The man was undressing!

"How old are you?" He had removed his shirt and was now unbuckling his gun belt.

"Just turned thirteen," she answered, keeping her eyes downcast.

"You're kinda puny for thirteen. You need to put some meat on your bones."

"All of us Stevensons are small-boned." She tried to will her legs to move, but they seemed as heavy as lead. I must leave! she told herself. I can't just stand here while he strips down to nothing! She managed a shaky step, but he placed a hand on her shoulder, halting her retreat.

"Virgil said that you and your brother aim to go to California. What do you two plan to do when you get there?" He laid his holster beside his shirt.

"I . . . I don't know," she stammered.

He sat down and tugged at his boots. "Damn! These can be a bitch to get off. Would you mind helping me?"

She gulped. "Help you?"

"Yeah. Put down that kindling."

Kneeling, she did as he requested. Her heart was thumping irregularly, and her hands were shaking so badly that she had to clasp them together.

When she didn't move, he asked a little gruffly,

34

"What's wrong with you, kid? Are you gonna help me or not?"

"Yes, sir," she answered, her voice almost inaudible. Standing, she stepped in front of him, and, once again, froze.

Impatient, Dru grumbled, "Turn around."

Doing so, she leaned over and grasped his outstretched foot. Grabbing a firm hold on the boot, she tugged ruthlessly. A silent gasp caught in her throat when he placed his other foot on her behind and shoved. The boot came off easily. The procedure was then repeated, and when both boots had been removed, she went back to her kindling. She planned to pick up the wood quickly and make her departure without further ado.

But, apparently, Dru still wanted to talk. Getting to his feet and undoing his trousers, he asked, "Did you have much trouble handling the team?"

"Team?" she echoed vacantly. If only he would let her leave!

Dru eyed her thoughtfully. The lad sure wasn't much of a conversationalist. "Virgil told me that Pete was teachin' you to drive the wagon."

"That's right," she mumbled, piling the kindling into her arms.

"Well?" he persisted testily.

Holding onto the wood and standing, she asked hesitantly, "Well, what?"

"Did you have trouble handling the team?" he repeated impatiently. Moving quickly, he took off his trousers.

Cassandra blushed effusively, but Dru was too occupied with discarding the rest of his clothing to notice.

"No . . . no, I didn't have any . . . trouble," she

35

replied, stumbling over her words. She stared into his face, not daring to drop her gaze.

"That's good," he answered. He grabbed the bar of soap and headed swiftly toward the river.

It took a while for Cassandra to regain her ability to move, during which time she watched, fascinated, as Dru waded into the water. She had never seen a man fully unclothed, and the sight of his masculinity aroused a desire in her that she'd never felt before. She was flushed, and an intense longing was flowing through her with a feverish force.

Then, regaining her mobility, she held securely to the firewood and headed back to camp on unsteady legs.

Russ was waiting for her. "What took you so long?" he asked. Seeing that she was flushed, he went on anxiously, "Are you all right?"

"I'm fine," she mumbled, placing the kindling beside the wagon.

Russ wasn't convinced, but he decided to let the matter rest. He gestured toward his bedroll and the one beside it. "I placed your blankets next to mine." He was speaking quietly, for several of the wranglers were already in their bedrolls. Russ had placed his and Cassandra's a short ways from the others', yet close enough not to draw suspicion.

She followed her brother over to their beds and lay down. Pulling the top blanket up to her chin, she told Russ good night, then rolled over onto her side. Despite her fatigue, thoughts of Dru had her wide awake. She closed her eyes, and a vision of Dru came to mind. She couldn't recall ever seeing a man as attractive as Dru Jensen. Remembering, vividly, everything that had transpired between them, she once again grew flushed. However, a tiny and mischievous smile played across her lips as she tried to imagine how Dru would react if he knew he had undressed in front of a woman. Would he be embarrassed? Suddenly her smile vanished. No, he probably wouldn't be in the least embarrassed, but most likely would be outraged. She had a sinking feeling that both of her new bosses would find her disguise no laughing matter. In their eyes, disguising herself as a boy was probably a serious offense.

She felt apprehensive and a little frightened, but knowing she needed a good night's sleep, she cleared her mind of her troublesome thoughts.

Cassandra was in the process of trying to will herself into a deep slumber when, all at once, she sensed another's presence. Her eyes opened cautiously, and through half-closed lids, she watched as Dru laid his blankets beside hers. Her heart thundered. He was planning to sleep next to her!

Unaware of being watched. Dru slipped into his blankets, rolled over and turned his back toward Cassandra.

She swallowed nervously. He was so close that she could reach out and touch him. It was unnerving to realize how badly she wanted to move over to his blanket and snuggle up intimately. The thought made her skin tingle as, once again, she was overwhelmed by a feverish longing.

Questions began to swirl through her mind. Was she falling in love with Dru Jensen? But how could she conceivably be in love with a man she barely knew? Why did his proximity affect her so strangely and send this fiery feeling flowing through her entire being?

Her confused musings switched to Silas Taylor. He had never made her feel this way, and they had even shared several embraces. She had been quite aware that her closeness stirred his desires, but, for some reason, his affections had always left her cold. She had begun to think that maybe she was incapable of returning a man's passion. Perhaps that was the reason why she had never told Silas that she'd marry him. She had dreaded their wedding night, for she was certain that he'd have found her a disappointment. If his kisses failed to awaken her passion, then his intimate fondling would certainly have failed also.

She pushed thoughts of Silas aside. He was now history. She'd probably never see him again. She must concentrate on the present.

Her gaze centered on Dru's turned back. Leisurely her eyes roamed over his tall frame, which was outlined beneath the top blanket. She decided that his build was perfect: masculine, strong, yet slender.

Then, suddenly, he shoved the cover down to his waist and rolled over onto his back. The moon was shining softly and she could see the thick dark hair on his bare chest. She held back the urge to reach over and run her fingers lightly through the curly mass. Slowly her perusal moved up to his face, admiring his handsome profile. His eyes were closed, and she noticed that his black lashes were so long that they curled up at the ends.

Cassandra was thoroughly enjoying her secret scrutiny, but when Dru turned so that he was facing her, she was afraid he might sense that he was being watched, so she quickly rolled to her side, presenting him her back.

Finally, after an hour or so of insomnia, Cassandra was able to drift off to sleep, but even in repose she was plagued by Dru, for he was in her dreams.

The next morning, Virgil awakened Cassandra before the sun had even crested the horizon. Leaning over and shaking her shoulder gently, he said firmly, "Wake up, Casey. It's time to start breakfast."

She was still sleepy, and rousing herself wasn't easy. She longed to stay in her bedroll and fall back to sleep. Dreading another long, tiring day, she managed to sit up, then get to her feet. Seeing that Dru's bedroll was gone, she figured he had taken a turn watching over the herd. She looked at Russ, who was sleeping soundly. She frowned somewhat petulantly. Apparently, a wrangler's job wasn't as demanding as a cook's.

Later, as Cassandra was preparing breakfast, Virgil informed her that the town of Silver Creek was close by. Following the morning meal, he planned for them to ride to town and buy some supplies. He said that Pete would drive the wagon, for they'd travel horseback and take two pack mules to carry their purchases. He assured her that they'd have no problem catching up to the herd, for it traveled slowly.

Virgil saddled a sorrel mare for his young cook, and Cassandra was grateful he had chosen a horse that looked as if it'd be easy to handle.

She was preparing to mount the mare when she realized that Dru was riding with them. Virgil had failed to mention that his nephew was planning to accompany them.

Struck with apprehension, she swung shakily into the saddle. Virgil had said that it was an hour's ride to Silver Creek. Dru's presence at breakfast had made her feel flustered, and now she had to ride with him all the way to town and back. By the time they caught up to the herd, she'd be a bundle of nerves.

Oh, if only he didn't have such a disturbing effect on her!

Mounted, Virgil rode over and handed her the reins to the mules. Then he and Dru spurred their horses into a trot, and Cassandra trailed behind.

As they traveled closer to Silver Creek, the landscape became more desertlike. The men's horses were soon stirring up loose dirt which, floating back to Cassandra, fell heavily across her face. She couldn't catch up and ride alongside the Jensens because the mules refused to hurry their pace.

Cassandra positioned her bandanna over her mouth, and although it helped somewhat, dust still flew into her eyes. She pulled her hat down low on her brow, and the dirt then settled on its wide brim.

Peeking out from under the hat, she watched ill-temperedly as the two Jensens rode in comfort while they talked to each other. It was as though they had completely forgotten that she even existed — let alone that she was being covered in their dust!

She decided heatedly that her bosses were inconsiderate cads! Well, her thoughts added, at least I don't have to worry about being too close to Dru. He certainly can't shake my emotions when I'm destined to spend the entire trip staring at his back through a dusty haze!

The town of Silver Creek was small, wild and rowdy. The sheriff was the only law officer, and he spent the largest part of his time in the saloon in a drunken stupor.

There were many such towns throughout the West, and because decent, God-fearing people never settled in them, they were destined to eventually become ghost towns.

Cassandra followed the Jensens to the hitching rail in front of the general store. As they were dismounting, Virgil told her to accompany him inside and help choose the provisions. Dru went across the street to the saloon.

It didn't take long for Cassandra and Virgil to buy their supplies and pack them on the mules. Now that the errand that had brought them to town was completed, Virgil suggested that they go to the saloon, and he headed across the street.

Cassandra had never been inside a saloon, and she followed a little hesitantly. Pushing aside the swinging doors, Virgil stepped back for her to precede him.

She went inside, her gaze going immediately to the bar where she saw a scantily clad woman hanging onto Dru's arm. Jealousy swarmed through her when she noticed that Dru was encouraging the strumpet's fawning.

Falling into stride beside Virgil, Cassandra stepped up to the bar. She made sure that Virgil stood between her and Dru. She preferred to keep her distance from him and his girlfriend.

"Whiskey, and a sarsaparilla for the boy," Virgil told the bartender.

As the man tended to the drinks, Cassandra cast a furtive glance at the woman with Dru. Her face was heavily painted, and her red dress was cut shockingly low. She continued to watch with amazement as the woman suddenly kissed Dru full on the mouth. When he responded by placing his hands on her hips, fusing her thighs to his, Cassandra looked away. She found herself actually envying the woman and wishing she were the one in Dru's arms.

Blocking their embrace from her mind, Cassandra glanced about the room. At this time of day there weren't very many customers, and most of the tables were unoccupied.

The bartender brought their drinks, and she turned back around and picked up her glass. She was on the verge of taking a big drink when the painting hanging on the wall behind the bar caught her attention. It was a drawing of a nude woman lying provocatively on a red velvet lounge.

Virgil had turned to look at his young companion, and seeing Cassandra's shocked expression, he guffawed. "Haven't you ever seen a naked woman before?"

Cassandra gulped, took a large swallow of her beverage and answered in a choked tone, "No, sir. I ain't never seen a woman without her clothes on." If you only knew! she thought amusedly.

Dru finished his shot of whiskey neatly, then asked Virgil, "Do you mind waitin' for me?" He grinned discernibly. "I won't be long."

"Go right ahead," Virgil said heartily. He nudged Cassandra with his elbow. "We don't mind waitin', do we, son?"

Dru, his arm wrapped about the woman's waist, was already heading upstairs when Cassandra managed to mumble sourly, "No, I don't mind waitin'."

Cassandra finished her drink as Virgil struck up a conversation with the bartender. She tried not to think about Dru, or envision him in bed with that woman. However, her attempts were futile. Deciding she could no longer stay in this establishment with Dru upstairs making love to a harlot, she moved away from the bar to head outside. She'd wait for Virgil and Dru in front of the general store.

Cassandra, her mood gloomy, was looking down at her feet as she walked toward the swinging doors. Suddenly, though, they swung open, causing her to raise her gaze. Her heart lurched as she looked up into Jubal Thurston's bandaged face!

Chapter Four

As Jubal Thurston entered the saloon, he was too involved with his thoughts to pay close attention to the lad he almost bumped into. He gave the boy a cursory glance, brushed him aside, and with his five brothers following on his heels, he lumbered to the bar.

Cassandra, shocked, stared wide-eyed as the Thurstons passed her without realizing who she was. She expelled a long grateful sigh, then darted outside. Thank God they hadn't recognized her!

She crossed the street to the general store, and hurrying to the side of the building, she looked around the corner. The Thurston brothers were still inside the saloon. She thought about the bandage on Jubal's face; it was so large that it completely covered his left cheek. She wondered how badly he was burned. Considering the size of the bandage, she had a feeling that the injury was extensive. He was probably scarred! Jubal Thurston had always taken pride in his good looks, and she was sure that he'd pursue her relentlessly.

Meanwhile, inside the saloon, Virgil suddenly realized that his young companion had disappeared. He'd been too busy talking to the bartender to notice when Cassandra had left. When the bartender moved away to take care of his new customers. Virgil had quaffed down his whiskey, looked to his side to talk to Casey and seen that he was gone. He wasn't surprised that the boy had left without saying anything. The lad was a strange kid.

Remaining at the bar, Virgil had three more drinks; then, figuring Casey was with the horses, he decided to join him and wait for Dru across the street. If he stayed in here, he'd continue to drink whiskey and end up inebriated.

Heading toward the doors, Virgil asked the bartender, "When my partner comes downstairs, will you tell him I'm waiting across the street?"

"Sure will," the man replied. "And good luck gettin' your herd of horses to Fort Laramie."

Jubal had been listening with little interest, but when the bartender mentioned Jensen's herd, he whirled about and said to Virgil, "Excuse me, mister."

Virgil stopped and looked at Thurston. "You talkin' to me?"

"Yeah. I heard the bartender say you got a herd of horses." Jubal and his brothers had found the Stevensons' wagon and signs of a herd passing close by. " 'Bout two days ago, did you come across an abandoned wagon? One with a broken axle?"

"Might have," Virgil mumbled. Although his interest was piqued, he didn't show it.

"I'm lookin' for a man named Russ Stevenson and his sister. They were travelin' in that wagon. Did you happen to see 'em?"

"Nope" was Virgil's terse reply. Russ Stevenson and his sister? Suddenly a humorous, imperceptible smile tugged at the corners of Virgil's lips.

Jubal spoke to the bartender. "How about you?

45

Have you seen 'em?"

As the man was answering, Virgil pushed aside the bat-wing doors and stepped outside. He crossed the street quickly, and searching for Cassandra, he found her still hidden beside the building.

His eyes were studying her closely as he asked. "Why are you standin' back here?"

"Just thought I'd wait in the shade," she answered, glancing away from his scrutiny and staring down at her feet. She didn't like the way he was looking at her.

Virgil held back a chuckle. Damn, how could he have been so blind? He supposed he was fooled because he had never really looked at his new employee. At their first meeting, he had mistaken Russ's sister for a boy and had never had any reason to think otherwise. But now, as his perusal grew even more intense, it became more and more apparent to Virgil that Casey Stevenson was a lovely young lady. Her features were too feminine for a thirteen-year-old lad, and her frame was too delicate. His thoughts went to Dru. His nephew wouldn't think Casey's disguise humorous, nor would he allow her and Russ to remain with the trail drive.

As Virgil continued to study Cassandra, he wondered why the men inside the saloon were looking for her and her brother. He had judged the men to be dangerous, and he was sure that the Stevensons were in deep trouble.

Cassandra's eyes were still downcast, and Virgil touched her arm to get her attention. Hesitantly, she raised her gaze and looked into his face. He gestured toward a group of trees in the near distance. "Let's go sit in the shade. I'd like to talk to you, and from over there we can see Dru when he leaves the saloon."

Cassandra, lengthening her strides, kept abreast of her boss as they walked to the cluster of trees. Virgil chose to sit beneath a large oak and beckoned for Cassandra to join him. Leaning back against the tree's trunk, he waited until she was seated before asking, "Why are those men in the saloon lookin' for you and your brother?"

Cassandra paled, stammering, "How . . . do you know . . . they're looking for Russ and me?" She felt sick. Did Virgil know the truth about her? Was he about to inform her that she and Russ were fired?

"One of 'em asked me if I came across your wagon. He said he was lookin' for Russ Stevenson and his sister." Virgil paused for a moment, then asked firmly, "You wanna tell me why you're passin' yourself as a boy?"

With tears brimming, Cassandra pleaded desperately, "Please don't be angry with me, or with Russ! We had no other choice! We were sure the Thurstons were following us, and we knew they'd never look for us on a trail drive. We didn't really plan to deceive you, but when you assumed that I was a boy, it gave us the idea. We knew you'd never allow a woman on the drive."

"Why are the Thurstons followin' you?"

At length, Cassandra told Virgil about the Thurston brothers, explaining the power they had in Clarksville; then she told him that Russ had won three hundred dollars from Jubal. She elaborated further, telling Virgil how Jubal had come to the farm, demanding that Russ give him back his money. Her words raced as she explained why she had panicked and thrown the scalding water.

"I didn't mean to burn his face!" she cried. "But he was going to shoot Russ, and I had no other way to

47

stop him. I just threw the water, and it happened to land on Jubal's cheek. Believe me, I wasn't aiming for his face! He was in horrible pain, but before he left, he swore that he'd kill us both. Russ and I had no other alternative but to run away."

She fell silent, and as she waited for Virgil's response, she was plagued with worry for her life and for her brother's. If they lost the protection afforded by the trail drive, the Thurstons would undoubtedly find them.

Finally, Virgil responded, "Why didn't you and Russ tell me the truth from the beginnin'?"

"If you had known I was a woman, would you have allowed me on the drive? Be honest."

He smiled wanly. "Nope, I don't reckon I would have."

She grasped his arm, and her eyes searched his beseechingly. "If you dismiss Russ and me, the Thurstons will find us! We haven't a chance against them. They'll kill us, and I shudder to think what Jubal will do to me before he finally takes my life! Please! Please help us!"

He patted her hand consolingly, then reached up and removed her wide-brimmed hat. Studying her short-cropped curls, he asked, "When did you cut your hair?"

"When you visited us at our camp my hair was tucked up beneath my hat, but after you left, I had Russ cut it."

"It's a beautiful color. How long was it?"

"About halfway down my back."

Virgil sounded regretful. "It's a shame you felt compelled to cut it."

"What other choice did I have?"

"None, I reckon."

48

"It'll grow back." She smiled somewhat ruefully.

His perusal left her hair, went to her pretty face, then trailed down to examine her delicate frame, but when his eyes came to rest questioningly at her chest, she blushed profusely.

Reading his thoughts, she said haltingly, "I . . . I tore up a sheet and . . . and binded myself."

Virgil chuckled heartily.

Her blush deepened. However, despite her embarrassment, she asked anxiously, "Are you going to dismiss us?"

"I don't know," he answered truthfully. "I gotta think about it. You just sit there and be quiet while I decide what I should do."

Complying, Cassandra replaced her hat, drew up her legs and folded her arms over her raised knees. She gazed over at the saloon. It was a good distance away, but from this vantage point, she had a clear view. She'd have no problem spotting the Thurstons if they came outside. What if Jubal was to look over this way and see her? Would he recognize her? No, of course not. If he failed to place her up close, he certainly wouldn't know her at this distance.

Her fear was not only justified, but also overwhelming. Placing her head on her folded arms, she closed her eyes and prayed that Virgil Jensen would protect her and Russ.

When her boss finally spoke, Cassandra was caught unawares, causing her to sit upright with a bolt. Her gaze probed his urgently.

"Casey isn't your real name, is it?"

"No. It's Cassandra."

"Cassandra," he began gently, "I've decided to help you and Russ get safely to Fort Laramie. But from there, you two are on your own. There'll be nothin' more I can do."

"Thank you!" she cried happily, throwing her arms about his neck and hugging him impulsively.

For a moment he allowed her embrace to linger; then he carefully unwrapped her arms from about his neck. Smiling fondly, he said, "If we're gonna continue passin' you off as a boy, you gotta remember not to be huggin' me."

"I'll remember. Haven't I done a good job so far? None of the men or Dru are suspicious."

"Dru," he groaned, frowning. "If he finds out, we'll both be in deep trouble. He'll be madder than hell. Most of the men wouldn't like it either. Some of 'em believe a woman is bad luck on a trail drive."

"Do you believe that?"

"No. I don't hold with superstitions."

"Why did you decide to help Russ and me?"

He grinned wryly. "I like your cookin'. If I fire you, I'll have to eat my own cookin' between here and Fort Laramie."

"I don't think my cooking had anything to do with it." She smiled gratefully. "You're a very kind, compassionate man. When I first met you, I had a feeling that you were God-sent. Now I know you were."

Virgil said somberly, "Hon, it won't be easy for us to continue foolin' Dru and the others. They'll liable to see through your disguise, and if they do, I won't have any control over what happens. If Dru's undecided, he'll put it to a vote, and if the majority of the men vote that you and Russ leave, then you two will have to move on."

"I understand," she answered softly. "But maybe it won't come to that."

Spotting Dru walking out of the saloon, Virgil stood and said, "Here comes Dru. Let's meet 'im at the horses and get the hell out of town. It wouldn't do for Jubal Thurston to run across you again. You're lucky he didn't recognize you when he came into the saloon."

Bounding to her feet, Cassandra asked anxiously, "Virgil, what if Jubal questioned Dru when he came downstairs? He may already know that I'm a woman!"

Virgil shrugged. "If he knows, we'll soon find out."

He headed toward the horses and Cassandra followed. As they drew closer to Dru, her heart began to beat rapidly. If Dru was now aware of her disguise, would he offer to help her and Russ? With clarity she recalled Pete's words. "Dru ain't no man to cross. Can be as mean as a rattlesnake when he's riled."

Dru was mounting his horse when they arrived. "Are you two ready to leave?"

"Yep, we're ready," Virgil drawled. Untying his horse's reins from the hitching rail, he asked as though it were merely an afterthought, "Did you notice those six mean-lookin' hombres at the bar?"

"Yeah, I saw 'em."

"Did they say anything to you?"

"No. Why do you ask?"

Mounting, Virgil replied evasively, "No particular reason."

Cassandra had been listening intently and was still poised at the hitching rail. Eyeing her impatiently, Dru said gruffly, "Casey, why are you just standin' there? Mount up, and let's get goin'."

She did so quickly. Learning that Jubal hadn't questioned Dru caused her heart to slow down to a normal beat. For now, she and Russ were safe.

Cassandra, holding the reins to the mules, planned

51

to once again follow the Jensens at a close distance, but Virgil motioned for her to ride alongside him.

"Come on up here, son," he called. "There's no reason for you to eat our dust." Virgil felt bad that, earlier, Cassandra had done just that.

As they rode out of town and onto the plains, Cassandra was relieved to be leaving the Thurstons behind.

They had traveled a couple of miles when Dru said to Virgil, "On our way back home, remind me to come back to Silver Creek. I promised Belle that the next time I was in town, I'd spend more time with her."

Virgil cast Cassandra a quick glance. Her expression was unreadable. Wary of what Dru might say next, he was about to steer their conversation onto a different course, but before he could, Dru continued.

"Belle's one of the best whores I've had in a long time. She was well worth the price. I'm lookin forward to the next time."

Virgil, his thoughts on Cassandra, grew uncomfortable. This was no subject for a lady's ears. Again, he was getting ready to change the topic when, suddenly, Dru remarked, "Pull up. I drank too much in town and now I need to stop and take a —"

Cutting in, Virgil ordered quickly, "Casey, keep on goin'. We'll catch up to you."

Although Dru found his uncle's order a little weird, he didn't bother to question it.

Continuing onward, Cassandra wondered why it hurt to think of Belle in Dru's arms. Why should Dru Jensen mean anything to her? She barely knew the man, had only spoken to him a few times. She supposed she was merely fascinated with him because he was so ruggedly attractive. How could any woman help but be totally entranced by a man as handsome as Dru?

She grew somewhat angry with herself. It was foolish for her to think about Dru in such a way. After all, he'd never know her as a woman. In his eyes, she was Russ's younger brother. If she continued thinking of Dru in a romantic fashion, she'd be heading straight for a heartache.

Banishing Dru from her thoughts, she turned her musings to Russ. She was anxious to tell him about seeing the Thurstons, and to let him know that Virgil was now their ally.

Riding at a good speed, the Jensens caught up to her, and to Cassandra's consternation, Dru guided his horse up alongside hers. His proximity had such a disturbing effect, she preferred that Virgil ride in middle. However, she now had Dru on one s Virgil on the other.

Cassandra tried to look straight ahead and i Dru's closeness, but against her will, she foun gaze sweeping over him fleetingly. Her quick praisal made her acutely aware of his blatant ma ness, emphasized by his tight-muscled hips, lon muscular legs, and his tall lissome frame. She was unable to keep her eyes averted from such male perfection, and her gaze went to his face.

Sensing her perusal, Dru's eyes met hers. She glanced away at once, but not before he saw a look of adoration in her eyes. However, he interpreted her expression as a young boy's admiration for an older, experienced man. The boy was probably looking forward to the day when he'd be old enough to drink whiskey and enjoy a woman like Belle.

"Don't worry, Casey," he said. "Your day's comin'."

"Wh-what?" Cassandra stammered, confused.

"You're anxious to grow up, aren't you? I know I was when I was your age."

"Grow up?" she muttered. What in the world had prompted him to ask such a silly question?

Dru frowned impatiently. The boy had an exasperating habit of answering a question with a question. It was impossible to carry on a conversation with the kid. He wondered if the lad was a little slow.

"Never mind," Dru grumbled, giving up on conversing with the boy. He spoke to Virgil. "I'm goin' to ride on ahead and catch up to the herd."

"All right," his uncle agreed.

Cassandra watched until Dru had galloped out of sight. Then, with a sigh of adoration, she said to Virgil, "Your nephew is such a handsome man."

"Don't get any romantic notions about Dru," he said kindly.

She looked at him questioningly.

"If you fall in love with Dru, all you'll get in return is a broken heart."

"Why do you say that?"

"Love's an emotion Dru's hardened himself against."

"Some woman must have hurt him terribly."

"Yeah, his wife."

"Wife!" Cassandra exclaimed. "Where is she?"

"She's dead."

"How did she die?"

"Maybe I'll tell you about her sometime, but for now, let's drop the subject. All right?"

Cassandra agreed, but she did so reluctantly. She was very curious about Dru's wife. Had Dru hardened himself against love because his wife's death had devastated him, or had his marriage been

54

a failure?

Belle was sitting at a table by herself, and leaving his brothers at the bar, Jubal walked over, pulled out a chair and joined her.

"I hope you don't mind," he said, flashing a warm smile.

She studied him closely. In spite of the large bandage, she could tell that he was good-looking. She returned his smile a little hesitantly as she wondered about his injury. Had he been burned? It would be a shame for a man as handsome as this one to be disfigured.

"I'm lookin' for my two cousins," Jubal began, deciding prudently that the best way to receive information was to pretend that the Stevensons were kin. That way, people were more apt to be helpful. "I was wonderin' if you had seen my cousin Russ."

Belle thought for a moment, then shook her head. "No, I don't recall anyone named Russ." Suddenly, her eyes lit up. "Wait a minute! A short time ago, there were two men and a boy in here. I took one of the men upstairs with me." She paused, heaving a deep, contented sigh as she reflected on Dru's visit to her bed. What a man!

Impatient, Jubal coaxed, "Go on."

"I asked 'im about the two cowboys with 'im. He said that one was his uncle and the other one was a kid he had hired a couple of days ago. He said that the kid and his brother were headed for San Francisco when their wagon broke down. Anyway, to make a long story short, he happened to mention the brother's name. He called 'im Russ. Could that be your cousin?"

Jubal didn't answer; he was too occupied trying to recall the lad he had almost bumped into. Could the kid have been Cassandra Stevenson? Was she disguising herself as a boy? Concentrating, he drew up the boy's image. Yes! Yes, it was Cassandra Stevenson!

Pushing back his chair, Jubal left the table, motioned for the others to follow, swung open the doors and darted outside.

When his brothers had joined him, Jubal said between gritted teeth. "That old geezer lied to us!"

"What old geezer are you talking about?" one of the Thurstons asked.

"The one with the horse drive. The Stevensons are workin' for 'im."

"A woman workin' on a trail drive!" the youngest brother exclaimed, his tone incredulous.

"The bitch is disguising herself as a boy. Dammit! I almost bumped into her when I was goin' into the saloon."

"What are you plannin' to do, Jubal?" the youngest asked.

"We're gonna follow that trail drive. The first time Russ Stevenson is away from the wranglers, I'll finish him off."

"What about the woman?"

"I got other plans for her."

"You ain't gonna kill her?"

Jubal's hand went to his bandage, caressing it gingerly. "I done changed my mind 'bout killin' her. I'm gonna give her the same thing she gave me." His eyes narrowed ruthlessly. "When I get through with her. she ain't gonna be beautiful no more."

Chapter Five

Cassandra was washing the supper dishes when Virgil walked over, picked up a towel and said, "I'll dry."

She smiled her thanks.

Watching her closely, he uttered in a low voice, "During dinner, I happened to notice the way you kept lookin' at Dru. A thirteen-year-old lad wouldn't be eyein' that nephew of mine with such devotion. Missy, you got to be more careful. What if Dru was to catch you lookin' at him in that way?"

"I'm sorry," she mumbled. "But I can't seem to help myself. Dru's the kind of man a woman finds herself admiring. He's handsome beyond words." She pouted fretfully. "I keep thinking about him and that woman Belle. He seemed awfully anxious to go upstairs with her. Is she the kind of woman that appeals to Dru?"

Virgil laughed softly. "Belle's a prostitute. Her type of woman appeals to Dru because there's no emotional strings attached."

"But doesn't he want to marry again and have a family?"

Virgil shook his head, saying somberly, "Dru's got to learn to put his past behind 'im before he can start over."

She handed him the last plate. "He must have loved his wife very much." She started to lift the heavy dishpan, but Virgil took it for her, stepped away, emptied it and returned.

"It's not as simple as Dru gettin' over his wife. It's more complicated than that." As Virgil was handing her the dishpan, they were interrupted by a wagon approaching the camp.

Cassandra was surprised to see that the visitors were a man and a woman.

"Damn!" Virgil cursed quietly, recognizing the pair.

Dru had been sitting at the campfire, and Cassandra watched as he walked over to the covered wagon. As the man halted the team, Dru reached up, placed his hands on the woman's waist and assisted her from the wagon. Cassandra's eyes widened with amazement when the woman suddenly flung herself into Dru's arms and hugged him enthusiastically.

"Who is she?" Cassandra asked Virgil, her gaze lingering on the lovely stranger in Dru's embrace.

"Vivian Lance," he answered. "Her ranch borders ours."

"What is she doing here?" Dru had now disentangled himself from Vivian's clinging hold and was leading her to the campfire.

"She's our partner. Half of these wranglers work for her. We didn't have enough ranch hands to round up a herd of this size, so Dru and I went into partnership with her." Stepping away, he said over his shoulder, "Bring two cups, will you? I'm sure our company will want some coffee."

Cassandra did so quickly, and when she reached the campfire, she poured coffee for their guests, then took a seat beside Virgil. She wanted to hear everything that was being said.

Although Vivian had been talking constantly, she had said nothing of any substance, but now she turned to Dru. He was sitting next to her, and from Cassandra's position across the fire, she could see the way Vivian batted her long lashes as she gazed sweetly into Dru's eyes.

"Dru," she began, her tone purring, "I know you're angry with me. But I just couldn't sit at home and bide my time while you took our herd to Fort Laramie. After all, I am a full partner, and I have every right to be here." She pouted attractively. "Please forgive me, darling."

Dru stood, grasped her hand and pulled her to her feet. "Vivian, I think we should talk alone."

Cassandra's eyes stayed on the couple as they headed away from the fire before disappearing into the surrounding darkness.

The man traveling with Vivian mumbled gruffly, "I tried to talk Mrs. Lance into stayin' at the ranch, but she was determined to make this trip. If I hadn't agreed to accompany her, she'd have taken off by herself." He looked at Virgil. "You know how stubborn she is."

"I know what you mean," Virgil replied.

Cassandra was barely listening, for her mind was on Vivian. She had never seen a woman more attractive. Her long auburn hair was full and lustrous, and her tailored western attire accentuated her voluptuous curves. Cassandra glanced down at her manly clothes, comparing them to the feminine outfit Vivian was wearing. The woman's split riding skirt and matching vest reflected a Spanish flair, black with gold braid. Her long-sleeved yellow blouse and ornately designed black boots completed the outfit.

Cassandra, immersed in thought, remained by the fire as the wranglers and the man accompanying Vivian laid out their bedrolls. A storm was brewing, and the men put on their slickers before crawling between their blankets. Russ, Pete and a couple of the other hands, were watching over the herd. They'd be relieved in a couple of hours.

Virgil was still seated beside Cassandra. He poured himself a cup of coffee, took a sip, and then, nodding toward the man traveling with Vivian, said quietly, "Carl's Vivian's foreman."

As a streak of lightning zigzagged across the sky, Cassandra stammered. "Is . . . is Dru involved with Vivian?"

"It all depends on what you mean by involved," Virgil replied. Thunder rumbled overhead, sounding ominous.

"She's in love with him, isn't she?"

Virgil didn't answer.

His silence didn't deter Cassandra, and she continued prying. "How long have they known each other."

"Quite a few years. After Dru lost his wife, he left the ranch and stayed gone for nigh on ten years. He mostly wandered from one town to another. He worked as a bounty hunter for a time, then became a deputy marshal. When the war broke out, he headed north and joined the Union. He didn't come back to the ranch until two years after the war. So he and Vivian didn't see each other for almost ten years."

"He fought for the Union?" Cassandra mumbled, but she was speaking more to herself.

Virgil didn't say anything. However, finding Cassandra's Southern loyalty humorous, he smiled inwardly.

Cassandra's concentration returned to Vivian.

"She must be older than I thought."

"I imagine Vivian's close to thirty."

"She's very beautiful."

"Vivian's a widow. She was married to Dru's best friend. Her husband's name was Stephen. He was from back East. Stephen and Dru grew up in the same neighborhood, so they were boyhood friends."

"Dru's from the East?" Cassandra queried, surprised.

"Dru was born in Boston. He didn't come West until he was sixteen. His parents died in a train accident, and since I was Dru's only kin, he came to live with me. My brother and I were as different as night and day. Our father owned a general store, and when he passed away, my brother took over the store and I headed West to sow my wild oats. I was a young man at the time. I fell in love with this land and settled here. I met a lovely young lady, and we were married. A year later, she died of cholera."

"I'm sorry," Cassandra murmured. "You never remarried?"

"No, I never tried it a second time. Anyway, to get back to Dru and Stephen, Dru had been livin' with me 'bout two years when Stephen came out for a visit. Dru and I invited him to stay on, and he took us up on our offer. The boys used to vie good-naturedly for Vivian's affections. Since her father and I were neighbors, we were good friends. We visited a lot, so Dru and Stephen saw Vivian often. I don't think either of 'em were in love with Vivian, but I could tell that Vivian was infatuated with Dru. Then, one summer, Vivian's cousin came for a visit. Her name was Anita, and she was as beautiful as an angel. Dru and Stephen both fell head over heels in love with her. But it was Dru who won her hand in matrimony. Shortly thereafter, Vivian and Stephen were married."

"Did they marry on the rebound?"

"Yep. Stephen married Vivian 'cause he couldn't have Anita, and Vivian married Stephen cause she lost Dru."

"It must've been an unhappy marriage."

"It was doomed from the beginnin'. But then, so was Dru's and Anita's."

"But why was Dru's marriage doomed?"

"Well, like I told you, Anita was as beautiful as an angel. But her beauty was only on the outside. On the inside, she was selfish, overbearing and nagged like a shrew. She'd been city-bred as well as pampered. She couldn't cope with the hardships connected with ranch life. She was constantly naggin' at Dru to move back to Boston. But Dru loves the West as much as I do, and he flatly refused to even consider movin'."

Virgil finished his coffee, then continued, "When Anita became pregnant, I was hopin' she'd stop complainin' and be happy bein' a wife and mother. She gave birth to a healthy baby boy. She and Dru named 'im Jonathan after my brother, but we called 'im Johnny. Well, bein' a mother didn't change Anita. She still longed to live in the East, but Dru held firm. He wouldn't even talk about returnin' to Boston. As far as he was concerned, it was out of the question."

Virgil grew silent, and Cassandra encouraged him. "Go on. Tell me the rest."

"Well, Stephen never got over losin' Anita — a fact I'm sure she was well aware of. To make a long story short, while Dru and I were away on business, the two of 'em ran away, takin' Johnny with 'em. They chose a bad time to head into the plains 'cause there were some renegade Sioux goin' on a rampage. When Dru and I returned home, Anita had left him a note, tellin' 'im that she was leavin' 'im for Stephen. We took out after 'em. 'Bout two days' ride from the ranch, we came across their wagon. It had been burned with their bodies inside."

"Johnny's too?" Cassandra gasped.

"All three of 'em," he murmured.

"My God!" she groaned, imagining how horrible and tragic it must have been for Dru and Virgil. "How old was Johnny?"

"Two years old."

"Now I understand why Dru can't put his past behind him, and why he's distrustful of love."

"After that, Dru left the ranch and I took to the bottle. I couldn't cope with losin' Dru and Johnny both. Vivian's father was a good friend, and he not only tried to bolster my spirits but kept loanin' me money to keep my ranch operative, but I just kept right on drownin' my sorrows in a bottle of whiskey. In time, the ranch began to fall to ruin. I didn't put the money in the ranch like I should have, I just bought more whiskey. When Dru finally returned, he was shocked to find a rundown ranch and a drunk for an uncle. But Dru got me back on my feet and on the straight and narrow. We're takin' this herd to the army 'cause we need the money to build the ranch back up. We didn't have enough wranglers or the finances to do it on our own, so that's why we brought Vivian in as a partner."

"What about her father?"

"He died 'bout a year ago." Virgil stood, took Cassandra's hand and helped her up. "Vivian wanted to come with us, but Dru said a trail drive was no place for a woman. She tried to change his mind, but he was adamant. We thought she had conceded to reason, but apparently we were wrong. I imagine she planned all along to catch up to us, knowin' it would be too late for Dru to do anything about it. I have a feelin' if Dru tries to insist that she turn back, she'll threaten to take half the herd and her ranch hands with her."

"Why do you suppose she wants to come along?"

"Now why do you think? She's wanted Dru for a helluva long time. Accompanying 'im on this drive is gonna place 'em in close contact."

"But what about the wranglers? Don't most of them believe a woman is bad luck on a trail drive?"

"Yep. They aren't gonna like it. But half of 'em work for her. If they say anything, they'll lose their jobs. The other half work for Dru and me. They're good men, and they won't leave us in a bind, regardless of their personal feelin's."

Still holding onto her arm, Virgil led Cassandra to the chuck wagon. He glanced up at the threatening sky. The storm was quickly approaching. "Considerin' the weather, you'd better sleep inside the wagon. In fact, it might not be a bad idea for you to start sleepin' there permanently."

"Won't the men think it strange?" she asked, keeping her voice low. "Why would a boy be opposed to sleeping outdoors?"

"Don't worry about what the others will think. They'll get used to the idea. Now, you climb on inside and get some sleep."

She started to comply, but turning back to Virgil, she mumbled, "I wonder what's keeping Dru and Vivian. They've been gone for a long time."

He smiled speculatively. "I already warned you not to fall in love with Dru. If you do, you're headin' for trouble."

"I can handle trouble," she replied. "I've handled it all my life. I've got more backbone than you might think. Unlike Anita, I'm not city-bred. Nor was I pampered." Her green eyes flashed querulously. "Besides, who said I was falling in love with Dru? After all, he's a damned Yankee!"

With that, she whirled about and climbed inside the wagon. Grabbing her rolled-up blankets, she found a place to spread them. Then, extinguishing the lantern, she lay down and drew up the top blanket.

I don't care, she told herself, if Dru and Vivian stay away all night! Against her own volition, she suddenly pictured them locked in a lovers' heated embrace.

As lightning flashed across the sky, followed by a loud clap of thunder, Cassandra hoped spitefully that the lovers would get caught in the rain and get soaking wet.

When Dru had led Vivian away from the camping area, his temper had been hanging by a mere thread. A trail drive was no place for a woman; furthermore, Vivian had deliberately deceived him. She had promised to stay at her ranch but had known all the time that she would follow him.

Dru had no patience with deceit, and Vivian's trickery didn't sit well with him.

When they came upon a small boulder, Vivian sat down. She knew Dru wanted them to be alone so he could try and convince her to go back home. Postponing the moment, she began a constant flow of small talk, and as her words raced, Dru, pacing back and forth, listened with little interest.

The moon's rays were blocked by the heavy cloud coverage, and the night was pitch black. But as streaks of lightning began illuminating the sky, Vivian was able to see Dru clearly.

Running out of things to say, Vivian fell silent. She watched, entranced, as Dru continued his pacing. She had adored Dru since she was a young girl, and her feelings hadn't changed with the passage of time. Years ago, she had lost him to Anita, and then for ten years he had disappeared from her life. Well, she wouldn't let him go again! She would become Mrs. Dru Jensen—one way or another!

Vivian Lance was determined to have Dru, and she wasn't about to let anything or anyone stand in her way. She'd get him to marry her even if she had to stoop to blackmail. However, she hoped it wouldn't come to that. But if she was left no other choice, she'd use blackmail. She thought about the legal papers back home in her safe. Yes, through them, she could convince Dru to marry her. She wondered if Dru even knew the papers existed. Probably not. More than likely, Virgil hadn't told Dru about them. He was probably hoping to take care of the debts himself.

Dru had stopped his pacing, and his eyes were probing Vivian's as he mumbled ill-temperedly, "In the morning, I want you to turn around and go back home." He hoped she'd agree to turn back without putting up an argument.

"I'm not going back," Vivian replied, her chin raised stubbornly. "Half of that herd is mine, and half of the wranglers work for me. I have just as much right to be here as you and Virgil." Actually, Vivian was dreading the arduous trip to Fort Laramie, for she certainly didn't relish living out of a covered wagon. However, she was willing to put up with discomfort to be close to Dru. Surely, before the drive was over, he would succumb to her beauty—her passion! She was no longer the naive, inexperienced young woman who had lost him to Anita.

"A trail drive is no place for a woman!" Dru argued.

"Don't hand me that male-biased excuse," she replied. "I'm not a greenhorn who can't take care of herself. I've lived in the West all my life."

He sat beside her. "Vivian, I don't understand why you're so determined to come along. Don't you trust me? Are you afraid that I'll try to cheat you?"

"I trust you implicitly," she answered, inching so close to him that their thighs were touching.

"Then why . . . ?"

"Why not?" she came back.

"As I said before, a trail drive is no place for a woman. You shouldn't be here."

"And, as I said before, I don't buy your male-biased excuse. I own half of that herd, and I have every right to be here."

"I'm sorry, but I'm gonna have to insist that you go home."

"In that case, I'll take my men and my half of the herd with me."

"Dammit!" Dru snapped. "Are you that determined to make this trip?"

"Yes, I am."

He stood, folded his arms across his chest and eyed her unyieldingly. "All right, Vivian. Have it your way. But when the goin' gets rough, don't come to me with your complaints. If you can't cope, you get left behind. I've got a deadline to meet, and I intend to deliver these horses on time."

She didn't want Dru to be too angry with her, so rising and standing close to him, she gazed warmly into his eyes. "If I find the trip too difficult, I promise you that I'll admit I was wrong and turn back. I won't take my men with me or my half of the herd." She smiled prettily and offered him her hand. "Is it a deal?"

He hesitated, then reluctantly accepted her handshake. "It's a deal."

Her fingers interlaced with his. "Dru, now that we have reached an understanding, can't we start being more pleasant to each other? After all, we go back a long way, you and I."

"Yes, we do," he replied somberly.

Her hand tightened within his. "Friends?"

"Friends," he answered with a half-grin.

Lightning zoomed overhead, defining Dru's irresistible, sensual smile, and, enchanted, Vivian slipped her arms about his neck, stood on tiptoe and pressed her lips to his.

Dru almost returned her ardor, but he suspected that Vivian wanted a permanent involvement. Although he found her desirable, he didn't want an emotional attachment between them, and he gently broke their embrace.

Seeing disappointment mirrored in her eyes, he said tenderly, "During this drive, I need to keep my mind on work, not romance."

"All work and no play makes a very dull Dru," she said teasingly.

"Perhaps," he answered. "But there's a time and a place for everything."

"And this isn't the time, nor the place?" she questioned pertly.

Dru knew there would never be a right place or time for him and Vivian, but he wasn't sure just how to tell her without hurting her feelings. However, Dru was saved by sudden drops of rain. Grabbing her arm, he said quickly, "Let's hurry back to camp before we get drenched."

They hurried through the low shrubbery, and keeping a firm hold on Vivian's arm, Dru ushered her to her covered wagon and helped her climb inside. Bidding her a quick good night, he went over to where Virgil had placed his bedroll. The man had on his slicker and was snuggled underneath a blanket.

Virgil was still awake, and as Dru knelt beside him, he asked, "Where's your slicker? You're gonna get soakin' wet."

"I loaned my slicker to Russ 'cause he didn't have one. I knew he'd need it out there with the herd. I'm gonna sleep inside the chuck wagon."

"But Casey's sleepin' in there!" Virgil exclaimed.

"So?" Dru questioned, wondering why his uncle seemed upset.

"So . . . So . . ." Virgil stammered, at a loss.

The rain was now falling harder, and anxious to keep dry, Dru dismissed Virgil's stammering, sprang to his feet and rushed to his bedroll, which he had stored under the chuck wagon. Grabbing it, he climbed over the backboard.

A streak of lightning flashed brilliantly, lighting the wagon's interior, and Dru saw that Casey had placed his bedroll in the center of the floor.

Impatient with the boy for taking up all the space, Dru mumbled gruffly, "Casey, move over and make room."

Chapter Six

Cassandra was lying on her side with her back turned toward the intruder. She had heard his entry and was about to sit up to see who it was when Dru issued his order to move over.

Her heart lurched and a gasp caught in her throat. Lord, surely he wasn't planning to sleep inside the wagon!

"Casey?" Dru grumbled. "Kid, are you awake?"

"Yes, sir," she whispered.

"Would you mind movin' your bed over and givin' me a little space. I'm sleepin' in here because I loaned my slicker to your brother."

Lightning flashed radiantly, and keeping her face turned away from Dru's watchful eyes, Cassandra rose and drew her blankets to the side. She was thankful that she had decided to sleep in her clothes. She had thought about sleeping nude, which would have been more comfortable. Thank goodness she had changed her mind!

Quickly she crawled back into bed. As Dru spread his blankets beside hers, she rolled over and turned her back. Her heart was thumping, and she wished it would slow down to normal.

Slipping between the blankets, Dru murmured, "Sorry I had to disturb you."

"That's all right," she mumbled. His closeness tormented her, and she ached to turn over and snuggle against his strong, manly frame.

Lightning flashed again, but this time it wasn't quite so bright, and the thunder that followed rumbled less ominously. The raindrops beating against the canvas began to dwindle. The storm was passing.

Dru emitted a long, weary sigh. Cassandra wanted to ask him if he was troubled, but decided she shouldn't pry. Then, when Dru sighed a second time, she could no longer suppress her curiosity.

"Is somethin' wrong, boss?" she asked, remembering to keep her voice an octave lower.

"I've got a lot on my mind, kid."

"Are you worried about Mrs. Lance?"

"Worried? That's puttin' it mildly. A woman doesn't belong on a trail drive."

"Do you believe a woman brings bad luck?"

Dru smiled. "No, of course not. But, Casey, you gotta realize that the wranglers like to feel free to say and do whatever they want. With a woman along, they have to watch their conduct. Furthermore, one beautiful woman in the midst of several men is liable to stir up trouble."

Cassandra didn't say anything; she was too involved in her own troublesome thoughts. What would Dru do if he knew the truth about her? She had a sinking feeling that he'd be furious.

"I'll be glad when this drive is over," Dru said softly. "Then Virgil and I can get back to the Bar-J and start turnin' it back into a ranch we can be proud of. During the war, it fell onto hard times."

"Yeah, I know," Cassandra mumbled. "Virgil told me 'bout his drinkin'."

Dru was surprised to learn that his uncle had taken

Casey into his confidence. "What else did Virgil tell you?"

"He also told me 'bout you and your wife."

"Vivian and Stephen, too?"

"He told me everything."

"It's not like Virgil to run off at the mouth."

"I hope you ain't mad at 'im," Cassandra uttered in her feigned dialect.

"No, I'm not mad. My life's no secret."

Cassandra swallowed nervously, hoping Dru would accept her condolences with grace. "Boss, I just want to say that I was sorry to hear 'bout your wife and son."

Silence ensued. Not even the raindrops could be heard, for the storm had passed completely. Cassandra was growing afraid that she had said too much when Dru remarked pensively, "Tomorrow Johnny would've been twelve years old."

She wished she could turn over, take Dru into her arms and console him.

"Well," he drawled, his tone now unemotional, "we'd better get some sleep. Good night, kid."

"Good night, boss," she mumbled.

Cassandra closed her eyes, but she knew sleep was far away. With Dru so close, relaxing and falling into a deep slumber was not going to be easy. She drew up her knees and snuggled beneath her blanket. She could hear Dru's deep breathing, and she wondered if he was asleep. She was tempted to roll over and look at him but was afraid that he might still be awake. Again, she questioned her feelings. Was she falling in love with Dru? I must be, she mused. I think about him constantly, and I have this overwhelming need to be in his arms. She tried to imagine how it would feel to be held in Dru's embrace. She was sure it would be heaven!

Suddenly, Cassandra's thoughts were interrupted by a horse racing into camp, the rider calling anxiously, "Dru! . . . Dru!" She recognized the voice as Pete's.

Leaping to his feet, Dru hurried outside. Cassandra considered following him, but then decided it might be best for her to stay inside. She hoped nothing was seriously wrong.

A few moments later, Cassandra was surprised to see Virgil climbing inside the wagon.

"What happened?" she asked.

She was still on her bedroll, and Virgil went over and knelt beside her. He spoke gently. "Hon, your brother's been shot."

"Oh, no!" she cried. She tried to leap to her feet, but Virgil's hands went to her shoulders, deterring her.

"He was shot by a sniper. The men are bringin' 'im into camp. Pete rode ahead to let us know what happened."

"Is he . . . Is he . . . ?" she stammered, her heart beating wildly.

"He's alive," Virgil replied quickly. His grip on her shoulders increased considerably. "Cassandra, when you go outside to see your brother, you've got to keep a tight hold on yourself. You can't carry on like a woman. You've got to remember to act like a boy."

She frowned petulantly. "I don't carry on! Now, let me up so I can go to Russ."

He helped her from her bedroll. "Do you think he was shot by the Thurstons?"

"I'm sure he was. Somehow, they found out that Russ and I are working for you."

She brushed past Virgil, and as she was leaving the

wagon, two wranglers arrived with Russ. They had him slung across his horse. She waited until Dru had eased Russ to the ground before hurrying to kneel at his side. He was unconscious. "How badly is he hurt?" she cried to no one in particular.

It was Pete who answered. "It looks pretty bad."

Joining her, Virgil quickly examined Russ's wound. He'd been shot in the back.

"We'd better get him to a doctor," Dru remarked.

"There's a doctor in Silver Creek," Virgil replied. "I don't know how good he is, but he's better than no doctor at all. Dru, get the wagon hitched."

"All right. I'll drive the team, and you and Casey can ride in the back with Russ." Dru moved away quickly, and motioning for Pete to help, he went about hitching up the horses.

Virgil, along with two of the wranglers, carried Russ inside the wagon and placed him on Cassandra's bedroll.

Meanwhile, Cassandra filled a basin with water; then, hurrying to her brother, she placed the basin at his side, grabbed a clean cloth and dipped it into the water.

Virgil dismissed the two wranglers. Then he carefully removed Russ's slicker and shirt, and using extreme care, he turned him over onto his stomach.

Her brother's wound was ghastly, and Cassandra cringed. "Oh, God, Virgil!" she moaned. Russ was bleeding copiously, and she washed his wound with haste, then pressed the cloth against the injury, blotting the flow of blood.

By this time, Dru had the team hitched and was ready to leave. The wagon took off with a sudden jolt.

"Dru!" Virgil called urgently. "We've got to hurry!

74

This man is dyin'!"

Jubal and his brothers knew they weren't being pursued, so they rode back to Silver Creek at an unhurried pace. Jubal was feeling complacent; he had gotten off a good shot and was sure that Russ Stevenson was dead. Due to the storm, sneaking up on the herd, locating Russ and shooting him in the back had been as easy as taking candy from a baby. Jubal could hardly believe his good luck.

Now that Russ had been disposed of, Jubal could start making plans to get even with Cassandra. He had no intention of simply shooting her. A quick death was too merciful. However, sneaking up to the wranglers' camp and abducting her would be too risky. With Russ being shot, the trail boss would certainly double security. Although Jubal was anxious to get his hands on Cassandra, he knew he had to be patient. Now that her brother was dead, she'd be even more determined to stay with the drive, for it was her best means of protection.

As Jubal continued riding toward Silver Creek, he decided to follow the drive to Fort Laramie before seizing Cassandra. When the wranglers reached the fort and sold their herd to the army, their security would grow lax. Then, kidnapping Cassandra should be relatively easy.

A wintry, calculating smile crossed Jubal's face. If he played his cards wisely, it would only be a matter of time before Cassandra would be his. He rubbed his hand lightly across his bandaged face. The bitch would pay dearly for burning him! First, he'd have his way with her, then give her to his brothers. Afterward, when they'd had their fill, he'd show her what it felt like to have scalding water thrown in her face.

75

No, he thought spitefully. Not scalding, but boiling! He'd give her worse than she had given him! He'd mete out his own dose of justice!

Cassandra paced the doctor's parlor, and, watching her, Dru said kindly, "Casey, why don't you sit down?" He was on the couch, and he gestured to the wing chair across from him.

She shook her head. She was too nervous to sit still and had been pacing for over an hour. Her eyes flew anxiously to the closed door leading off the parlor. Upon their arrival, the doctor had told Dru and Virgil to carry Russ into that room. Virgil had remained with the doctor, but Dru had come back into the parlor, closing the door behind him. Cassandra had gotten a quick glimpse of her brother lying on a bed with the doctor leaning over him; then Dru had shut the door.

Standing, Dru stepped to Cassandra, laid a hand on her shoulder and detained her pacing. A pine side table was in the corner, and a bottle of whiskey and three glasses were placed on top of it.

"Would you like a drink?" Dru asked. "It might do you good."

Cassandra was about to decline, but then changed her mind. "Thanks," she answered. "Maybe it'll help me relax." Cassandra was not only worried about her brother's life, but was also concerned about the doctor. The man was unkempt and looked incompetent.

Dru poured the drink quickly and brought it to Cassandra. "Here, kid. Turn it up and drink it all."

She took the glass, she supposed it held a couple of shots. She'd never tasted whiskey before and was somewhat leery. Tipping the glass to her lips, she took a deep breath and drank its full contents. The potent brew burned her throat, and while suppressing a cough, she handed the glass back to Dru.

"Another?" he asked.

"No . . . No, thanks," she managed to reply. Her throat was still burning and the hard liquor was making her eyes water. Heavens! Why would anyone want to drink that horrible stuff? It was awful! However, despite its terrible taste, Cassandra realized that it did have a soothing effect, and she was beginning to feel more calm.

The door to Russ's room opened, and stepping into the parlor, the doctor announced, "The patient is out of danger."

"Thank God!" Cassandra exclaimed.

The man poured himself a liberal amount of whiskey. Now that the operation was over, his hands began to tremble. Lifting the glass, he downed the drink, poured another and then said to Dru and Cassandra, "If it weren't for the booze, I could've been a great surgeon." He shrugged as though resigned to his fate, turned up the glass and quaffed the whiskey. He refilled the glass, draining the bottle. As soon as everyone had left, he'd make a quick trip to the saloon and replenish his supply.

"May I see Russ?" Cassandra asked.

He nodded. "Sure, son. He's awake. But don't stay long. He needs his rest."

She fled into the room. Virgil was seated beside the bed, but at Cassandra's entrance, he stood and offered her his chair.

Thanking him, she sat down and asked her brother, "How are you feeling?"

"Terrible," he whispered hoarsely, his smile weak.

"The doctor says you're going to be all right."

"Cassandra," he began feebly, "I want you to stay with the trail drive." He was free to call her by her true name, for earlier in the day Cassandra had found the opportunity to tell Russ that Virgil was aware of her disguise.

"I can't leave you!" she cried.

Virgil decided to leave them alone, and touching Cassandra on the shoulder, he said, "I'll wait for you in the parlor."

As Virgil was leaving the room, Russ insisted, "Cassandra, you must leave. With the Thurstons in the vicinity, it's too dangerous for you here in Silver Creek. At least on the trail, Virgil can look out for you. He's already promised me that he would. As soon as I'm well enough to travel, I'll meet you at Fort Laramie."

He gestured toward his trousers, which were hanging over the chair in the corner. "Our money is in my pants pocket. Take half of it with you. You'll need it for lodging until I can get to the fort. I'd give you more than half, but I'll need money to pay the doctor and travel to Fort Laramie."

Cassandra was unwilling to leave her brother. What if Jubal was to learn that Russ was still alive? Would he return to Silver Creek and try to kill him? "But, Russ," she cried, "what if Jubal finds out that you're here?"

"I'm not worried about Jubal finding me, I'm worried about you. Besides, he probably thinks I'm dead."

"But what if he comes back to Silver Creek?"

"There's no reason for him to come back here." Russ spoke with feigned certainty, for he knew the Thurstons' return to Silver Creek wasn't that unlikely. He wanted Cassandra out of town. Bedridden, he couldn't protect her.

Conceding somewhat reluctantly, Cassandra murmured, "I'll do as you want. But, Russ, do you really believe Jubal won't find out that you're here?"

"I'm certain," he answered, for he knew his sister wouldn't leave him if she thought he was in danger.

Rising, she went over to Russ's trousers, took half the money and slipped the bills into her pocket. Returning, she leaned over the bed and placed a light kiss on her brother's brow. "I'll wait for you at the fort."

"I should be able to travel in a couple of weeks. The Thurstons might follow the drive to Fort Laramie, so while you're at the fort stick close to Virgil. He promised me that he'll stay with you until I get there."

Cassandra wondered what excuse Virgil planned to give Dru for lingering at Fort Laramie. She was sure that Dru would want to head for home as soon as the sale was completed.

Russ was growing tired, and it was becoming an effort for him to keep his eyes open.

Seeing her brother's fatigue, Cassandra uttered warmly, "I'll leave now." She held back her tears. "I love you, Russ."

"Love you too, sis," he whispered; then closing his eyes, he fell asleep.

Forcing herself to leave her brother's side, Cassandra turned and walked out of the room. Her gaze swept over the three men in the parlor before coming to rest on Virgil.

"Did Russ tell you that he wants you to stay with the drive?" Virgil asked.

She nodded, mumbling, "Yeah, he told me."

"Well? Did you agree?"

Her eyes communicating secretly with Virgil's, she answered, "All things considered, I reckon it's best if I go on with you to Fort Laramie."

"Good," Virgil remarked. He went over and took her arm. "Come on, Casey. We need to get back to camp and get some sleep. We'll be movin' out early in the mornin'."

She looked at the doctor. "Are you goin' to let my brother stay here while he's convalescing?"

"He'll be more than welcome," he replied sincerely.

"Thank you," she murmured.

As Virgil was leading Cassandra from the parlor, Dru approached the doctor and said quietly, "I know you said that Russ is goin' to make it, but if something should go wrong, send me a wire at Fort Laramie. My name's Dru Jensen."

Receiving the doctor's promise to do so, Dru followed the others outside. As Virgil was stepping up into the back of the wagon behind Cassandra, he didn't notice the six men heading into town. However, they spotted him and quickly guided their horses into the dark shadows.

Dru climbed up onto the seat, picked up the reins and set the wagon into motion.

Meanwhile, the six men waited until the wagon was out of sight before emerging from the darkness.

"Wasn't that the same man we saw in the saloon?" one of the Thurstons asked Jubal.

"Yeah, that was him, and he's the one headin' the trail drive."

"Ain't that the doctor's house?" another one asked.

"Yep, it sure is. Which means Russ ain't dead."

At that moment, the doctor left his house and headed in the direction of the saloon.

Jubal grinned. "Mighty obliged to the doc for makin' this easy for me." His gaze flitted over his brothers briefly. "Wait here. I got some unfinished business to take care of."

He galloped his horse to the hitching rail in front of the physician's home, dismounted and entered the house stealthily.

A few minutes later, Jubal slipped out the front door, hurried to his horse, mounted, and rode back to his brothers.

"It was just like I figured," Jubal remarked. "I found Stevenson alive."

"Did you kill 'im?" the youngest asked.

"I put a pillow over his face and held it there 'til he stopped breathin'." Jubal laughed gleefully, but his laughter stopped abruptly. "I won't be that merciful with his sister!"

Chapter Seven

Dru drove the wagon into camp and pulled back on the reins. Glancing back at Virgil, he asked him if he'd mind unhitching the team. As his uncle complied, Dru jumped to the ground, went to the back of the wagon and said tersely, "Casey, I want to talk to you."

Cassandra was apprehensive. Why did Dru want to talk to her? Had he somehow caught on to her masquerade? She climbed over the backboard a little shakily, stood before him and mumbled. "Yes, sir?"

Dru frowned good-naturedly. "Casey, you don't have to call me sir."

She didn't say anything.

Dru continued. "Son, I want you to be honest with me. Are you and Russ in some kind of trouble? Are you two bein' chased?"

"Why . . . Why would you think that?" she stammered.

He ignored her question and pressed on, "Casey, if you know who shot Russ, then you need to tell me. If there's a chance that someone's gonna take a shot at you, I want to know beforehand. Tonight when Russ was shot, it's a wonder that the gunshot didn't start a stampede."

Cassandra looked at him disdainfully. He didn't

care about her life or Russ's, he only cared about his horses stampeding!

Reading her thoughts, Dru said hastily, "Don't misunderstand me, kid. I certainly don't want anything to happen to you, and I'm glad that your brother's all right. But if there's a sniper followin' us, I intend to get rid of him."

Should she tell Dru about Jubal and his brothers? Could she explain why they were after her and Russ without revealing her secret? She supposed she could manage an explanation and guard her disguise at the same time. However, she suddenly realized that she was tired of pretending that she was a boy—especially when she was with Dru.

She gazed deeply into Jensen's piercing blue eyes; he was watching her closely. Yes, she'd be honest with him. He'd be angry, but after his temper cooled, he'd understand.

Dru was growing impatient. "Dammit, Casey! Answer me! If there's someone followin', tell me so I can do something about it."

"Do what?" she asked.

"I'll find the bastard and turn him over to the law."

"What if there's more than one?"

He eyed her suspiciously. "You do know something, don't you?"

Before she could answer, they were interrupted by Vivian calling sweetly, "Dru, darling?"

Cassandra watched as the woman appeared around the corner of the wagon. She was amazed to see that Vivian was wearing a sheer dressing gown.

Dru's eyes narrowed angrily. "Vivian, don't you think your attire is inappropriate? I bet every man in this camp was ogling you as you walked over here!"

"Honestly, Dru, if I didn't know better, I'd think

you were jealous."

Dru's temper blew. "These wranglers have been without a woman for quite some time, and you walk around in front of them wearing a gown that leaves little to the imagination!" He turned his gaze upon Cassandra. "Now do you understand why I don't want a woman along? A woman on a trail drive is nothing but trouble!"

Vivian, misconstruing his anger for jealousy, remarked in a sugar-coated tone, "Well, darling, at least you have only one woman to worry about."

"One is one too many!" he thundered.

Cassandra edged away from Dru and stood back in the shadows. She was now afraid to tell him the truth. He'd be so furious that he'd never forgive her. She had let her heart overrule her better judgment. She mustn't make that mistake again.

"Casey!" Dru spat sharply.

She stepped out of the shadows.

"I'm takin' Mrs. Lance back to her wagon. Wait here, 'cause I'm not through talkin' to you."

For the first time, Vivian took a close look at Cassandra. "You know, you're almost too pretty to be a boy."

Grasping Vivian's arm, Dru ushered her away from the wagon. As they were leaving, Cassandra heard Dru grumble, "Don't you know you shouldn't tell a boy that he's pretty?"

Cassandra couldn't hear Vivian's reply, but it didn't matter. She couldn't care less what the woman thought. Furthermore, she didn't like her, and the way she fawned over Dru struck Cassandra's jealousy to the core. Disguised as a boy, she couldn't even compete with Vivian.

Cassandra was so immersed in her thoughts that

she didn't hear Dru's return. His voice startled her. "Casey, who's after you and Russ? Or is it only Russ who's in trouble?"

"No one's after us," she muttered, glancing down at her feet.

"Boy, you better not be lyin' to me," Dru warned. "I'm a fair man to work for, but I expect my men to be honest with me. If I find out you aren't tellin' me the truth, I'll send your butt back to Silver Creek. Do you understand me, son?"

On the verge of tears, she nodded quickly, turned about and hastened inside the wagon. She couldn't let Dru see that she was about to cry. A thirteen-year-old boy wouldn't be so emotional.

She went to her bedroll and lay down. Dru's blankets were still placed beside hers. Now that it had stopped raining, he'd probably decide to sleep outdoors. When he came to get his bedroll, she'd pretend to be asleep. That would stop any further questioning.

Later, when Dru slipped quietly inside and gathered his blankets, Cassandra feigned sleep. She heard him leave, and the moment he was gone, she surrendered to her tears and let them roll down her cheeks unhindered.

She had never felt so depressed or so troubled. She knew she'd worry about Russ and wonder if he was all right, if he'd make it safely to Fort Laramie. Then there was Dru. She no longer questioned her feelings for him. She was in love, there was no doubt in her mind. How ironic that she should love a man who would never see her as a woman!

Cassandra had finally discovered the man of her dreams, only to find that he was beyond her reach.

* * *

Jubal was sitting in the saloon with his brothers when he happened to glance up and recognize the man who had just walked inside and was sauntering up to the bar.

"Well, I'll be damned!" Jubal exclaimed.

"What's wrong?" one of the Thurstons asked.

He pointed toward the man at the bar. "That's Roy DeLaney."

"It is him!" two of them chorused. They were as surprised as Jubal to see DeLaney in Silver Creek.

During the war, Jubal, two of the older Thurstons, and Roy DeLaney had fought under the same command. The three younger Thurstons had joined the Union Army later and were assigned a different company than their brothers'.

Jubal pushed back his chair, got to his feet and headed toward DeLaney. The saloon was packed, and although several men crowded the bar, Belle and another woman had made their way to Roy's side. Jubal wasn't surprised; DeLaney was exceptionally handsome, and women were drawn to him like moths to a flame.

"DeLaney!" Jubal called heartily.

Roy whirled about swiftly. Despite Jubal's bandaged face, he recognized him instantly. "Thurston!" He shook his hand enthusiastically. "What the hell are you doing in these parts?"

"I was about to ask you the same thing."

Roy, anxious to rehash old times with his army buddy, dismissed Belle and the other woman; then, buying a bottle of whiskey, he grabbed up two glasses and led Jubal to an empty table.

When they were seated, Roy asked, "How's your two brothers?"

86

"Joe and Charlie are with me. They're sittin' over there at that table with my other brothers."

"Invite them over," Roy suggested.

"Later," Jubal replied. "First, let's have a couple of drinks and talk about the good old days."

DeLaney chuckled. "Dammit, Jubal! You enjoyed the war, didn't you?"

"I admit that I liked killin' Johnny Rebs. Is there anything wrong with that?"

Roy hadn't enjoyed killing; however, he didn't pass judgment on Jubal. DeLaney leaned back in his chair and studied Thurston's bandaged face curiously. "What happened to you?"

"I'll tell you about it later," he replied gruffly, tipping his glass to his lips and emptying it. Pouring himself another drink, he asked, "How come you're in Silver Creek?"

Roy smiled wanly. "I was on my way to San Francisco, but the last town I passed through drained my finances. I got into a poker game that was way over my head."

"Roy, you never could play cards worth a damn."

"You'd think by now I'd have enough sense to avoid 'em." He shrugged as though unconcerned. "I'm almost broke, so I guess I'll look for a job. It'll probably take me a helluva long time to save enough money to get to San Francisco."

A plan began to take shape in Jubal's mind. Maybe he wouldn't have to wait for Cassandra to reach Fort Laramie before capturing her. Although Roy was a failure at cards, Jubal knew he had always been highly successful with women. His tall, muscular frame was perfectly proportioned. His features were sensual: full lips, high cheekbones and dark brown eyes framed by long lashes. His sandy-colored hair was thick and wavy. During the war, Jubal and Roy had made a handsome pair and had seduced many a Southern belle. Impressed with the two good-looking soldiers, several women had forgotten their loyalty to the Confederacy.

Jubal rubbed a hand gingerly over his bandage. Thanks to that bitch Cassandra, women would no longer find him handsome, but repulsive!

As his plan took root, Jubal continued to scrutinize DeLaney. Could he convince the man to help him seize Cassandra? Roy owed him a favor, he had saved his life during the war. If necessary, he'd remind him of the debt.

"Roy," he began, "I need your help."

"I'll be glad to help you if I can."

"You can do me a great favor, and, in the meantime, make yourself some money."

DeLaney's interest was aroused. "I'm all ears."

"My brothers and I live in Clarksville. Do you know where it is?"

"Isn't it close to the Arkansas-Texas border?"

"That's the place." Taking a deep breath, Jubal began elaborating on the story he had craftily devised. "Well, a few weeks ago, I got into a poker game with a Southerner named Russ Stevenson. He'd won three hundred dollars before I caught 'im cheatin'. He drew a gun on me, knocked me over the head and left while I was unconscious. When I came to, I went to his farm and snuck into the house. He and his sister were in the kitchen discussin' running away. When I barged into the room and demanded that Russ give me back my money, his sister threw a pot of steaming water in my face."

"My God!" Roy groaned. "How badly are you burned?"

88

"The doctor said I'd be scarred for life."

Roy was genuinely concerned. "I don't know what to say."

Jubal finished his drink, then refilled his glass. "Stevenson and his sister Cassandra left the farm. My brothers and me have been followin' 'em. They joined up with a trail drive that's takin' a herd of horses to Fort Laramie."

"A woman on a trail drive!" Roy remarked incredulously.

"She's passin' herself off as a boy."

Roy couldn't help but smile.

"Earlier tonight, we slipped up to the herd. Stevenson was on duty. We confronted the bastard and told him we were takin' him back to Clarksville to stand trial. He tried to run away, and my youngest brother panicked and shot him. I'm kinda ashamed to admit that he shot Stevenson in the back. He wasn't dead, so his trail boss brought him to town and delivered him to the doctor."

Jubal nodded toward the physician, who was sitting alone at a corner table. He had drunk himself into a stupor. "The doc came in the saloon a short time ago and said that his patient had died. He was really shook up, 'cause he thought his operation had been successful. He said he has no idea why Stevenson died but figures complications set in. The goddamn drunk probably couldn't set a broken arm without killin' his patient."

"It's too bad about Stevenson. But how can I help you?"

"That Stevenson bitch is still free. I intend to take her back to Clarksville. She should pay for what she did to me!" Jubal wasn't about to tell Roy what he really had in mind for Cassandra. He knew DeLaney

89

well and was perfectly aware that he wouldn't condone such violent vengeance, especially on a woman.

Reaching into his pocket, Jubal withdrew a wad of bills. After suffocating Russ, he had gone through his victim's trousers and confiscated the 150 dollars. He placed it on the table. "If you'll agree to help, and if you're successful, this money will be yours."

Roy eyed the bills hungrily. He needed funds desperately. "What do you want me to do?"

Jubal spoke briskly. "Catch up to that trail drive and talk the boss into hirin' you. Then, put your charms to work and convince Cassandra that you're her friend. Don't let her know that her brother's dead, 'cause if you do, you won't be able to talk her into returnin' to Silver Creek."

"How am I supposed to convince her to come back?"

"Prey on her conscience. Make her start feelin' guilty 'bout leavin' her brother. Hell, Roy, you can talk a woman into anything. My brothers and I will follow the drive, but we'll stay a couple of days behind. You persuade that bitch to leave with you and head back toward Silver Creek. We'll meet up with you."

"I don't understand why you don't simply go to the trail boss and tell him that she's wanted by the law. I should think he'd hand her over and let you take her back to Clarksville."

Jubal frowned. "The boss probably knows she's a woman. He won't simply hand her over to me and my brothers. Besides, there's no tellin' what kind of cock-and-bull story she's told him." He shook his head. "No, I can't take the chance that me and my brothers will be shot if we try to take her by force. You convincin' her to leave on her own accord is

90

better."

Again, Roy eyed the money hungrily. "All right, Jubal. I'll help you."

Thurston smiled broadly. "Thanks, Roy."

"I owe you one," he replied. "I haven't forgotten that you saved my life."

Jubal eyed DeLaney cautiously. "Roy, Cassandra Stevenson is not only beautiful, but she's also cunning. If she decides to tell you what happened between me and her brother, she won't tell the truth. She'll lie through her teeth. Don't be taken in by her act of innocence."

"No woman, regardless of how beautiful, has ever pulled the wool over my eyes. I not only need money, but I also owe you a tremendous favor. Don't worry, I'll deliver Cassandra into your hands. I agree that she should stand trial for what she did to you." Roy sighed sympathetically. "Scarred for life! Damn, Jubal, what a tough break! I don't blame you for demanding justice."

Jubal gleamed inwardly. He'd get justice all right! That bitch would pay! As he envisioned Cassandra totally at his mercy, he smiled with anticipation.

After leaving the chuck wagon, Dru had placed his bedroll beside the campfire. He was sound asleep when the touch of a hand on his shoulder brought him wide awake. Sitting up, he was surprised to see Vivian kneeling at his side.

"Is something wrong?" he asked quietly, not wanting to wake the wranglers sleeping close by.

"I must talk to you," she whispered, tugging at his arm. "Please, it's urgent. Let's go to my wagon so we won't disturb anyone."

Dru complied somewhat aversely. He was wary about being alone with Vivian. She had made her amorous intentions obvious, and he was opposed to a romantic involvement between them. Personally, he had nothing against Vivian; in fact, he found her very attractive. However, he knew that she wanted a permanent relationship. He wasn't in love with Vivian and knew he never would be. If he were to succumb to temptation and enjoy her charms, she'd probably misinterpret the union as an act of love.

Vivian tucked her arm in Dru's as they headed toward her wagon. Neither of them was aware of the figure emerging from the foliage that grew thickly behind the chuck wagon.

Cassandra had awakened a few minutes earlier, and needing the privacy afforded by the shrubbery, she had slipped outside. She was on her way back when she caught sight of Dru and Vivian.

Her silent steps halted abruptly, and a sob caught in her throat. She watched teary-eyed as the man she loved ushered Vivian into her wagon. I won't cry! she told herself. Crying won't change anything!

She climbed inside and returned to her bedroll. A vision of Vivian and Dru sharing a lovers' fervent kiss flashed before her. Oh, how she envied the woman!

If only I could be myself and compete for Dru's affections! she cried inwardly. But I can't let him see me as a woman!

She buried her face in her pillow. I love you, Dru! I love you! Holding back tears, she tried futilely not to think about the romantic interlude taking place inside Vivian's wagon.

Meanwhile, as Cassandra's heart was breaking, Dru was watching Vivian closely. She was still wearing her sheer dressing gown, and the soft rays from the lantern illuminated her voluptuous curves. He reached over and extinguished the light, for he knew it was casting their silhouettes on the canvas. If someone were to see their shadows, he might get the wrong idea.

Vivian assumed, erroneously, that his turning off the lantern was a prelude for the passionate union that was about to follow. She was standing close to him, and reaching out into the darkness, her hands found his chest. Sliding them upward and about his neck, she whispered provocatively, "Darling, I knew if I were to make the first move, you'd cooperate. I was lying here in my bed, debating if I should come to you. Finally, I decided to throw my pride to the wind, go to you, and bring you back with me. Make love to me, Dru. I want you so desperately!"

Gently, Dru removed her hands and stepped back. "Vivian, if you brought me here to seduce me, then you not only wasted your time, but also mine."

Exasperated, she cried, "Dru, don't you find me attractive?"

"Of course I do. But, Vivian, there can never be anything between us except friendship."

"Why?" she pleaded. "Is it because I remind you of Anita and Stephen?"

"Maybe," he murmured. "I'm not sure."

"Dru, if you'd only give me a chance, I could make you forget about Anita and what she and Stephen did to you. I got over their betrayal, why didn't you?"

"I did get over Anita. It's the loss of my son that still haunts me."

"I can give you another son!" she entreated.

His tone was hard, unyielding. "I don't want any more children."

"Why?"

"It hurts too badly to lose a child. I never intend to go through that pain again!"

"Then we won't have any children," she said hastily. "Dru, to be perfectly honest, I don't even like children. They get on my nerves."

Dru moved with stealth, and due to the dark, she didn't realize that he was leaving until he pushed aside the canvas, letting in the moonlight. Jumping lithely over the backboard, he uttered tersely, "Good night, Vivian."

His brusque departure infuriated her. Well, if she didn't soon win his devotion through seduction, she'd use blackmail to persuade him to marry her. He was leaving her no other choice. He'd be angry and marry her reluctantly, but he'd quickly come to his senses and realize his good fortune; once he got a taste of her passion, she was confident that he wouldn't be able to live without her.

Chapter Eight

Pete decided that Casey was now capable of handling the team, and, for the first time, Cassandra was on her own. Doubting her capabilities, she spent the first half of the day driving the wagon gingerly. However, as the day wore on, she grew more confident, and by the time the sun had begun its descent, she was handling the job with relative ease.

She was glad that the chuck wagon was expected to follow the large herd at a distance; otherwise, she'd be traveling through a dusty haze stirred up by the horses' hoofs. But more importantly, removed from the others, she was free to relax and be herself. She didn't have to worry about sitting or moving like a boy, and because the only wrangler who had ridden back to visit had been Virgil, it hadn't been necessary for her to slip back into Casey's role. Vivian's wagon was in front of the herd, and when it came time to stop, the wagon would circle the herd and come back to the campsite.

Now, as Cassandra kept the team moving at a steady pace, she knew Virgil would soon return to let her know that it was time to set up camp. It had been a long day, and she was anxious to be finished with her evening chores, then go to bed.

The sky was clear, and the sun's hot rays had dried

the wet earth. It was as though last night's storm had never taken place.

As Cassandra guided the wagon over the dry terrain interspersed with sagebrush and mesquite, her thoughts weren't on the land, but on Dru and Russ. They had been on her mind all day. If she wasn't thinking about one, she was thinking about the other.

She missed her brother, and, more than once, she had considered leaving the trail drive and returning to Silver Creek. She felt that she had deserted Russ, abandoned him in his time of need! Should she go back and stay at his bedside until he was well? She was tempted to do so but knew he would be terribly angry with her for disobeying his instructions.

Cassandra sighed wistfully. She knew her brother had no idea how difficult it was for her to stay with the drive and be forced to watch Dru's and Vivian's blooming romance. She must find a way to control her feelings where Dru was concerned; if she didn't, she'd only end up with a broken heart. It's almost comical, she thought testily, that Dru has the power to break my heart, and he doesn't even know it!

A deep frown creased her brow. If only there was some way that Dru could see her as a woman. She'd give anything to be in his arms, even for one night! It would be a memory she could lock away in her heart and treasure forever. Just imagining herself in Dru's embrace accelerated her heartbeat. Silas Taylor's advances had left her feeling nothing, but despite her inexperience, she was sure that Dru would awaken her passion. The mere thought of sharing a lovers' embrace with him caused a feverish longing to course through her.

The sound of a horse's hoofs advancing from the

rear brought Cassandra's musings to an abrupt end. Who was coming up behind her? Jubal Thurston? A cold chill prickled the back of her neck. Her eyes flew to the double-barreled shotgun resting at her feet. Virgil had given it to her for protection. She wasn't a very good shot, but he had assured her that with this gun's wide pattern she couldn't possibly miss. He also let her know that he'd ride at the back of the herd, and if he heard a shot, he could reach the wagon in a matter of moments.

Cautiously Cassandra lifted the shotgun, but her hands were trembling so badly that she almost dropped it. As the rider came up alongside the wagon, she let out the breath she'd been holding and laid the gun across her lap. It wasn't Jubal, but a stranger.

"Howdy," he said. "Where can I find the trail boss?"

"We have two bosses. They're up ahead with the herd." She noticed that the man was looking at her a little strangely. Her hat was pushed back from her brow, and she quickly lowered it. Had he seen through her disguise? Had she remembered to deepen her voice? She wasn't sure. Dropping her tone, she asked, "Are you lookin' for a job?"

"Yes, I am."

"Well, Virgil Jensen will be comin' back most anytime to set up camp." Moving as though she were perfectly at ease, she placed the shotgun at her feet.

"In that case, I'll wait for him." Taking Cassandra by surprise, he grabbed ahold of the wagon, swung out of the saddle and onto the seat. Smiling at her startled face, he settled himself beside her.

"Ain't you worried 'bout your horse?" she asked. "He might run off."

"He'll follow the wagon." The stranger offered her his hand. "My name's Roy DeLaney. What's yours, son?"

Cassandra sighed inwardly as she accepted his handshake. Thank goodness he hadn't caught on to her disguise. "The name's Casey."

"Glad to meet you." Roy suppressed a smile as he surreptitiously perused his companion. There was no doubt in his mind that he had just met the malicious little vixen Jubal was pursuing. Her boy's disguise was good, and if he hadn't been aware of her masquerade, it might even have fooled him. Thurston had said that she was beautiful. Dressed in a man's clothes, which were a size too large, it was hard to judge the shape of her figure. As he continued his furtive perusal, he glanced at her face. He could see that she had rubbed in a light coat of dirt in an effort to cover her peaches-and-cream complexion. She had thought of everything, down to the last detail. Apparently, she was as cunning as Jubal had warned.

Meanwhile, as Roy was carrying out his secret examination, Cassandra was doing likewise. She was quite impressed with DeLaney's good looks. He was indeed handsome. Her hopes soared. Maybe Vivian would find Roy DeLaney so irresistible that she'd use her lascivious charms on him instead of on Dru. This man's appeal was sensual, whereas Dru's was rugged. Which would Vivian find more attractive? Suddenly, Cassandra's hopes plunged. Vivian had wanted Dru for years, and there was no way that some stranger was going to come along and change her mind. Not even one as handsome as Roy DeLaney.

"I was in Silver Creek last night," Roy began, striking up a conversation. "The bartender told me about this drive to Fort Laramie. I'd like to go to San

98

Francisco, but I don't have the funds. I thought if I could get a job as a wrangler, I could make enough to join one of the wagon trains that stop at the fort."

"That's where my brother and I are goin'," Cassandra replied.

"San Francisco?"

"Russ has wanted to go there for a long time."

"Is he a wrangler on this drive?"

"He was." A lump rose in her throat. "Last night, he was shot by a sniper. He's at the doctor's in Silver Creek. As soon as he's well, he's gonna meet me at the fort."

"Maybe the three of us can travel to San Francisco together." He smiled infectiously.

Responding, Cassandra answered eagerly, "That's not a bad idea."

Catching sight of Virgil riding back to the wagon, Roy asked, "Who's that?"

"Virgil Jensen. You can ask him for a job."

"Put in a good word for me, will you? I need this job."

"You shouldn't have any trouble gettin' it. With my brother in Silver Creek, the Jensens are short one man. I hope you know something about horses."

He grinned charmingly. "Well, I know which end is which."

Cassandra laughed lightheartedly. She like Roy DeLaney and hoped that Virgil would hire him. The man's warmth and pleasant personality boosted her spirits, and with Russ in Silver Creek and Dru infatuated with Vivian, she desperately needed someone to keep her mood lifted. She had a feeling that Roy DeLaney was just the medicine she needed.

* * *

As Cassandra washed the supper dishes, she kept glancing over at the campfire. Vivian was sitting beside Dru, her arm locked familiarly in his as, along with Virgil and the wranglers, they listened to Delaney talk about himself. Roy's easygoing and charming manner had not only gotten him a job, but new friends as well; everyone seemed to have taken an instant liking to him.

Watching Vivian, Cassandra wondered if the woman was impressed with DeLaney. Although Vivian's eyes would periodically sweep openly over Roy's handsome physique, she nonetheless continued to hold onto Dru possessively.

Turning away from the people gathered about the fire, Cassandra finished her chore, then emptied the dishpan. Her mood was sullen. Despite Roy DeLaney's good looks and winning personality, Vivian was still entranced with Dru. Cassandra didn't blame her. How could any man compare with Dru?

Deciding to gather kindling for the morning, Cassandra left the camp and walked into the surrounding foliage. Branches and twigs were plentiful, and as she knelt to pick them up, she heard someone coming up behind her. Startled, she leapt to her feet and whirled about.

"I didn't mean to scare you," Roy said, coming to her side.

She swallowed heavily. Why was he here? She hoped he hadn't stepped into the shrubbery for privacy. She must hurry and gather the kindling and make a quick departure.

Cassandra was about to carry out her intentions when Roy remarked quite calmly, "Casey, I know you're not a boy, but a beautiful young lady."

"Wh-what?" she stuttered, paling.

DeLaney had decided the best way to become good friends with Cassandra was to pretend that he had caught on to her disguise, then promise to guard her secret.

"You heard me," he replied. "I know you're a woman. Your disguise is good, almost perfect. But I have an eye for beauty, and your masquerade didn't fool me." He smiled tenderly. "Don't worry, Casey. I won't tell anyone."

"Why are you protecting me?"

He shrugged insouciantly. "I'm sure you have a good reason for passing yourself as a boy. I don't see where your disguise is hurting anyone. So why should I get you in trouble? Besides, I make it a point to mind my own business." Moving slowly, he reached over and took her hand, holding it snugly within his. "I considered not telling you that I know the truth, but then I thought that you might need a friend. Someone you can be yourself around. This constant pretending must be difficult for you."

"Virgil knows I'm a woman," she answered. "But no one else knows."

He squeezed her hand fondly, then released it. "Do you want to tell me how you came to be on this trail drive?"

"There are some men pursuing my brother and me, and we joined this drive because we thought they wouldn't find us. When Virgil realized that I'm a woman, he decided to keep my secret. Russ and I believed we were safe, but somehow these men learned that we were working for the Jensens. They slipped up to the herd and shot my brother."

"Who are these men, and why are they after you and Russ?"

"They're the Thurston brothers. The oldest one,

101

Jubal, is determined to kill Russ and me. Back in Clarksville, he came to our farm, demanding that Russ give him back the three hundred dollars that he'd won from him in a poker game. Jubal was going to shoot Russ, and in order to save my brother, I threw a pot of scalding water in Jubal's face. I didn't mean to burn him, but it was the only way I could save Russ. Jubal was going to kill him in cold blood."

Roy watched her thoughtfully. That was probably the same story she had told Virgil to gain his sympathy. If Jubal hadn't already warned him that she was cunning, he would have fallen for the story himself. Roy sighed inwardly. Although he wasn't overly anxious to deliver Cassandra to Jubal, he needed the money Thurston planned to pay him; furthermore, Cassandra had scarred the man and should be held to account.

Roy believed Jubal over Cassandra, and playing his role to perfection, he said with a warm smile, "The man was going to kill your brother. You did the only thing you could."

"I still feel terrible about burning Jubal's face. I just wish that it had never happened."

He patted her shoulder soothingly. "Everything's going to be all right. And I promise I'll take care of you."

Cassandra felt better. "I'm glad I have you and Virgil as friends."

"Speaking of Virgil," Roy began, "it might be better if you don't tell him that I know the truth about you."

"But why not?"

Roy didn't want Virgil knowing that he was aware of Casey's true identity. The man would probably suspect his motives and start watching him like a hawk. When he and Cassandra talked alone, Virgil would question her, wanting to know what was said. He couldn't let Virgil learn that he was trying to persuade Cassandra to ride back to Silver Creek.

"Why don't you want me to tell Virgil that you know I'm a woman?" Cassandra pressed him.

"He'll order me to stay away from you, and I want us to be friends."

"I don't understand why you think Virgil would object."

He wondered if she was really as naive as she sounded. "He'll be worried about your virtue."

Cassandra blushed. "Oh, I see," she stammered.

"But don't worry. You're safe with me. Not that I don't find you attractive, but I pride myself on being a gentleman."

Feeling somewhat flattered, she asked haltingly, "Dressed the way I am, how . . . how can you tell if I'm attractive?"

"I already told you. I have an eye for beauty. I'm surprised that no one has caught on to your disguise, especially Dru. He doesn't seem to be the kind of man who is easily fooled."

Cassandra's green eyes sparkled peevishly. "Dru can't see any farther than Vivian!"

Roy studied her speculatively. Her apparent infatuation with Dru would undoubtedly make his job harder. She'd be reluctant to leave Dru to return to her brother. He must start making her feel guilty about leaving Russ before this crush got out of hand.

"How seriously was your brother wounded?"

"He almost died."

"Are you sure he's now out of danger?"

"The doctor said that he'd be all right."

Roy appeared apprehensive, pretended that he was

about to say something, then acted as though he had changed his mind.

"Is something wrong?" Cassandra asked, seeing his indecision.

He spoke hesitantly. "Well, while I was in Silver Creek, I saw the doctor in the saloon. He was drinking himself into a drunken stupor. You'd think he would have been home with his patient. In cases such as your brother's, complications can set in. I saw that happen more than once during the war." He paused a long moment, then lied convincingly, "In fact, I had a good friend who was wounded in battle. The doctor operated and said that he'd recover. Twenty-four hours later, my friend died."

"That's terrible," Cassandra replied. "But I'm sure Russ is fine."

"Well, I guess if you're sure," he said, gazing intensely into her eyes.

A pang of fear coursed through her. "God!" she moaned. "I can't be sure!"

Now that he had her worrying about her brother, Roy decided to let the matter rest. It was still too soon to convince her that she should leave with him. First, he must win her trust and make her believe that he was truly her friend.

Kneeling, he began to gather up kindling. "We'd better get back to camp," he said. "Virgil's liable to start wondering what's keeping you and come looking."

As Cassandra helped Roy with the kindling, her thoughts were on Russ. She shouldn't have left him! Regardless of his wishes, she should have stayed in Silver Creek!

* * *

When Roy and Cassandra returned to camp, the wranglers were in their bedrolls and Vivian had gone to her wagon; however, Virgil and Dru were still sitting at the fire.

DeLaney told Cassandra good night, then found a place to spread his blankets. Cassandra started to climb inside the chuck wagon, but concern for Russ had her wide awake, and she knew she'd merely toss and turn as sleep eluded her. Moving slowly, she went to the fire to join Virgil and Dru.

As she approached, Virgil stood up.

"Are you goin' to bed?" she asked him.

"No, I'm takin' a watch over the herd." He smiled warmly. "I'll see you in the mornin', Casey."

She waited until he had walked away before sitting beside Dru. A pot of coffee was brewing over the open flames, and she poured herself a cup of the hot brew. Plagued with concern for Russ, she was totally immersed in her thoughts.

Taking note of Casey's somber expression, Dru asked considerately, "Is something botherin' you, son?"

"I'm worried about Russ," she answered.

"Your brother will be fine. Virgil was with the doctor when he operated, and he said that the man did a remarkable job."

"But that's no guarantee that Russ won't take a turn for the worse."

Dru was about to try and lift Casey's spirits when he became aware of a slight disturbance in camp. The wranglers, still ensconced in their bedrolls, were sitting up and whispering to each other. Noticing that their gazes were on Vivian's wagon, he looked to see what was capturing their interest.

Vivian's lantern was lit, and its soft rays were casting her silhouette on the white canvas. She was taking a sponge bath and was completely nude. Her voluptuous curves were clearly defined.

Dru leapt to his feet, cursing heatedly, "Dammit!"

Cassandra's gaze was also on Vivian's wagon. She wondered if the woman knew that the lantern was outlining her shadow. Was she purposefully arousing Dru's jealousy? If that was her intent, Cassandra could tell by the fury on Dru's face that Vivian's ploy was successful.

Storming away from the fire, Dru headed for Vivian's wagon. His temper was boiling.

Vivian wasn't surprised when Dru suddenly yelled her name. She knew the lantern was casting her silhouette and had been expecting Dru's arrival. Grabbing her dressing gown, she slipped it on, then went to the back of the wagon and parted the canvas. She smiled sweetly at Dru. "Is something wrong?" she asked innocently.

"The next time you take a bath, do it with the lantern off!" he grumbled.

"Dru, what in the world are you talking about? And how did you know that I was bathing?"

"Don't you realize that at night a lit lantern will cast your shadow onto the canvas?"

Vivian pretended to blush. "Oh, my goodness! I didn't realize!"

"When you're undressing, extinguish that damned light! This is a trail drive, not a damned strip show!"

"I'm sorry, Dru. It won't happen again."

"Make sure that it doesn't!" he growled, turning away.

Vivian was pleased. She was certain that she had fired up Dru's jealousy, and even better, he had seen everything she had to offer. Her image would haunt him and arouse him to the point that he'd soon come to her. She was confident.

As Dru returned to the fire, his temper began to cool somewhat. He wished he could find a way to convince Vivian to go home. Dammit, a woman didn't belong on a trail drive! Her presence could only stir up trouble, especially one as beautiful as Vivian. He wondered how many of the wranglers were now envisioning themselves making love to Vivian. He was sure that it was only a matter of time before one or more of them tried to have his way with her.

Cassandra was still seated at the fire, and glaring down at her, Dru mumbled his thoughts aloud. "A woman on a trail drive is nothing but trouble!" Whirling about, he went to his bedroll.

Leaving the fire, Cassandra walked to the chuck wagon and climbed inside. Imagining the full extent of Dru's anger if he were to find out that she was a woman made her thankful that she now had Roy for a friend as well as Virgil; this way, if Dru learned of her deceit, she wouldn't be forced to face his wrath alone.

107

Chapter Nine

Cassandra waited until Virgil had finished his breakfast before motioning for him to come over to the chuck wagon.

"What do you want?" he asked.

She looked at him and said with a note of secrecy, "Virgil, will you teach me to shoot?"

He was surprised. "Why do you want to learn to shoot?"

"I was thinking about it last night and again this morning. I believe it's important that I learn to protect myself. You can't shield me every hour of the day, and if Jubal's following, it's only a matter of time before he confronts me. If I'm armed, I can at least defend myself."

Virgil concurred. "You're right. I should've thought of it myself." He wondered if she was totally inexperienced. "Have you ever shot a rifle?"

"Yes. Before Russ left to join the army, he gave me a few lessons. But I'm not a very accurate shot."

"I'll have Pete drive the wagon, and we'll stay here. You might as well have your first lesson this mornin'. Afterwards, we'll catch up to the herd, and you can take over drivin' the wagon. We'll repeat the procedure every mornin', but since you've already used a rifle, it shouldn't take too many lessons."

"I also want you to teach me to shoot a pistol." She could tell that Virgil was opposed. Raising her chin in a stubborn fashion, she said determinedly, "A rifle is too cumbersome to carry around with me. I plan to strap on a gun belt."

Virgil quirked a brow. "A gun belt?"

"I intend to buy one in the next town, or at the next trading post. Whichever comes first."

Virgil lowered his voice, chastising grumpily, "A lady doesn't wear a gun strapped to her hip!"

"If this lady doesn't wear one," Cassandra returned, "she's liable to find herself at Jubal Thurston's mercy!"

He conceded, albeit reluctantly. "All right. I'll teach you. Have you ever fired a handgun?"

"No," she admitted, hoping her inexperience wouldn't alter his decision.

Virgil grinned. Despite his reluctance, he admired Cassandra's spunk. Patting his holstered pistol, he said half-seriously, "I reckon you also want me to teach you to be fast on the draw. Right, missy?"

Cassandra smiled fondly. When they were alone, Virgil often referred to her as "missy." She didn't mind his using a pet name.

"Fast on the draw?" she pondered. "Yes, why not?" There was a bright twinkle in her jade green eyes.

The day had been long and exhausting, and by the time Cassandra completed her evening chores, she was totally fatigued. Although she was bone-tired, she was in good spirits. Her first lesson had gone well. Handling Virgil's Winchester hadn't been difficult, and she had hit more targets than she had missed. Virgil's revolver had been a different story. Unfamiliar with a handgun, Cassandra had found it extremely difficult to hit what she was aiming at. However, by the end of the lesson, she had shown considerable improvement. Virgil had told her that she had a natural ability to become a good shot, and she had accepted his praise with pride.

Cassandra was about to climb inside the chuck wagon when the wranglers seated around the camp-fire suddenly broke into hearty fits of laughter. She had noticed earlier that the men seemed to be in high spirits, joking and laughing more than usual.

Virgil was standing a short way from the others, and going to him, Cassandra asked, "Is it my imagination, or are the men in unusually good spirits?"

"It's not your imagination. They're in a good mood 'cause we're two days away from Colorado Territory, and once we're in Colorado, we're only a week from Good Times."

She looked at him quizzically.

"Good Times is a boomtown located close to the railroad."

"Why are the men so anxious to get there?"

" 'Cause Good Times lives up to its name. We'll camp outside the town for twenty-four hours; that way all the men will get a chance to go to town and visit Violet's."

"Violet's?" she questioned.

"It's a cathouse." Dru said, his sudden appearance startling Cassandra and Virgil. He had walked up so soundlessly that they hadn't heard him.

"Dammit, Dru!" Virgil complained gruffly. "Don't sneak up on us like that!"

"Why?" Dru asked archly. "Have you two got something to hide?"

110

"Of course not." Virgil was quick with his denial.

Dru turned to Cassandra and smiled. His smile was so sensual that it took her breath away. Her heart fluttered, and a feverish tingling sensation swept through her. Slowly, she gazed up into his eyes. The soft moonlight made their azure pupils shine like two brilliant sapphires.

"Virgil told me that he's teaching you to shoot," Dru began, unaware that his listener was totally mesmerized. "It's about time you learned to handle a gun. A boy your age should already be a fairly good shot."

Cassandra offered no reply. She didn't want to talk to Dru about guns; she wanted to be in his arms with him whispering sweet endearments in her ear.

Suddenly, the wranglers seated about the fire laughed gustily, capturing Dru's interest. He turned away from Cassandra, and she followed his gaze.

Glancing at the wranglers, Cassandra noticed that DeLaney was absent. Apparently, he was one of the men who were now watching over the herd. Her eyes came to rest on one cowboy in particular. His name was Perry, and he was a loudmouth, but harmless.

Aware that the young cook was looking at him, Perry grinned largely. "Hey, Casey!" he called, his tone blustering. "When we get to Good Times, you wanna go to Violet's with us?"

"No, thanks," she mumbled. Cassandra was glad that the night hid her blushing cheeks.

Perry continued his ribbing. "Boy, ain't it about time you got your wick wet? Why, when I was your age, I was already a-dippin' my wick."

The other wranglers joined in, agreeing with Perry that Casey should visit Violet's. They voiced their opinions boisterously and with good humor.

Perry's voice rose above the others'. "Casey, after one of Violet's girls initiates you, you're gonna find that your hand's a poor substitute."

At this point, Virgil's temper blew. "That's enough!" he bellowed. "Perry, open your mouth again and I'm gonna stick my fist in it!" His gaze swept furiously over the other wranglers. "That goes for all of you!"

Dru and the wranglers were shocked by Virgil's unexplained anger.

Turning to Cassandra, Virgil ordered brusquely, "Casey, get in the wagon!"

She obeyed at once, for Virgil's tone had brooked no argument.

Dru waited until Cassandra was inside the wagon before saying testily, "What's wrong with you, Virgil? Perry and the others didn't mean any harm. They were just joshin'. Dammit! You hover over Casey like a mother hen!"

Virgil knew that his nephew was right. Perry's teasing had been in fun, and if Casey were really a boy, he wouldn't have given Perry's gibing a second thought.

Virgil apologized. "Sorry, men. I didn't mean to blow my top."

As the wranglers were accepting their boss's apology, Perry got hastily to his feet and stormed away from the fire. He soon disappeared into the surrounding darkness.

Walking always cooled Perry's temper, and as he strolled aimlessly, his anger began to diminish. He couldn't understand why Virgil had jumped down his throat. If Casey couldn't take a little teasing, then the

112

boy didn't belong on a trail drive. Dru had been right: Virgil hovered over the lad like a mother hen.

Perry, deciding to forget the whole incident, switched his thoughts to Violet's. Because he was still young and fairly good-looking, he knew the girls at Violet's would be more than willing to accommodate him. Just imagining the fun he was going to have aroused him sexually. Damn! If he didn't get to Violet's soon, he was sure to burst right out of his trousers!

A twig snapping arrested Perry's full attention, and he wheeled about alertly. He was taken aback to see Mrs. Lance emerging from the nearby shrubbery. The moon-drenched night shadowed her shapely form, and golden moonbeams danced in her shiny auburn tresses. She was desirable beyond words.

Vivian had stepped into the heavy foliage for privacy and was returning to her wagon. The sight of Perry brought her steps to an abrupt halt. Her thoughts began to flow shrewdly as she studied Perry, who was watching her with unmistakable hunger. Should she use this man to agitate Dru's jealousy? Yes! Why not? Bathing with her silhouette shadowed on the canvas had certainly aroused Dru's temper; he wouldn't have been that angry if he didn't want her for himself. He was foolishly fighting his desires because Anita had made him distrustful of love. Surely if she once again stirred up Dru's jealousy, he'd come to realize how badly he wanted and needed her.

Moving gracefully, with her hips swaying provocatively, Vivian covered the short span between her and Perry. She paused in front of him and looked up into his face. Her gaze was an open invitation.

Perry's eyes traveled over her feverishly. Her leather riding skirt hugged her feminine thighs, and her blouse, partially unbuttoned, revealed her deep cleavage.

He reached for her, and she seemed to float into his arms. Drawing her close, Perry bent his head and captured her lips, kissing her wildly, passionately.

She allowed his kiss to linger for a long moment; then, taking him unaware, she broke loose, and pounding her fists against his chest, she began to scream shrilly.

Vivian's piercing screams carried to the campsite, and Dru, with Virgil on his heels, hurried to her rescue.

Cassandra had also heard the screaming, and leaving the chuck wagon, she followed Dru and Virgil at a distance.

Vivian, still shrieking, continued pounding her fists against Perry's chest, and he was trying vainly to calm her when the Jensens arrived.

Seeing Dru, Vivian shoved Perry aside and rushed into Dru's arms. Clinging, she cried brokenly, "That man was . . . was trying to molest me!"

Perry, totally dumbfounded, stood riveted.

In the meantime, Cassandra came upon the scene so quietly that her presence went undetected. Vivian, cuddled in Dru's embrace, penetrated Cassandra's heart to the core.

Keeping Vivian close, Dru glared at Perry and shouted angrily, "What the hell's wrong with you?"

Vivian snuggled intimately, placing her head on Dru's shoulder. Pretending hysterics, she broke into heaving sobs.

Dru said tenderly, "Don't cry, you're safe now."

Cassandra had seen and heard all that her heart could stand. Turning about, she slipped away as stealthily as she had arrived.

Meanwhile, Perry had emerged from temporary shock. Meeting Dru's unwavering gaze, he remarked strongly, "I didn't try to molest her. Hell, she came on to me!"

"Oh, you vile monster!" Vivian cried. She lifted her face to Dru's, gazing helplessly into his eyes. "He's lying!" Then detecting Dru's uncertainty, she pleaded, "You believe me, don't you?"

Perry had worked for the Bar-J for over two years; he was a good wrangler and had never caused any trouble. Also, Dru had never known the man to lie. However, he knew that Vivian was perfectly capable of deceit. But why should she lie about something like this? Was it a ploy to arouse his jealousy? Dru didn't put it past her.

Speaking to Virgil, Dru asked, "Do you mind takin' Vivian to her wagon? I want to talk to Perry alone."

"No, I don't mind," he replied, going to Vivian and taking her arm firmly. Like Dru, Virgil suspected that Vivian had initiated the unfortunate incident.

Dru waited until they were gone before stepping to Perry. "Tell me exactly what happened."

"I was takin' a walk, tryin' to cool my temper. Virgil's jumpin' down my throat had me kinda upset. Well, Mrs. Lance came out of the shrubbery. For a moment, she just stood there lookin' at me. As I stared back, I was thinkin' about seein' her silhouette on the canvas. But I swear that I didn't approach her. She came to me and looked up into my eyes like she was just a-dyin' for me to kiss her. I reached for her, and she went into my arms willingly. I kissed her, and she responded. Then, all at once, she stopped kissin' me and started screamin' and poundin' my chest. She was like a wild woman." He looked at his boss directly. "Dru, I swear I'm tellin' the truth."

"I believe you, Perry. But, hereafter, keep your distance from Mrs. Lance."

"I will," he replied hastily. "You can bet I will!"

"You'd better hit the sack," Dru suggested.

Perry took a step to leave, hesitated, and uttered sincerely, "Thanks, boss, for believin' me."

Dru responded with a terse nod. Damn Vivian! She was nothing but trouble!

When Dru returned to the campsite, he saw Casey sitting alone at the fire. The lad's expression was sullen, and he wondered if the boy was still worried about his brother.

Joining him, Dru asked, "Son, are you thinkin' about Russ?"

Russ hadn't been in Cassandra's thoughts; she'd been thinking about Vivian in Dru's arms, remembering how protectively he had held her. Having no choice but to evade the truth, she mumbled, "Yeah, I was thinkin' about Russ."

"I'm sure Russ is fine." Dru reached into his shirt pocket and removed a cheroot.

As he put a stick into the flames to light his smoke, Cassandra took advantage of his preoccupation to study him closely. He was so irresistibly handsome! His hair and trimmed mustache were as black as ebony, and their dark color made the blue in his eyes stand out prominently. Furtively, she allowed her perusal to roam over his tall, tight-muscled frame. In her opinion, Dru Jensen was flawlessly handsome. She also admired his character, and the only fault she could find with him was his foolish infatuation with Vivian. Couldn't he see that beneath her beauty she

116

was cunning and untrustworthy? Was he going to make the same mistake with Vivian that he had made with Anita?

Sensing that he was being watched, Dru turned to look at her, but she quickly glanced away.

He wondered why the boy had been staring at him. Casey was a strange kid. He wanted them to be friends, but the boy remained aloof, except with Virgil. The two of them were apparently very close.

Cassandra, knowing it wasn't wise for her to remain in close proximity to Dru, got hastily to her feet. She must try to keep distance between them, for if Dru was around her too much, he'd most assuredly catch on to her disguise.

"Good night," she muttered.

Moving quickly, she went to the chuck wagon and hurried inside. Going to her pallet, she sat down and sighed despairingly. Pretending to be a boy in Dru's presence was becoming more and more difficult. She was falling so deeply in love that she literally ached to be held in his arms.

She removed her hat, picked up her hand mirror and studied her reflection. Frowning, she brushed a hand through her short-cropped locks. Even if she could let Dru know that she was a woman, he probably wouldn't find her attractive, not with her hair cut as short as a boy's.

Placing the mirror aside, she glanced down at her figure, comparing it to Vivian's. Her rival was voluptuous, whereas she was tall and slender. Although her breasts weren't buxom, they were firm and full. Her slim hips were well-rounded, and her legs were long and shapely. If Dru were to see her unclothed, would he find her desirable? Or did he prefer a woman who was full-figured?

She exhaled deeply. There were no answers to these questions, so why was she tormenting herself? Furthermore, if Dru ever did see her as a woman, he'd be so furious with her for deceiving him that he wouldn't care if she was attractive or not.

Her mood pensive, Cassandra stretched out on her blankets and wiped away a tear in the corner of her eye. Dru could never be hers, except in her dreams.

Chapter Ten

It seemed strange to Cassandra to set up camp while the sun was still midway in the sky. But they were now a couple of miles outside of Good Times and would remain camped for twenty-four hours. During this time, every wrangler would have his chance to go into town. Half of the men would watch over the herd for the first twelve hours, and then the others would take the second shift.

Cassandra wondered if Vivian planned to go into town. Last night she had mentioned doing so, but Dru had advised her against it, telling her Good Times was no place for a lady. Lady? Didn't Dru realize that Vivian Lance was no lady, but a manipulative, cunning she-devil? Why were men so blinded by beauty?

The drovers had eaten a hearty meal, and the ones going to town, Dru among them, were now down at the river washing and changing into clean clothes. Cassandra had just finished drying the dishes when Virgil walked up to her.

"Missy," he said, his voice lowered, "I want you to ride into town with Pete and buy whatever supplies we're low on." Seeing her hesitancy, he assured her, "Good Times doesn't get too rowdy 'til after dark. Besides, you and Pete are just goin' to the general store and then head straight back. You'll be all right. I'd go into town and get the supplies, but I have an old friend who owns a homestead about ten miles from here. I plan to leave shortly to visit 'im, and I won't be back 'til mornin'." He could see a shadow of worry on her face. "If you're worried about the Thurstons, they aren't in this vicinity. I've backtracked for the past week and there's no signs of anyone followin'. If they're behind us, they're at least two days back."

She smiled affectionately. "So that's why you haven't been riding with the herd, you've been searching for the Thurstons. Why didn't you tell me before now?"

"I wanted to make sure they weren't anywhere around before letting you know what I was up to."

"What excuse did you give Dru for backtracking?"

He rubbed a hand over his full beard, chuckling softly. "I told 'im it was none of his business."

"I doubt if he accepted that for an answer."

"He didn't. So I told 'im I was worried about rustlers followin' us. He bought my story 'cause he thinks that's why Russ was shot."

She clasped his hands, squeezing them fondly. "Oh, Virgil, what would I do without you?"

He glanced about cautiously and was glad to find that no one was watching. He favored Cassandra with a quick wink, then withdrew his hands. "I'll go saddle the horse you rode to Silver Creek." His eyes gleaming, he added, "Your very own mare."

"My mare?" she questioned.

He grinned expansively. "I've decided to give you the horse."

Cassandra's face brightened. "I don't know what to say!"

120

"Thank you will do quite nicely," he answered, still grinning.

"I do thank you!" she exclaimed. "Does Dru know you're giving me the horse?"

"He knows, but he kinda objected. He said that a docile mare wasn't a fittin' horse for a boy your age. He suggested that we give you a horse more spirited." Virgil laughed jovially. "Dru said if I didn't stop coddlin' you, I was gonna turn you into a sissy. He hinted that I should put a skirt on you and be done with it."

Cassandra giggled merrily. "If he only knew!"

Virgil's mood sobered. "If he ever finds out, we're both in deep trouble. He's gonna think we made a fool of 'im."

"But we aren't! Not really."

"He won't see it that way." Virgil shrugged. "Well, there's nothin' we can do about it."

Cassandra's consternation was apparent. Virgil smiled encouragingly, and it lifted her mood. "Don't worry, missy. Regardless of what happens, I can handle that stubborn nephew of mine. Well, I'll go saddle your mare. The men will be leavin' soon, and you and Pete can ride to town with 'em. I'll see you in the mornin' when I get back from visitin' my friend."

As Cassandra watched Virgil leave, she was suddenly struck with how dearly she loved him. She had never been especially close to her father; he had been too reticent and severe. Now, all the love she would have given a father was bestowed upon Virgil.

It was a warm, pleasant day, the sky etched with scribbles of billowing clouds, and the sun was a dazzling yellow blur drifting lazily toward the western horizon.

As the riders traveled speedily across the dusty terrain, their horses' pounding hoofs sent small burrowing animals scurrying wildly for shelter.

Cassandra and Pete brought up the rear, and as Dru and the wranglers kept up their hurried pace, Cassandra wished they'd slow down. Apparently, she bristled, saloons and prostitutes made men anxious fools! She didn't admit to herself that her peevishness was ruled by jealousy. The prospect of Dru bedding one or more of Violet's girls was so painful that she refused to think about it.

Her mood testy and her spirits drooping, Cassandra rode in silence. A few times Pete tried to engage her in small talk, but his attempts proved futile, and he finally gave up.

The wranglers whooped boisterously as they rode into town. It had been built with good times in mind, and as the riders entered the main thoroughfare, Cassandra was astounded by the number of saloons that bordered the street. A couple of clapboard hotels, a mercantile, a gunsmith's, a barber shop, a public bath, and a general store were placed here and there as though they had been included as an afterthought.

Cassandra didn't doubt that Good Times would be doomed when civilization conquered the West; the town would cease to exist.

As the wranglers headed toward the stables, Cassandra and Pete, leading two pack mules, guided their horses to the general store. Dismounting, Cassandra caught a glimpse of Dru and was surprised to see that he hadn't accompanied the others but was riding in her direction. He edged his horse to the hitching rail, dismounted, and said. "I'll stable my horse later."

Although Cassandra's face remained impassive, she was disturbingly aware of Dru's rugged, masculine appeal. Her eyes raked him furtively. His dark trousers, fitting like a glove, accentuated his long legs and manly thighs. An ivory-colored Western shirt was stretched tightly across the width of his strong shoulders, the top laces untied to reveal an apex of dark curly hair. His Colt revolver was strapped on securely, the thong tied loosely about his leg. His black hat, worn low on his brow, shadowed his strikingly blue eyes and handsome face.

Dru, totally unaware of Cassandra's hungry perusal, turned and motioned for her and Pete to follow him inside the store.

As Cassandra stepped through the doorway, Dru caught her arm and said hastily, "Casey, pick out the supplies you need, then let Pete load 'em on the mules. I want you to go someplace with me."

"Where?" she asked. The touch of his hand was sending fire through every nerve in her body.

"You'll see," he replied, his grin devilishly handsome. When Cassandra remained riveted, he gave her a gentle but impatient shove. "Go on, son. Pick out the supplies. I don't have all day."

Dru waited at the doorway, and as Cassandra told the store owner what she needed, she could feel Dru's eyes watching her every move. However, she hid her apprehension well, and outwardly she seemed totally relaxed. Inwardly, though, she was a nervous wreck. Where did Dru plan to take her? Had he caught on to her disguise? Did he intend to take her someplace where they could be alone so that he could fully unleash his rage? The thought was somewhat frightening.

Completing her shopping, Cassandra drew a nervous breath and went to Dru. Her heart was pounding as she followed him outside. He slowed his steps, and as she came abreast of him, he matched his strides to hers.

They had walked only a short distance when Dru halted, remarking, "Well, here we are."

Cassandra was surprised to see that they were standing in front of a gunsmith's. Dru opened the door, gesturing for her to precede. She stepped inside a little hesitantly. Why had Dru wanted her to accompany him to a gun shop?

A tall, lanky man stood behind the counter, and smiling cordially, he asked, "What can I do for you gents?"

Cassandra held back, and grasping her arm, Jensen drew her forward, taking her to the counter with him. Speaking to the proprietor, he remarked, "I'd like to see a Starr Double-Action Army Forty-four. Do you have one in stock?"

"Yes, sir, I sure do." Opening one of the gun cabinets, he reached in and withdrew the pistol, then gave it to his customer.

Dru held it for a moment, balancing its weight in his hand. Then, turning to Cassandra, he said with a smile, "This gun's a double-action revolver. Here; it's yours." He handed her the pistol.

Dru thought Casey would be exultant, and when the lad merely stared at the gun as though he'd never seen one before, Dru uttered crankily, "Didn't you tell Virgil that you planned to buy yourself a revolver?"

"Yes, sir," she mumbled.

"Well, you can save your money, I'm buyin' it for you."

Cassandra swallowed heavily. She knew Dru was

expecting her to thank him jubilantly. She was touched by his gift; however, the deceitful web she was weaving was becoming more entangled. If Dru were to learn the truth about her, this day would most assuredly add fuel to his anger.

Forcing herself to smile brightly, she said excitedly, "Thanks boss! I can't wait to try it out!"

"Son, will you take some advice?" Dru queried.

"Sure," she muttered.

"If you're good with a pistol you might deter would-be trouble, but if you ever find yourself facing a gunfight and you have a choice of weapons, it makes good sense to reach for a rifle or a shotgun. At long ranges, you need a rifle with a calibrated sight, and at close range a sawed-off shotgun is the most fearsome weapon you can own. A load of buckshot at close range can practically cut a man in two."

Cut a man in two? Cassandra cringed inwardly. "Thanks, boss. I'll remember what you said." Her tone, however, was devoid of emotion.

A small frown furrowed Dru's brow. He didn't know why he kept trying to build a relationship with Casey. He'd never met a kid so close-mouthed and distant.

"Casey," he began, "you're still too young to carry a gun. I suppose it won't hurt if you wear it on the trail, but hereafter, when you go into a town, leave your gun at camp."

"Sure, boss," she mumbled.

Looking away, Dru spoke to the proprietor. "The boy needs a gun belt."

The man's eyes swept over Cassandra. "He's kinda puny, but I think I've got one that will fit."

Dru, anxious to stable his horse and get a room at the hotel, asked for ammunition, and then he quickly

125

paid for his purchases.

He kept out some of the cartridges, handed the box to Cassandra, then inserted the bullets into the gun belt before giving it to her.

She strapped in on, then slipped her pistol into the holster. It felt heavy and awkward about her waist.

Dru moved brusquely to the door, gesturing tersely for her to follow. As they stepped outside, he told her to return to camp and he'd see her in the morning.

Without further ado, he walked away, leaving her gazing lovingly at his departing back. Tears threatened, but she held them back. She knew that Dru was disappointed. He had thought his gift would thrill her, and if she had really been a thirteen-year-old boy, she supposed she would have been elated. She didn't even like guns, but she believed learning to use them was the only defense she had against Jubal Thurston.

With a despairing sigh, she glanced across the street, and as her gaze centered on the mercantile, she became aware of the elegant gown hanging in the window. Her pretty face puckering into a pout, she glanced down at her new gun, then back at the gown. I'd rather have a new dress! she thought glumly.

She started across the street, paused halfway for a buggy to pass, then hurried to the mercantile. She stood in front of the window, gazing at the gown with longing. It was an evening dress of white silk, trimmed with pink lace. It was designed to fall gracefully off the shoulders, fit tight at the waist, then flare into soft, billowing folds. Judging its size, she was sure that it would fit perfectly.

Daydreaming, Cassandra envisioned herself in the gown, waltzing gracefully over a dance floor with Dru as her partner. Oh, if only he could see her in such elegant attire!

She had made a half-turn to head back to the general store when, suddenly, she stopped dead in her tracks. A special gleam had come to her eyes and her thoughts were flowing fluidly. She slipped her hand into her pocket as though to reassure herself that she still had her 150 dollars. The money was stuffed deeply into her pocket, and as her thoughts continued to race, her fingers wrapped unconsciously about the bills.

She was sure the dress was terribly expensive, and she shouldn't spend her money on something so frivolous. Furthermore, if she bought the dress, she'd have to buy all the accessories.

Thoughtfully, she nibbled at her bottom lip. What if she were to purchase the gown, get a room at the hotel, then confront Dru? Would he recognize her dressed in her new gown? No! She was certain that he wouldn't!

Her thoughts continued. She'd tell Pete that she had decided to stay in town and for him to take the supplies back to camp. She was glad that Virgil had decided to visit his friend; otherwise, he'd come to town looking for her.

Her mind made up, Cassandra hurried away from the mercantile and headed for the general store. Pete had the supplies packed on the mules and was waiting for her. Informing Pete of her decision to stay in town, she handed him her box of cartridges, asking him to take them back to camp.

Pete, knowing how protective Virgil was of Casey, was reluctant to leave the lad.

Before he could voice his objections, Cassandra rushed off, giving him no choice but to leave without her.

Hurrying back to the mercantile, Cassandra glanced over her shoulder to check on Pete. Her heart fluttered joyfully when she saw that he was leaving. The first part of her plan had been put successfully in motion. She hoped desperately that the rest would run as smoothly.

Opening the door, Cassandra darted inside. The proprietor, a middle-aged woman, was hanging a new supply of dresses. She glanced at the door and was surprised to see that her customer was a young boy. Certain that he wouldn't make a substantial purchase, she asked somewhat coolly, "Can I help you find something?"

"Yes. I want the dress in the window."

She arched her brows. "Son, are you quite sure you want to buy an evening gown?"

Cassandra looked closely at the woman. Her face was heavily painted, and her hair, worn in an upsweep style, was so blond that it was almost white. Cassandra had never seen hair that color, and she wondered if the woman was wearing a wig. Upon closer perusal, she decided that she was indeed sporting a wig. Giving the store a quick appraisal, she was elated to see that there were several wigs for sale. She had been wondering what to do about her short hair, but now that problem was solved. She'd buy a wig!

The owner was growing impatient with the boy. "Are you sure you want that gown?" she asked again.

"Yes. How much is it?"

The woman's clientele consisted mainly of Violet and her girls, and the dress in the window was too conservative and tasteful for women of their profession. They preferred gowns more revealing and colorful. White was too virginal. Ordering the gown had been a costly mistake, and the garment had now been hanging in the window for months.

She eyed the lad thoughtfully. If she priced the gown too high, he wouldn't be able to afford it. However, she needed to make a profit. "I'll sell it to you for fifty dollars."

Cassandra realized the price was extremely low, but as badly as she wanted the dress, she was now having second thoughts. Sensibly, she knew she shouldn't spend her money so frivolously.

Mistaking the reason behind her customer's hesitancy, the woman lowered the price even more. "Forty dollars, and that's my final offer. If I go any lower, I may as well give it to you."

Forty dollars! Cassandra couldn't refuse! "All right, I'll buy it."

As the proprietor stepped to the window to get the dress, she asked, "Who's the lucky lady?"

"Ma'am?" Cassandra mumbled, confused.

"Who are you buying the dress for?"

"My . . . my sister," she stammered.

"She'll be delighted to receive such a beautiful gift.

"I also want to buy lace underthings, a petticoat, shoes, and cologne."

Carrying the gown to the counter, the woman exclaimed. "My goodness, you're really splurging, aren't you?"

Cassandra, offering no comment, stepped over to study the wigs. She chose a honey blond color that was close to her own shade. The wig was styled in long, draping curls which would touch her shoulders with feathery softness.

Cassandra was now growing anxious and could hardly wait to stand in front of a mirror and see her transformation.

Turning and facing the proprietor, Cassandra said

briskly, "I'll take this wig and a hairbrush. I also need rouge."

The woman, suddenly growing suspicious, asked sharply, "Boy, is this some kind of joke? Did some drunken cowboys dare you to come in here and pull my leg?"

Cassandra went to the counter, drew out her money and said curtly, "Ma'am, it's no joke."

Cassandra got a room at a hotel and stashed her purchases. Then hurrying back outside, she took her mare to the stables and paid for a night's keep. Returning to the hotel, she ate a hurried supper before going upstairs. The bath was located at the end of the hall, and seeing that it was unoccupied, she dashed into the small room and quickly took a bath. She slipped back into her boy's clothes for the short walk down the hall to her room.

She unlocked her door and went inside. Her purchases were on the bed. She was carrying her gun belt, her revolver tucked in its holster. She laid it aside and gave her new clothes her full attention.

She dressed with care, loving the way her new attire made her feel like a woman. She was so tired of wearing men's clothes.

She studied her appearance in the full mirror that hung beside the dressing table. She had never owned a gown so beautiful, and while admiring her reflection, she twirled about gracefully, the movement sending the long folds flowing about her ankles.

The blond wig was on the dresser, and picking it up, she placed it on her head. She secured the hairpiece with pins, then ran her brush carefully through the honey-colored tresses. When she was finished, she studied her reflection closely. She knew no one would guess that she was wearing a wig. She dabbed rouge sparingly on her cheeks and lips, then sprinkled cologne behind her ears, remembering to splash a little on each wrist.

Groomed and ready to leave, Cassandra wondered where the most logical place was to find Dru. Violet's? She shuddered. She couldn't possibly go there!

Deciding her best recourse was to walk about town on the chance that she might spot him, Cassandra drew a deep, apprehensive breath and left her room.

Chapter Eleven

As Cassandra walked out of the hotel, she was somewhat amazed to find the main thoroughfare so congested. Several cowboys on horseback were galloping down the street whooping jubilantly, their horses' hoofs sending clouds of dust swirling thickly through the night air. Men of all shapes and sizes crowded the sidewalks, and as Cassandra stepped away from the hotel, these men, startled by such unexpected beauty, trailed her with their eyes. A few tried to speak to her, but Cassandra looked straight ahead, ignoring them. She took long, determined strides as though she knew exactly where she was going and was in a hurry to get there.

As she moved quickly down the wooden walkway, Cassandra was beginning to experience second thoughts. Regardless of how badly she wanted Dru to see her as a woman, going about it in this fashion might be too dangerous. In towns like this one, only prostitutes walked the streets unchaperoned. What if one of these cowboys were to forcefully stop her and insist that she spend the night with him? What would she do? All at once, she wished she hadn't left her revolver in her room. If she had it with her, she'd feel a lot safer.

Warily, Cassandra approached a saloon located

close to the hotel. Although a piano was blaring a lively tune, the sounds of men's voices intermingled with women's shrill laughter carried over the loud music.

She paused outside the saloon's swinging doors. If she were to peek over the top, would she spot Dru? If she did, then what? Could she possibly muster the nerve to step inside?

Beads of perspiration dotted Cassandra's brow, and her heart started to pound apprehensively. No! She couldn't make herself step inside such an establishment! Not even for Dru!

If he's in there, she decided desperately, I'll just stay here and wait for him to come outside.

She was about to look over the doors when a gruff voice seemed to come out of nowhere.

"Howdy, doll. Are you lookin' for someone?"

She wheeled about awkwardly. The man was standing so close that her breasts brushed against his brawny chest. Stepping back, Cassandra looked up into his bearded face. His eyes were traveling up and down her as a lustful grin spread across his lips, revealing tobacco-stained teeth. Fear gripped her heart!

His words slurred drunkenly. "What's your price, baby-doll?"

"Wh-what?" she stuttered, inching away from his appalling presence.

"How much do you charge for a roll in the hay?" he asked, his tone now impatient.

Cassandra paled; then, taking the man unawares, she darted past him. His arm flailed out to stop her, but she moved too swiftly. Seized with panic, she ran blindly across the street, causing her to barely miss colliding with an oncoming buggy. The

133

driver, jerking back on the reins and bringing his team to an abrupt halt, hurled angry obscenities at her back.

Cassandra ignored the driver's offensive tirade, and the moment she reached the other side of the street, she dared to look back to see if the man who had accosted her was following. She was relieved to catch a glimpse of him going inside the saloon.

Her foolish plan to confront Dru suddenly hit her with startling force. How could she have planned something so foolhardy? Was she completely out of her mind? Was her love for Dru making her so desperate that she'd lost all common sense?

She chastised herself severely and was on the verge of returning to her hotel when she happened to glance back across the street. The tall man stepping out of the saloon arrested her full attention. Dru! It was Dru!

She was so delighted that she almost called out to him. Luckily, she caught herself in time and his name died on her lips. The mere sight of him lifted her spirits, and his presence made her feel safe. She was no longer afraid, and as Dru sauntered away from the saloon, she crossed over and followed him at a distance.

She wondered where he was going. She knew she had to find a way to confront him before he reached his destination, for if he was heading for another saloon, she wouldn't dare follow him inside—no matter what!

However, to Cassandra's surprise, Dru, his long strides remaining steady, walked past saloons without giving them so much as a cursory glance.

They were soon at the edge of town, and the

roisterous sounds of Good Times faded only to be replaced by music and voices coming from a large, two-story clapboard house.

The brightly lit home, surrounded by a white picket fence, sat prominently at the end of the street. Several horses were tied to the long hitching rail that ran the full length of the house. Cassandra had a sinking feeling that this place belonged to Violet.

Knowing she must stop Dru before he entered the house, she lifted the hem of her dress and began to run. She was so anxious to catch up to Dru that she didn't notice the two men who had ridden up to the hitching rail.

They, however, were very conscious of her. The two cowhands frequented Violet's, and not recognizing Cassandra, they took for granted that she must be a new girl that had been hired since their last visit.

The drovers dismounted hastily, waited until Cassandra was within their reach, then they stepped in front of her, blocking her path.

"What's your hurry, sweetheart?" one of them drawled. "Are you that eager to get to work? I bet Violet charges a pretty penny for you." His gaze undressed her. "Hell, I don't give a damn how much you cost, I'm gonna pay it. Honey, you're the prettiest, sweetest-looking whore I ever set eyes on." His callused hand shot out, capturing her wrist in a viselike grip.

Trying vainly to wrest free, Cassandra pleaded, "Let me go! Please! You don't understand!"

Meanwhile, Dru had paused to light a cheroot, but when he saw what was happening, he slipped the unlit cheroot back into his pocket.

His eyes steely, his movements as stealthy as a panther's, Dru moved soundlessly toward the two men and Cassandra.

"Come on, honey," the drover was saying, tugging at Cassandra's wrist. "Let's go inside and up to your room."

The drover's friend came up behind Cassandra and circled his arm about her waist. Pressing her back flush against his hard chest, he uttered huskily, "We'll make it a threesome. Violet charges more for unusual entertainment, but we got paid today so we can afford it."

"Honey," the other one said anxiously, "we'll be gentle, but I promise you that we'll give you the time of your life."

"No!" Cassandra cried desperately. She tried wildly to pull away, but her attempts were futile.

"Excuse me, gentlemen," a deep voice suddenly cut in.

Recognizing the voice, Cassandra froze as her eyes flew frantically to Dru. He was poised calmly, and every nerve in his body seemed totally relaxed. He wasn't looking at Cassandra; the drovers held his undivided attention.

The man holding Cassandra released her brusquely, and she managed to move shakily out of his reach.

Dru, his tone quiet but deadly serious, continued, "I don't think the lady's interested in a threesome. So why don't you two just mosey on into the house and find yourselves another playmate?"

"Mind your own goddamn business!" one of them yelled, his face beet red with rage.

The other man, moving furtively, reached for his holstered pistol.

But Dru had read his intent, and before the drover's hand had ever touched his weapon, Dru's gun was drawn and aimed at this opponent's heart.

Mistaking Dru for a gunman, the man said hastily to his comrade, "Come on; let's go inside. Ain't no whore worth dyin' over. Not even a whore as pretty as this one."

His friend agreed, and they walked away quickly. Dru waited until they were inside Violet's house before holstering his pistol. He turned slowly, and for the first time he looked closely at the woman he had rescued. Her loveliness was breathtaking, and his eyes glinted with masculine interest. He found something vaguely familiar about her, and he wondered if they had met before. He dismissed the chance. It would be impossible to forget someone as beautiful and as enticing as this enchanting minx.

Cassandra, her heart beating irregularly, watched him silently, and his fiery blue eyes stared back, studying her with something more than mere physical attraction.

"Are you on your way to work?" he asked suddenly, breaking the silent tension. He nodded tersely toward Violet's house.

"Work?" Cassandra repeated vacantly. Like the drovers, he had mistaken her for one of Violet's girls. "No. . . . No, I'm not on my way to work." Nervous perspiration broke out on her palms.

"Is this your night off?"

"Yes," she lied quickly, not giving her better judgment a chance to cast out a warning.

Dru smiled lazily. "Well, since this is your night to do with as you please, I don't see any reason for you to go inside. Do you?"

"No." She answered so softly that he barely heard her.

"If you'll spend the night with me, I'll make it well worth your time. Price is no object."

She could see the hungry passion radiating from the blue depths of his eyes. Oh, she had waited so long for Dru to look at her in this way!

Slowly, he reached over and curled a honey blond curl about his finger, never imagining that the shiny tresses weren't truly hers.

Excitement mounting within her, Cassandra shivered imperceptibly. Her eyes, filled with desire, met his, and his intense gaze held her spellbound.

Moving with catlike grace, Dru's hands spanned her waist, drawing her against his tall frame. His hunger came in a heated gush as he pressed every inch of her supple body to his. Bending his head, his lips descended lightly to hers; then, as his passion sparked into flames, his mouth claimed hers so fervently that his kiss was almost savagely brutal.

A wild surge of pleasure coursed through Cassandra as she surrendered willingly to the lips taking such wonderful possession of hers. For weeks she had wished for this moment, but not even in her wildest dreams had she imagined that Dru's kiss would be this electrifying, this thrilling!

Taking his mouth from hers, he kissed the soft hollow of her throat, his lips whisper-light. "Come to my room with me," he said, his tone laced with urgency.

Cassandra's heart cried to leave with him, to experience the full pleasure of his love, to hoard the memory forever and savor it on lonely nights. However, her better judgment demanded that she turn away, run to her hotel room and lock the door before it was too late.

Again, his mouth moved over hers in a sensuous, breathtaking exploration, and his fiery kiss destroyed her better judgment. Her heart emerged victorious, and as his lips left hers, she whispered timorously, "Yes, I'll go to your room."

He smiled, and it was so disarming and full of warmth that it went straight to Cassandra's heart. Daringly, she placed her hand on the nape of his neck and pressed his mouth down to hers. As his tongue darted between her teeth to explore the deep recesses of her mouth, nothing could have prepared her for the explosive sensations that swept through her entire being. She loved his intimacy, and despite her inexperience, she fitted the contours of her body to his as though she had done it a thousand times before. She could feel his male hardness straining against her, and she instinctively pressed her thighs so close to his that they seemed fused together.

Disrupting their embrace, Dru stepped back and said with a shaky grin, "Little one, we'd better take it easy, or I won't be physically able to walk to my room." Taking her hand, he pressed her palm against his hard arousal, "Just feel what you do to me."

A blush colored Cassandra's cheeks, but she didn't move her hand away. She wanted to touch every inch of his tall, masculine frame.

He lifted her hand to his lips, placing a light kiss on her palm; offering her his arm, he asked, "Shall we?"

She slipped her hand into the crook of his arm, and as they walked away from Violet's, Cassandra forced herself not to dwell on what she was about to do. She pushed her conscience to the farthest corner of her mind. Tomorrow she'd free her conscience and let it plague her, but not tonight. Tonight she'd give herself to the man she loved, to the only man she could ever love this passionately, this desperately!

"How long have you worked for Violet?" Dru inquired, his question cutting into Cassandra's thoughts.

"Not long," she mumbled evasively.

Detecting a Southern drawl, he asked, "You're from down South, aren't you?"

Cassandra gulped. Had he recognized her voice as Casey's? Was he merely playing cat and mouse?

"Yes," she answered softly. "My home's in the South."

"I thought I detected a Southern drawl. What brought you to Good Times?"

"Circumstances," she mumbled. Apparently, he hadn't recognized her as Casey, but she wished he'd stop asking so many questions. She had no answers.

"You're not much of a conversationalist, are you?"

"No," she replied.

Dru chuckled pleasantly. "Good! I don't pay a woman of your profession for her conversation but for her favors."

Sudden tears stung Cassandra's eyes, but she forced them back. She didn't want Dru to pay for her favors, she wanted him to love her. She longed to hear him whispering sweet endearments in her ear, pledging his heart for an eternity. A surge of anger rose. What did she expect? She had come to him as a prostitute, not as the woman who loved

140

him with all her heart and soul! She was getting exactly what she deserved!

Suddenly, though, the true meaning of "prostitute" thundered through her mind, bringing her steps to an abrupt stop. She was still a virgin, and Dru would certainly know that she had never been with another man! He'd be outraged and demand an explanation.

"What's wrong?" Dru asked, wondering why she had stopped so unexpectedly.

"N-nothing," she stammered, resuming her steps. What should I do? she cried inwardly. Her thoughts began running turbulently, and she was soon totally involved.

Cassandra remained so immersed in her troublesome reverie that she didn't even realize that they had entered the heart of town. When Dru suddenly paused in front of the hotel where she was staying, her mind was in such a turmoil that it took a moment for her to recognize where they were.

Dru opened the lobby door, and stood back for her to precede him. "I have a room here," he explained.

She entered on shaky legs. She had an overwhelming impulse to turn and run outside. Would he follow, catch her and demand that she explain her erratic behavior? Maybe he wouldn't pursue her, or if he did, maybe she could lose him in the crowded streets.

Cassandra was about to attempt a frantic escape when Dru slipped an arm around her waist, his hold tenacious. Had he somehow sensed her need to flee?

He rushed her across the small lobby and up the stairs. His grip remained firm as he guided their steps down the dimly lit hall and to his room. Keeping one arm about her waist, he reached into his pocket, brought out a key and unlocked the door.

Cassandra's eyes darted desperately to her own room, which was three doors down. If only she had stayed in there instead of carrying out this foolhardy plan! The words "prostitute" and "virgin" danced across her mind as Dru ushered her inside.

He locked the door, then crossed the uncarpeted floor, placed the key on the night table and lit the lamp. He adjusted the wick down to a romantic glow.

Cassandra, standing riveted, watched wide-eyed as Dru moved to the bed and drew back the covers.

"Would you like a drink?" he asked, looking at her for the first time since they'd entered the room. "You seem a little pale. A drink might help."

"Drink?" she echoed shakily. "Yes. . . . Yes, I need a drink."

"Whiskey all right? That's all I have."

"That's fine," she answered quickly. She recalled Dru giving her whiskey at the doctor's house in Silver Creek. The liquor had indeed calmed her nerves, and she hoped it would do so again.

He brought her a half-filled glass and was amazed when she tipped it up and drank the full contents. Apparently, the little minx enjoyed her spirits. Following suit, he finished off his own drink, taking it neatly.

Handing Dru her empty glass, she said urgently, "I'd like another, please."

He quirked a brow. "Are you sure?"

"I've never been more sure of anything."

Dru obliged, and he watched somewhat amused as she drained her second drink.

Cassandra gave him back the glass, and during the time it took him to carry it to the dresser and return to her side, the potent whiskey had hit her full force.

The room began to spin before her eyes, and she could feel a heavy layer of perspiration spreading across her forehead.

Her face turned deathly pale, and when she tottered precariously, Dru moved swiftly and lifted her into his arms.

He carried her to the bed and laid her down carefully. Stretching out beside her, he drew her close. "Are you all right?" he asked.

"Yes," she whispered, feeling somewhat better. However, the bed seemed to be rocking gently, and a warm tingling sensation was spreading through her limbs.

Rising up on one elbow, Dru gazed down into her face. Color had returned to her cheeks, and they were once again rosy. "You're very beautiful," he murmured. "What's your name?"

"Cassandra," she replied.

"My name's Dru."

Slowly he lowered his lips to hers, kissing her with exquisite tenderness. "Cassandra," he moaned huskily. "I can't recall ever wanting a woman as much as I want you. I can understand why Violet hired you. There's an aura of innocence about you that's very seductive. If I didn't know better, I'd never imagine that you do this for a living."

Cassandra's conscience suddenly broke free. She must tell Dru the truth! Pretending to be a boy in his presence was bad enough, but pretending she was a prostitute was more than she could bear!

She was trying to think of the best way to confess

143

when, demandingly, his mouth crushed against hers. His wild, hungry kiss swept all thoughts from her mind, and returning his ardor, she laced her arms about his neck. His thrusting tongue aroused fiery sensations within her, and her tongue boldly entwined with his. He moved over her, and his hardness pressed against her thighs fanned her awakening passion into leaping flames that were totally consuming.

"I must have you now!" he groaned urgently.

Standing, he drew her to her feet. His anxious fingers fumbled at the tiny buttons on her dress, and when he finally had them undone, he removed her gown with an air of impatience.

As he continued disrobing her, Cassandra regained a semblance of composure. She must tell him the truth! Now! . . . Now!

When she was left wearing only her lace panties and chemise, Dru once again lifted her onto the bed.

As he quickly slipped off his clothes, Cassandra's conscience demanded that she tell Dru who she really was, but her vocal chords refused to cooperate. Transfixed, her mind muddled with whiskey, she could only stare with wonder as Dru's manly physique was revealed. Oh, he's so perfectly handsome! she cried inwardly. And I love him so much!

He knelt on the mattress and slowly, seductively, removed her underthings. She could see desire mirrored in his blue eyes and knew that he found her attractive.

Dru lay beside her, and turning to him, she brushed her fingers across the dark curling hair of his chest. He kissed her urgently, and his tongue ravaged the sweetness of her mouth. She clung to him tenaciously, wanting the kiss to go on and on and on.

Every curve of her body molded against his as his hand caressed her bare back, trailing a blazing path down to her rounded buttocks. Then, tantalizingly, his fingers traveled across her soft thighs and to her womanly core. She was hot, moist, and his finger slid easily into her velvety depths. He prodded rhythmically, and she writhed wildly, arching against his stimulating invasion.

As his intimate caress drove her to ecstatic heights, Dru's lips traveled down her neck to her breasts, where he gently kissed and suckled each taut nipple.

His passion was dangerously surpassing the point of control, and raising himself up, he moved over her delicate frame. He parted her legs with his knees, and as his hard arousal sought entrance, Cassandra's senses returned and she stiffened against him.

She had to tell him that she was a virgin! Now! Before it was too late! "Dru!" she cried softly. "Wait! I must talk to you."

But Dru was beyond listening, and he drove deeply within her, robbing her innocence in one quick thrust.

As Cassandra released a small whimper, Dru's entire body grew taut. He froze, and staring down into her face, he gasped, "What the hell!"

"I tried to tell you," she said weakly.

"The hell you did!" he grumbled.

Anger radiated from his icy blue eyes, and she turned her face away. Her bottom lip trembled as she fought back tears.

Dru's heart softened, and he said with a note of

kindness, "What's done is done, and I can't give you back your innocence. But, sweetheart, you'd better have a good explanation."

He started to withdraw, but her warm heat was too pleasurable and he found himself delving deeper into her moist warmth.

She responded and instinctively wrapped her legs around him, pulling him into her. His thrusts were slow, measured, and her hips lifted in sensuous surrender.

Engulfed now in mindless ecstasy, Cassandra returned his passion with abandon, and her hungry intensity encouraged Dru to take her demandingly.

His electrifying aggression spiraled Cassandra to erotic heights, and she wished such rapture would never end.

Dru's lips, tongue and deep thrusting drove her helplessly to passion's brink, and shuddering beneath him, she reached for final fulfillment. Cresting love's peak, Cassandra cried aloud as a starburst of ecstasy exploded through every nerve in her body.

With a husky groan, Dru suddenly jerked inside her, finding and achieving his own breathtaking completion.

He lay atop her until his ragged breathing slowed to normal; then he withdrew and stretched out at her side.

Cassandra remained perfectly still, thoughts spinning through her head. Should she tell Dru the truth, or think up a plausible lie? She gave an inward, bitter laugh. A virgin pretending to be a prostitute? Barring the truth, there was no conceivable explanation.

In the meantime, Dru's rampant thoughts were

flowing. The enticing little vixen had made a fool of him! Her treachery was infuriating. Furthermore, guilt was intermingling with Dru's anger. He had taken her innocence, and he felt bad about it. However, his wrath was the stronger of the two emotions, and leaving the bed brusquely, he quickly slipped into his trousers.

He turned to Cassandra, his eyes glaring furiously into hers. "I don't like to be made a fool of, young lady! Nor do I have any patience with deceit!" His tone was severe, inflexible. "Now, I want an explanation! And it had better be good!"

Chapter Twelve

Cassandra's heart pounded against her rib cage. She knew Dru's temper was hanging by a mere thread, and if she told him that she and Casey were one and the same, she feared his reaction. She shuddered inwardly as she tried to imagine the full extent of his anger. He'd be so furious that he'd never forgive her.

Her delicate frame trembled as she sat up and swung her long legs over the side of the bed. She felt a wet, sticky sensation, and glancing down, she saw a patch of blood between her thighs.

All at once, Cassandra felt terribly dejected. She had just surrendered her innocence to the man she loved, and this moment should be filled with tenderness. She wanted Dru to hold her close and whisper loving words. But, instead, he was standing aloof, glaring at her with barely controlled wrath. She couldn't even ease her misery by placing part of the blame on him; the entire guilt lay with her.

Cassandra rose and picked up her undergarments, and as she slipped them on, she cast Dru a cautious glance. She had hoped that his anger was cooling, but his furious glare told her otherwise.

I must find a way to get out of here! she

thought frantically. I can't tell him the truth! I just can't! He'll hate me for tricking him! I can take his anger, but I'd rather die than suffer his hate!

Drawing a deep, apprehensive breath, she dared to meet his heated gaze. Timorously, she murmured, "I need to go to the bath."

His eyes narrowed suspiciously.

"Please!" she pleaded weakly.

He shook his head, stepped to the dresser and poured himself a drink. He quaffed down the whiskey, then turned and faced her. His countenance was hard, unforgiving. "I'm waiting for an explanation!" His voice tinged with rage, he added, "And I'm not a patient man!"

Cassandra's vision darted desperately to the locked door, then flitted back to Dru. "Please," she implored. "I must go to the bath and . . . and clean up."

Stifling his rage, Dru relented; however, he did so hesitantly, and finding his shirt, he handed it to her. "Wear this," he said gruffly.

Taking the garment, she looked at it disconcertedly. "Why do you want me to wear your shirt? Why can't I wear my gown?"

"If you leave your dress, petticoat and shoes, I know you won't try to run away. You can't very well walk through town dressed in your underwear and my shirt. You'd be molested before you got halfway down the street."

Cassandra searched his face. His lips were curled into a cold, confident grin. She suppressed her own smile of relief. He was giving her permission to leave the room! She could hardly believe it!

Dru stepped to the night table, grabbed the key, went to the door and unlocked it.

Quickly Cassandra slipped into Dru's ivory-colored shirt. It was entirely too large: the long sleeves fell past her hands, and the tail hung almost to her knees. She gave her beautiful gown a forlorn glance. It had cost a large hunk of her stored money, and now she was being forced to abandon it. She had never owned a garment so elegant, and leaving it behind was depressing.

Dismissing the gown, she moved warily to the open door, hardly believing her escape was going to be this easy. When Dru's hand snaked out, grasping her shoulder, her heart sank. Had he changed his mind? Was he about to insist that she explain herself?

Dru's anger was diminishing, and he spoke calmly, somewhat tenderly. "Cassandra, I can't begin to imagine why you gave up your virginity so easily. But I'm sure you think you had a good reason. Was it for the money? Are you or your family in some kind of financial trouble?"

Financial trouble? Yes, now that she had spent most of her money, she and Russ were dangerously low on funds. She was glad that, this time, she didn't have to tell a lie. "Yes, I'm in need of money," she answered softly.

His grip on her shoulder became gentle, consoling. "Hurry and clean up, then I'll take you to dinner. We'll discuss your financial troubles over a good meal. Maybe I can find a way to help you."

Placing both hands on her shoulders, he turned

her so that she was facing him. "Hon, selling yourself isn't the solution to your problems. I have a large herd of horses close by, and if necessary, I'll check about town and see if I can find someone to buy a few of 'em. I'll give you the money I receive. Considering what happened between us, it's the least I can do."

A shadow of abject misery darkened his handsome face, and Cassandra's heart ached for him. She had brought this anguish upon Dru, and she despised herself!

He removed his hands, smiled disarmingly and encouraged her to hurry and wash so they could go to dinner.

Cassandra took a step to leave; then, wanting to feel his lips on hers one last time, she flung herself into his arms and kissed him. Her heart jumped for joy when he drew her flush to his tall frame and returned her kiss fervently.

Releasing her with reluctance, Dru gazed down into her upturned face. He looked deeply into her beautiful green eyes, and for a moment, he inexplicably felt as though he had gazed into these same green eyes in another time, another place. He shook the feeling aside. If he had met her before, he'd certainly remember.

By now Dru's anger was completely dissolved and had been replaced with mixed emotions. He felt terrible about taking her innocence, but his feelings went deeper than that. This lovely, mysterious vixen had struck a tender cord deep within his heart.

Dru's compassion tore painfully into Cassandra's

conscience. Moving quickly, she crossed the threshold and started down the hall. When she heard his door close, she went to her own room. She had hidden the key under the mat, and retrieving it, she unlocked her door and rushed inside.

She undressed with haste. There were a water pitcher and basin on the dresser, and she quickly washed herself. She wrapped her undergarments and her other articles in the paper that had protected her gown. Her movements remaining hurried, she donned Casey's attire, strapped on her gun belt and placed her wide-brimmed hat on top of her short curls. Picking up her wrapped bundle and Dru's shirt, she went to the door. As her hand touched the knob, she detected heavy footsteps moving down the hall, heading for the bath.

She pressed her ear to the closed door. Loud, insistent knocks sounded on the bath's door, and as she listened, Cassandra's body tensed, her nerves on edge.

"Cassandra!" she heard Dru call impatiently. When she heard the door to the bath opening, she froze. Soon, though, she detected Dru's steps going back down the hall and his door slamming shut.

She waited a long moment before daring to peek into the hall. It was empty, and she stepped quickly to Dru's room and dropped his shirt in front of his door. Then, she hastened to the rear stairway, vaulted down the steps and hurried out the back entrance.

Wanting to leave Good Times as fast as possible, she ran all the way to the stables, saddled her mare and rode speedily out of the roisterous town.

She had traveled a good distance before pulling up and dismounting. She was too overwhelmed with guilt to practice precaution. Stopping on the plains late at night was perilous, but Cassandra was too overwrought to care if danger was lurking in the darkness.

The night was black, and the moon, obscured by one cloud after another, was casting moving shadows across the dark landscape. A gentle breeze whispered plaintively through the tall, rustling treetops, and in the distance a lone coyote's howling answered the wind's forlorn melody.

The woebegone scenario was in perfect harmony with Cassandra's mood, and leaning her head against the mare's sleek neck, she released her sorrow in a gush of tears. She cried until her eyes ran dry and her throat was raw from such deep sobbing.

Her movements sluggish, she remounted and headed the mare toward camp. She was plagued with guilt and knew there was only one solution. She must confess everything to Dru. He'd be outraged and would probably never forgive her. He might even hate her. The possibility seared Cassandra's heart like a red-hot iron.

Nevertheless, she'd clear her conscience and tell Dru the whole truth, regardless of the repercussions.

The next morning the sun had fully crested the horizon before Cassandra awakened. She stretched

153

sleepily, her eyes opening slowly. The brightness inside the wagon brought her awake with a start. My goodness, she had overslept! She should already have breakfast cooking!

She was about to hurry and dress when, suddenly, last night's memory came flooding back. Groaning, she remained on her pallet and drew the top blanket over her head as though she could smother her troublesome thoughts. Lord, it had really happened! She had tricked Dru into taking her to his room and making love to her!

A warm flush coursed through her, and throwing off the cover, she sat up and rested her arms over her raised knees. She could see her wrapped bundle, and she stared at it vacuously. Oh, how could she have been such a fool? Why hadn't she listened to her better sense instead of her heart?

Finding her guilt too depressing to dwell on, she allowed her thoughts to drift onto a different course. Remembering the ecstasy she had found in Dru's embrace caused a pleasant tingling sensation to sweep through her body. It had been heaven! What she wouldn't give to be in his arms right now, this very minute!

Resolutely, Cassandra thrust such dreams aside. She'd never again share a lovers' embrace with Dru! When she told him the truth, he'd despise her and never forgive her. She had lost him, and she might as well find a way to accept it.

Lose him? she pondered bitterly. How can I lose what I never had? Dru was never mine, not really.

"Casey?" Virgil suddenly called from outside, knocking loudly on the rear of the wagon. "Are you still asleep?"

"No," Cassandra answered quickly. "I'm getting dressed."

"Well, hurry up. You need to get started on breakfast. There's some hungry drovers out here."

Cassandra left her pallet and slipped hastily into Casey's attire. When she climbed down from the wagon, Virgil was waiting for her.

"Are you all right?" he asked, studying her closely.

Her answer was a quick nod. She started to walk past him, but his hand grasped her arm.

"I've been back for about an hour. I talked to Pete, and he told me that you didn't come back with him yesterday. He said you had decided to stay in town, then he saw you ride into camp late last night."

Cassandra looked away from his searching gaze. "So?" she mumbled.

"Don't get impertinent with me, missy!" he chastised paternally. "I promised your brother that I'd take care of you. But, dammit, you're more to me than a responsibility. I reckon I love you like a daughter, and speaking as a father, I want you to tell me why you stayed in town."

"I can't," she muttered quietly, guiltily.

He eyed her speculatively. "Did it have something to do with Dru?"

"Please, Virgil!" she pleaded pathetically. "Don't question me about last night!"

He was too worried to relent so easily and was getting ready to say more when Dru suddenly rode into camp.

155

They watched silently as he dismounted, walked over to the campfire and poured himself a cup of coffee.

The sight of Dru wrenched Cassandra's heart, and her stomach coiled into tight knots. She loved him so desperately! How could she find the courage to confess her deceit? But I must! I must! she thought wretchedly.

Virgil's eyes flitted back and forth from Dru to Cassandra. They both wore sullen, somber expressions. It doesn't take a genius, he speculated to himself, to know that something happened between those two.

He touched Cassandra's shoulder, gaining her attention. She gazed sadly up into his kind face.

"Missy, I've got a fairly good idea what happened. I don't know how you worked it, and I don't care to know. But I got a feelin' you got tangled in your own web." He looked her deeply in the eye, his meaning clear. "You'd better start untangling that web before it's too late."

"I will," she whispered.

"Don't put it off too long."

"I think it'll be easier if I wait a couple of days." She had a feeling that Dru was still terribly angry about last night. She had run away, leaving him without explaining herself. If she postponed her confession for two days, maybe three, it'd give his temper time to mellow. Then, she hoped, he wouldn't be quite so furious with her.

Virgil decided to let the matter rest — for now. "You'd better start breakfast."

She tried to will her legs to move, but they

156

wouldn't budge. "I can't," she groaned. Dru was at the fire, and she didn't want to be in close proximity with him. Just the thought made her hands tremble, and her body break out in a cold sweat. "I'm sick," she uttered weakly. "You'll have to make breakfast."

Without further explanation, she turned about and climbed inside the wagon. Going to her pallet, she fell across it. Dru's presence had ripped into her heart, shearing it into pieces. She hadn't lied to Virgil. She was sick; she was heartsick!

Outside, Virgil ambled away from the wagon and paused beside Dru. His eyes moved briefly over the wranglers. "Looks like I'm gonna be the cook today."

Virgil was answered by murmurs of protests.

"Sorry, men. I know I'm not much of a cook, but I'm all you got. Unless one of you want to volunteer for the job."

None of them did.

"What's wrong with Casey?" Dru asked.

"The boy's sick," Virgil grumbled.

Dru, like the drovers, dreaded Virgil's cooking. He hoped Casey wouldn't be under the weather too long. As he refilled his cup, a deep frown knitted his brow. He had a feeling this wasn't going to be his day. His mood was steadily plunging from bad to worse.

He sipped his coffee, letting his musings turn to Cassandra. Thoughts of the little minx had kept him awake for most of the night. He had tossed and turned as he tried to make sense out of what had happened. Why had she given him her inno-

157

cence, only to run away? If she needed money, he would have helped her. Hadn't he promised her that he would? So why did she disappear? And how the hell had she managed to leave the hotel dressed the way she was? She had even returned his shirt.

Dru had considered the possibility that she might have a room at the hotel, and this morning he had questioned the desk clerk. The man had assured him that no one matching Cassandra's description had checked into the hotel. Only two women were registered, and they were elderly ladies with their husbands. The rest of the patrons were men, except for a teenage boy.

Dru, certain that he'd never see the beautiful minx again, swore to forget her. However, he had a somber feeling it wouldn't be all that easy. Her memory was implanted deeply in his mind and would probably haunt him for a long time.

Banishing Cassandra from his thoughts, Dru put down his cup and got to his feet. He'd go check on Casey. The boy might be seriously ill and need a doctor.

Catching sight of Dru leaving, Virgil called. "Where are you goin'?"

"To see about Casey," he said over his shoulder.

Virgil came close to stopping him but changed his mind. Dru had to see Cassandra sooner or later. There was nothing he could do to keep them apart.

Dru didn't bother to announce his presence; he merely stepped up into the back of the wagon. Cassandra was lying on her bed. "How are you

158

feelin'?" Dru asked.

Her back was turned, and she hadn't been aware of Dru's intrusion until he spoke. The sound of his voice caused her to freeze, and her heart seemed to stand still.

She swallowed nervously, found her voice and muttered, "I feel a little sick at my stomach. Must've been something I ate."

Dru sat beside her pallet. Her back was still facing him. "Roll over, son."

"Why?" she asked so quietly that he almost didn't hear her.

"I don't like talkin' to your back," he complained, his tone cranky.

She was afraid to turn over. The memory of Cassandra was still too fresh in his mind. If he were to look at her closely, at such proximity, would he recognize her?

"Dammit, Casey!" Dru grumbled. "Roll over and look at me! What's wrong with you?" He'd never encountered a boy so exasperating.

As she slowly obeyed, her heart was beating so loudly that it thundered in her ears. She was scared to meet his gaze, but her eyes seemed to have a will of their own, and they went straight to his.

For a long moment, he became lost in the depth of her jade green eyes, his thoughts groping for a certain memory. At first it was hazy; then suddenly the memory became crystal clear and he was back in his hotel room looking deeply into the same pair of green eyes. His stomach muscles tightened, and his heart lurched. My God! How could he have been so blind? Anger surged, but it was aimed more at himself than Cassandra. He silently cursed his stupidity, his blindness!

Meanwhile, Cassandra was staring at him with bated breath. She was wary of the strange expression on his face. Had he recognized her? Lord, she hoped not. She didn't want him to learn the truth this way. She wanted to prove her sincerity by telling him herself.

Dru turned away from her questioning gaze. Taking a deep breath, he composed himself. The deceitful little chit deserved to be taught a lesson. She liked playing games, did she? Well, why the hell not? A mischievous gleam came to his blue eyes. Then, drawing an inscrutable mask over his features, he returned his gaze to hers.

Speaking calmly, he asked, "When did your stomach ache begin?"

Cassandra sighed inwardly. Thank goodness, he hadn't recognized her! "It started a few minutes ago," she answered.

The moment you set eyes on me, Dru thought, repressing a sarcastic grin. He was sure there was nothing wrong with Cassandra—except for a guilty conscience and maybe a bad case of nerves. Glancing about the wagon, and locating the medical kit, he reached over and picked it up. Since she enjoyed playing games, he'd play along with her, only this time they'd play by his rules.

Eyeing the medical kit, Cassandra asked warily, "What are you going to do?"

"I'm gonna give you something that'll help your stomach ache."

"I don't need anything," she mumbled. There was nothing wrong with her stomach, it was her heart that ached.

"Of course you do," he insisted. Reaching into the kit, he withdrew a bottle of castor oil. "A dose of this will fix you right up."

Cassandra, her nose wrinkling, protested, "No! I don't want any castor oil. It tastes horrible! If I take that, it'll make me sick! I'll throw up!"

"But if you throw up, you'll feel better." He opened the bottle, and as the medicine's odor wafted beneath Cassandra's nostrils, she frowned distastefully.

Sitting up, she scooted back until she was braced against the side of the wagon. She thrust out her arm, pushing the bottle aside. "I won't take it!" she said stubbornly, her lips pursed into a pout.

Dru's eyes raked her. God, it was tempting to draw her into his arms and kiss her beautiful, pouting mouth. With difficulty, he fought the urge and said firmly, "Casey, grow up and take your medicine like a man." He emphasized the word "man."

She wished she could call him a despicable, arrogant, and demanding bully, but she knew that a thirteen-year-old boy wouldn't express himself in such a way.

"I won't take castor oil!" she insisted, before childishly clamping her mouth shut.

Dru arched a brow. "In that case, I'll get a couple of the men to restrain you while I pour a good dose down your throat."

Anger flamed in her green eyes.

"Casey," he began, using an authoritative tone. "I don't have time to argue with you."

"I won't take it!"

"Yes, you will!" he persisted. "Now, do you take it like a man, or do I call for help?"

He had her on the spot. She could find no way out, so she lifted her chin bravely although she felt as though she'd rather take a beating than a dose of castor oil. "All right. You win. I'll take the damn stuff!"

A shadow of a smile fell across his face as he tipped the bottle to her lips. "Take a big swallow, Casey."

Holding her breath, Cassandra took a liberal amount. As it flowed slowly down her throat, the horrible taste made her shiver uncontrollably. Gagging, she choked out, "It's terrible!"

Dru capped the bottle. "If you aren't better by this evening, I'll have to give you another dose." His tone sounded a bit cynical.

Her eyes widened. "I'm sure I'll be fine."

"Do you think you'll feel like cooking supper?"

"I'm certain," she hastened to assure him. The thought of taking another dose of castor oil sent a shiver up her spine.

"Good," he remarked, placing the bottle aside and getting to his feet. "If the men have to eat Virgil's cookin' for breakfast and supper both, there won't be enough castor oil to go around."

His sudden grin was askew, and there was a special twinkle in his eyes that Cassandra failed to notice. "Casey, I've decided that Virgil coddles you

162

too much. So I'm gonna make it my personal business to turn you into a man. A trail drive is no place for a mama's boy."

As Dru left the wagon, he could feel Cassandra's eyes shooting daggers into his back. He laughed inwardly. The little vixen hadn't been taught a lesson yet—not by a long shot!

Chapter Thirteen

Pete, believing Casey was ill, volunteered to drive the chuck wagon, and Cassandra gratefully accepted his offer. Throughout the long and tedious day, she stayed under the canvas, avoiding Dru's disturbing presence and Virgil's questioning eyes. However, when it was time to set up camp, she climbed down from the wagon and resumed her job as cook. Although she dreaded facing Dru and Virgil, she dreaded a dose of castor oil even more; she didn't doubt that Dru would carry out his threat and force the vile-tasting concoction down her throat.

As Cassandra started her evening chore, Virgil kept his distance and she was able to prepare the meal without any distractions.

The drovers, along with Virgil and Vivian, ate heartily, but Cassandra didn't join them; she had no appetite. Knowing that she must soon confess everything to Dru had her nerves on edge and her stomach tied into knots. Would he hate her? God, she hoped not!

Meals were always eaten in two shifts because the herd was never left unattended. The wranglers who had the first watch left the camp, mounted their horses and rode out to relieve the others.

164

A few minutes later, the men arrived for supper. Dru was among them, and as he ambled to the fire and dished himself a plate of stew, Cassandra, poised at the rear of the wagon, watched his every move. She was fully aware of his rugged, masculine appeal, and she had to turn away from the surging power of his presence.

Dru, showing no interest in Casey's recovery, sat between Virgil and Vivian and began eating his meal. Vivian was soon flooding him and the others with small talk, and outwardly Dru seemed to be listening. Inwardly, though, his thoughts were centered on Cassandra. She had been on his mind all day, and remembering the times she had made a fool of him had added fuel to his anger. His wrath wasn't directed solely at Cassandra, but also at Virgil. He didn't doubt that his uncle was in cahoots with Cassandra. No wonder he hovered over the young cook like a mother hen! He was protecting her for more reasons than one. Well, in a couple of days, he'd insist that the pair explain themselves, but for now, he'd bide his time. He was still too angry to confront them, his temper needed to cool. He didn't want to say or do anything that he might later regret. He loved his uncle too much to hurt him, and if he tried to talk to him now, his anger could very well drive him into saying things that he'd later wish he could retract. Dru was perfectly aware that his temper was short-fused, and once it was lit, it was likely to explode before it could be extinguished.

As Vivian kept up a constant flow of words, Dru frowned impatiently and blocked out her voice. In Dru's opinion, Vivian had always talked too much, and her steady yapping never failed to grate on his nerves.

His gaze moved slowly to Cassandra. She was standing at the large water basin, washing dishes. She wasn't wearing a hat, and for a long moment he stared at her short hair. He wondered why she had gone to such lengths to disguise herself and why she and Russ had hired on to this drive. Why would a woman be willing to pass herself for a boy and take on such a strenuous job? And, more confusing, why would her brother approve?

Dru looked away from Cassandra. In a couple of days he'd know the answers to these questions, for he planned to insist that she and Virgil be totally honest with him, Also, when he talked alone with Cassandra, he intended to find out why she had given him her innocence so easily. She was beautiful, desirable, and each time his thoughts relived their rapturous union, the vision would stir his deepest passion. However, he wasn't about to be taken in by her beauty and her sweet facade. Obviously, she had an ulterior motive for surrendering her virginity. Was she planning to inveigle him into marriage? But why would she want to marry him? He certainly wasn't rich. His confused musings drifted to Anita, and for a moment he remembered that her beauty had also been coupled with a misleading aura of sweetness. Were she and Cassandra two of a kind?

He shrugged as though unconcerned. Some men didn't learn from their past mistakes, but he had learned his lesson well. An angry glint came to his blue eyes, turning them icy cold. No woman would ever again make a fool of him! He had paid too severe a price for Anita's treachery; it had cost him his son's life!

"Dru? . . . Dru?" Vivian's voice infringed on his thoughts. "Have you been listening to me?" She sounded perturbed.

He turned his head and looked at her. Anger was still radiating from the depths of his eyes. "Excuse me," he said tersely, getting to his feet.

Vivian, taken aback by his abrupt mood, watched as he moved toward the chuck wagon. What was wrong? Had she said something upsetting?

Cassandra's back was turned, and Dru stepped soundlessly to her side. She was completely unaware of his proximity until he said, "Here's my plate."

His nearness was unsettling, and her heart pounded. She couldn't muster the nerve to meet his eyes, and keeping her gaze turned away, she held out her hand. "Give me your plate," she muttered in her boyish tone.

He slapped it into her palm. "How are you feelin'?" he asked, his scrutiny intense.

"Fine," she mumbled. As she dipped the plate into the water, it slipped from her shaky grasp and sank beneath the suds. She wished she could disappear as easily.

His arms akimbo, his posture relaxed, Dru remarked calmly, "Casey, I've been thinkin' about you all day."

"Thinkin' about me?" she echoed, a slight quiver

in her voice.

"I decided it's about time you learned something besides cookin'."

Still withholding her gaze, she asked warily, "What do you mean?"

"Like I told you this morning, Virgil coddles you too much. He's turnin' you into a mama's boy. A boy your age needs to start actin' like a man." His caustic grin was imperceptible. "You don't want to be a mama's boy all your life, do you?"

"I'm not a mama's boy!" she uttered, in lieu of anything better to say.

"Of course you aren't," Dru readily agreed. "But if Virgil has his way, he'll keep you tied to this chuck wagon. Personally, I think it's about time we severed that tie. Don't misunderstand me. I don't aim to change your job. I want you to continue bein' our cook, but I'm gonna tell Pete to drive the wagon." He paused, watched her closely, then floored her with his news. "I decided it's high time you learned to be a drover."

"A drover!" she gasped, facing him. Oh, no! Not that! She didn't want to learn to herd horses!

Reading her thoughts, he grinned inwardly. "I knew you'd be thrilled. A boy your age doesn't want to be tied to a job as borin' as cookin'. I know when I was thirteen, I wouldn't have liked it. In the mornin', after Virgil gives you your shootin' lesson, ride out to the herd and find me so I can put you to work." He slapped Cassandra on the back in a gesture of camaraderie. "Son, I'll make a damned good drover out of you!"

He moved away quickly. Although Cassandra deserved to be taught a lesson, being close to her wasn't easy. He had to continually fight the urge to draw the deceitful little minx into his arms.

Cassandra, her face noticeably pale, her eyes opened wide, watched as Dru returned to the fire. She couldn't imagine herself herding wild horses; the mere thought was unnerving. I must tell him the truth! she cried silently. I must do it now! No, it's still too soon! He'll be so furious there's no telling what he might do!

In the morning, I can pretend to be sick, she thought suddenly. She quickly dismissed the idea. He'd merely insist that she take another dose of castor oil, and given a choice, she'd rather herd horses.

Cassandra's small chin lifted defiantly. Whoever said that only men could be drovers? Why couldn't a woman be just as proficient? It couldn't be that difficult. Russ had never herded horses, and if he could learn, why couldn't she?

She smiled confidently, then went back to washing dishes.

Dru stayed at the fire long enough to drink a cup of coffee; then he wandered from camp and into the surrounding darkness. He went to a towering cottonwood, sat down, and leaned back against its trunk. The treetops stirred with the whisper of a summer breeze, and the full moon, resplendent in the cloudless sky, cast a golden hue over the quiet landscape.

Dru lit a cheroot, and as he enjoyed his smoke, his thoughts floated to Cassandra. His mind conjured up her image, and he saw her as she was in Good Times. She had been so beautiful in her white evening gown, long honey blond tresses draping to her shoulders. A tiny smile curled his lips. She had worn a wig, of course. But the color of her own hair was very close to that of the wig's. He wondered how long her hair had been before she had cut it.

His smile widened as he remembered Cassandra's reaction to his decision to teach her to be a drover. She had taken the startling news like a trooper. The lady has grit, he mused.

Dru, however, hadn't been serious about making her herd horses. The work was too tiring and treacherous for a woman. He'd simply assign her a position at the rear of the herd, let her eat dust for a couple of hours and then send her back to the chuck wagon. Then, tomorrow night, he had one last lesson to administer. He planned to take the little spitfire across his knee and give her a thorough spanking. Afterward, he'd demand an explanation from her and Virgil.

The snapping of a twig arrested Dru's attention, and as his hand went to his holstered pistol, he heard Vivian call, "Dru . . . Dru, where are you?"

Dru frowned testily. Damn! Why the hell had Vivian followed him?

"Dru? . . . Dru?" she called again, her voice growing closer.

"I'm over here," he announced.

He watched as she came into sight. Vivian was

170

lovely in the moon-drenched night: the golden rays made her hair shine with auburn highlights, and her western skirt clung seductively to her full thighs. She wore a matching vest, and the material was stretched tightly across her ample bosom. The top buttons on her blouse were open, drawing attention to her deep cleavage.

Sitting beside Dru, she asked, "Why are you out here by yourself?"

"I wanted to be alone," he answered candidly.

His answer was perturbing, but Vivian wasn't about to be deterred by such frank honesty. Dru's aloofness had finally brought her patience to an end. She wanted him for a husband, and she was determined to have him. She would let no one stand in her way, not even Dru himself. She'd try seduction one last time, and if she failed, she'd throw her pride to the wind and stoop to blackmail.

Leaning against him, she placed a hand on his arm. "Dru, you seem troubled. Is there anything I can do to help?"

"No, thanks. I have to work this out in my own way."

"Then let me help you forget whatever is bothering you. I mean, I can make you forget temporarily." Boldly, she slipped her arms about his neck, pressing her breasts against his hard chest. "Kiss me, Dru," she purred.

He reached up and unwrapped her arms. Placing her hands on her lap, he pinned them there. "Vivian," he began tolerantly, "I've already told you that we can never be more than friends. So

171

why do you keep trying to seduce me?"

"Why do you keep fighting me?" she pleaded. "Oh, Dru, can't you see that we're perfect for each other? Why must you be so blind? If you'd just lower your defenses, I could prove how passionately you need me!"

"It takes more than passion for a couple to be compatible." He patted her hands kindly. "Vivian, you don't want a one-night union, you want a permanent relationship. For that to work, we would have to be in love."

"But I do love you, Dru!" she cried.

He answered gently, "But I don't love you."

"You could learn to love me!"

He shook his head. "It'd never work."

"You're wrong!" she remarked firmly. She rose to her feet, placed her hands on her hips and eyed him directly. "Dru, if you were to share my bed every night, you'd soon be very much in love with me. I know how to please a man, to drive him wild with passion."

"I already told you, there's more to love than sex."

"I disagree," she answered. "And since you've left me no other choice, I'll have to prove my point. Dru Jensen, when this drive is over and we return home, you'll marry me."

He watched her guardedly. "Why do you think that?"

"Because if you don't marry me, I'm going to foreclose on your ranch."

Standing, Dru threw down his cheroot and demanded, "What the hell are you talking about?"

172

"All those years when you were gone, wandering from one town to another, and fighting a war that didn't even concern you, Virgil drowned his troubles in whiskey."

"I know that," he replied impatiently.

"But you don't know that during those years he borrowed money from my father. Separately, they are small debts, but totaled they're enormous. Virgil accepted my father's loans pridefully and insisted on legal papers. Of course, he put the Bar-J up as collateral. Virgil's debts came due six months ago, and if I'm not paid in full, I'll foreclose."

"How much?" he asked, gritting his teeth. "How much do we owe you?"

"Ten thousand dollars." She raised her chin arrogantly.

"We don't have that kind of money!"

"Of course you don't. But I'm willing to make a deal."

"Deal?" he repeated, his eyes narrowing distrustfully.

"Marry me, Dru. I wouldn't foreclose on my uncle-in-law, would I?"

"Dammit, Vivian! I'm not for sale!"

"Oh, I think you are," she said calmly. "You love Virgil very much, and you know as well as I do that losing the Bar-J would destroy him. You're still young enough to start over, but Virgil's an old man. What can he do? Where can he go?"

He reached out and grasped her shoulders, his hold so tight it was almost painful. "Vivian, you damned fool! Under these circumstances, what kind of marriage would we have? Do you really want a husband who'll despise you?"

"You won't despise me," she replied confidently. "In time, you'll even fall in love with me."

"Surely you don't believe that!"

"But I do. And there's nothing you can say or do that will change my mind."

"You're crazy!" he uttered furiously, releasing his grip on her shoulders so brusquely that she tottered backward.

"Yes, I'm crazy!" she cried. "Crazy in love with you!" Desperate, she clutched his arm, her fingers digging into his flesh. "Dru, someday you'll realize I'm doing what is best for you! My ranch is more prosperous than the Bar-J so you'll have plenty of money. Also, you'll have a wife who loves you more than anything on this earth!"

"The answer's no," he grumbled. "I won't marry you!"

She turned, took a few steps, then whirled about and faced him. Her eyes were challenging. "So your pride is more important to you than Virgil. Very well, Dru, have it your way. Save your pride and destroy your uncle. That is, if you consider it a fair exchange." She paused, giving her words time to sink in. "Now, if you'll excuse me, I need to talk to Virgil. It's only fair that I inform him that he's about to lose his ranch."

She took a step to leave, but Dru detained her. "Wait!" he demanded. "Give me a moment to collect my thoughts."

Dru turned away from her watching eyes, moved back to the cottonwood, placed his outstretched

174

arms on the trunk and leaned forward. Staring down at his feet, he breathed in deeply in an effort to calm his inner rage. This was no time to lose his temper.

Vivian's blackmail was almost too much for him to grasp. Her desperation was incredible, unsound! But, despite her disturbed mind, she was right about Virgil. Losing the Bar-J might very well destroy him.

Ten thousand dollars! Dru groaned inwardly. The sale on the horses wouldn't cover the debt. Dru realized he needed time to think, to try and come up with a solution. But for now, he had to placate Vivian. He wanted to keep this from Virgil, and he knew the only way to do so was to tell Vivian that he'd marry her. However, he had to find a way to persuade Vivian to postpone the marriage.

Vivian, anxious for Dru's answer, stepped to his side and touched his arm. "I'm growing impatient. What's your decision?"

Stepping away from the cottonwood, he gazed thoughtfully down into her face.

She waited with bated breath, her eyes searching his classically handsome features.

"All right, Vivian, I'll marry you."

She smiled victoriously, but his next words rocked her triumph.

"However, there's a stipulation."

"Oh?" she questioned, her brows raised.

"That we get married three months from now." It wasn't much time, but he knew Vivian would never agree to an extended period. However, a reprieve would give him time to work something out. Perhaps he could return to his old line of work as a bounty hunter. In three months, he could never earn enough money to pay Virgil's debits, but at least he could make enough for him and Virgil to start over. With his money added to the sale of the horses, they could move north to Montana and buy another ranch. The winters were frigid, but the land was cheap. Losing the Bar-J would be hard on Virgil, but Dru was determined to see him through it.

"Wait three months?" she remarked sternly. "Not on your life! The marriage will take place as soon as we return home."

He shrugged calmly. "Then the deal's off. Run back to camp and tell Virgil you plan to take the Bar-J. I won't try to stop you." He was bluffing.

Believing him, she stammered uncertainly, "I don't understand why . . . why you need three months."

"I have some personal business to take care of. This business will take me away for about three months."

"Where are you going?"

"I told you, it's personal."

She shook her head. "No, I won't agree to your terms. You won't return in three months, you'll skip out on me."

"I might do that to you, but I wouldn't do it to Virgil."

She was weakening. "I don't know. I'm not sure I can trust you."

"We either do it my way, or we don't do it at

176

all." He sounded adamant.

Vivian conceded, reluctantly. "Very well, Dru. But I swear if you don't return in three months, I'll foreclose on the Bar-J, and your uncle will be left with nothing."

He eyed her unyieldingly. "I'll be back, you can count on it."

Her spirits lifted, and taking his hand, she said gaily, "Let's hurry to camp and tell everyone that we're getting married."

He drew back. "Is it necessary?"

"For years I've dreamed of announcing our engagement, and now that it has come to pass, I'll not be denied the pleasure."

He followed hesitantly. The news would come as quite a shock to Virgil. He already knew that his uncle would try to talk him out of it. Convincing Virgil that he was serious about marrying Vivian wasn't going to be easy, but he didn't want his uncle to know of Vivian's blackmail until he had the money for them to head to Montana. He wanted to protect him from Vivian's heartless ploy as long as possible. Virgil had accumulated the debts while he was drinking, and when he learned what his drinking had cost him, he was going to be awfully hard on himself.

As they walked into camp, hand in hand, Dru saw Cassandra and Virgil sitting at the fire. The wranglers had retired to their bedrolls.

Virgil was telling Cassandra that, regardless of Dru's instructions, there was no way he was going to allow her to herd horses when, suddenly, he became aware of Dru and Vivian.

Cassandra followed Virgil's gaze. Dru and Vivian holding hands like lovers cut sharply into her heart.

Vivian, her steps bouncing, came to the fire, placed an arm about Dru's waist and declared eagerly, "Virgil, Dru and I are getting married!"

Her declaration was followed by stunned silence.

Chapter Fourteen

Vivian, finding the silence exasperating, exclaimed, "Virgil! Say something! Aren't you pleased?"

Virgil was far from pleased, and he couldn't bring himself to utter congratulations. "When's the weddin'?" he asked dryly.

"In three months," Vivian announced, her eyes sparkling. "I want a big wedding, so as soon as I get home I'll start sending out invitations."

Virgil's vision locked on Dru. "This is kinda sudden, ain't it?"

"Very sudden," Dru replied quietly, looking away from his uncle's disparaging gaze.

Cassandra got slowly to her feet, mumbled a quick good night and moved away from the fire. She was heading toward the chuck wagon when her course veered and she disappeared into the bordering darkness.

Meanwhile, Roy DeLaney, ensconced in his bedroll, had overheard Vivian's announcement and had seen Cassandra's departure. A pleased smile crossed his face. He had been waiting for the opportune moment to present itself. He knew that Cassandra was infatuated with Dru, and now that he was engaged to another woman, convincing Cassandra

179

to leave should be easy.

He sat up, slipped on his boots, and moving undetected, followed the path Cassandra had taken. The full moon lit his way, and he traveled quickly. As soon as he was a safe distance from camp, he called softly, "Cassandra? Cassandra?"

"Roy?" he heard her respond. Her voice was close, and he soon located her; she was standing in a small clearing.

Stepping to her side, he said as though sympathetic, "I wasn't asleep, and I heard what Mrs. Lance said. I've always known how you feel about Dru, and, honey, I'm sorry."

Roy took her hands into his, squeezing them gently. "It's always a severe blow to lose someone you love. But you'll get over it; believe me, you will. It'll take time."

Cassandra was profoundly touched by his concern. Since the day Roy had joined the trail drive, he had gone out of his way to show her kindness and warmth. She thought him a very gentle, compassionate man.

"Thank you, Roy," she murmured, withdrawing her hands. "I hope you're right, and that in time I'll get over losing Dru." She sighed heavily. "But I have a feeling it's going to take a very long time. Seeing him and Vivian every day isn't going to make it any easier." Her voice took on a desperate note. "I dread watching those two together, day after day! It's more than I can bear!"

"You don't have to bear it," Roy said quickly.

She looked at him dubiously.

"Cassandra," he began anxiously, "let's quit this

drive and head back toward Silver Creek. By now, your brother's headed this way. We'll meet up with him, and then the three of us can travel to Fort Laramie together. From there, we'll make arrangements for San Francisco."

"But, Roy, how can you quit this job? You need the money."

"I don't need it so badly that I'm willing to stand back and watch Jensen callously hurt you time and time again."

"He doesn't mean to hurt me," she replied. "Dru doesn't know that I'm in love with him. God, he thinks I'm a thirteen-year-old boy!"

"That's beside the point," Roy argued. "Apparently, he's in love with Vivian Lance and wants to marry her. Even if he knew you were a woman, it wouldn't change his feelings."

"I suppose you're right," she mumbled defeatedly.

"Well?" he persisted, his tone eager. "What do you say? Let's go back and find your brother."

"Russ!" she exclaimed softly. Yes, why not? She needed her brother, and she missed him terribly. Suddenly, though, the Thurstons came to mind. "What if Jubal and his brothers are following this drive to Fort Laramie?"

"That's all the more reason why we should find Russ. Alone, what chance would he have against the Thurstons?"

"But what if Jubal finds us before we find Russ?"

Roy wished she weren't so sensible. He had no logical answer, so he chose to prey on her con-

181

science. "Well, if you're more concerned with your own welfare than your brother's, then there's no way I can convince you to leave."

His innuendo struck her to the core. "Roy," she began hesitantly, "I'll think about it. But I need a little time. Leaving is a big step, and I shouldn't make such a decision on the spur of the moment."

Roy concealed his disappointment. "All right, hon. You think about it, but don't take too long. Your brother's life might be on the line."

She could have done without such a remark, and as he took her arm, ushering her back to camp, she envisioned the Thurstons ambushing Russ. The vision was frightening, and she willfully banished it.

As they were entering the quiet camp, Cassandra noticed that the fireside was empty. She saw that Virgil was in his bedroll. She was wondering about Dru's whereabouts when she caught a glimpse of him escorting Vivian to her isolated wagon. Watching intently, Cassandra paused. Roy, seeing what had captured her interest, halted beside her.

Vivian's constant chattering had Dru's nerves on edge, and he had to bite his lip to keep from telling her to shut her mouth. When they reached her wagon, he mumbled a terse good night and was about to make a hasty retreat, when reading his intent, Vivian grasped his arm.

"Aren't you going to kiss me?" she asked, leaning toward him provocatively.

He eyed her incredulously. "Woman, you've got

bats in your belfry!"

She was enraged. "Another remark like that, and I'll go straight to Virgil and tell him everything!"

"Don't threaten me," he said between gritted teeth.

"Don't anger me, and I won't threaten you."

He quirked a brow, grinning indolently. "You're right, Vivian. I should kiss you. After all, we are engaged."

Moving incredibly fast, he drew her roughly into his arms, pinning her so tightly against his hard frame that his hold was cruelly painful. Bending his head, his lips came down on hers, their pressure brutal instead of passionate.

Dru's embrace was torturous, and Vivian tried vainly to wrest free, but he wouldn't relent. His strong arms wrapped about her, digging into her ribs and cutting off her breath. When his teeth penetrated her bottom lip, drawing blood, a moan of pain sounded deep in her throat.

From Cassandra and Roy's position, Dru's angry embrace appeared to be one of unbridled passion. Cassandra couldn't bear to watch, and grasping Roy's hand, she led him away from camp and back into the surrounding tableau.

Finally, Dru released Vivian none too gently. She took a step backward, her face red with rage, her breathing labored. Drawing back her arm, she slapped his cheek soundly. "You bastard!" she seethed.

He smiled cynically. "I'm sorry, darlin'. But my passion verges on cruelty."

"Verges?" she cried. Her hand went to her bleed-

183

ing lip, caressing the wound gingerly. "In the future, I hope you'll be more gentle."

"I'll try," he remarked. "But I can't make any promises." With that, he walked away, leaving her staring heatedly at his departing back.

Returning to the clearing, Cassandra stopped, looked at Roy and said, "I don't need to think about it any longer. I'm ready to leave whenever you are."

"We'll quit in the morning," he replied, secretly triumphant.

"No," she remarked strongly. "Virgil won't let me quit. We'll have to slip away undetected."

He agreed. "I have the second watch tonight. I'll leave my post, saddle your horse and meet you back here. Say two o'clock?"

"I don't have a watch. How will I know when it's two o'clock?"

He drew his timepiece from his pocket. "Here; take mine. The second watch starts at one-thirty. It should only take half an hour for me to slip away from the herd, get your horse and meet you."

"Don't take the mare. She was a gift from Virgil, and leaving under these circumstances, I don't feel right about taking her. Do you know which horse belongs to my brother?"

"I think so."

"Saddle that one for me. Also take the two mules that belong to Russ and me. I'll pack provisions and fill a couple of extra canteens with water."

184

Roy touched her arm, saying persuasively, "We'd better get back to camp. It wouldn't do for Dru or Virgil to catch us out here."

Submissively, she let him usher her away. They parted company at the edge of camp, Roy stepping furtively to his bedroll as Cassandra climbed quietly into the chuck wagon.

Going to her pallet, she sat down, raised her knees and cupped her chin in her hands. She knew leaving the drive was dangerous. But Roy had been right. She mustn't be selfish and think only of herself. Alone, Russ had no chance against the Thurstons. He needed her and Roy.

Her worry lightened. Maybe Jubal and his brothers had returned to Clarksville. When Virgil was backtracking, he'd found no traces of them.

Virgil! she thought sadly. She would miss him. She hoped he wouldn't be too upset. He'll worry about me, she mused, sensing a pang of guilt. Thinking about Virgil was depressing, so she quickly set her mind onto a different course.

Against her will, Dru entered her thoughts. She wondered if she'd find a way to stop loving him. Roy had said that it'd take time. However, deep within the depth of her soul, Cassandra knew that time could never completely erase Dru from her heart. He was there to stay.

Cassandra and Roy rode through the night, and by the time the sun had fully risen, they had put a good distance between themselves and the drive. The verdant, pastoral countryside was dotted with mesquite trees, their short trunks indented with deep forks and branches so full that they seemed to touch the ground. The omnipresent cottonwoods grew thickly, their cottonlike seeds floating weightlessly on the summer breeze. Clumps of sagebrush dotted the vast landscape, and small rolling hills could be seen on the far horizon.

The unblemished countryside was breathtaking in its virginal beauty, and Cassandra was beginning to understand why so many pioneers loved the untamed West, and why the native Indians fought so hard to keep it.

Cassandra was tiring, for they had traveled nonstop, and Russ's horse added to her fatigue. Unaccustomed to its present rider, the spirited steed balked at her commands. More than once it had tried to take off with a bolt, causing her to hold a tight rein. Her arms had begun to ache, and a constant, gnawing pain was centered between her shoulder blades.

She looked wearily at her companion. "Roy, can't we stop and rest for a while?"

He could see her exhaustion. "Yes, I suppose it's all right. We'll eat breakfast, then get a couple of hours of sleep."

They found a good place to camp, and as Cassandra built a small fire, Roy watered the horses and the mules. Turning them loose to graze, he sat down beneath a cottonwood and watched Cassandra. She was totally preoccupied with cooking breakfast.

Roy's brow furrowed thoughtfully. It was hard for him to imagine Cassandra maliciously scalding

Jubal. He supposed she could be as cunning as Jubal had warned and that her sweetness was merely a facade.

In an effort to ease his conscience, Roy tried to convince himself that Cassandra deserved to return to Clarksville and stand trial. However, he couldn't find her guilty beyond a doubt. He knew there was a vicious streak in Jubal; he had seen it several times during the war. Had Thurston lied to him about Cassandra? Had she burned Jubal because he was about to kill Russ in cold blood?

Cold sweat broke out on Roy's forehead. If Cassandra was innocent, he didn't want any part of delivering her to the Thurstons. Suddenly, though, greed got the better of him. He needed the 150 dollars Jubal had offered.

Also, he reminded himself, Jubal saved my life. I wouldn't even be alive if it weren't for him.

Roy decided to cast his gnawing suspicions aside. He owed Jubal his loyalty; not Cassandra. He waited for his decision to bolster his spirits and clear his conscience. However, to his dismay, the feeling of relief failed to materialize.

Cassandra had slept a couple of hours, and as she and Roy rode away from their temporary camp, she was refreshed. Roy, however, had stayed awake. His better judgment had continued to nag until, finally, he'd had to admit that Cassandra's guilt was highly unlikely. Roy considered himself a good judge of character, and he couldn't believe that Cassandra's amiable personality was merely a fraud. Jubal had warned that she was cunning, but Roy was beginning to suspect that, in this case, it was Jubal who was cunning.

Roy was practically destitute and needed the money Jubal had promised, but he didn't want it badly enough to turn over Cassandra. Especially if she was innocent, and he sensed intuitively that she was.

Roy remained buried in his deep thoughts, and they had traveled quite a distance before Cassandra began to wonder if he was troubled.

"Roy?" she asked. "Is something bothering you?"

He pulled up his horse, gesturing for Cassandra to do likewise.

She was watching him intently, and he turned away from her angelic face, her trusting eyes. He couldn't bring himself to deliver her to Thurston, even if she was guilty, which he seriously doubted. He drew a long breath. "Cassandra, we have to talk. There's something I must tell you."

Roy had decided to be perfectly honest, to confess everything. Afterward, if she felt she could still trust him, he'd take her back to the trail drive. Although he dreaded telling her about himself and Jubal, letting her know that Russ was dead was going to be a lot more difficult. Inwardly, he cursed himself. What a helluva time to change his mind! Why didn't he have these seconds thoughts before persuading her to leave with him?

You did have them! he told himself. You just wouldn't listen! You couldn't see any farther than the reward money!

Growing impatient with Roy's silence, Cassandra

said pressingly, "What do you want to talk about?"

Suddenly, Roy caught a movement out of the corner of his eyes, and he twisted quickly about in the saddle.

A lone horseman was riding in their direction, his black stallion's powerful strides covering the distance with amazing speed.

Recognizing the rider, Cassandra gasped breathlessly, "Dru!"

"Damn!" Roy grumbled. "I was hoping he wouldn't follow."

Cassandra was astounded. She didn't think Dru would want her and Roy back bad enough to come after them. Well, she reminded herself defiantly, he can't make us return!

Arriving, Dru reined in so abruptly that his magnificent steed had to lean back on its haunches to manage a complete stop.

Dru swept the pair with a piercing, anger-filled glare.

Watching, Cassandra tensed. She felt threatened by his presence, and a feeling of uneasiness whirled inside her. Finding Dru's angry silence unbearable, she began nervously in Casey's voice, "Dru, we aren't goin' back. And you don't have no right to stop us."

For a brief moment, his steely gaze fell over her like a cold shadow. It sent a chill up her spine, and she shivered involuntarily. She was familiar with Dru's anger, but she had never seen it this intense. His body was rigid, and his jaw was clenched tightly. There was an unmistakable aura of danger about him, and she suspected that his temper was barely controlled. But why? Why was he so enraged?

Dru looked squarely at Roy. He spoke with deadly seriousness. "Get out my sight before I pull you off your horse and beat the hell out of you."

Roy's own anger emerged. "You might not find it that easy."

Quickly, Cassandra cut in, "Dru, just 'cause we quit without warnin' doesn't give you the right to . . ."

"Stay out of this!" Dru shouted furiously.

"Casey's right," Roy remarked. "You've got no right to harass us."

"No right?" Dru questioned harshly. "Does two injured wranglers give me the right?"

"Wh . . . what?" Roy stuttered. "What the hell are you talking about?"

"You left your post last night without tellin' anyone."

"So?" Roy asked archly.

"A cougar slipped up to your side of the herd and charged, causing the horses to stampede. They headed straight toward camp, and the men couldn't turn 'em. Virgil and Pete managed to get the chuck wagon out of the way, but Mrs. Lance's wagon was demolished. Carl and Perry thought she was inside, and they were nearly trampled to death tryin' to save her. They didn't know that she wasn't in her wagon."

Dru didn't bother to explain that Vivian had been with him. He had tried to convince her to drop her blackmail threat and give him an extension on Virgil's debts. His attempt, however, had proved futile. She had refused to relent.

Dru stared unsympathetically at Roy's paling face. "If you had been at your post, the cougar wouldn't have charged. Because of your negligence, two men are seriously injured."

Cassandra felt sick. God, she was also to blame! If she hadn't agreed to slip away, none of this would have happened.

Dru continued, "DeLaney, this is my last warnin'. Get the hell out of my sight before I do something I may later regret. The way I feel right now, I'd just as soon shoot you as look at you."

Roy wanted to say that he was sorry, but he realized that it would sound hollow, meaningless. Furthermore, Jensen wasn't interested in his apology. Roy turned to Cassandra. "Casey, let's go."

"Casey's goin' back with me," Dru remarked firmly.

"The boy's got a right to make his own decision."

"He's goin' back," Dru insisted flatly.

Roy was about to argue, but he quickly changed his mind. Cassandra was better off with the trail drive. The Jensens were her best defense against Jubal and his brothers. He wondered if he should tell her that Russ was dead, but he couldn't do so without admitting that he was working for Jubal. Furthermore, he couldn't speak freely in front of Jensen, and Roy knew that Dru wouldn't give permission for him to talk to Cassandra alone.

Roy looked at Cassandra and smiled encouragingly. "Casey, I think you should stay with the drive."

"But what about Russ?" she asked. She feared for his life. What if the Thurstons were to ambush him?

Although he despised himself for doing so, Roy lied, "I'll keep riding until I meet up with Russ. Don't worry, we'll join you at Fort Laramie." Knowing he was pressing his luck with Jensen, Roy decided he'd better leave without further delay. He offered Cassandra the reins to the pack mules.

"No, you keep the provisions. You and Russ will need them. Just give me my bag."

Roy detached her small carpetbag and handed it to her. Then he turned his horse about and took off in a fast trot.

Cassandra, avoiding facing Dru, watched Roy as he rode away. She hoped desperately that he'd find Russ. She felt that Russ would stand a better chance of reaching the fort safely if Roy was with him.

Roy's shape soon diminished to a mote on the horizon, and Cassandra could no longer postpone meeting Dru's eyes. She turned to him and was surprised to see that his face was now devoid of anger. "Are . . . are Carl and Perry going to be all right?" she asked haltingly.

"I don't know. Virgil and a couple of the men took them to Fort Lyon in the chuck wagon. The fort's about a day's ride south."

"Dru," she began, remembering to talk like Casey, "if Roy and me had known somethin' like this was goin' to happen, we wouldn't have left."

He merely stared at her with an expression she couldn't discern.

She felt uncomfortable. "I . . . I just wanna say that I'm sorry."

"It's not your fault. You didn't know any better, but DeLaney knew the danger in leaving his post."

"I don't think he did." Cassandra believed what she said.

"Maybe," Dru gave in. He changed the subject. "There's a way station about ten miles to the west. We'll stay there tonight, then head back to camp in the morning."

"Why stay there? Why don't we just camp out?"

"You gave the provisions to DeLaney, remember? And I didn't bring any with me. So if you wanna eat a substantial meal, we head west."

"All right," she agreed. Unable to meet his eyes, she looked away. She felt terrible about Carl and Perry, and she prayed that they'd make a complete recovery.

Dru read her thoughts. "Casey, hereafter remember that driving a herd of horses can be hazardous. Every man has a job, and it's important that he doesn't neglect it." He controlled a sudden urge to dismount, lift her from her horse and take her into his arms.

"I understand," she said softly. "And I won't forget."

"We'd better leave," he said. "I'd like to reach the way station before dark."

"Dru?"

He eyed her levelly. "Yes?"

"Why did you come after me?"

From the moment Dru had realized that she was gone, he'd been hellbound to go after her, but he

193

wasn't sure about the force that had driven him. He only knew that, for some reason, he couldn't bear the thought of losing her.

Drawing a mask over his dubious feelings, he grinned wryly and quirked a brow. "I didn't wanna eat Virgil's cookin'."

"Was Virgil upset when he found out I was gone?"

"Upset is puttin' it mildly. Come on, kid. I don't know about you, but I could use a hot meal." Dru set his horse into motion.

Cassandra quickly attached her bag to the back of her saddle; then she caught up to Dru.

Chapter Fifteen

As Cassandra and Dru rode up to the way station, the sun was making its descent into the west. The station's primary purpose was to offer food and sleeping accommodations to stagecoach passengers, but it was also open to the general public.

It had been years since Dru had last visited the rural inn, and as he brought his horse up to the hitching rail, he noticed that the two-story building was showing signs of deterioration. He supposed it had fallen on hard times during the war. Not many people had traveled during those years.

A stagecoach, its team unhitched, stood close to a corral, and Dru hoped the inn wouldn't be so filled that he and Cassandra couldn't get rooms for the night.

They dismounted, and remembering to bring her carpetbag, Cassandra followed Dru up the steps, across the porch and into the building.

The large room was partitioned into two parts. The eating area was on one side, and the other side had a counter loaded with odds and ends that were for sale. Also, there were two high shelves filled with merchandise.

The stagecoach driver, the man riding shotgun, and five passengers sat about the dining table. The proprietor, a brawny man with a ruddy complexion, was seated with his guests, but seeing Dru and Cassandra, he got to his feet and walked over to greet them.

Recognizing Dru, he said heartily, "Dru! Dru Jensen! It's good to see you again. How long has it been?"

"Seven or eight years," Dru replied evenly. "How have you been, Dobbs?"

"Fine, fine," he replied.

Dru shook hands with Dobbs, but he did so without much enthusiasm. Dru had never especially liked the man.

"What are you doin' in these parts?" Dobbs asked.

"I'm takin' a herd of horses to Fort Laramie." He nodded toward Cassandra. "The boy and I need a couple of rooms for the night."

"Sorry, but I only have one room left. You and the boy will have to bunk together."

Dru could well imagine Cassandra's alarm, and he grinned inwardly. "One room will be fine." He looked amusedly at Cassandra. "We don't mind bunkin' together, do we, Casey?"

She swallowed heavily. "No, I guess not."

"You can have the room at the end of the hall on the left. But before you go up, you better have some grub."

Numbly, Cassandra followed the proprietor and Dru to the table. A heavyset woman entered from the kitchen carrying plates, utensils and cups.

A long bench ran the length of the table, and Dru and Cassandra sat at one end. Cassandra placed her bag at her feet as the woman heaped their plates with stew. Although the fare was tasty, Cassandra was too nervous to do her dinner justice, and she merely picked at her food.

Dru, eating heartily, congenially joined the conversation at the table. A couple of times, he encouraged Cassandra to stop picking at her dinner. She ignored him.

Finishing their supper, the other patrons retired to their rooms. Dru, the owner and Cassandra were left alone.

Dru lit a cheroot, then said to the proprietor, "Tell your missus that dinner was delicious."

Dobbs smiled broadly, but when he noticed that Cassandra had eaten very little, his grin disappeared and he said gruffly, "No wonder the boy's so puny. He don't eat enough to keep a bird alive."

Dru hid a humorous grin. "Casey's kinda finicky." He turned to Cassandra, asking, "Son, are you feelin' sick?"

"No," she mumbled. "I just ain't hungry."

"Sure you aren't sick?" Dru pressed, smiling stealthily. He knew the real reason behind her loss of appetite.

A frown creased her brow. "I told you, I'm not sick!"

"Well, in that case, why don't you go on upstairs while I unsaddle our horses and take them to the stables."

The owner cut in, "Hell, Jensen, you don't have to do that. I got a boy workin' for me. He can take care of your horses. He'll feed 'em and water 'em." The man called loudly over his shoulder.

"Badge, get in here!" When his call went unanswered, he yelled furiously, "Badge, you goddamned bastard, you better haul your ass!"

The boy suddenly appeared from the direction of the kitchen. He was a handsome lad, his black hair was collar length, and his frame, although lanky, was tightly muscled. Studying him, Cassandra judged his age at twelve or thirteen.

Speaking roughly, the proprietor complained. "Damn you, Badge! When I call, you come runnin'! You hear me, boy?"

"Yes, sir," he mumbled, his head bowed submissively.

"There's two horses out front. Take 'em to the stables, unsaddle 'em and tend to 'em."

The lad hurried outside.

Dru didn't approve of Dobbs's harshness, but he saw no reason to butt in. "How did you come by the boy?"

"A little over a year ago, a Colonel Haley stopped here for the night. He had the boy with 'im. The colonel had resigned his commission and was returning to his home in St. Charles, Missouri. I had supper with Haley, and he told me that he'd been takin' care of the boy for two years. A bunch of Sioux had been rounded up and taken to the reservation. The boy was among 'em. He'd been raised by the Sioux. The colonel felt sorry for the boy, and took 'im into his own home. Haley and his wife didn't have any kids, so they kinda adopted the boy. Well, shortly after they took in the kid, Mrs. Haley came down with a fever and died. The colonel kept the boy with 'im; then, when he turned in his resignation, he decided to take the boy back to Missouri."

Dobbs paused, then continued, "Durin' dinner, Colonel Haley said he wasn't feelin' well. He went on to bed, and shortly thereafter, the boy comes runnin' downstairs. He tells me that the colonel's ill. I hurry up to his room. The man's havin' a heart attack. There weren't nothin' I could do. I ain't no doctor. The colonel died. He's buried on the hill out back. I contacted the army, but the man didn't have no kin. So nobody ever came to claim the body. The boy didn't have no place to go, so I told him he could stay here and work for his room and board."

"Why do you call him Badge?" Cassandra asked. "It's such a strange name."

"The Sioux named 'im Badger, but the colonel called 'im Badge."

"You're kinda hard on the boy, aren't you?" Dru implied.

"I don't run no home for the homeless," he grunted, resenting Dru's remark. "The boy's got to earn his keep."

"I'm surprised he hasn't tried to return to the Sioux," Dru replied thoughtfully.

"Hell, he ain't about to run back to them Indians. He weren't never adopted into their tribe. He was a slave."

"God!" Dru groaned. "Except for the time he was with the colonel, the boy's had a helluva life."

"Maybe so," the man agreed. "But I ain't no Samaritan. If the boy don't work, he don't stay!" The man stood up, ending the discussion. "You

199

two had better turn in. Breakfast is ready at six."

Dru agreed. Tomorrow he and Cassandra had a long day facing them. He got to his feet. "Go on up, Casey. I think I'll help Badge with the horses. I'll be up in about thirty minutes or so."

Grabbing her bag, Cassandra darted out of the room and up the stairs. She didn't dare glance back to see if Dru was watching, for she was afraid her expression would reveal her anxiety. Hurrying down the narrow hallway, she went to the last room on her left. The door was unlocked, and she stepped inside and lit the lamp. As she had suspected, there was only one bed. Fortunately, it was huge and could easily accommodate two people. She'd merely sleep far to her side, leaving a large space between herself and Dru.

The room was adequately furnished: there was a chest of drawers against the wall, and a wardrobe stood in one corner. A filled water pitcher and a bowl stood on the night table accompanied by a washcloth and a towel.

Cassandra opened her carpetbag and hastily withdrew a change of clothes. Dru had said he'd be outside about thirty minutes; that should give her plenty of time to take a quick sponge bath and slip into her clean attire.

The door locked from inside, and she hurriedly slipped the bolt in place, then took a thorough bath and put on her clothes. She returned to the door, unlocked it, scampered to the bed, drew back the covers and lay down. Except for her boots, she planned to sleep fully clothed.

She lay still for a moment; then she began to

squirm uncomfortably. Moving briskly, she got up and began searching for a chamber pot. She was on her hands and knees peering under the bed when Dru suddenly opened the door and stepped inside.

"What are you lookin' for?" he asked.

A blush colored her cheeks, and keeping her face turned away, she rose to a standing position. She couldn't possibly tell him what she had been searching for without dying of embarrassment! "I'm not lookin' for nothin'," she mumbled.

As usual, Dru read her thoughts. Repressing a chuckle, he egged her on. "What do you mean nothing? Why were you peeking under the bed if you weren't tryin' to find something?"

Damn him and his everlasting questions! "What I was lookin' for isn't important."

Dru carried his bedroll, and placing it on the bed, he unrolled it and removed a set of clothes. "I guess I'll wash away this trail dust."

As he removed his shirt, Cassandra kept her eyes averted. Surely, he wasn't planning to strip down completely!

"Casey?" he said.

"Yeah?" she muttered, her back facing him.

"In rural establishments such as this one, when nature calls one has to go around back to the outhouse."

"I know that," she lied, covering her inexperience in such matters. Trying to sound indifferent, she continued, "I reckon I'll mosey on outside while you wash up."

She didn't see Dru's knowing smile. "Hurry

back, son. We need to get some shut-eye."

She slipped on her boots and hurried out the door.

When Cassandra returned, Dru was partially dressed in his clean clothes. His shirt was unbuttoned, the tail hanging over his trousers. He was sitting on the bed, leaning back against the large headboard, smoking a cheroot.

She could feel his eyes on her as she locked the door and crossed the room. Going to her side of the bed, she sat on the edge and removed her boots. She fluffed her feather pillow, then stretched out on her side, turning her back to Dru.

She was acutely aware of his nearness, and her heart began to thud like a drum. The woman inside her started to come alive; she could feel the magnetic pull of his masculinity.

Foreseeing a sleepless night facing her, Cassandra sighed deeply. Lord, how was she to share this bed with the man she loved and remain on her own side of the mattress? She longed to turn over and slide into his arms so desperately that it took all her willpower not to do so. If only she didn't love him so much!

Maybe I should tell him the truth, she suddenly thought. However, she wasn't sure if this was a good time. There'll never be a good time, she told herself testily. Virgil warned you not to wait too long to untangle the web you weaved. You should've taken heed.

Dru's voice broke into her troubled reverie. "Cassandra, do you plan to sleep in your clothes?"

With a short gasp, she sat upright, her eyes staring into his. "Wh . . . what did you call me?"

"Cassandra. That is your name, isn't it? Or did you lie about that, too?"

"How long have you known?" she asked weakly.

"Long enough."

"That . . . that night in Good Times, did you know I was Casey?"

"No," he replied, his expression impenetrable.

"Then when . . . ?"

He took a drag in his cheroot, then answered, "The next morning when I returned to camp and visited you in the chuck wagon, I took one good look at you and knew."

Cassandra's sudden anger was more powerful than her apprehension, and leaping from the bed, she placed her hands on her hips and spat furiously, "You made me take that castor oil out of spite, didn't you?"

His grin was cocky. "You apparently enjoy playing games, so I decided to play along, only by my own rules. Furthermore, you deserved to be taught a lesson."

"I suppose teaching me to be a drover was going to be another lesson?"

Dru put out his smoke, and in one catlike movement he slid to her side of the bed. "You escaped that lesson by running away. I had only one more lesson to teach you."

"Oh?" she questioned.

He was now close enough to reach out and grab her. A sly smile curled his sensuous lips. "I

203

planned to take you over my knee and give you a sound spanking."

"You wouldn't stoop so low!"

"Yes, I would," he replied calmly. Then, striking with the quickness of a snake, he sat up, grasped her arm and pulled her across his lap.

Struggling, Cassandra shouted, "Damn you, Dru! Let me go!"

"Not on your life, you deceitful little minx. You've got a good spanking comin', and I'm gonna relish givin' it to you."

"You beast! You bully!"

Despite her struggles, Dru easily positioned her across his knees. His strong hand slapped her bottom so hard that she cried out sharply. "Ow! That hurt, damn you!"

"Would you believe me if I told you this is goin' to hurt me more than it hurts you?"

"You cad! I hate you!"

"I don't think you do, but that's beside the point. Now, Casey, I hope you'll take your punishment like a man."

She started to flood him with insults, but before she could finish, Dru lived up to his word and gave her a solid spanking.

Then, setting her on the bed, he got up, folded his arms across his chest and eyed her levelly. "You've got some explaining to do, and it had better be good."

"Go straight to the devil!" she spat. She tried to stand up, but Dru's hands were suddenly on her shoulders, pressing her back onto the bed.

"Why are you passing yourself for a boy, and

why did you sign on to my trail drive?"

Stubbornly, she clamped her mouth shut. She'd never forgive him for spanking her as though she were a child. She bet he'd never treat his darling Vivian that way!

Dru was losing his patience. "Dammit, Casey, answer me!"

"My name isn't Casey!"

"You've got a choice, Casey," he said, putting sarcastic emphasis on the name. "You either give me a thorough and candid explanation, or I'll take you back over my knee."

"You wouldn't dare!"

He quirked a brow. "Try me."

She believed him. Although she hated giving in submissively, she wasn't about to let him get the better of her. "All right, I'll tell you everything. I've been wanting to tell you since that night in Good Times, but I could never find the right opportunity."

"Right opportunity?" he repeated skeptically. "Is that why you ran away with DeLaney? Were you looking for the right opportunity?"

"When I decided to leave with Roy, I didn't think I'd ever see you again."

"Does DeLaney know the truth about you?"

"Yes," she answered.

"How long has he known?"

"He guessed the truth from the beginning."

"Apparently, the man's more perceptive than I am." Dru wondered if DeLaney was in love with Cassandra. The possibility angered him, but he wasn't sure why.

Gingerly, Cassandra attempted to stand up, and when Dru made no move to stop her, she rose quickly and stepped to the foot of the bed. Her bottom stung, and she rubbed it tenderly.

Dru moved around her and went to the night table, where he relit his cheroot. Sitting and leaning back against the headboard, he met Cassandra's gaze. "I'm waiting for an explanation."

Cassandra took a deep breath, and her story began to unfold. She told Dru about Jubal Thurston, his brothers and Russ. She elaborated in detail, even letting Dru know that she suspected it was Jubal who had shot Russ. However, she didn't explain why she had planned their intimate interlude in Good Times. She wasn't about to let him know that she was hopelessly in love with him. He was arrogant enough without giving him encouragement. Besides, he was infatuated with Vivian!

Finishing her story, Cassandra grew silent as she waited anxiously for Dru to say something. Would he refuse to let her return to the trail drive? If he did, what was she going to do? By now, Roy was too far away for her to catch up to him.

Dru smashed what was left of his cheroot in the ashtray. Cassandra, still standing at the foot of the bed, was directly in his line of vision. He looked at her, and she could see an odd mingling of curiosity and amusement in his piercing blue eyes.

"Didn't you forget something?" he asked.

"I don't know what you mean," she said evasively. She knew exactly what he was leading up to.

"Have you already forgotten what happened between us in Good Times?"

"Of course I haven't forgotten," she whispered, glancing away from his unwavering scrutiny.

"Why did you do it?" he demanded, his tone suddenly hard.

She fought back tears. "It was a mistake. Let's just leave it at that, all right?"

"No, it's not all right." He pounced from the bed with the grace of a panther, and in two quick strides, he was at her side. His hands grasped her shoulders firmly, and gazing steadily down into her face, he insisted, "Tell me why you were so willing to lose your innocence!"

She refused to answer.

His patience gone, Dru shook her roughly. "Tell me, dammit! Don't you realize that I feel rotten about what happened?"

Dru didn't mean it exactly the way it sounded. He felt bad about mistaking her for a prostitute. Also, he had stolen her innocence, she should have saved her virginity for her husband.

Cassandra erroneously assumed that he felt rotten because he had bedded a naive, foolish young girl instead of a professional prostitute. Her lost innocence was probably tormenting his damnable conscience. Well, she didn't want or need his pity! That went double for any obligation he might feel!

Mustering a surge of strength, she pushed his hands from her shoulders and stepped back. Lifting her chin proudly, she remarked coolly, "I'd been curious about sex for a long time, but Russ always watched me like a hawk. Then Virgil took it upon himself to be my watchful guardian. Well, when I found myself in Good Times, and away from Russ

207

and Virgil, I decided it was time for me to get some experience. I chose you because I knew you well enough to know you wouldn't try to abuse me."

Dru didn't like her answer; in fact, it infuriated him. However, he now knew that she hadn't instigated their interlude to inveigle him into marriage. That he had even suspected such a thing made him feel a little ridiculous.

"Why the hell did you have to pick me? Why didn't you let DeLaney take your innocence?"

"Roy's too much of a gentleman." She wanted to burst into tears, fling herself into his arms and tell him that she was spouting nothing but lies. She had given him her innocence because she loved him! But he would throw her love back in her face!

As his anger simmered, Dru's eyes raked her with a fiercely possessive look. "So it's experience you want, eh? Well, since I'm not the gentleman DeLaney is, I'll help you achieve that experience."

He took a step toward her, and she backed away tentatively. "Leave me alone," she said weakly, a little in awe of him.

He eyed her with a scorching intent, his heated gaze rendering her speechless. She was powerless to move, and when he suddenly jerked her into his arms, she fell against him helplessly.

Swiftly, he lifted her and carried her to the bed. Placing her on the mattress, he looked down at her with a predatory expression, and Cassandra felt as though she were his captured prey to do with as he pleased. Strangely, the sensation was primitively

208

arousing, and as she watched him fling off his clothes, a wild surge of desire suddenly coursed through her veins.

Chapter Sixteen

Dru stood before Cassandra unclothed, and she was mesmerized by his male magnificence. He was so strikingly handsome that she longed to reach out and touch every inch of his tall, masculine frame.

Moving decisively, Dru took her hands and pulled her to her feet. "God!" he groaned intensely. "I want to make love to you!"

She gazed deeply into his eyes, and the passion smoldering in their depths made her heart beat wildly. She needed him with every fiber of her being. Taking the initiative, she slid her arms about his neck and brought his lips down to hers.

His mouth was warm, demanding, and she responded fervently, pressing her hips seductively against his rigid maleness. Her trousers didn't prevent her from feeling his urgency; he wanted her as powerfully as she wanted him!

Together, moving impatiently, they stripped away her boyish attire, and when Dru saw the torn sheet binding her beautiful breasts, he removed it and threw it to the floor as though he found it distasteful. When she was freed of her restricting clothing, Dru pressed her soft, supple body to his.

His mouth claimed hers savagely, and her lips

opened fully, welcoming his thrusting tongue. They clung to each other; then, pulling away with tearing reluctance, Dru lifted her onto the bed.

A rasping moan of longing escaped her lips as he lay beside her, drawing her close. She trembled against his virile body, and his whispered endearments calmed her as his fingertips caressed her silky skin with featherly softness.

Overwhelmed with fiery, molten shafts of desire, Cassandra slid her hands searchingly over his naked flesh, and when she touched his male hardness, a passionate gasp sounded deep in Dru's throat.

When her fingers tentatively encircled him, he moved his hand over hers, showing her how he wished to be caressed. Her electrifying stimulation awakened a primitive hunger so consuming that Dru's mouth came down on hers with a demanding force.

Her arms went about him, and placing her hand on the nape of his neck, she accepted his kiss eagerly, her tongue clashing with his in sensual warfare.

Exultant waves of pleasure washed over her as Dru's hand traveled heatedly over her body, touching, caressing her velvety skin. Giving him full rein, she parted her legs so that his finger could delve deeply. She arched against his probing, her hips moving with a feverish pitch.

Dru, his need aroused to the fullest, raised himself up and moved over her slender frame. His hardness sought entrance, then penetrated with one quick breathtaking thrust.

He made love to her aggressively, demandingly,

possessing her fully. Cassandra surrendered with untethered rapture and held onto him as tightly as she could.

Dru's exciting, steady strokes spiraled Cassandra to an erotic climax, and her body trembled convulsively as she peaked love's fulfillment.

Simultaneously, Dru reached his own uncontrollable completion, and grasping her hips firmly, he shoved himself deeply within her, achieving breathless satisfaction.

Without withdrawing, Dru rolled to his side, and pulling Cassendra with him, he cradled her close.

Emitting a heavenly sigh, she snuggled intimately. She felt as though she could make love with him for an eternity and still be anxious for more. There was no end to her passion for Dru; it was unquenchable.

Dru's feelings coincided exactly with Cassandra's. No woman had ever stirred his passion so completely. She held some kind of magical power over him, and it was taking control, ruling his heart as well as his mind. More disturbingly, though, his feelings for her went much deeper than a mere physical need.

He sighed heavily. He was falling in love, and the revelation was disconcerting. Love meant marriage and children. His thoughts drifted uneasily to Anita and to their son Johnny. He had tried marriage, and it had brought him nothing but heartache. Anita's betrayal and his son's death had been so painful that he'd sworn never to love again. Love made one too vulnerable. In time, his wife's betrayal had ceased to hurt and his heart had healed completely. But time failed to ease the loss of his son; the wounds were too deeply embedded.

Dru's thoughts returned to Cassandra. If he were to ask her to marry him, what could he offer her except an uncertain future? Asking a woman to accompany him and Virgil on a perilous journey to Montana would be asking an awful lot.

Willfully, Dru thrust all his plaguing doubts aside. Worrying about them now was merely a waste of time. The answers would have to wait until he was more certain of his feelings. For now, he'd remain elusive and guard his emotions.

Bolstered by his resolve, he reached over and lightly kissed Cassandra's brow. "We'd better get some sleep. We've got a long day facing us."

To Cassandra, his perfunctory kiss was like a slap in the face. How could he treat her so indifferently? Didn't the love they had just shared mean anything to him?

Love? she questioned bitterly. On Dru's part, it was male lust and nothing more! He doesn't love me, he loves Vivian! She's the one he plans to marry! I'm nothing more to him than an easy conquest!

Forcing herself to hold back a harsh retort, Cassandra asked evenly, "A long day facing us? Does that mean you're going to let me remain with the drive?"

He was astounded. "Surely you don't think I'd leave you here in the middle of nowhere!" He grinned teasingly. "Besides, I already told you that I don't want to eat Virgil's cookin'."

Cassandra, silently cursing his insensibility,

turned away and rolled to her side of the bed. She was too proud to tell him how she felt, and she wrapped her pride about her like a thermal cocoon.

Dru came close to drawing her back into his arms, but his own stubborn pride intervened. If she'd wanted to sleep next to him, she wouldn't have moved away. Not realizing that he had inadvertently hurt her feelings, he reached over and extinguished the lamp.

They both lay still, neither wanting to disturb the other. It was a long time before their troubled minds gave way to sleep.

A shaft of sunlight infiltrating in the room brought Cassandra awake. She was confused to find that she was cuddled close to Dru. He had an arm wrapped about her, and her head was nestled on his shoulder. She supposed she had snuggled against him in her sleep.

Gingerly, she inched her body away from his, and leaning up, she gazed into his face. He was alert, his eyes watching her.

She blushed noticeably. "How . . . how long have you been awake?"

"A few minutes."

"Why didn't you wake me?"

"I was enjoying watching you sleep."

Watching her while she slept? The thought was somewhat embarrassing, and moving quickly, she scooted to her own side of the bed. She sat up with intentions of retrieving her clothes and dressing with haste. To her dismay, she suddenly realized that her discarded apparel was on the other side. Keeping her back turned, she asked timorously, "Would you mind handing me my clothes?"

"What?" he teased. "And miss watching you walk around the bed to get them? I have no intention of missing such a lovely sight."

"Damn your ornery hide!" she seethed, steaming.

"I don't know why you're so bashful. It's not as though I haven't already seen your beautiful attributes."

"I refuse to parade around in front of you without a stitch of clothing on! I'm not an exhibitionist!"

Taking Dru by surprise, Cassandra grasped the sheet and jerked it to her side. She wrapped it about her, leaving him fully exposed.

Chuckling, Dru stood up and gathered his clothes. Cassandra's noticed that he didn't seem in the least embarrassed. Against her will, her eyes traveled the full length of him, and his superb maleness was sensually disturbing. Her pulse began to race, and a warm, tingling feeling awakened her senses. She cursed her weakness. Apparently, she had no defense against Dru; the mere sight of him aroused her passion!

Dressed, Dru turned and looked at her. He grinned devilishly, and with a mock bow, said, "I'll behave as a gentleman and let you dress in private." He went to the door and opened it. "I'll meet you downstairs for breakfast." He stepped across the threshold, but wheeled about and added, "By the way, Casey, don't forget my bedroll. My other clothes are wrapped in it."

"My name isn't Casey," she uttered petulantly.

He didn't say anything. He simply grinned, stepped into the hall and closed the door.

Cassandra put on her boyish attire; then, using the back stairs, she paid a quick visit to the latrine. She reentered the inn by the same exit, went to her room, strapped on her gun belt and donned her floppy-brimmed hat. Picking up her carpetbag and Dru's bedroll, she hastened to the front stairway and descended it quickly. She was surprised to see Dru waiting at the bottom. He was leaning leisurely against the wall.

She was so physically aware of him that an almost imperceptible shiver ran through her. The power he had over her was infuriating, and she silently berated her vulnerability. Tentatively, she met his gaze. Amusement still lurked in his eyes, and his lazy, sensual smile lifted the corners of his black mustache.

"You know," he began casually, "you look kinda cute dressed that way."

"Cute!" she scoffed. "Is that supposed to be a compliment?"

He shrugged insouciantly. "Well, I've never tried to compliment a lady in a man's clothes with a gun strapped about her waist. Cute seems fitting, don't you think?" His gaze, hardening, centered on her gun belt.

Cassandra knew what he was thinking. He was remembering that day in Good Times when he had taken her to the gunsmith's. "Dru," she began uncertainly, "I never wanted to deceive you. Please

216

don't feel that I tried to make you look like a fool. If you want the gun back, you can have it."

"Keep it," he mumbled evenly.

"You're angry, aren't you? Virgil said that you'd think we made a fool of you."

"Let it rest, Casey. Talkin' about it only gets my dander up." He stepped away from the wall. "Badge already has our horses saddled and tied out front." He reached over and took her carpetbag and his bedroll. "I'll put these on the horses and then we'll eat breakfast."

Before Dru could leave, the front door opened, admitting Dobbs and another man.

"Jensen!" Dobbs said heartily. "I'd like you to meet my brother. Owen, this is Dru Jensen."

The man held out his hand, and Dru placed his bundles on the floor.

Owen, a close replica of Dobbs, shook Dru's hand firmly. "I've heard 'bout you, and it's a pleasure to finally meet you. In case you don't know it, when you were bounty huntin', you made quite a reputation of yourself." His sudden grin was somewhat challenging. "Are you really as fast as I've heard?"

"Probably not," Dru answered, his tone flat.

Cassandra could feel a certain tension between Owen and Dru, and she wondered if Dobbs's brother was considering egging Dru into a gunfight. Did he want to prove that he was faster?

Suddenly, Dobbs's bellowing voice broke the tension. "Dammit! I told Badge to mop this floor! The goddamn, lazy no-account! I'll box his ears!" He called thunderously, "Badge! Badge, where the

217

hell are you?"

At that moment, the boy, carrying a bucket and a mop, entered by way of the back door. "Did you call me, Mr. Dobbs?" he asked, his gray eyes revealing fear.

"Why ain't you mopped this floor?" Dobbs demanded.

"I saddled Mr. Jensen's horses," he answered. "I'm gonna mop the floor now."

"I don't want to her no damn excuses!" he roared. Moving lithely for a man his size, Dobbs stepped forward, drew back his powerful arm and slapped the boy on the side of the head.

Badge, reeling under the severe blow, fell to his knees.

Dobbs was about to rain more blows on his young victim, but Dru suddenly edged his way between them.

"Stay out of this, Jensen!" Dobbs grumbled. "It ain't none of your business!"

"If you lay a hand on this boy again, I'll break your damned arm."

Dru's back was facing Owen, and using it to his advantage, the man moved his hand stealthily to his holstered pistol.

Cassandra, seeing the man's furtive intent, reached quickly for her own revolver, and although she drew it speedily, Jensen had already drawn, spun around and had his gun pointed at Owen.

Cassandra could hardly believe that anyone could move so swiftly. Furthermore, Dru's back had been turned, so how had he known that Owen was reaching for his gun?

Dru was surprised to see that Cassandra had covered his back, but he was also proud of her. He wondered if she'd had the nerve to pull the trigger.

Owen's gun was half in and half out of his holster. His hand was hovering uncertainly over the weapon.

"Owen!" his brother bellowed. "Get the hell out of here and go back home! You stupid idiot! You ain't good enough to confront Jensen!" He nodded tersely toward Cassandra. "You can't even outdraw this kid!"

Knowing Dobbs was right, Owen turned on his heel, swung the door open and darted outside.

"I apologize for my brother," Dobbs said, as Dru holstered his pistol. "The man ain't too bright." He eyed Badge, who was getting to his feet. "I'll tend to you later!"

Cassandra, glad that the incident was over, slipped her pistol back into her holster.

Dru started to pick up Cassandra's carpetbag and his bedroll, but he stopped suddenly and spoke to Badge. "Would you like to come to work for me?"

The boy's face lit up. "For how long?"

"For as long as you want." Certain that he and Virgil would lose the Bar-J, Dru added, "I can't promise you an easy life, but it'll be a helluva lot better than this one."

"Yes, sir!" Badge exclaimed. "I'll be glad to work for you!"

"Dammit, Jensen!" Dobbs fussed. "You ain't got no right to come in here and take away my hired help!"

219

Dru cast the man a cold, unwavering stare. "You wanna try and stop me?"

Dobbs backed down quickly. "No . . . No, of course not. I ain't gonna tangle with you."

Dru turned to Badge. "Go pack your things. Do you have a horse?"

"No, sir," he answered hesitantly, hoping that wouldn't change Jensen's mind.

"That's all right. We have plenty of horses, and I'll pick out a good one for you. For now, Casey can double with me, and you can ride his horse." When the boy stood as though riveted, Dru encouraged warmly, "Go on, son. Get your clothes packed."

Badge jumped over the bucket and made a beeline up the stairs and to his room in the attic.

Dru picked up his bundles and stepped outside. Following, Cassandra watched as he attached them to the horses. Moving to Dru's magnificent stallion, she rubbed the steed behind its ears.

"He's such a beautiful horse. What's his name?"

"Impressive," Dru answered.

Cassandra smiled. "I can understand why."

Dru, resting an arm on the saddle, caught her gaze and said sincerely, "Thanks for covering my back."

"You're welcome," she murmured.

"Tell me something, Casey."

"What?"

"Could you have pulled the trigger? Are you capable of shooting a man?"

"I'm not sure," she replied honestly. "Maybe I could. Why do you want to know?"

He shrugged. "Just curious."

She looked at him inquisitively. "How did you know Owen was going to draw on you? Your back was turned so you couldn't have seen him.;"

He chuckled. "It's called second sense. I acquired it when I was a bounty hunter."

Cassandra started to say something, but changed her mind. Dropping her gaze, she stared down at her feet.

"Is something on your mind?" he asked gently.

Keeping her eyes lowered, she said quietly, hesitantly, "Dru, what I told you last night wasn't true. I didn't instigate our interlude in Good Times because I was curious about sex." Her voice quavered slightly. "I just wanted you to know, so you wouldn't think badly of me."

"Then why did you instigate it?" he pressed, his tone caring.

"I'd rather not say." Certain he'd scorn her love, she couldn't bring herself to tell him the truth.

"All right, Casey," he relented. "We won't talk about it again until you're ready."

She lifted her gaze. "Thank you." Anxious now to change the subject, she said quickly, "I think what you're doing for Badge is very nice."

"I can't see leaving the boy at Dobbs's mercy." He stepped away from his horse. "Let's go have breakfast."

"You mean, we're going to eat here after what happened? Aren't you worried that Dobbs will try something?"

"Like what?" he asked.

"Like shooting you in the back."

221

Dru chuckled good-humoredly. "I'm not worried, I've got you to cover my back. Come on; I don't know about you, but I'm starving."

Chapter Seventeen

At noon, Dru decided to stop for lunch. At the way station, he had purchased a couple of cans of beans, a pan, three plates and utensils. They soon had a small fire burning and warmed the food.

Later, deciding to rest for a few minutes, Dru found shade under a nearby cottonwood, sat down and leaned back against the tree's sturdy trunk. Cassandra and Badge had remained seated at the fire. They were facing Dru, and catching Badge's eye, Jensen asked, "How old are you, son?"

"I'm not sure," he replied. "Twelve or thirteen, I guess. I was just a babe when the Sioux kidnapped my ma and me. I don't remember anything about it, but from what I've gathered, I was only with Ma about a year, and then I was sold to another tribe."

"You never saw your mother again?" Dru queried.

"I saw her a few times. She married the chief's son, Tall Tree, so she was one of the People. But I was a slave, so she never talked to me. When our tribes visited, I only saw her from a distance."

Astounded, Cassandra exclaimed, "She never made any attempts to talk to you?"

He shook his head, answering solemnly, "She

didn't want anything to do with me. I guess she was ashamed of me."

Dru, seeing the boy's sadness, changed the subject. "You speak English very well. Did Colonel Haley teach you?"

"Yes. sir." Thinking about the colonel brought tears to his eyes. He had loved Colonel Haley like a father, and he still missed him.

The boy's sorrow didn't escape Dru. Apparently, his attempts to lighten Badge's depression hadn't worked. Considering the distressing life the boy had led, any subject concerning his past was bound to be oppressive. Dru felt an acute pang of sympathy for Badge and silently swore that, if it was in his power, the lad's future would be considerably better than his past.

Cassandra had little knowledge of the Western Indians, and she was curious about them. "Was it terrible being a slave? Did the Sioux mistreat you?"

"No, not really. As long as I remembered my place, they treated me all right. Living with the Sioux was better than living with Dobbs. I stayed with Dobbs 'cause I didn't have anyplace to go, or any way to take care of myself."

Dru studied the boy closely. He was a handsome lad; his black hair was full and wavy with an unruly curl falling over his forehead. His gray eyes, the color of charcoal, were framed by arched brows and lashes so long that they were almost effeminate.

"Mr. Jensen," Badge said, "I want to thank you for givin' me a job."

Dru smiled warmly. "Call me Dru."

Badge turned to Cassandra. "Your name's Casey, right?"

She found it hard to lie to Badge, and averting her eyes from his, she stammered, "Yes . . . yes, my name's Casey."

Dru noticed her hesitancy. He wondered why she had difficulty deceiving Badge when she had found it so easy to deceive him. Well, it was time to end her masquerade. "Badge," he began, "there's something you should know."

He looked questioningly at Dru; so did Cassandra.

"Casey's real name is Cassandra. There's a young lady under those boy's clothes."

Badge wasn't surprised. "I kinda suspected it."

"You did?" Cassandra gasped.

Dru chuckled. "Casey, you might be dressed like a boy, but ever since we left the way station, you've been movin' and talkin' like a girl. You forgot to play your role."

Cassandra realized that he was right. She had been so at ease with Dru and Badge that she'd completely forgotten to act like Casey.

"I know it's none of my business," Badge began, "but why are you pretendin' to be a boy?"

As simply as possible, she told him about Russ and the Thurstons, explaining why she and her brother had hired on for the drive.

When she was finished, Dru asked Badge if any men fitting the Thurstons' descriptions had stopped at the way station.

"No," he answered. "Except for you two, there's been no one but stagecoach passengers."

"Maybe the Thurstons gave up and returned to Clarksville," Cassandra said hopefully.

"Don't count on it," Dru replied. "From what you've told me about Jubal, he doesn't sound like the type to give up."

Cassandra's hopes sunk. Jubal's stalking shadow hovered over her like a dark, threatening cloud. She almost wished that he'd confront her and get it over with.

"Don't worry," Badge told Cassandra. "When we reach camp, I won't let anyone know you're a girl."

"That won't be necessary," Dru remarked. "It's time to unveil Casey's true identity."

"Why?" Cassandra asked, astonished.

"There's several reason why. For one, I don't intend to lie to the wranglers. They have a right to know. Also, now that Vivian's wagon was demolished, she'll have to sleep in the chuck wagon with you. If she thinks you're a boy, she's going to insist that you sleep outside."

The mere mention of Vivian managed to spark Cassandra's anger. Share the chuck wagon with that she-devil! She'd rather share it with a rattlesnake! Her eyes squinting angrily, Cassandra mumbled, "I don't mind sleeping outside."

"But I do mind," Dru returned.

"Don't I have a say in this?" she questioned irritably.

"No," he answered firmly. "The subject is closed. You're sleepin' in the wagon with Vivian."

Cassandra's temper got the better of her, and she spoke without thinking, "Won't my presence in the wagon put a damper on yours and

Vivian's romance?"

Listening, Badge's eyes flitted back and forth from one to the other. Their bickering made him feel a little uneasy.

Dru laughed at Cassandra's remark, but his apparent mirth merely increased her anger. Oh, he was such an inconsiderate cad! Last night he had made love to her, but tonight he'd go anxiously into Vivian's awaiting arms! Well, she'd be damned if she'd play second fiddle! As far as she was concerned, the pair deserved each other!

Dru got to his feet. "Badge, put out the fire. If we leave now, we'll reach the herd by nightfall."

Cassandra also rose, and looking staunchly at Dru, remarked, "I've decided to ride the rest of the way with Badge."

Dru understood her anger; she resented his relationship with Vivian. He didn't blame her. However, this wasn't the right time for them to discuss Vivian. So he didn't argue with her. "Suit yourself, Casey."

"Why do you keep calling me Casey?" she spat.

He grinned wryly. "I reckon the name kinda grew on me, and habits are hard to break." His gaze swept over her indolently. "Besides, the name fits you. It's cute, just like you are."

Night was blanketing the landscape when Roy spotted a campfire in the distance. He was sure it was Jubal's, but just in case it wasn't, he approached cautiously.

He was drawing close when, unexpectedly, a tall

227

figure stepped out of the shrubbery. Cocking his rifle, he warned, "Hold it right there, mister."

Roy, recognizing the voice, said with a grin, "You wouldn't shoot your old army buddy, would you?"

Jubal moved in front of DeLaney's horse so that he could get a good look at its rider. "Roy!" he exclaimed jovially, but his jubilation was short-lived. "Where the hell's Cassandra?" he grumbled.

The Thurstons were cooking dinner, and smelling the savory aromas, Roy replied, "I'll tell you what happened over supper and a cup of coffee."

Jubal agreed and led him into camp. The moment Roy was seated, his plate heaped with beans and bacon, Jubal sat beside him and demanded, "How come you ain't got that damned bitch with you?"

Between mouthfuls of food, Roy gave a full explanation. However, he failed to mention that he believed Cassandra's story over Jubal's. He didn't want hard feelings between himself and Thurston.

"Godammit!" Jubal raged. "You mean, you two were actually on your way here when Jensen caught up to you?"

"I'm afraid so," Roy replied, sounding disappointed.

"I bet Jensen knows she's a woman! Furthermore, he's probably gettin' between her legs. Why else would he come after her?"

DeLaney didn't agree but kept it to himself.

One of the brothers cleared his throat loudly.

Eyeing him sharply, Jubal grumbled, "Joe, you got something to say?"

228

"Yeah, I do," he answered, obviously hesitant. "The others and me, we've been talkin'."

When Joe's voice faded, Jubal insisted, "Talkin about what?"

"Well, we decided if DeLaney didn't bring the woman, we were gonna turn around and go back home. We got wives and kids back in Clarksville, and they need us. When we joined up with you, we never thought we'd be away from home this long. If you're smart, you'll come back with us. You ain't never gonna catch that woman. She's got Jensen and all them wranglers to protect her."

Jubal was outraged. "I can't believe what I'm hearin'! My own brothers are gonna turn tail and run out on me!"

The youngest one spoke up. "I ain't gonna leave you, Jubal. I ain't got no wife or kids."

A look of affection crossed Jubal's bandaged face. His youngest brother, Dave, was his favorite. He could relate to him because he was a younger version of himself. "I knew you wouldn't run out on me, Dave. You believe in blood ties. It's too bad the others ain't got no brotherly loyalty."

"This ain't got nothin' to do with brotherly loyalty," Joe argued. "We got responsibilities to our wives and kids. In the mornin', we're goin' back."

"Don't wait 'til mornin'!" Jubal raged. "Leave now! Get the hell out of my sight! Go on, before I forget you're my kin and blow your asses to hell!"

The brothers' exchanged glances conveyed a unanimous agreement to leave at once.

As the Thurstons busied themselves packing, Jubal turned to DeLaney and asked gruffly, "What

229

about you, Roy? Are you gonna run, too?"

"I plan to head for Fort Laramie, where hopefully I can acquire a way to San Francisco. Since we're traveling in the same direction, I don't see any reason for us to split up." Roy's remark was partially true. He did plan to go to Fort Laramie, but Cassandra was his true reason for staying with Jubal. Traveling with Thurston, he'd know when he was ready to seize Cassandra. He intended to find a way to spoil Jubal's plan.

Roy, finishing supper, didn't see the suspicious glint in Jubal's eyes. Thurston wasn't sure if he could trust DeLaney. He intended to keep a close eye on him.

Shortly following the evening meal, Dru called Vivian and all the wranglers, except for the few watching the herd, to the fire. Telling them to sit down, he stood with Badge and Cassandra poised behind him. Virgil had returned from Fort Lyon with the good news that Carl and Perry would make a complete recovery. Now, wondering why Dru had called a meeting, he stepped to the fire and took a seat beside Vivian.

First, Dru introduced Badge and explained why he had hired him. Then, girding himself for their shocked reactions, Dru announced that Casey wasn't a boy, but a young lady.

For a long moment, his declaration was met by stunned silence; then, as the drovers began to whisper among themselves, Virgil looked at Cassandra and caught her eye. She gave him a small smile.

Meanwhile, Vivian was bristling. Casey a woman? No wonder Dru had been so determined to go after her! She wondered bitterly if they were lovers.

Dru regained everyone's attention, then let them know why Cassandra had found it necessary to pretend that she was a boy.

The wranglers had all come to like and respect the young cook, and now as they listened to Dru talk about the Thurston brothers, they didn't blame Cassandra for hiding behind her disguise. They sympathized with her plight and agreed unanimously to let her remain. Although a few of them actually believed that a woman on a trail drive brought bad luck, under the present circumstances, it seemed immaterial. They already had a woman accompanying them: Mrs. Lance.

Dru suggested that everyone get some sleep, for they'd be pulling out early in the morning. As the men gathered up their bedrolls, Dru beckoned to Vivian.

Emphasizing the sway of her hips because she knew Dru was watching, she stepped to his side. Badge and Cassandra were still behind him, and, stealthily, Vivian cast Cassandra a cold glance.

"Vivian," Dru began, "you and Cassandra will sleep inside the chuck wagon."

"Why should I share the wagon with her?" Vivian questioned sharply. "If it weren't for her and DeLaney, my wagon wouldn't have been trampled! She should have to sleep outside and suffer the elements!"

"I don't intend to argue with you about this,"

Dru replied, his tone adamant.

Vivian conceded. She knew she had no other choice. Rising on tiptoe, and catching Dru unawares, she kissed him soundly on the mouth. "Very well, darling. I'll share the wagon. Good night, sweetheart."

She swept grandly past Cassandra and Badge, paused at the rear of the wagon and asked Cassandra in a sugar-coated tone, "Aren't you coming to bed, dearie?"

The term infuriated Cassandra. "Don't call me 'dearie'!" she snapped.

"Casey," Dru began firmly. "Control your temper and go on to bed." In his opinion, Vivian's cattiness deserved to be ignored.

Cassandra, believing he was siding with Vivian, uttered testily, "I should've known you'd stick up for your fiancée!"

Leaning close to her, Dru whispered, "Casey, stop thinking you know so much." He winked, then said with a wry smile, "Good night, and sweet dreams."

Thoroughly confused, Cassandra followed Vivian inside the wagon. What had Dru meant? Why would he tell her to stop thinking so much? It made no sense whatsoever.

Deciding to dwell on it later, Cassandra removed her gun belt and hat, found a stack of blankets and made herself a pallet far to one side of the wagon.

Vivian did likewise, but instead of extinguishing the lantern, she sat down and stared at Cassandra's turned back.

Feeling the woman's eyes on her, Cassandra rolled over and met her cold gaze.

Slowly, deliberately, Vivian began unbuttoning her blouse. Her voice tinged with honey, she asked, "Aren't you going to undress for bed?"

"Yes, after you turn out the light. You might enjoy casting your silhouette on the canvas for all the men to gawk at, but I have no intention of doing so."

She gave Cassandra's tall, slender frame a quick, sneering appraisal. "No, I don't suppose you would enjoy revealing yourself, since you have so little to reveal." Smiling, she rubbed her hands over her blouse, caressing her ample bosom. "You know, Dru likes large-breasted women. Tell me, dearie, is it terrible to be so flat-chested?"

Sitting up, Cassandra reached under her shirt, removed the sheet binding her and threw it on the floor. The act brought her little satisfaction, for although her breasts were full, she certainly wasn't as voluptuous as Vivian.

"Well, now that everyone knows you're not a boy, you won't have to bind yourself anymore." Vivian smiled maliciously. "It's a shame no one will notice the difference."

"If you don't turn out that light and shut up, I'm liable to forget I'm a lady and knock the living daylights out of you!"

"You're a very rude little girl, aren't you? Didn't your mother teach you any manners?"

"I'm not a little girl. I'm twenty years old. And, yes, my mother taught me manners! She especially taught me to be polite to my elders. So, ma'am, I apologize if I've offended you." With that, Cassandra lay down on her pallet, rolled over and turned her back to Vivian.

Vivian, fuming, reached over and turned off the lamp.

When Dru finished bedding down his horse and Cassandra's, he found Virgil sitting at the fire. Joining him, he poured a cup of coffee.

"I suppose you're upset with me," Virgil said.

"I was, but I'm not anymore. After Cassandra explained everything, I understood why you protected her."

"Did she tell you she was a woman, or did you guess it?"

"I caught on without her tellin' me. Last night, at the way station, I insisted that she give me an explanation."

Virgil nodded toward the chuck wagon. "Puttin' those two women together is kinda like placin' two sticks of dynamite side by side, lightin' the fuses and waitin' to see which one blows up first."

Dru smiled good-humoredly. "Considerin' Cassandra's temper, her fuse is bound to be shorter."

"Dru," Virgil began carefully, "I don't mean to stick my nose where it doesn't belong, but just for the record, "I've got something to say."

"Go on; say it."

"I'm against you marryin' Vivian."

"I know," Dru replied.

"I don't believe you're in love with her. So why the hell are you plannin' to marry her?"

"I'd rather not talk about it."

"Dammit, Dru, don't you clam up on me!"

Dru put down his coffee cup and got to his feet.

"Where are you goin'?" Virgil asked testily.

"To bed. I'm tired."

As Dru headed for his bedroll, Virgil fussed to himself, but loud enough for Dru to hear, "If he's so damned set on gettin' married, I wish he had enough sense to marry Cassandra."

Crawling inside his bedroll, Dru chuckled softly. His uncle's wish might very well come true. It seemed with each passing minute, he was falling more and more in love with Cassandra. Did she share his feelings? Deep in his heart, he felt that she did.

Chapter Eighteen

The next few days passed uneventfully. Cassandra saw very little of Dru; he'd ride with the herd all day, then eat a hurried supper, take the first watch and not return to camp until after Cassandra had gone to bed.

Although she missed being with Dru, she had one consolation. Vivian wasn't seeing very much of Dru either.

Traveling and sleeping in the same wagon with Vivian tried Cassandra's patience. The woman was infuriating. If she wasn't nagging or complaining, she was making snide remarks. More than once, Cassandra had to grit her teeth and count to ten to keep from striking her. She abhorred physical disputes, but Vivian was enough to drive a preacher to violence. If only the woman would shut up! But her mouth never took a rest. Cassandra couldn't imagine why Dru loved her, let alone why he wished to marry her. She supposed there was no accounting for taste.

Although she missed spending time with Dru, she had Virgil and Badge for company. Their presence lightened the dreary days and made the long journey less tedious. She loved Virgil, and was now growing extremely fond of Badge.

Cassandra was not alone in missing Dru; Vivian literally ached to be near him. Her feelings, however, were mixed. One part of her was hurt by his aloofness, but the other part resented his cold withdrawal. How dare he treat her indifferently!

Suffering sleepless nights, tossing and turning on her pallet, she'd recall Dru's savage kiss. His passion had been so unbridled that it had actually been brutal. When he was kissing her, he certainly hadn't found her indifferent! What had happened to cause him to make such a complete turnabout? Was it because of Cassandra? Did he no longer desire her because the little tart was satisfying his sexual needs? Well, Dru was a virile man, and if her suspicions were true, he'd soon seek out Cassandra and take her someplace where they could be alone. She'd guard their activities closely so she'd know when, or if, the secret interlude took place. If Dru was two-timing her, she'd get rid of Cassandra.

If the Thurstons were following, and she felt certain that they were, she'd help them seize Cassandra. Of course, she would have to do it stealthily so Dru wouldn't know that she had taken part in Cassandra's capture. Then, with Cassandra out of the picture, Dru would turn to her to appease his passion. She believed, emphatically, that once Dru made love to her, he'd be hers for the asking. She had every confidence in her ability to please a man sexually, and in her disturbed, perverted mind, she believed Dru would fall prey to her irresistible charms.

As Cassandra washed the supper dishes, Badge stood beside her, drying them. Although he worked willingly and without complaint, he nonetheless found the work disappointing. He wanted to be a drover, but Dru had assigned him to the chuck wagon.

Noticing Badge's sullen face, Cassandra asked, "What's wrong?"

"Nothing," he mumbled.

"I know something is bothering you," she insisted.

He decided to confide in her. "When Dru offered me a job, I was hoping he was gonna let me be a drover."

"I see," she answered, understanding. "Working with me isn't very exciting, is it?"

He hoped it hadn't hurt her feelings. "Don't misunderstand me," he hastened to reply. "I like you a lot, Cassandra. But cookin' and cleanin' is work for women and old men."

She smiled warmly. "You want a man's job, right?"

He nodded, then asked expectantly, "Will you talk to Dru for me? Will you ask him to let me be a drover?"

Talk to Dru? Lately, he seemed to be avoiding her like the plague. Holding his attention long enough to discuss Badge might not be easy.

"I'll try," she answered. "But Dru doesn't seem to have time for me anymore."

"He's workin' extra hard because he's behind schedule. Virgil told me that the army expects the

238

herd to be delivered on time."

At that moment, Vivian climbed down from the chuck wagon. Cassandra watched as she moved gracefully to the campfire, dished herself a plate of food, then squeezed in between Dru and Virgil. She placed a hand familiarly on Dru's arm, said something to him, then laughed seductively.

Cringing, Cassandra looked away.

Badge had also been watching Vivian. "Mrs. Lance reminds me of a story I once read," he began. "The colonel gave me the book when I was learning to read. It was about a witch who was beautiful on the outside, but was evil on the inside."

"That's Vivian, all right!" Cassandra agreed. "What happened to the witch?"

"She was burned at the stake and died screaming."

Cassandra laughed lightly. "Well, I don't wish such a terrible fate on Vivian, but I do wish she'd climb on her broom and fly away."

"I heard that!" Vivian's voice suddenly shrieked.

Cassandra and Badge had been so involved in their conversation that they hadn't heard Vivian walking up to them.

Although Badge's embarrassment was evident, Cassandra was undisturbed. There was nothing she'd say behind Vivian's back that she wouldn't say to her face.

Meeting the other woman's angry eyes, Cassandra said evenly, "I don't care if you did hear. I meant what I said."

"You smart-mouthed little bitch!" Vivian raged,

her voice so shrill that it carried to the campfire.

The wranglers stopped eating to stare openly at the two women. All of them, except for one, were hoping Cassandra would take Mrs. Lance down a peg. Even the men who worked for Vivian didn't especially like her. She was the type who grated on everybody's nerves.

However, the wrangler called Hawk, who was half Sioux and half white, wasn't interested in the ladies' dispute and didn't care about the outcome. He had worked for Vivian for six months. When he had taken the job, he had done so on a temporary basis. Working for a woman wounded his male pride, and he intended to quit as soon as they reached Fort Laramie. Hawk was a stoical, unemotional man. He intentionally went through life without making close friends. He was a wanderer and a loner, and he preferred it that way. A good wrangler, he did his job and minded his own business.

Now, as the other wranglers watched the women, Hawk stepped quietly away from the fire and went to his bedroll.

Meanwhile, Dru and Virgil were also staring at Cassandra and Vivian. Knowing they might have to interfere, they were ready to leap at a moment's notice.

Cassandra's temper was boiling, but she hoped to keep a lid on it.

Precariously composed, Cassandra said with a degree of calmness, "Vivian, I might have a smart mouth, but unlike yours, it doesn't run continually."

Cassandra's retort was met by the wranglers' hearty laughter.

Vivian was furious. How dare the men laugh at her! She had never hated Cassandra as much as she did at this moment. Her face beet red with rage, she spat nastily, "You despicable little tramp! You might have everyone fooled with your helpless, innocent facade! But I'm not fooled!"

"What do you mean?" Cassandra demanded.

"I know you've been sleeping with Dru! And considering how close you are to Virgil, you've probably been wallowing in the grass with him too! That's why both of them are so willing to give you shelter; you're their little whore!"

"Uh-oh," Virgil remarked to Dru. "I told you it was like placin' two sticks of dynamite side by side."

As Virgil was speaking, Cassandra's temper did indeed explode. Whirling about, she lifted the sudsy dishpan, heaved it over Vivian, and turning it upside down, let it slip from her grasp.

The woman shrieked as the heavy pan landed on top of her head. With streams of dishwater running down her hair and onto her clothes, Vivian looked a sight.

Badge, his mouth agape, stared wide-eyed. The wranglers, however, were amused and broke into gusty fits of laughter.

Vivian went into hysterics, and as Virgil reached for her, she slapped wildly at his hands. Virgil was proud of Cassandra, and because he was finding it difficult to hold back his own laughter, it took him a while to control Vivian.

In the meantime, Dru had grasped Cassandra's arm, and as he pulled her away from the wagon, he said gruffly, "Casey, you're comin' with me!"

She tried to wrest free, but his hold was too firm. "Don't you think you should be consoling your fiancée, instead of harassing me?"

Forcing her to keep abreast of him, he ignored her implication and said with a note of amusement, "I'm surprised you didn't draw your gun and shoot her."

"I thought about it!" she spat halfheartedly. As he continued to guide their steps away from camp and into the surrounding darkness, she demanded petulantly, "Where are you taking me?"

"Where we can be alone."

"I'd rather be alone with a polecat!" she humphed.

Deciding they were far enough from camp, Dru paused, placed his hands on her shoulders, gazed down into her enchanting face and asked with a delightful grin, "Casey, what am I going to do with you?"

Still perturbed, she snapped, "You can stop calling me Casey!"

"Never," he answered warmly.

Detecting his warmth, she lost her anger as she looked confusedly into his blue eyes. "You aren't mad at me?" she asked timorously.

"Why should I be mad?"

"Well, I just poured dishwater over your fiancée's head. I should think you'd be outraged."

"Didn't I tell you to stop thinking so much?"

"Yes," she replied hesitantly. "But I don't understand what you mean."

Dru came close to telling Cassandra that he was falling in love with her. But his past suddenly took control, making him overly cautious. There was no reason to rush into anything. Besides, a trail drive was no place for a romance. He'd wait until they reached Fort Laramie before confronting his feelings. In the meantime, he'd ask Cassandra to be patient and to trust him.

"Sweetheart," he began gently, "delivering this herd to the army on time is a big responsibility, and I should give it my full concentration. When the drive is over, we'll have a long talk. Until then, I hope you'll be patient and trust me. I also hope you'll stop drawing your own conclusions. You don't know as much as you think you do."

"I know you're impossible!" was her riposte. "Be patient and trust you? On what grounds?"

"On this," he replied huskily, drawing her quickly into his arms and kissing her passionately.

With a small whimper, she opened her mouth beneath his and returned his ardor fully.

Involved totally in their fervent embrace, they weren't aware that Vivian was poised close by. She watched them for a long moment, her eyes glazed furiously. Then, whirling about, she hurried quietly back to camp. Oh, she'd get even with Cassandra! And she'd do it soon!

Dru relinquished Cassandra reluctantly and said with a half-grin, "I'm tempted to lower you to the ground and take you here and now. But I respect you too much to jeopardize you. There's no guarantee that someone wouldn't come across us. Furthermore, if we stay away from camp too long, the men are liable to start talkin'." Placing a hand under her chin, he tilted her face up to his. "I promise you when we reach Fort Laramie, we'll settle everything between us."

She smiled wanly. "And until then, I'm supposed to be patient and trust you."

"Can you?"

"I'm not making any promises, but I'll try."

Leaning over, he kissed her sweetly, and then, taking her arm, began leading her back toward camp.

"Dru," Cassandra began unyieldingly, "I don't care what you say, but I'm not sleeping in the wagon with Vivian."

He started to argue with her; he didn't like the idea of her sleeping outdoors. But Dru knew Cassandra well enough to know when her mind was set.

"All right," he relented. "But place your bedroll beneath the wagon."

She was a little surprised that he gave in so easily. Suddenly, she laughed merrily.

"What's so funny?"

"I was just remembering how Vivian looked with dishwater all over her."

Dru chuckled. "You know, I've been wanting to do something like that to Vivian for years?"

She eyed him intently. "If you feel that way about her, then why did you ask her to marry you?"

"I didn't ask her to marry me." Dru brought their steps to a stop. "Vivian's using blackmail to

try and get me to marry her. Virgil knows no[?]
about this, and I don't want him to know. I'll
him about it later." Quickly he told her about his
uncle's debts and Vivian's threat to foreclose.

"Virgil loves the Bar-J. It'll break his heart to
lose it."

"I know, but losing it is unavoidable. Vivian will
carry out her threat."

"When do you intend to tell Virgil?"

"When the sale on the horses is completed, I
plan to resume my old occupation as a bounty
hunter. Hopefully, between what I can make and
what we can get from the army, we'll have enough
money to build another ranch."

"Is that when you plan to tell Virgil that he's lost
the Bar-J?"

Dru nodded. "I'm afraid if I tell him now, then
while I'm away, he'll return to the bottle."

"I don't think he would."

"You wouldn't say that if you had known him
when he was drinking."

As they started back to camp, it was on the tip
of Cassandra's tongue to ask Dru where she fit in
his plans, but she had told him that she'd try to be
patient and trust him. So, with effort, she held
back the question. However, patience was not one
of Cassandra's stronger points.

Then, remembering she had promised Badge she
would talk to Dru, she let Dru know that Badge
wanted to be a drover. Dru said he'd consider it.

The campsite was quiet as Vivian slipped silently

huck wagon. The wranglers and Virgil, their bedrolls, were deep in slumber. der the wagon, Vivian saw that Cassan- ound asleep. She stood still, her eyes moving briefly over the reposeful scene. She didn't have to worry about Dru, for he was with the herd. Daring to move away from the wagon, and hoping no one would awaken, she stepped furtively past the sleeping wranglers.

Hawk had placed his bedroll away from the others, and when Vivian reached it, she knelt. As she reached out to touch Hawk's shoulder, she looked down into his face and was startled to see that his open eyes were staring into hers. For a moment, her outstretched arm hung suspended; then she let it drop to her side and whispered, "Hawk, I must talk to you."

He showed no emotion. "What do you want, Mrs. Lance?"

"Please, we must talk privately." She nudged his arm, hinting for him to get up.

Rising to a sitting position, he flung off the top blanket and put on his boots.

"Come with me," Vivian encouraged conspiratorially.

As Hawk followed her past the sleeping wranglers and into the bordering darkness, his curiosity was piqued. He couldn't imagine why Mrs. Lance wanted to talk to him.

The sky was cloudless, and he could see her plainly in the moon-draped night. She was wearing her sheer dressing gown, and the transparent garment merely shadowed her feminine curves. Hawk could feel himself responding to her tempting beauty, but the feeling was purely physical.

They had walked a good distance from camp when, coming upon a small boulder, Vivian sat down and gestured for Hawk to join her.

He remained standing, measuring her with his dark, stoical eyes.

The man exuded a savage, dangerous air that sent a cold chill up Vivian's spine. He made her nervous, and she was in awe of him. Vivian hadn't hired Hawk; her foreman had given him the job. She had berated Carl for doing so, telling him that the half-breed frightened her. Carl had laughed at her fear, assuring her that Hawk wouldn't go on the warpath and take her scalp.

Now, as she watched him closely, she became acutely aware of his primitive yet sensuous magnetism. She had felt it before when in his presence, and the feeling always unnerved her.

"Hawk," she began, her tone shaky, "Carl has told me that you are a superb tracker. Is that true?"

He didn't answer.

She went on nervously, "Would you be interested in making yourself five hundred dollars?"

This time, she received a response. "What do you want me to do?"

"You were listening when Dru explained that the Thurston brothers might be following Cassandra. I want you to find the Thurstons and set up a meeting between Jubal and me."

Hawk's sudden smile resembled a cold sneer. "You want to get rid of Cassandra so you can have

Dru."

"Do you disapprove?" she asked, on her guard.

"I don't care what happens to Cassandra," he answered truthfully.

His answer delighted Vivian, and she carried on anxiously, "After I help Jubal kidnap Cassandra, I want you to ride with them. Dru will most assuredly pursue the Thurstons, and I doubt if they can cover their tracks well enough to fool Dru. He's too sharp. But if you're as good as I've heard, then you can cover your tracks so well that not even Dru can follow. I'll pay you two hundred dollars now; when I return from Fort Laramie, come to my ranch and I'll give you the remaining three hundred."

Hawk decided it was an easy way to make five hundred dollars. "All right, Mrs. Lance."

"You'll do it?" she questioned urgently, hardly believing getting rid of Cassandra was going to be so simple.

"I'll leave in the morning, find the Thurstons, set up a meeting, then return."

"Dru will want to know where you're going. What should I tell him?"

"There is a Sioux burial ground close by. Tell him I went to visit my dead mother." A demonic glint suddenly shone in his feral eyes.

Despite the warm night, his demonian aura sent a shiver through Vivian. Standing, she said uneasily, "In the morning, before you leave, I'll give you the two hundred dollars."

She made a half-turn to head back to camp, but when Hawk didn't move, she looked back at him.

The lustful expression in his eyes made her heart stand still. His heated gaze, penetrating her sheer gown, was devouring her shapely form. Vivian swallowed heavily, apprehensively. Used to getting her own way through her sexual attractiveness, she had purposely worn the transparent dressing gown. She suddenly felt that her lascivious maneuver had backfired. Hawk was not a man to tease, cajole, then be put off. A part of her was frightened by what she imagined his prowess to be, yet the other part was sexually aroused. She couldn't help but wonder what it would be like to make love to this strange, savage man.

Slowly he stepped toward her, his eyes caressing her silhouetted curves. "There will be an added payment to the five hundred dollars. You can deliver it now."

Unconsciously, she backed away from his stalking approach. Her heart slammed against her ribs. Although she found him disturbingly attractive, she was nonetheless afraid.

Moving with lightning speed, he jerked her into his arms. She felt crushed by his strength. His mouth captured hers in a kiss so filled with aggression that it stole her breath away.

Hawk, unconcerned with his partner's needs, undressed her quickly and lowered her roughly to the ground. Kneeling between her legs, he undid his trousers, then rammed his hardness into her with a brutal force.

His entrance was painful, and Vivian cried out as tears spilled from her eyes.

He pounded into her madly, his hips pumping

rapidly. When, at last, he jerked inside her, releasing his seed, Vivian was thankful that it was over.

As he leapt to his feet, drawing up his trousers, Vivian spat furiously, "You beast! You animal!"

He laughed cynically.

Rising awkwardly, Vivian threatened, "If you ever touch me again, I'll have you killed!"

"I won't want you again, Mrs. Lance. Once was enough." He moved away, saying over his shoulder, "I'll leave in the morning, after you give me the two hundred dollars." Then leaving her to make her way back to camp alone, he disappeared into the darkness.

Chapter Nineteen

Cactus Bend was a typical town, busy with the usual noon hour activities when Vivian and Hawk rode away from the livery stable.

Vivian could barely restrain her excitement. Knowing she was about to meet Jubal Thurston had her pulse racing and her heart pounding.

Everything had worked about splendidly. It had taken Hawk only four days to find Thurston, set up this meeting, then return to the trail drive. At that time, the drive had been two days away from Cactus Bend. Hawk had let Vivian know that Jubal would catch up to the herd, circle it, then veer into town, where he'd meet her at the saloon.

This morning Vivian had informed Dru that she planned to ride to Cactus Bend with Hawk and purchase herself a new wagon. Although it had been a pretext to leave the drive, she nonetheless intended to go through with it. Dru would be suspicious if she came back without a wagon. She had been worried that he might refuse to give her permission to leave, but, instead, he had told her that getting her own transportation was a good idea.

When she and Hawk had reached Cactus Bend, they had gone straight to the livery stable, where she had purchased a sturdy wagon. It hadn't been necessary to buy a team, for she had brought her horses with her.

Now, as they arrived at the hitching rail in front of the Gold Nugget saloon, Vivian could hardly believe that everything was running so smoothly. She'd soon be permanently rid of Cassandra, and then Dru would be all hers!

Pushing open the bat-wing doors, Hawk stood aside for Vivian to precede him. She swept past him with an unmistakable air of indignation. She had every intention of getting even with the savage half-breed! She was suffering his hated presence simply because she needed him. But soon she'd no longer have need of his services, and then he'd pay dearly for raping her!

Jubal and his youngest brother were seated at a corner table. Vivian's seductive beauty instantly sparked Jubal's desire, and as she came toward him, he ogled her with lustful eyes.

However, it wasn't a mutual attraction, for although Vivian supposed he was a handsome man, she found the huge bandage forbidding. He must be horribly disfigured, she thought with a shudder. She could easily understand why he hated Cassandra.

Hawk, without uttering a word, walked away from Vivian and went to the bar.

Pausing at the Thurstons' table, Vivian said with a cool composure, "Let's omit the formalities and get straight to business."

Jubal, admiring the way her Western skirt and blouse adhered to her voluptuous curves, said huskily, "Sit down, Mrs. Lance."

As she complied, her passionless gaze met Jubal's fervent one across the span of the table.

"Get lost," Jubal mumbled tersely to Dave.

Although the youngest Thurston was annoyed, he pushed back his chair and got to his feet. Dammit, he wanted to hear what the woman had to say! He stalked away angrily and joined Hawk at the bar.

"Hawk informed me that your other brothers deserted you," Vivian said, starting the conversation.

"Yeah. They got wives and kids back in Clarksville."

"Then there's only you and your one brother?"

"We got another man ridin' with us," Jubal replied, referring to Roy. Since Mrs. Lance was acquainted with DeLaney, he decided it might be best not to mention his name.

"Where is this other man?" she asked.

"A few days ago, his horse pulled up lame and we had to leave 'im behind. His horse should be healed by now, so he'll be catchin' up to us most any day."

"I see," she replied. "Well, you won't need him in order to capture Cassandra. I have a plan worked out for you."

Jubal's visage was cautious. "Mrs. Lance, why are you helpin' me? You got something against Cassandra?"

"I despise the little tart!" she said vehemently. "She's sleeping with Dru Jensen, who happens to be my fiancé."

Jubal's grin was humorless. "I kinda suspected the bitch was gettin' Jensen to protect her by

253

spreadin' her legs for 'im."

Vivian, anxious to explain her plan, said crisply, "Mr. Thurston, if you'll do as I say, capturing Cassandra will be as easy as taking candy from a baby. Naturally, I don't intend to pay you. Seizing Cassandra is payment in itself. However, I do wish to hire your services for an entirely different matter. I'll pay you one hundred dollars now, and if you complete the job successfully, I'll wire you another hundred dollars to the bank in Clarksville."

Jubal's interest was aroused. "What do you want me to do?"

"Hawk will help you kidnap Cassandra, and he'll also ride away with you. Dru's an experienced tracker, and you need a man like Hawk to cover your tracks. When, in your opinion, you have traveled a safe distance, I want you to kill Hawk. But you must be sure you're far enough away that Dru can't pick up your trail."

"I got no use for Indians or half-breeds. Killin' Hawk will be a pleasure." He studied her curiously. "Why do you want 'im dead?"

"That's my business," she answered coolly.

Jubal shrugged. Why she wanted the half-breed dead didn't really interest him. His concern lay with Cassandra. "Tell me this plan you have for kidnappin' the Stevenson bitch."

"It's very simple," she said, smiling confidently. "Every morning when the herd pulls out, Virgil Jensen and Cassandra stay behind." Her smile became shrewd. "It's just the two of them . . . all alone."

Jubal was surprised. Why hadn't DeLaney told

him about this?

Vivian went on, "Virgil is giving Cassandra shooting lessons. Sneaking up on them should be unbelievably easy. However, I don't want Virgil killed. Knock him unconscious, but leave him alive." If Virgil were dead, Vivian knew her blackmail threat would be useless. Dru would simply let her have the Bar-J and ride out of her life.

"All right, Mrs. Lance. I won't kill the old man."

"I hope I can trust you," she remarked, watching him dubiously.

"I said I won't kill 'im, and I won't." Jubal suddenly grinned derisively. "I never break my word to a lady."

His remark was so farfetched that she wanted to laugh in his face, but keeping her countenance impassive, she replied, "There's no reason to procrastinate. I'll expect you to kidnap Cassandra tomorrow morning."

"No problem," he uttered confidently.

"Mr. Thurston," she began, somewhat hesitantly, "considering what Cassandra did to you, I'm sure you plan to, shall we say, make her pay dearly? Save your revenge until you have put a great distance between yourself and Dru. To lose him, it's imperative that you travel quickly and do as Hawk advises. You can get even with Cassandra later, and at a more appropriate time."

"That bitch will pay her dues when we cross into Arkansas."

"Good," she declared, satisfied. "I plan to leave Hawk here with you. When I return to the drive,

I'll tell Dru that the man quit on me without notice. Dru knows that Hawk is very strange, so he'll not be suspicious."

She reached into her skirt pocket, brought out a small wad of bills and placed them on the table. "Here's your first payment; as I said before, I'll wire you the rest,"

"How you gonna know whether or not I killed the half-breed?"

She spoke calmly. "Because if you don't kill him, he'll kill you. I'm merely paying you two hundred dollars to beat him at his own game."

"What makes you think he's gonna kill me?"

"Because he'll suspect that you have it in mind to murder him."

Jubal guffawed heartily. "Damn, woman, you're talkin' in circles!"

"Listen to me!" she spat furiously, resenting his laughter. "Men like Hawk kill before they can be killed. The man is a savage, he'd cut out your heart just for the pleasure of watching you bleed. Heed my warning, Mr. Thurston, be on your guard. And as soon as you've put ample ground between yourself and Dru, kill that savage beast before he kills you."

Her chilling warning sent an icy shiver through Jubal. He turned his gaze to the bar. Hawk was watching him, his feral eyes as unfriendly as a panther's.

"All right, Mrs. Lance," Jubal said, returning his attention to Vivian. "I'll stay on my guard."

"See that you do," she declared firmly, standing. "I must leave. I need to go to the livery stable, pick up my wagon and then catch up to the herd. I have no time to waste."

Jubal got to his feet. "Do you think you can manage?"

She raised her chin arrogantly. "I might be a woman, but I'm not helpless." She had spoken with feigned certainty. She was apprehensive about driving back to the herd, but she was willing to risk her own safety to be rid of Cassandra.

Thurston's lust-filled gaze swept over her in an insolent fashion. "You're a woman, all right. And I bet you ain't one bit helpless."

Vivian found his lewd scrutiny insulting. How dare the low-bred clout take such liberties with his evil eyes! She whirled about and marched across the floor. She and Hawk had finalized their business, and since there was no reason for parting words between them, she pushed aside the swinging doors and left.

Dru was riding a short distance in front of the herd when Virgil rode up to him.

"The river's about ten miles ahead," Virgil began. "Do you wanna camp there for the night and cross the herd in the mornin'?"

"That's what I had in mind," Dru answered.

They rode in silence for a few minutes; then, watching his nephew out of the corner of his eye, Virgil remarked, "You know, I've been givin' your engagement to Vivian a lot of thought. I know damn good and well that you aren't in love with her. So I kept askin' myself, why the hell are you marryin' her?" He paused for a long moment before stating speculatively, "I think I know why you told her you'd marry her."

Dru waited, but when his uncle didn't say any more, he encouraged, "Well, go on. Don't stop now."

"After much deliberation, I came to the conclusion that Vivian's pressurin' you into marriage."

"Why do you say that?" Dru questioned, his surprise evident.

"I know Vivian. She's selfish, overbearing and would do most anything to snare you into marriage. So once I narrowed it down to Vivian's less than admirable character, the pieces to the puzzle fell into place. I then asked myself, what could she use to force you into marriage? The answer was simple. When I was livin' for the bottle, I accumulated a lot of debts. Her pa kept loanin' me money."

Virgil's voice faded, but following a moment of silence, he went on, "When Adam loaned me money, I insisted on putting the Bar-J up as collateral. I would've told you about these debts if I had thought it was necessary. Now, I bet Vivian is threatin' to foreclose if you don't marry her."

"Dammit, Virgil!" Dru fussed. "Why didn't you tell me we were in debt? Why did you wait and let me find it out through Vivian?"

Virgil's face lit up. "So I'm right? She is usin' those debts to pressure you into marriage?"

"Answer me!" Dru persisted. "Why didn't you tell me we owe Vivian ten thousand dollars?"

" 'Cause we don't owe her ten thousand dollars.

258

We don't owe Vivian one red cent."

Dru was dumbfounded. "What?"

"A couple of days after Adam's funeral, his lawyer came to see me. Adam had a new will drawn up a few weeks before he died. The will stated that all my debts to him were forgiven. Those notes Vivian's holdin' aren't worth the paper they're written on."

"Surely Vivian knows!"

"I doubt it. The lawyer told me that Vivian waived the actual readin' of the will. She only wanted to know if her father had left everything to her. When he told her she was the sole heir, she couldn't have cared less about Adam's last will and testament. The will's locked in the lawyer's safe."

Virgil drew a long breath. "I feel badly about those debts, and Adam absolvin' them kinda hits me where it hurts. My drinkin' didn't cost us our ranch, but it did cost me my pride. I guess Adam was afraid that Vivian would demand payment, and to prevent something like that from happening, he erased my debts." Virgil sighed pensively. "Adam and I went back a long way together. He was a good friend."

"We'll pay your debts in full," Dru hastened to reply. "Only Vivian will have to take the payments in installments. We won't be in debt to her or anyone else."

Virgil agreed. "I'm glad you feel that way. Now that we have that taken care of, why didn't you let me know that Vivian was blackmailin' you?"

Candidly, Dru told him his reasons for withholding the information, and also elaborated on his plans to make extra money as a bounty hunter so they could build themselves another ranch.

Virgil was quiet for a couple of minutes, then murmured, "I can understand why you were afraid that I'd turn to the bottle. I can't guarantee you that I wouldn't, but I can say honestly that I don't think it would have happened. Losin' you and Johnny was a terrible blow, and I turned to the bottle for consolation. I don't think I'll ever make that mistake again, regardless of what happens."

Suddenly Dru smiled expansively. "When Vivian finds out about her father's will, she's gonna be madder than a hornet."

Virgil chuckled. "You can say that again."

An idea occurred to him, and Dru remarked hastily, "I'm gonna ride ahead to the river."

He started to turn his horse about, but Virgil detained him. "You're goin' in the wrong direction. The river's in front of us, not in back of us."

"I plan to invite a certain young lady to accompany me," Dru explained.

Virgil, smiling, yelled to Dru's departing back, "If you've got the sense God gave a billy goat, you'll marry that certain young lady!"

Cassandra, driving the chuck wagon with Badge sitting beside her, caught sight of Dru riding in their direction. Her eyes sparkled, and a smile lit up her face. She loved him so much that just seeing him was thrilling.

Reaching the wagon, Dru steadied his horse to a walk. Speaking to Badge, he asked, "Son, do you think you can manage the team?"

"Sure," he replied.

"Good." He looked at Cassandra. "Casey, would you like to ride ahead with me to the river and take a bath?"

"A bath?" she exclaimed, elated. Envisioning herself fully immersed in a bed of water was heavenly. She was so tired of quick sponge baths. "I'd love to!" she remarked.

"Grab a towel, a bar or soap and a clean set of clothes."

She handed the reins to Badge, then climbed into the back of the wagon. Stuffing everything she would need in her carpetbag, she hurried back over the seat.

Guiding his horse closer to the wagon, Dru offered her his arm and helped lift her from the seat and onto the back of his saddle.

"Badge," Dru began, once Cassandra was settled, "if you still have your heart set on bein' a drover, I'll start trainin' you in the mornin'."

The boy was ecstatic. "Thanks, Dru!"

"It's hard work."

"I'm not afraid of hard work. I've worked hard all my life."

"I know, son," Dru replied soberly. "Well, we'll see you later."

He spurred his horse into a fast gallop, and sliding her carpetbag over her arm, Cassandra held firmly to Dru's waist.

Traveling quickly, they soon left the herd far behind. It was a warm, sunny afternoon, and Cassandra could hardly wait to reach the river. She'd not only bathe, but swim to her heart's content.

"So far, this has been a wonderful day," she declared impetuously.

"Why is that?" Dru asked, his feelings the same as hers.

"Vivian left this morning to go into Cactus Bend, so I haven't had to endure her presence, and now the river awaits! I'm going to indulge myself and stay in the water until I'm as wrinkled as a prune. You don't have to worry that I might drown, for I can swim like a fish."

Dru laughed cheerfully. "Listen closely, my innocent little fish. I'm not taking you to the river so you can spend all your time in the water. I have other plans for you."

"Oh?" she asked saucily. "My goodness, what could you possibly have in mind?"

He took her hand from his waist and placed it on his aroused manhood. "This," he answered.

"Why, Dru Jensen, I do believe you intend to take advantage of me." She blew softly into his ear.

Her teasing, plus the touch of her hand, was so stimulating that he took her hand and returned it to his waist.

"What's wrong?" she questioned pertly. "Are you afraid you can't wait until we reach the river?"

"Exactly," he answered with a grimace, his loins aching.

"Dru," she began smoothly, "I thought you said that you wouldn't jeopardize me."

"Do you have to remember everything I tell you?"

"Of course."

He smiled. "Well, what I said is true. However, the wranglers are far behind, so we're safe from watchful eyes. Besides, today is an exception."

"Why is it exceptional?"

Quickly he told her about Adam's will absolving Virgil's debts.

"That's wonderful!" she exclaimed. "Now you don't have to return to being a bounty hunter. And more importantly, you and Virgil won't lose the Bar-J." She waited, hoping he'd let her know where she fit in his future plans.

Dru's thoughts, running parallel to Cassandra's, were in a turmoil. He didn't have a cowardly bone in his body when it came to something he could see or touch, but love scared the hell out of him. Since Anita's betrayal and his son's death, he had avoided the emotion like a child once burned stays away from fire.

Now, without warning, Cassandra had managed to slip into his life, reviving emotions he thought had died with his son.

It took courage for Dru to lay his feelings on the line, to leave himself vulnerable. "Cassandra," he said tenderly, "I love you."

His declaration, spoken so unexpectedly, took Cassandra by surprise. "You love me?" she gasped.

"Yes," he whispered. "I love you with all my heart."

"Oh, Dru!" she cried gloriously. "I love you too!"

As his past came back to haunt him, delving into unhealed wounds, he skirted talk of marriage and said briskly, "I don't know about you, but as far as I'm concerned, the sooner we get to the river, the better." He sent his horse into a full run, ending any further discussion.

Cassandra wasn't discouraged. Dru had actually declared his love. Considering his past, she knew confessing his love had been a big step. Surely, with a little more time, he'd ask her to marry him!

Chapter Twenty

Kneeling at the river's edge, Cassandra dipped her hand into the water. It was refreshingly cool, and she could hardly wait to fully immerse herself.

Standing, she threw off her hat, unbuckled her gun belt and let it drop gently to the ground. She was unbuttoning her shirt when Dru, having turned the horses loose to graze, came up soundlessly behind her. Drawing her back flush to his chest, he bent his head and kissed her earlobe with featherlike softness.

The touch of his lips sent a rush of warmth all over her, and turning, she slid her arms around his neck

His mouth came down on hers, and his fervent kiss quickened her pulse.

Releasing her tenderly, Dru gazed down into her enchanting face and murmured with a wry grin, "I think we'd better bathe. Otherwise, we might never get around to it."

Cassandra gave him a saucy smile and said teasingly, "You can go farther downstream to wash while I bathe here."

He quirked a brow, staring at her as though she were daft. Then suddenly detecting a mischievous gleam lurking in the depths of her green eyes, he responded playfully, "When was the last time you were stripped and thrown into a river?"

"Never," she answered, inching away from him.

"Well, my teasing little minx, there's a first time for everything."

Moving extremely fast, he lunged forward, seized her arm and jerked her against him. As he began to unceremoniously strip away her boyish attire, she fought him halfheartedly.

All their worries and cares ceased to exist as they became totally involved in their frolicsome play. By the time Dru lowered Cassandra onto the grassy bank to remove her undergarments, she was laughing so hard that she was too weak to struggle.

When she lay before him fully unclothed, Dru let his eyes devour her tempting beauty. In his opinion, she was the picture of perfection and more desirable than words could adequately describe.

Anxious now to take her to the river, he began to hastily shed his own clothing. Cassandra watched, glorying in his superb maleness.

Dru grabbed the bar of soap, then lifted Cassandra into his arms.

He carried her into the rippling water, but when it was waist-high, he pitched her forward without warning.

Screaming, she went under with a splash, but then came up quickly and threatened good-humoredly, "Dru Jensen, I'll get even with you!"

"We'll see about that," he came back, his tone challenging. Keeping an alert eye on Cassandra, he quickly washed himself. However, she made no advances. This wasn't the right time to get even; she'd have to wait for the opportune moment.

Finishing, Dru threw her the bar of soap as she made her way to more shallow water. Dru plunged deeply into the river, swam out to deeper depths, then broke the surface, turned over onto his back and floated. Basking in the cool water, he closed his eyes against the sun's rays and was soon totally contented.

Meanwhile, Cassandra had bathed and washed her hair. Her short tresses, curled into tight ringlets, gave her a delightfully impish look.

She pitched the soap onto the bank before stealthily moving farther out into the stream. She kept a close watch on Dru. He was still floating on his back, and as soon as the water was deep enough, she took a long breath, then dived beneath the surface. Using long, graceful strokes, she swam underwater with amazing speed.

Cassandra was perfectly at ease. Her home had been close to a river, and worried that she might fall in and drown, Cassandra's father had taught her to swim well at an early age.

When she was directly beneath Dru, Cassandra pushed herself upward, grabbed ahold of Dru's leg and pulled him under.

Releasing him quickly, she swam out of his reach, broke the surface and filled her lungs with needed air. Treading water, she waited for Dru to make his way back up. However, the undulating waves remained unbroken. Frightened, she inhaled deeply, then plunged downward into the river's depths.

Her eyes open, she searched frantically for Dru,

panicking when she couldn't find him. She was about to go up for another breath of air before continuing her search when, suddenly, she was grabbed from behind.

Dru, his strong arm encircling her waist, took her with him to the surface.

While she gasped for air, she managed to say breathlessly, "Damn you, Dru! You scared me half to death! I thought you had drowned!"

"Not likely," he laughed. Then, as a sensuous smile curled his lips, he suggested, "Well, my little mermaid, shall we swim to the bank?"

Understanding his intentions, her heart skipped a beat. The mere thought of making love with Dru sent a trembling thrill racing through her.

"Are you cold?" he asked, her trembling not escaping his notice.

"No," she answered, looking at him with longing. "It's anticipation that makes me tremble."

"Darlin'," he rasped, drawing her supple body against his hard frame. Holding her close with one arm, he used the other to take them to shallow water. When it was hip-level, he slipped her legs about his waist.

His splendid hardness touching her womanly core was exciting, and embracing him, she murmured seductively, "Oh, Dru, now! Take me now!"

"Cassandra!" he groaned huskily, shoving his manhood deeply into her warm depths.

His entry was exhilarating, and she cried out with unrestrained pleasure. Locking her ankles, she rode him with abandon, her passion so wild that she had no control over it.

Dru was thrilled by her unbridled response, and without disrupting their thrusting rhythm, his lips seized hers in an aggressively passionate kiss.

Her desire was primitive . . . raptuous, and he could feel the thundering pounding of her heart beating against his chest. As overpowering sensations wafted through him in heated flashes, he slid his hands under her hips and molded her thighs to his.

Making love with a hungry intensity, they surrendered to their fiery appetites, reaching, then gloriously finding, an all-consuming moment of shared ecstasy.

Dru kissed her endearingly; then, sweeping her into his arms, he carried her out of the river and laid her on the grassy bank. He stretched out beside her, and resting in each other's arms, they allowed the warm sun to dry them.

"Dru?" Cassandra murmured, her head nestled on his shoulder. "What did you do with my evening gown?"

"Gown?" he questioned.

"The dress I wore in Good Times," she explained.

"Why do you ask?"

"I've always wondered what happened to it, but I could never find the right time to ask you."

"I left it with the desk clerk. I thought you might come back to the hotel to claim it."

She sighed wistfully. "It was such a beautiful gown."

"And you were so beautiful in it," he added.

"Are you still angry about what happened in

Good Times?"

"Which incident are you referring to? The gun-smith's, or the clandestine visit to my hotel room?"

"Both," she answered.

He hugged her gently. "No, darlin'. I'm not angry about either incident." He chuckled. "I still can't believe that you fooled me so completely. How could I have been so blind?"

"Oh, Dru," she began intensely, "you have no idea how terrible it was for me. I desired you so desperately and could do nothing about it because I was supposed to be a boy."

"Is that why you planned our romantic interlude in Good Times? Because you desired me so desperately?"

"Yes," she said with a smile, glad to get the truth in the open.

Rising up on one elbow, he gazed down into her face. "You must love me very much."

"I do!" she exclaimed. "Dru, you mean the world to me. I swear it's the truth."

In spite of her candid confession, Dru's past still held him in its unyielding grasp; yet deep down inside he burned with his love for Cassandra. If only he could break down the protective shield he had built around his emotions and give his heart freely.

She sensed his torment and wished she could take away his doubts with promises, but she knew actions spoke louder than words. Slipping her arms about his neck, she whispered, "Let me show you how much I love you."

When he bent his head, she met his lips halfway

as she moved against him in a suggestive body caress. Her mouth was smothered by his ardent kiss, his tongue entering her mouth with such urgent passion that her lips opened fully beneath his.

He moved his lips to the hollow of her throat, then downward to her soft breasts, finding and kissing her hardened nipples. Slowly, his tongue etched a blazing path over her stomach and to her most sensitive area.

A rasping moan of pleasure escaped her lips as she was swept away by a new, ecstatic experience. Giving herself to him without inhibition, she arched against his heated caress. His passion demanded her full surrender, and wrapped in mindless ecstasy, she achieved her ultimate desire.

He rose over her, and she welcomed him into her body, her legs locked firmly about his waist. His thrusting was deep, consuming, and she lifted her hips to his, wanting him ever deeper.

He took her with him to a rapturous, heart-stopping climax, and she trembled as wondrous sensations coursed through her.

Sated, Dru gazed into her flushed face. "I love you," he whispered, his breathing labored.

Her hands feathering over the muscles of his back, she murmured throatily, "I love you too."

Studying her, he suddenly smiled. "Your short hair makes you look like a mischievous little imp."

"I hate my hair. I can't wait for it to grow long."

"I don't know," he said, grinning. "I think it's kinda cute. Maybe someday short hair will be the fashion for women."

"Never," she disagreed. "Why would women ever

cut their hair willingly?"

Dru kissed the tip of her nose; then, breaking their intimate joining, he stood, took her hand and brought her to her feet. "Let's enjoy another swim before the herd gets here."

Taking Dru unawares, she shoved him aside, and running toward the river, she yelled over her shoulder, "Last one in is a rotten egg!"

Dru and Cassandra were fully dressed and sitting on the bank when they detected the sounds of horses approaching. It sounded like distant thunder.

Cassandra sighed inwardly and edged closer to Dru. She didn't want this afternoon to end; it had been too heavenly.

His feelings the same as hers, Dru kissed her tenderly, then murmured, "Sweetheart, we'll be together like this again. I promise you."

His words made her feel somewhat better, but she wanted more than another afternoon like this one. She wanted them to spend the rest of their lives together. Be patient, she told herself. Dru will ask you to marry him. Just give him a little more time. She sighed audibly and let her thoughts drift to Russ.

"Is something wrong?" Dru asked.

"I was just thinking about Russ. I'm worried about him."

"Are you afraid the Thurstons will find him?"

"Yes. I certainly hope that Roy meets up with Russ."

He wished he could lighten her worries with encouraging words, but he was aware of all the hazards that could befall her brother on his way to Fort Laramie. To try and assure her that Russ wasn't in danger would be giving her false hope.

Virgil, riding a good distance in front of the herd, was the first to reach the river. As he rode up to Dru and Cassandra, they got to their feet.

Dismounting, he said, "Vivian and Hawk haven't caught up to us yet. It'll be dark in another hour." He looked at Dru. "You reckon I should go look for 'em?"

"That's all right. You rest. I'll find 'em."

A feeling of melancholy washed over Cassandra. Dru was leaving. The afternoon was now officially over. She'd commit every wonderful moment of it to memory, and on lonely nights, she'd relive their shared Utopia, time and time again.

As Dru was heading toward his horse, they suddenly spotted Pete riding speedily toward them. Arriving, he announced, "Mrs. Lance just showed up, only Hawk ain't with her. She said he quit and stayed in Cactus Bend."

"I'm not surprised," Virgil replied. "That Hawk's a strange one."

"When the chuck wagon gets here," Dru said to Pete, "I want you to drive it across the river. We'll camp on the other side, but wait and cross the herd in the morning."

Pete dismounted and started talking to Virgil. Using their preoccupation to his advantage, Dru touched Cassandra's arm and urged her to walk with him a short way downstream.

273

Pausing, he met her questioning eyes and said gently, "Hon, I know you realize that a trail drive is not the proper setting for a romance. We'll have to keep our feelin's for each other under control. I don't intend to give these wranglers, or Vivian, reason to start waggin' their tongues about us. This afternoon alone will give them reason to speculate." He got the distinct notion that she wasn't truly listening. "Are you paying attention to what I'm sayin'?"

"Yes. I heard every word, and I understand."

"Then why do I have the feelin' that there's something else on your mind?"

She smiled affectionately. "I just realized how much I love your voice. Especially your accent, which is a cross between a Bostonian pronunciation and a Texas drawl. It's very appealing."

"Oh yeah?" he grinned, his blue eyes twinkling.

"Furthermore, did you know that I've been in love with you for years? A long, long time ago, my mind conjured up the image of the man I would love, and you fit my dream lover's description perfectly."

He chuckled good-naturedly. "Casey, you're a delight!" Dru was somewhat amazed when he suddenly realized that it had been years since he'd been so happy, so at ease. Cassandra was a ray of sunshine, casting out the dark shadows of his past.

Chapter Twenty-one

Early the next morning, the wranglers rounded up the herd and sent them across the river. Cassandra's shooting lesson had to wait until the drive was a good distance away. A gunshot at close range could start a stampede.

Cassandra was feeling a little ill as she watched Virgil line up some empty cans to use as targets. Ambling back, he said, "Let's see how many of those you can hit."

When she remained unresponsive, he looked at her questioningly. "Is something wrong, missy? You seem a little pale. Are you sick?"

Cassandra was slightly nauseous. "I'm not feeling too well," she answered.

"Are you comin' down with a cold?"

"I don't think so."

"Maybe we'd better cancel your lesson. You can spend the day restin' in the chuck wagon. Pete can drive the team."

She smiled weakly. "I'm sure I'll be all right."

He touched her brow. "You don't have a fever. That's a good sign."

"Mr. Jensen!" Hawk suddenly called from the other side of the bank.

They turned and watched as the half-breed

forged his horse across the river.

"I wonder what he's doin' here," Virgil mumbled.

"He probably changed his mind about quitting and wants his job back."

Reining in, Hawk dismounted, and walking up to them, uttered amicably, "Good mornin'." Then, taking the pair totally by surprise, he drew his gun with amazing speed and slammed it against Virgil's temple.

The severe blow knocked Virgil unconscious. As he dropped limply to the ground, Cassandra screamed. She fell to her knees beside him, but Hawk's strong hand, grasping her arm, jerked her back to her feet.

He drew her pistol and tucked it in his belt. Cassandra's horse and Virgil's were saddled, and shoving her toward the mare, Hawk ordered tersely, "Mount up!"

"Why are you doing this?" she demanded incredulously. God, why would this man want to kidnap her?

"Keep your mouth shut and get on your horse," he mumbled.

Disobeying, she turned to him, ready to fire more questions.

Showing Cassandra that he meant business, Hawk slapped her face so powerfully that she reeled backward. Holstering his gun, he grabbed her under her arms and heaved her onto the mare. Snatching the reins, he led the horse over to his own, mounted and, taking his captive with him, fled back across the river.

Cassandra's cheek was burning, and her ears

276

were ringing from Hawk's brutal slap. As the mare began its swim across the river, Cassandra glanced back at Virgil. He hadn't moved. She prayed he wasn't dead!

Reaching shallow water, the horses' hoofs touched the river's muddy bottom, and getting their footing, they climbed the short embankment.

As they reached ground, Hawk spurred his steed into a fast, loping run. His stallion's pace was too exhausting for Cassandra's delicate mare, and her horse was soon laboring under the unrelenting speed.

Afraid Hawk would force the mare to run until she dropped, Cassandra was considering pleading with him to slow down when, suddenly, two horsemen broke through the shrubbery, blocking the path.

Hawk pulled up so abruptly that the mare bumped against the stallion's flanks.

The collision sent Cassandra sliding, and she came close to falling before regaining her balance. She looked at the two riders, and as recognition flashed in her mind, her eyes widened with fright. Jubal and his brother! Her heart pounded.

Jubal edged his horse alongside Cassandra's. He grinned cruelly as his hate-filled eyes roamed over her boyish attire.

"Well . . . well," he drawled. "If it ain't Miss Stevenson. You done changed a lot since we last met. You don't look like such a smug Southern bitch anymore. In fact, you look downright comical in them clothes." He placed a hand on his bandage. "I don't look so good anymore either."

Suddenly, he laughed mercilessly. "When I get through with you, bitch, your face is gonna look worse than mine!"

Hawk interrupted, "You can threaten the woman later. We need to move out. Head west. I'll bring up the rear and cover our tracks."

"West?" Jubal argued. "I ain't headin' west. I'm goin' south."

"Which is the exact direction Jensen will expect you to take. To throw him off, we need to head west before veering south.

Dave spoke up. "Jubal, Mrs. Lance told you to take Hawk's advice. So far, he's been right. Didn't he tell ya that he could get Cassandra without any problem?"

Vivian! Cassandra fumed. How had she managed to contact Jubal and set up this abduction? Cassandra's eyes went to Hawk. Of course, she had done this while in Cactus Bend! That's why Hawk didn't come back with her.

Hawk pitched the mare's reins to Jubal. "Head your ass west," he ordered gruffly.

Hawk's insolence infuriated Jubal. He was looking forward to killing the smart-mouthed half-breed!

The Thurstons, their captive in tow, spurred their horses into motion. Due to their pack mules, they set such an easy pace that Cassandra's mare was able to keep up without tiring.

As tears threatened, Cassandra wondered if Dru would find her. She had a foreboding, however, that not even Dru, with all his experience, could find her in this vast, uninhabited land. Especially with a man like Hawk covering their tracks.

Dru, leaving Badge's training in the capable hands of one of his wranglers, circled the herd and rode back to the chuck wagon. He was surprised to see Pete still at the helm; he had expected to find Cassandra.

Keeping his horse alongside the wagon, Dru asked Pete, "What do you suppose is keeping Virgil and Cassandra?"

"I don't know, but I'm gettin' kinda worried."

"I'm gonna ride back and check on 'em."

As Dru began riding toward the river, he was certain that, at any moment, he'd spot the pair heading in his direction. Still, the terrain remained unblemished. Becoming worried, Dru spurred his horse into a faster canter.

It took him nearly an hour to reach his destination. When he spotted Virgil's prone body, a stab of fear cut into his heart like a knife.

Pulling up, Dru leapt from his mount before it could come to a complete stop. A deep moan sounded in Virgil's throat, and kneeling, Dru elevated his uncle's head. "Virgil!" he exclaimed.

Touching the ugly gash at his temple, Virgil mumbled confusedly, "Wh . . . what happened?"

"Apparently, somebody knocked you out. Where's Cassandra?"

Virgil tried to make sense out of his muddled thoughts. Slowly, his confusion cleared. "Hawk," he remembered. "He came ridin' in, dismounted, and walked up to me like he wanted to talk. Then before I knew what was happenin', he drew his gun and slammed it across my head." Pushing himself into a sitting position, he asked excitedly, "Did Hawk take Cassandra?"

"It looks that way," Dru answered, assisting Virgil to his feet. He swayed unsteadily for a moment.

"Why the hell would Hawk kidnap Cassandra?" Virgil asked, grimacing against the pain throbbing at his temple.

"He must be workin' for Thurston," Dru speculated.

"How do you suppose he managed to team up with Thurston?"

Dru, rigid, his eyes glazed with fury, uttered fiercely, "Vivian! She's behind this! I should break her damned neck!"

"Losin' your temper won't get Cassandra back," Virgil said, hoping to cool his nephew's anger.

With effort, Dru heeded his uncle's advice and controlled his rage. He looked closely at Virgil. "Are you well enough to ride?"

"I can make it," he answered, although his head was hurting something fierce. "What do you plan to do?"

"Return to the drive, pack some provisions, extra ammunition, and then hope to God that I can find Cassandra before Jubal kills her. If it were only the Thurstons, trackin' them would be easy, but Hawk's another matter."

"I'm goin' with you," Virgil decided.

"You're staying with the herd. We can't leave the men without a trail boss. Also, you probably have

280

a mild concussion. You need rest."

"Dammit, Dru!" Virgil fussed. "That little gal means the world to me!"

"Virgil, I don't have time to argue with you."

"All right," he conceded. "If you won't take me with you, then take a couple of the men."

"We're too shorthanded. Besides, I travel better alone." With that, Dru moved to fetch Virgil's horse.

The moment they reached the herd, Dru told Pete to gather supplies and extra ammunition and load the goods on a packhorse. As Pete carried out his order, Dru paid a visit to Vivian.

Standing outside her wagon, Vivian, filled with apprehension, watched as Dru's long strides brought him quickly to her side.

Feigning concern, she hastened to say, "I just heard that Cassandra's been abducted! The poor child!" She forced an angry frown. "Is it true that Hawk is the one who kidnapped her?"

"It's true," Dru replied stiffly.

"The beast!" she spat. "My goodness, why do you suppose he did such a thing?" Vivian was enraged with Hawk for showing himself to Virgil. Now, Dru would suspect that she was somehow involved.

"I think you know why Hawk took Cassandra. You paid him to take her to Thurston, didn't you?"

"Heavens no!" she claimed.

His hand shot out, grasping her arm. Tightening

281

his grip, he uttered between gritted teeth, "Where's Thurston?"

"I have no idea," she answered, trying to pull away from his crushing hold.

"So help me God, if anything happens to Cassandra, I'll make you pay!"

"I tell you, I had nothing to do with Cassandra's abduction!"

"I don't believe you," he replied, releasing her brusquely. He started to leave, but turned back and said, "I suggest you have a talk with Virgil. He has something to tell you concerning your father's will."

"Father's will?" she questioned. "What are you talking about?"

He didn't bother to explain, but wheeled about and headed back to the chuck wagon. By now, Pete should have his supplies packed. Dru was anxious to be on his way. Each passing minute took Cassandra farther away.

Darkness was cloaking the landscape when Jubal decided it was time to stop for the night. He found a good place to camp, and soon he and Dave had a fire burning.

Cassandra was seated close by, under a tree, her tied hands resting in her lap. Not only was she bone tired, but the nausea she'd experienced this morning was still with her.

Supper was warming over the flames when Hawk appeared. Dismounting, he moved to the fire and sat down. "We can't be tracked," he said to no one in particular. "Not even Jensen can follow."

As she listened, Cassandra's heart sank. If Dru didn't find her, she'd soon be totally at Jubal's mercy. She didn't dare try to imagine what he had in store for her; the possibilities were too horrifying.

Jubal dished up a plate of food and carried it over to Cassandra. He sat beside her and untied her hands. Then, offering her the plate, he said with a cold grin, "You gotta eat to keep up your strength."

She accepted the proffered fare. She had no appetite, and her stomach was queasy. Still, she knew Jubal was right. She needed nourishment.

Jubal's grin widened. "By the way, I think you should know that I killed Russ."

"You shot him in the back," she muttered, sounding angry. She wasn't about to let him know that his shot hadn't been fatal.

"I ain't talkin' about shootin' him in the back. I know you and the Jensens took him to the doctor. I saw you leavin' the doc's house. You weren't gone no time 'til the doctor left. While he was gone, I slipped into the house and finished your brother off for good."

Cassandra paled. "No! You're lying!"

"Russ is dead. I smothered him with his own pillow."

"No!" she cried again.

He took the plate from her limp hands. "I reckon you done lost your appetite."

Jubal was about to get up when Cassandra suddenly turned on him. Wildly, her fists pounded against his chest. "You murderer! . . . Damn you!"

Throwing down the plate, he captured her hands, grabbed the rope and securely tied her wrists. He shoved her roughly, and she fell over, her face slamming flat against the ground.

She waited until she heard his footsteps move away; then, rolling to her side and turning away from her captors, she gave in to her sorrow. Tears flooded her eyes and ran down her cheeks in a steady stream. Russ dead! It was almost more than her distress-filled mind could grasp.

"Oh, Russ! Russ!" she moaned weakly, her heart breaking. Cassandra wept until she finally cried herself into a restless slumber, her dreams filled with Russ.

A couple of hours later, she was awakened by a chill. She sat up, shivering. The night breeze was cool and she wished for a blanket. She looked toward the fire. Seeing that Jubal and his brother weren't sleeping, she considered asking them for cover. Before she could do so, Dave began talking to Jubal.

"Are you really gonna kill that half-breed?"

Cassandra looked about. Hawk was nowhere in sight, and she guessed he was standing guard.

"You're damned right, I'm gonna kill him," Jubal was saying.

"He's a mean one. You better be careful."

"I ain't scared of no half-breed Indian."

"When do you aim to do it?" Dave asked expectantly.

"Mrs. Lance told me to wait 'til we was a safe distance ahead of Jensen, but, hell, I ain't worried about that ignorant cowboy. In a couple more days we won't need Hawk anymore, and then I'm gonna put a bullet right betwixt his eyes." He nudged his brother with his elbow. "You better get some sleep. You got the second watch."

Neither the Thurstons nor Cassandra were aware of the man hidden nearby, his huge form shrouded in darkness. As Dave went to his bedroll, Hawk, crouched behind a heavy bush, crept back to his post.

He took a stance beside a large boulder, and leaning back against it, he propped his rifle at his side. Folding his arms across his wide chest, he stared thoughtfully into the distance.

That Vivian had told Jubal to kill him didn't surprise Hawk. He had suspected her to do just that.

A flicker of a smile curled the corners of his lips, then disappeared as though it had never been there.

Meanwhile, Cassandra had decided that she'd rather freeze than ask Jubal for a blanket. Lying down, she curled up into a tight ball and tried to draw a measure of warmth from her own body heat.

It was a long time before she was able to fall asleep.

In the morning, Cassandra was awakened by Jubal's foot jabbing into her ribs.

"Wake up, bitch!" he ordered.

She sat up gingerly. Every muscle in her body

ached from sleeping on the hard ground.

Jubal thrust a strip of jerky into her bound hands and placed a canteen at her side. "Here; we ain't cookin' no breakfast."

As he moved away, she looked down at her meager food. She swallowed heavily, fought back a feeling of nausea and took a tentative bite. Knowing she must eat to survive, she chewed the dried meat thoroughly. She had to force herself to swallow each biteful before washing it down with gulps of water. She still felt queasy, and she hoped she wouldn't throw up. She concentrated fully on her food, not letting herself think of anything else. Cassandra knew if she allowed her thoughts to dwell on Russ, she'd start crying so heavily that she wouldn't be able to eat.

The men busied themselves saddling the horses and loading the pack mules. Finished, Jubal returned to Cassandra, grasped her arm and jerked her roughly to her feet.

Leering down into her watching eyes, he said with a lewd chuckle, "I bet you need to relieve yourself, don't ya? Even genteel Southern ladies has got to answer when nature calls."

Cassandra hated herself for blushing. However, her bladder was full, and she desperately needed privacy.

Jubal guffawed. "Am I embarrassin' you, Miss Stevenson?"

"Please," she whispered. "May I step into the shrubbery?"

"I ain't lettin' you out of my sight. You got to go, then you do it right here. Pull down them

286

trousers and squat."

"No!" she gasped, appalled.

"Jubal," Hawk intervened, walking up to them. "We don't have time for you to get your thrills."

Thurston's face reddened with rage.

Brushing Jubal aside, Hawk went to Cassandra and untied her hands. "Come; I'll take you to the shrubbery."

Keeping a firm lock on her arm, he led her away from camp and into the surrounding vegetation. Pointing at a full bush, he said, "Go behind there."

She took a step, but he suddenly touched her shoulder, detaining her. "I want to hear that bush rustling the entire time you're behind it. If I don't hear it, I'm coming after you."

She nodded, moved away and went behind the shelter nature had provided. Carrying out Hawk's instructions, she shook the bush as she took care of her needs.

Stepping out from the shrubbery, Cassandra was surprised to see that Hawk, his back turned, was leaning leisurely against a large boulder. She didn't consider running; she knew it would be futile. Suddenly, a slithering movement on the rock's surface caught her eye. A rattlesnake, dangerously close to Hawk's shoulder, was coiling stealthily, readying itself to sink its poisonous fangs into its unsuspecting victim.

"Hawk!" Cassandra cried. "Watch out! There's a snake behind you!"

The half-breed, moving with incredible speed, spun around, drew his pistol and shot the reptile, severing its head.

"What happened?" Jubal yelled from camp.

"Nothing!" Hawk called back. "I just shot a rattler."

Averting her eyes from the bloody mess that was once a snake, Cassandra moved to return to camp, but Hawk stepped in front of her, blocking her way.

"Why did you call out and warn me? Even if the bite wasn't fatal, it would have made me too sick to cover our tracks. Don't you want Jensen to find you?"

"Of course I do. But I didn't stop to think about such things. My instincts are to save human life, not destroy it."

His feral eyes regarded her with a measure of respect. "I am grateful to you."

"I don't want your gratitude," she replied testily.

"It is the way of the Sioux to be grateful."

"If you're really grateful, you'll help me get away from Jubal!" she cried.

"I'll think about it," he answered stonily.

"Well, don't take too long thinking about it. I heard Jubal talking last night, and he plans to kill you."

"I know."

"You know?" she gasped. "Then why aren't you doing something about it?"

"I will, when the time is right." Through talking, he shoved her gently toward camp.

Cassandra longed to question him more, but she intuitively knew that Hawk had said all he was going to say.

288

Chapter Twenty-two

Cassandra lay still, listening vaguely to the nocturnal sounds. Jubal had tied her hands, taken her to a tree and shoved her to the ground, telling her not to get up.

It had been a long, arduous day, and Cassandra was so weary that the slightest movement was an effort. Lying on her back, she gazed up through a canopy of branches, watching a crescent moon accompanied by a myriad of twinkling stars. Her eyelids grew heavy, and she was about to give in to sleep when Jubal lumbered over with her supper. He placed the food beside her, turned around and walked back to the fire.

Sitting up with a tired grimace, Cassandra found that her bound wrists made it difficult for her to pick up the tin plate. Balancing it on her lap, she stared down vacuously at her meal, which consisted of a fatty hunk of bacon surrounded by greasy beans. Managing clumsily to grasp her spoon, she filled it, brought it halfway to her mouth, then dropped it back onto the plate. Her stomach was churning, and for a moment, she thought she might actually throw up. The spell passed, and she put her supper aside and lay down.

Concentrating, she tried to make some sense out

of her nausea, for she'd been sick at her stomach now for two days. Could she have contracted some disease? She didn't think so; she wasn't running a fever. Then why? Why? What was wrong with her?

A possible cause for her queasiness suddenly hit her with such a tremendous force that she gasped aloud. She quickly counted back to her last monthly, remembering it had occurred a couple of weeks before the drive had reached Good Times. That night, in Dru's hotel room, had they conceived a baby? Cassandra didn't know whether to be happy or to panic. If she was pregnant, how would Dru take the startling news?

God! she groaned inwardly. Why am I worrying about Dru's reaction? He'll probably never even know. If Hawk doesn't help me escape, Jubal will kill me! She pressed her hands against her stomach. When Jubal killed her, would he be taking two lives? A chilling shudder coursed through her.

She rolled to her side, pillowing her cheek against her clasped hands. Her abduction, Russ's death and now her possible pregnancy were too much to cope with. Tears ran down her face, and her shoulders shook with her deep, grief-stricken sobs.

Moments later, a hand touching her arm brought her weeping to an abrupt stop, and turning over, she expected to find Jubal's bandaged face leering down at her. However, it was Hawk who was kneeling at her side.

"Why are you crying?" he asked. Although his tone wasn't gentle, there was no trace of hardness in it.

Sniffling, she whispered, "I don't want to die."

He picked up her plate. "You should eat."

"I'm not hungry."

He shrugged as though unconcerned, stood up and took her plate back to the fire. "I'm tired," Cassandra heard him tell the Thurstons. "So I've decided to take the last watch."

Cassandra kept her eyes on the burly half-breed as he ambled to his blankets. Then rolling to her side, and resuming last night's position, she curled up into a tight ball. She berated herself for letting Hawk leave without asking if he had decided to help her.

The man's words flashed across her mind. "It is the way of the Sioux to be grateful." Oh, God! she prayed desperately. Please, please let him mean what he said!

But her better sense took over. He's half white, she thought, her hopes plunging. She quickly uttered a second prayer, this time praying that it was his Sioux blood that dictated his way of life.

In Cassandra's nightmare, Jubal had decided to burn her face with a branding iron. She was on the ground, tied spread-eagle, which rendered her totally helpless. Jubal hovered over her, and she stared up into his vicious eyes. As his mouth lifted into a menacing, demonic smile, he lowered the red-hot iron closer and closer to her cheek until it was so near that she could feel its fiery heat against her flesh. Before she could release a blood-curdling scream, her dream vanished and she awoke with a start.

Dawn was breaking, and, sitting up, Cassandra was surprised to see that she had slept through the night. A shiver ran up her spine as she recalled her nightmare. She forcefully blocked it from her mind; it had been too terrifying . . . too real!

She turned to check on the Thurstons, expecting to find them breaking camp. Her eyes widened and a gasp caught in her throat when she saw that Hawk was kneeling beside Dave's bedroll. A bloody knife was dangling from his hand. She watched, paralyzed, as the half-breed moved furtively to where Jubal lay sleeping.

As Hawk placed the bloodstained knife against Jubal's throat, she heard him say gruffly, "Wake up. You're gonna meet your Maker."

Thurston's eyes flew open, and becoming aware of the deadly blade resting against his Adam's apple, he turned so ghostly pale that his face was almost as white as the bandage covering his scarred cheek.

"I should cut out your heart, chew it up and spit it in your face." Hawk spoke without emotion. "Mrs. Lance was stupid to hire a greenhorn like you to kill me."

"Kill you?" Jubal stammered shakily. "I . . . I don't know what you're talkin' about. She didn't hire me to do no such thing. I swear it. Ask Dave, he'll tell you."

"Your brother's dead," he mumbled coldly. "And so are you." With one quick flick of the wrist, Hawk slit Jubal's throat.

Gagging, Cassandra looked away, and getting to

her knees, she bent over and heaved convulsively. Then, weakly, she managed somehow to stand up. Her legs buckled, and she would have fallen if Hawk hadn't reached her in time.

Grasping her shoulders supportively, he said tersely, "Let's go." Quickly he untied her wrists.

"Go where?" she asked feebly.

"Never mind," he said, moving away. Going to the Thurstons' horses, he untethered them and swatted their flanks. Startled, they took off with a bolt. Then he hastily loaded the supplies onto the two pack mules and saddled his horse and Cassandra's.

Meanwhile, Cassandra had remained motionless, her eyes glued to Hawk's every move.

Turning to her, he mumbled impatiently, "Come on; mount up."

Her strength returning, she moved as quickly as possible, and swinging into the saddle, she pleaded, "Please tell me where we're going!"

"You'll see," he said, mounting.

His answer was not only confusing, but also unnerving. Had he saved her from the Thurstons for his own evil purposes? She wondered if she was still in grave danger.

Hawk handed her the reins to the mules; then, kneeing his horse into a trot, he warned her to stay close behind.

Urging the mare forward, she followed. As her horse's hoofs moved closely past the Thurston brothers, Cassandra didn't dare drop her gaze to look at their lifeless bodies. Recalling how easily and swiftly Hawk had snuffed out their lives sent a whisper of terror through her. Could he have a worse fate in mind for her? She tensed, and her heart thumped apprehensively. She didn't know if Hawk was her friend or her enemy.

She mustered the courage to ask. "Hawk! Please, you must tell me! Are you my friend or my enemy?"

"Neither," he muttered flatly.

His answer wasn't very soothing.

The sun was directly overhead when Hawk led Cassandra into a fertile meadow shaded by tall, billowing trees. A steep, vegetation-covered hill loomed over the area, and a rippling stream of water flowed down the gradual slope. Wild flowers, reflecting the colors of a rainbow, where scattered over the verdant glade.

"Did you know about this area?" Cassandra asked Hawk.

"Yes," he answered.

"Did you bring us here intentionally?"

"Yes," Hawk replied again, swinging down from his horse.

"But why?" Cassandra questioned testily, finding his terse, uninformative answers exasperating.

"Because you'll be safe here."

"Surely you aren't going to leave me here alone!" she exclaimed, dismounting.

Dividing the supplies equally, Hawk remarked, "You have plenty of food, water and grazing for your mare. You'll be all right until Jensen finds you."

294

"How can he find me?" she demanded. "You covered our tracks, remember?"

"Yesterday, and then again today, I left a track that even a greenhorn can follow."

"But Dru will have to pick up our trail from yesterday. What if he doesn't find it?"

"If Jensen is half the tracker I think he is, he'll find it. He should be here by tomorrow, maybe the next day." He put her supplies and a blanket on the ground. "All you have to do is sit tight and wait. Don't try to find your way to the herd. You'll only get lost, and then Jensen will have a helluva time finding you. Besides losing your way, you might confront dangers that you couldn't handle. Also, don't allow your mare to wander too far away. Keep a close watch on her, and she will warn you of danger, whether it be man or beast." He had her pistol tucked into his belt. Removing it, he gave it to her.

"Hawk," she began urgently, holstering the gun, "if you'll take me back to the herd, Dru and Virgil won't do anything to you. Not after I tell them how you saved me from Jubal."

He acted as though he hadn't even heard her. Mounting his horse, he said, "Do as I told you. Stay here and wait for Jensen."

"Where are you going?" she cried.

"I have something I must do. Then I'm going into the Black Hills to visit my mother's people." He started to leave, but pulling back on the reins, he measured her with a level look. "You saved me from a snakebite. Now I have saved you from the Thurstons. We are even." With that, he urged his

295

horse into a trot, and taking the two mules with him, he rode away.

Cassandra watched until he was out of sight, and then she gave her surroundings a quick appraisal. Hawk had found her the ideal location to hole up in for a day or two.

Picking up the supplies Hawk had left, she carried them to the hillside and stored them under a tree. She intended to heed the half-breed's warning and stay where she was. She knew if she tried to find the herd, she'd most certainly get lost.

She unsaddled the mare and watched as the horse romped playfully over the green meadow before returning to nuzzle her shoulder.

Laughing, Cassandra patted the mare affectionately. "You know, I haven't even given you a name. You're such a beautiful lady that I think I'll call you Lady."

The horse whinnied as if it understood that it was now officially named.

Cassandra suddenly felt very alone and vulnerable, and drawing comfort from the mare's presence, she wrapped her arms about the horse's neck.

Hawk had sounded so certain that Dru would find her. But what if he didn't? She couldn't stay here indefinitely!

"We'll wait two days," she said to Lady, preferring to speak her thoughts aloud. "If Dru doesn't show up by then, we'll leave and head northwest. If we keep going in that direction, we should eventually find Fort Laramie."

She refused to think of all the dangers that could befall a woman traveling across such vast

296

terrain. If it became necessary for her to leave, then she'd do so and face the dangers when or if they arrived.

Sitting beside the small campfire, Cassandra watched as the sun sank steadily over the horizon. She was dreading full dark, when the meadow would be shrouded in black shadows. Would the night hold unseen terrors? Was this cougar territory? She wished she had remembered to ask Hawk. He had made a point of telling her that the mare would warn her of danger—man or beast. He must have been referring to cougars. Or maybe wolves! she thought suddenly. But hadn't she read somewhere that wolves never attacked man? She wasn't sure; however, she was sure that cougar attacks were not that uncommon.

She placed a hand on her holstered pistol; it gave her a feeling of security. She had the mare close by, tied to a tree. Now, checking her, Cassandra saw that the horse was relaxed. Apparently, at the moment, there was no predator lurking about.

Cassandra, having taken a nap during the afternoon, had decided to stay awake through the night. She had a feeling it was much safer to sleep during the day and remain on guard after darkness fell.

She had gathered ample kindling and had it piled at her side. She didn't intend to let the fire burn out. She had considered that a burning fire might attract outlaws, hostile Indians or other unsavory characters; however, given the alternative of sitting through the night in pitch darkness, Cassandra had decided to take her chances with the fire.

Now, raising her knees and cupping her chin in her hands, Cassandra sighed heavily as the sun disappeared, taking its comforting light with it. Shortly thereafter, full darkness fell.

Cassandra wished she could be brave and not be afraid of the dark. She had always believed that she had courage and grit, but now that it was time to put these traits to work, she felt as though they had deserted her. She frowned, angry with herself for fearing the night. I just won't let myself be scared! she told herself.

She was mentally preparing herself to make it bravely though the night when, suddenly, the mare whinnied nervously.

Leaping to her feet, Cassandra drew her pistol. Stepping to the horse, she place her free hand on the mare's neck. A strong tremor ran through the animal's body.

The mare was undoubtedly frightened, and as Cassandra glanced about cautiously, she wasn't sure who was more afraid—her or the horse.

In the shadows beyond the fire, Cassandra spotted a pair of yellow, feral eyes watching her. A cougar? she wondered, aiming her pistol, ready to fire if the predator was to leap.

When the animal made no sudden moves, Cassandra inched her way to the stacked kindling, picked up a large stick and threw it at the wild beast. By chance, she hit her target, and she detected a canine-like yelp before the animal's eyes disappeared and she heard it scuttling away. Obviously, it had been a lone coyote or wolf.

Lady calmed down, and Cassandra returned to sitting at the fire. She was somewhat proud of herself, considering she had handled her first crisis with a cool head.

Holstering her gun, she poured a cup of coffee. Taking the blanket, she draped it over her shoulders. She let her thoughts drift back over the day, reflecting on the Thurstons' violent deaths. A chill prickled the back of her neck as she remembered how Hawk had taken the lives of two men. Although she didn't condone murder, she wasn't sorry that Jubal was dead. Jubal had killed Russ in cold blood and had planned to horribly disfigure her before taking her life. She could feel no sympathy for Jubal. He had murdered Russ and deserved his punishment.

Thinking of her brother brought hurtful tears to Cassandra's eyes. She didn't want to cry, so she tried to think about something else, which caused her musings to turn to her possible pregnancy. Except for this morning, she hadn't experienced any queasiness all day. She supposed it'd take a couple more weeks before she'd know if she was going to have a baby. She tried to imagine how her and Dru's child would look. However, she couldn't quite conjure up a cross between the two of them. As she moved her hand to her stomach, she felt excited realizing that a life might be growing in her womb. At first, she hoped it was a boy and would look just like Dru; then, considering how wonderful it would be to have a daughter, she quickly decided that she didn't care about the child's sex. Boy or girl, either one would make her gloriously happy. Her spirits tumbled as she wondered if Dru would share her happiness. He might not want a wife and child. He had never even hinted at marriage.

Feeling herself growing depressed, she wiped thoughts of her possible pregnancy aside. She didn't even know yet if she was with child. Furthermore, she was judging Dru unfairly. He would probably be just as happy about the baby as she was.

Suddenly, a lone coyote's forlorn howl sounded in the distance. Cassandra smiled, quite certain that it was the same coyote who had visited her camp, only to be turned away so inhospitably.

As the coyote let lose with another wail, Cassandra took a large swallow of coffee. She was glad that she had plenty more and could refill the pot, for she had a feeling that it was going to be a long night.

Chapter Twenty-three

At first light, Dru broke camp and tried to pick up the Thurstons' trail. Hawk had done a remarkable job of covering their tracks, and even with Dru's experience, he failed to find a sign of their passing. He had spent the first day searching aimlessly, trying one direction and then another. Finally, on instinct alone, he had decided to head due west.

Now, Dru had traveled only a couple of hours when he suddenly found signs of a trail. The tracks were flagrantly visible, and Dru knew that Hawk had left them intentionally.

Tracking was now so easy that Dru was able to travel quickly, making exceptionally good time. The sun had climbed midway into the sky when Dru caught sight of a flock of vultures circling overhead. The carrion-eating birds were hovering over their find. Fear gripped Dru's heart as he watched the vultures soar through the air, then dive out of his vision.

He spurred his horse into a faster canter, desperate to reach the vultures' prey, yet fearing what he might find. God, had Jubal killed Cassandra? Was he about to come upon her body?

Cold sweat beaded his brow profusely and panic

swept through him. A vision of Cassandra, dead, left behind for the vultures, flashed in his mind, causing a violent tremor to shake his body.

As Dru reached the death-infested area, the grounded vultures squawked loudly, flapped their black wings and were quickly airborne.

Dru's heart was pounding as he dismounted, his eyes sweeping briefly over the Thurstons' bodies still ensconced in their bedrolls. Although he felt as though his legs were made of lead, dragging him down, he nonetheless moved incredibly fast as he searched the grounds for Cassandra. Failing to find her, his heart slowed back down to normal and his taut muscles relaxed.

Calmed, he tried to ascertain what had happened. Walking over to Dave's body, he saw that the man's throat had been cut; stepping to Jubal, he saw that he had died in the same way. Dru was quite certain that Hawk was their murderer. However, his reason for killing the Thurstons totally deluded him. He couldn't begin to imagine what had prompted the half-breed to turn on his partners.

Dru, not really caring why Hawk had killed them, hurried to his horse and mounted. His only concern lay with Cassandra. Looking about, he wasn't too surprised to see that Hawk had left an intelligible trail. For some mysterious reason, the half-breed wanted to be found. Or else, Dru decided, he intends to leave Cassandra somewhere and is making it easy for me to find her.

Dru urged his horse into a steady lope, and as soon as he was a safe distance away, the squawking vultures returned to their find. Dru didn't bother to think about the Thurstons' bodies being exposed to the carnivorous birds. Finding Cassandra was the only thing on his mind.

Cassandra stretched sleepily, awakening to a bright shaft of sunlight falling across her face. Sitting up, she stretched again as she glanced about. When she saw that the mare was grazing nearby, apparently undisturbed, Cassandra knew that nothing was amiss.

Knowing there were no predators in the close vicinity, Cassandra stood up and unbuckled her gun belt. Placing it on the ground, she turned and studied the small stream of water cascading down the hillside. She felt unbearably filthy and wished for a bar of soap.

Cassandra dismissed such a luxury with a shrug of her shoulders. There was no sense in wishing for something she didn't have. However, the thought of the cool stream was too inviting to discard, and she quickly slipped off her boots. She was tempted to remove her clothes and let the water run over her naked flesh, but she knew undressing could prove to be a crucial mistake. There was no guarantee that someone might not come upon her while she was under the stream. She knew if she were to be discovered, her best defense was her boy's attire. Nakedness, under a waterfall, would certainly blow that disguise!

Leaving her gun belt and boots beside the burned-out fire, she darted to the cascading stream and stood under it. The cool water splashing over her was wonderfully invigorating, and turning this way and that way, she was soon thoroughly soaked.

Cassandra's shower was interrupted suddenly by Lady's whinny. Dashing out from beneath the water, she rushed to her gun belt, and as she was strapping it on, two riders appeared over the nearest ridge.

Cassandra, filled with misgivings, watched as the two horsemen drew steadily nearer.

When they were close enough to speak to her, the taller of the two said amicably, "Howdy, son. Whatcha doin' out here in the middle of nowhere?"

"Waitin' for my brother," she mumbled, the lie coming to her instantaneously. "He'll be along any time now."

The man nodded toward the waterfall. "We need to fill our canteens."

Keeping her hand close to her holstered pistol, she said, "Go ahead, then be on your way."

The men dismounted, and as they sauntered to the water, the one who had done all the talking replied, "Boy, there ain't no reason for you to be so unfriendly. You don't own this goddamned countryside."

After filling their canteens, they moved over to Cassandra. The two drifters were usually harmless, but as their eyes were drawn to Cassandra's wet shirt clinging to her full breasts, lustful expressions crossed their weather-toughened faces.

Cassandra glanced down quickly, gasping softly when she realized that her soaked shirt was giving away her disguise.

"Well, well," the tall man drawled. "Just look what we got here."

"We got us a little gal," the other one uttered, ogling Cassandra.

A look of deadly intent flashed in Cassandra's green eyes as she drew her pistol with a speed that rendered the men speechless.

Holding the gun on them, she ordered, "Get on your horses and leave. If you so much as look back, I'll kill you."

Deciding she could shoot a gun as accurately as she could draw one, they moved swiftly to their horses. As they were mounting, the tall one whispered to his comrade, "Jake, we'll sneak back and take her unware. I want a piece of that good-lookin' ass."

Jake was about to agree when a lone rider leading a packhorse rode into sight.

Cassandra, recognizing the rider, smiled radiantly. Dru! Dru! she cried silently, wishing she could holster her gun and run to greet him. But despite her exultance, she knew it was imperative that she keep her pistol on the two strangers.

As Dru rode in closer, Jake got a good look at him. "Jensen!" he exclaimed. "He used to be the best bounty hunter in these parts. I never met 'im, but I seen 'im a few times. Let's get the hell out of here. Jensen ain't no man to tangle with."

They started to make tracks, but Dru was now close enough to call out a warning: "Stay right where you are!" Slipping his rifle from its scabbard, he placed it across the front of his saddle.

Arriving, Dru looked at Cassandra, and noticing

305

how her wet shirt outlined her breasts, he turned to the drifters and said coldly, "If you so much as touched her, I'll . . ."

"They didn't bother me," Cassandra cut in quickly. "Please, just tell them to leave."

"You heard the lady. Get the hell out of here."

"Gladly" was Jake's hasty reply. He sent his horse into a gallop, his companion following suit.

As Dru was dismounting, Cassandra holstered her gun and ran to him. Sweeping her into his arms, he swung her around, saying jubilantly, "Thank God you're alive and well!"

"Oh, Dru!" she cried. "I'm so glad to see you!"

He lowered her to her feet before claiming her lips with a kiss so urgent that it left her shaken. Holding her as tightly as possible, he declared emotionally, "Cassandra, I love you! God, how much I love you!"

Tears of happiness flooded her eyes. "I love you too! I was so afraid I'd never see you again! I have so much to tell you." She took his hand and led him to where her blanket was spread.

When they were seated, Dru remarked, "You can start by telling me why your clothes are soaking wet."

She explained quickly; then in detail she elaborated on her abduction. Tears trickled down her cheeks as she let him know that Russ was dead. He held her close, and nestling her head on his shoulder, she told him why Hawk had decided to help her and that he had killed Jubal and his brother.

"I found their bodies," Dru said, purposely omitting any mention of the vultures.

306

As Dru suddenly got to his feet, Cassandra cried with alarm, "Where are you going?"

"I'm gonna make damned sure your two visitors are really gone. I'll be back in a few minutes." He favored her with a loving smile. "You'll be pleased to know that my supplies include a bar of soap. When I return, you can take a real bath."

"Wonderful!" she sighed.

He turned to leave, but she detained him. "Dru, how is Virgil? Hawk hit him awfully hard."

"He was fine when I left."

She watched as Dru stepped to his horse, mounted, and rode off in the same direction the two men had taken. A few minutes later, he returned.

"Are they gone?" she asked, hurrying to meet him.

"There's no sign of 'em. I'm sure we've seen the last of those two." Dismounting, he unsaddled the stallion, then unloaded the packhorse and turned both animals loose to graze.

Cassandra, anxious to bathe, had Dru find her the soap. Taking it, she hurriedly slipped out of her clothes and dashed to the waterfall.

Watching, Dru was pleased that she was no longer shy in his presence. He quickly shed his own clothes and joined her. She was through sudsing, and he waited until she had rinsed before reaching for the soap.

Refusing to hand it over, she said pertly, "Darling, I'm going to thoroughly pamper you and wash you myself."

He smiled with anticipation. "I can hardly wait."

Slowly she moved the bar over his manly chest and arms, sudsing them sufficiently. Her ministrations were physically arousing, and Dru could feel himself responding. He extended his hand, insisting that she give him the soap. Quickly he finished washing, then stepped under the waterfall and rinsed away the clinging suds.

He returned to Cassandra, and she smiled invitingly. With a fevered groan, Dru brought her into his arms. His lips swooped down on hers aggressively, his tongue entering her mouth with urgent passion. She leaned against him, her hips pressed tightly against his.

Lifting her into his arms, Dru carried her to the blanket and laid her down gently. Then leaning over her, he lowered himself between her legs and entered her deeply.

His maleness filling her felt so wonderful that Cassandra gasped as her hips rose to meet his. She wrapped her legs about him, and together they soared blissfully into love's paradise.

Cassandra, her queasiness gone, ate a hearty supper. She had a feeling, though, that in the morning her nausea would return. Sitting near the fire, with Dru's arm draped about her shoulders, she wondered if she should tell him that she might be pregnant. She considered it for a moment, then decided to wait until she was certain.

"Dru," she began, her thoughts drifting elsewhere, "how far are we from the herd?"

"We're a lot closer than you think. After Hawk

killed the Thurstons, he made a wide circle to avoid running into me, then veered back toward the river. We should catch up to the herd in two days."

"How long will it take to reach Fort Laramie?"

"About two weeks."

"So soon?" she whispered despondently.

He moved her so that he could look down into her face. "Why do you sound so sad?"

Her eyes turned misty. "I feel secure on the trail drive, but when we reach the fort, I'll be alone."

"Alone?" he questioned.

"I have no one now that Russ is gone."

He hugged her gently. "You won't be alone. You'll have Virgil and me. Do you think we'd desert you?" He placed a hand beneath her chin, tilted her face up to his and said with a mirthful smile, "You're the best cook who's ever worked for me. I'm not about to let you go."

A feeling of happiness rose wonderfully inside her. Were his words a teasing invitation to marriage?

Dru, reading her thoughts, could see her love for him mirrored in her beautiful eyes. As he gazed into their deep green pools, the impregnable wall he'd built around his emotions began to weaken. Although he had loved Anita, his love had been mild when compared to his feelings for Cassandra. His heart and soul belonged to this lovely woman, and his whole world now revolved around her

"Casey," he murmured, his tone caressing the name, "I love you."

"I love you too," she whispered, her breath held, hoping he was about to propose.

"Will you marry me?" he asked softly.

"Oh, yes!" she cried ecstatically, her heart beating with joy.

He drew her tightly into his arms, holding her extremely close. A feeling of uneasiness came over him, casting a darkness over his mood. Marriage meant children. Had he truly put the loss of his son behind him? Was he ready to be a father again? He banished such disturbing thoughts from his mind. He'd face his feelings when the time came.

Turning to Cassandra, his lips reached hers, kissing her in a manner that clearly defined his need to make love to her.

Yielding, she leaned into his arms, pressing her breasts against his strong chest. Her passion as urgent as his, she moved her hand downward, finding and caressing his rigid hardness.

Easing her down onto the blanket, Dru hurriedly removed her clothes, then impatiently discarded his own. The soft moonlight shone down upon Cassandra's naked beauty, and Dru's eyes roamed ravenously over the seductively smooth textures of her body.

He lay beside her, and sliding her arms about his neck, she turned and molded herself against him. His throbbing maleness touching her thigh sent a flash of desire coursing through her, centering itself at her feminine core.

Dru kissed her demandingly as his hand mapped a blazing trail over her exquisite curves, fondling her breasts before dipping down between her alabaster thighs. His finger probed intimately, and her body was soon aching for complete fulfillment.

He rolled to his side, and wordlessly she turned to him, sliding her hand down his back to his tightly muscled buttocks. Then, daringly, her hand ventured to his hard member, and encircling him with her fingers, she stimulated her man with an up-and-down motion.

Dru's passion was almost out of control, and moving over her, he possessed her fully. His entry was thrilling, and as her legs went about his waist, he penetrated even farther inside her.

His deep thrusting sent her senses reeling and her head swimming with ecstasy. Utterly consumed with pleasure, Cassandra responded eagerly, her rapidly moving hips driving Dru to an explosive climax.

Taking Cassandra with him to love's wondrous culmination, Dru lunged forward aggressively, spiraling Cassandra to such ecstatic heights that she cried aloud with uncontrollable joy.

Simultaneously, sighs of satisfaction coursed through Dru's body as he achieved his own glorious completion.

He moved to lie at her side, and she went into his arms, cuddling intimately. Sated, they lay in silence, wonderfully contented.

Later, they drifted into sleep, awoke, and made love again.

Chapter Twenty-four

Vivian lay in her wagon, tossing and turning as sleep eluded her. In detail, she reflected on her conversation with Virgil. Taking Dru's advice, she had gone to Virgil and asked him about her father's will. Now, she silently damned her father for absolving Virgil's debts. Thanks to his generosity, she had probably lost Dru for good. She had tried seduction and failed, and now she had no grounds for blackmail. What was she to do? Surely there was some way she could win Dru's love.

A hopeful glint came to her eyes. She sat up and lit the lantern. With Cassandra out of the picture, she should find it easier to inveigle Dru. She couldn't begin to fathom why Dru was apparently so infatuated with the little tart. Well, it was a long way from Fort Laramie to Texas. During the return trip, she'd try again to seduce Dru, and this time she was confident that she'd succeed. After all, it shouldn't take too long for him to get over Cassandra. In Vivian's opinion, Cassandra was the kind of woman that, once out of a man's sight, was soon out of his mind. She wondered how long Dru would search for Cassandra. Surely he'd give up in another day or so and return to the drive. She hoped Hawk was doing his job accurately and was leaving no intelligible tracks.

Vivian, her spirits now improved, extinguished the lantern and settled down for a good night's sleep. Everything would work out favorably, she was confident that it would.

Suddenly, she seemed to sense another's presence. The wagon's interior was pitch black, and her heart began thumping rapidly as she turned onto her back. Staring into the darkness, she made out a huge shadow hovering over her. She was about to scream when the intruder clamped a large hand over her mouth.

"Hello, Mrs. Lance," he murmured throatily.

She recognized the voice. Hawk! Why had he returned? Damn the man for disobeying her orders! Had he slipped into her wagon to force himself on her? If so, she decided to let him have his way and submit meekly. If she were to cry out and alert the wranglers, Hawk would undoubtedly tell Virgil that she had paid him to help the Thurstons capture Cassandra. Then Dru would be so furious that she'd never win his love.

She relaxed, and Hawk removed his hand cautiously. "Mrs. Lance, you were very foolish to hire Jubal Thurston to kill me." Hawk's icy tone was chilling.

"I don't know what you mean," she denied, suddenly very frightened.

Her denial meant nothing to him. "Jubal and his brother are dead."

"You killed them?" she asked weakly.

"I slit their throats and they bled like stuck pigs."

313

"Why . . . why did you come back?" she cried softly. Fear gripped her tenaciously, its force binding her chest and making breathing difficult. She wheezed laboriously, erratically.

"I came back to kill you," Hawk said. He spoke as calmly as though he were giving her the time of day.

A crippling pang of fear shot through Vivian, rendering her temporarily motionless. Then, fighting for her life, she doubled her hands into fists and pounded Hawk's chest as she attempted to scream.

But Hawk's hand was instantly on her mouth, muffling her frantic cry. Keeping that hand clamped firmly, he moved the other one to her slender neck. His strong fingers tightened about her throat in a death grip, and he squeezed until she ceased to breathe.

Cassandra awakened to the aroma of coffee brewing. She stretched sleepily, sat up on her bedroll and glanced at Dru. He was sitting at the fire, pouring a cup of morning brew. Her eyes glazed with admiration as she perused the man she adored. He was handsome beyond words.

Sensing her scrutiny, Dru turned and looked at her. Smiling warmly, he murmured, "Good mornin', hon."

"Good morning," she replied.

"You want a cup of coffee?"

She started to accept when, all at once, her stomach churned. She swallowed hard, fought back her nausea and answered, "No, thanks."

He came and sat beside her. "You aren't sick, are you?"

She glanced away from his searching gaze. "No, I'm fine," she assured him. Should she tell him of her possible pregnancy? She decided not to. She'd wait until she was certain.

He placed a hand under her chin, turning her face to his. "Are you sure you're all right?"

"Yes, I'm sure," she said, giving him a cheerful smile.

Convinced, he kissed her brow, then murmured deeply, "I love you, Casey."

Snuggling against him, she replied happily, "I love you, darling."

He took a sip of coffee. "In a few minutes, I'll saddle the horses. I wish we could stay here for a day or two, but I need to get back to the herd. Also, Virgil's awfully worried about you. He'll be glad to see you."

"Dru?" she began. "There's something I haven't told you."

"What's that?"

"Vivian hired Hawk to help the Thurstons kidnap me."

"I'm not surprised," he answered heavily.

"She must hate me very much."

"I always knew she was spoiled and selfish, but I never dreamed she could be so cruel."

"I'm afraid she'll keep trying until she finds a way to come between us."

"Never," he said, draping an arm about her shoulders. "No one can come between us, Casey.

We're too much in love."

His words warmed her soul and thrilled her heart.

Dru and Cassandra, traveling at a steady pace, made exceptionally good time. They stopped at dusk, set up camp, ate supper, then made love and fell asleep in each other's arms. Arising early, they continued following the trail drive and had traveled a couple of hours when they came upon a fresh grave. Its only marker was a pair of sticks tied together in a crisscross fashion.

Reining in, Dru and Cassandra stared at the solitary grave for a long moment before turning to each other. Their thoughts were on the same wavelength. Had Virgil's head injury been worse than they had imagined?

Cassandra's eyes turned misty, and she swallowed back the lump in her throat. Please, God, don't let it be Virgil! she prayed silently.

Dru's heart pounded against his rib cage, and every muscle in his body was taut. He considered finding a way to dig up the grave to see whose body was inside, but then decided against it. Whoever lay there should be left to rest in peace.

"We'll catch up to the herd shortly after sunset," Dru said, his voice hoarse. "Then we'll know who's buried here."

Cassandra merely nodded; a lump was once again in her throat and speaking was difficult.

As they moved onward, Cassandra turned and glanced over her shoulder. Tears were in her eyes,

316

causing her to see the grave through a blurry haze. Again, she prayed that the burial site, which appeared starkly forlorn on the vast landscape, wasn't Virgil Jensen's final resting place.

As Dru and Cassandra neared the drovers' camp, the light from their fire was a flickering red glow on the horizon. 't was a welcoming sight, and they hurried their tired horses into a fast canter.

Aware of their arrival, the wranglers sitting about the fire got to their feet and watched the pair as they rode in closer. Badge hastened away from the chuck wagon to greet them, and pitching his horse's reins to the lad, Dru dismounted, stepped to Cassandra and helped her down.

Dru's eyes scanned the campsite, searching desperately for his uncle. Failing to spot him, he was about to question Badge when Virgil emerged from the chuck wagon.

"Thank God!" Cassandra cried, spotting Virgil at the same time as Dru, who, sighing with profound relief, grasped Cassandra's arm and ushered her quickly toward the chuck wagon.

Virgil was grinning broadly. "Missy! It's sure good to see you're alive and well!"

He held out his arms, and Cassandra hurried into his embrace, hugging him eagerly. "Oh, Virgil!" she exclaimed. "Dru and I were so afraid that you were dead!"

"Dead?" he questioned, perplexed.

She moved out of his arms, and gazing up into his warm blue eyes, she murmured, "I'm so thankful you're all right."

Virgil looked at Dru. "Why did you think I was dead?"

"We came across a grave," he explained.

Cassandra clarified further. "We were afraid that Hawk might have hit you harder than we thought."

Virgil was quiet for a moment, his features sober. "Night before last," he began, "Vivian was killed. Hawk was seen slippin' away from her wagon. I took a couple of the men with me, and we tried to run 'im down, but he lost us."

Cassandra gasped. "Hawk told me he had something to do before going into the Black Hills. My God, I never dreamed that he intended to murder Vivian!"

Dru shook his head sympathetically. "Poor Vivian. This time she tried to dupe the wrong man. Hawk's a killer and can snuff out a life as easily as steppin' on a bug. Especially if he's been double-crossed."

"I was just about to rustle up some grub," Virgil said, changing the subject. "While I get started, you can tell 'bout the Thurstons." He glanced directly at Dru. "And how you managed to find Cassandra."

Cassandra touched Virgil's arm, gaining his attention. "You and Dru can sit at the fire and talk over a cup of coffee. I'll cook supper."

Virgil smiled. "Thanks, missy." He chuckled good-naturedly. "I know the men are gonna be mighty glad you're back. My cookin' leaves a lot to be desired."

Cassandra was about to leave and get started on

318

dinner, but catching a glimpse of Badge, she paused. The boy was still holding the horses' reins. His gaze was centered on Dru, his face anticipating Dru's acknowledgment. Cassandra knew the lad idolized Dru, and she hoped he would take a moment to greet the boy warmly.

Dru turned to tell Badge to bed down the horses. But he caught a fleeting glimpse of the boy's adoration before Badge had time to lower his eyes.

"How's your trainin' coming along?" Dru asked him.

"Fine," he answered, raising his gaze.

"It won't be long," Virgil put in, " 'til he's a full-fledged drover."

"After you tend to the horses," Dru told Badge, "come on over to the fire and talk to me."

The youngster's face brightened. "I sure will, Mr. Jensen!"

"Dru, remember?"

"Yes, sir. I remember."

Dru grinned. "And drop the sir, will ya?"

Smiling, Cassandra moved to the chuck wagon. Apparently, Dru was very sensitive and considerate. It was no wonder that she loved him so much.

Cassandra had missed sleeping in Dru's arms, and when she awoke inside the chuck wagon, her mood was somewhat gloomy. She dressed sluggishly as she wished the long, arduous drive were over. Then she and Dru could marry and get on with their lives. She wondered if Dru intended for them to get married at the fort or wait until they returned to Texas. Her musings drifted suddenly to Virgil. My goodness, last night she had forgotten to tell him that she and Dru were engaged! She'd tell him first thing this morning. He'd be thrilled!

She chastised herself for not letting Virgil in on such marvelous news. But then last night had been hectic. Virgil had insisted on hearing all about the Thurstons and Hawk, and by the time she and Dru had filled him in, he'd had to leave to watch over the herd.

Cassandra left the wagon, and finding Virgil at the fire pouring a cup of coffee, she hurried over.

He saw her coming and filled a second cup. Handing it to her, he asked, "How ya feelin' this mornin', missy?"

She felt a little nauseous, but it was mild when compared to the last few mornings. "I'm fine," she answered. She took a tentative sip of coffee. She hoped it would stay down.

She looked at Virgil, her green eyes shining brightly. "I have something wonderful to tell you."

A large grin spread across his face. "I already know what you're goin' to say."

"You do?" she exclaimed.

"Yep. Dru rode out to the herd last night and told me that he asked you to marry 'im."

"You're pleased, aren't you?"

"Pleased is puttin' it mildly. I couldn't be happier. If any two people were ever made for each other, it's you and Dru."

"Where is Dru?" she asked, glancing about.

"He's with the herd. He'll show up for breakfast."

"Good. I forgot to ask him if we're getting married at Fort Laramie or when we return to Texas."

"He told me he wants to get married at the fort."

Cassandra smiled radiantly. "Oh, Virgil, I can hardly believe that Dru and I are getting married! I love him so desperately! Everything would be so wonderful if only . . . if only." A despondent shadow fell over her face.

"If only Russ was alive?" Virgil murmured.

"Yes," she whispered tearfully.

Taking her cup, Virgil placed it beside the fire along with his own. Then, taking her into his arms, he held her close. Resting her head on his comforting shoulder, Cassandra wept heartbrokenly.

She cried until her tears ran dry. Gently Virgil moved his hands to her shoulders, and gazing down into her red, swollen eyes, he said quietly, "Missy, it takes time to get over losin' a loved one. But the pain lessens with each passing day. Meanwhile, you need to look to the future."

"I will," she whispered.

He smiled encouragingly. "You'd better start breakfast." He glanced at the wranglers still in their bedrolls. "I'll rouse these cowboys and tell 'em to rise and shine." He looked meaningfully at Cassandra. "The sooner we get movin', the sooner we get to the fort."

Her spirits lifting considerably, she added, "And the sooner I become Mrs. Dru Jensen!"

The hot sun shone down inexorably, bathing the

chuck wagon with dazzling light. As Cassandra handled the team, she removed one hand from the multiple reins and wiped her perspiring brow. Driving the wagon was hot work, for the large canvas blocked the refreshing breeze that was drifting lightly.

Spotting two horsemen leaving the herd and riding in her direction, Cassandra shaded her eyes with her hand and tried to make them out. However, the bright sun made it difficult for her to see clearly, and the riders were almost upon her before she was able to recognize Dru and Pete.

The sight of Dru sent a thrill racing through her. She wondered if Dru would always have this effect on her, even after they had been married for years. She had a feeling that he would.

As they reined in, Cassandra brought the wagon to a stop and looked questioningly at Dru.

Grinning, he remarked, "I thought you might enjoy a break. Pete's goin' to drive the wagon. I need to ride ahead and scout around. Would you like to come with me?"

"I'd love to," she declared, her elation evident.

"You can ride Pete's horse."

Pete dismounted and climbed up on the wagon seat. As Cassandra was descending, he told her, "My horse won't give you no trouble. He's as docile as a kitten, but one helluva cow pony."

"Thanks, Pete," she said, mounting and taking up the reins.

As she and Dru turned their horses about, Pete called after them, "See ya later!"

They rode off swiftly, circled the herd and

headed into the countryside.

Cassandra found the brisk ride invigorating. The wind whipping about her face was cooling, and she removed her wide-brimmed hat so that the breeze could blow through her short tresses. She was glad that her hair grew so fast. She was anxious for it to be long and feminine.

As Cassandra was worrying about the length of her hair, Dru, watching her, was finding her short blond tresses enticing. He loved the way her short curls gave her a delightful impish look.

They slowed their horses down to a walk, and Cassandra replaced her hat while speaking her thoughts aloud. "I'll be so glad when my hair is long again, and I stop looking like a tomboy."

Dru chuckled. "But you're such a cute tomboy."

"Dru Jensen!" she fussed. "Will you please stop telling me I'm cute!"

He was about to continue his teasing when he caught sight of smoke billowing. The vapor, drifting over a distant hill, was too dark to be coming from a campfire.

Following Dru's line of vision, Cassandra asked, "What do you think is burning?"

"I don't know. It might be a barn or a house." The smoke thickened and turned darker.

"Indians?" Cassandra gasped.

"Sioux, most likely." His expression stern, he said, "Stay close to me, and if I tell you to do something, do it and don't argue."

"All right," she agreed. "Are we going to the fire?"

"We have to. Hopefully, that fire is comin' from

a barn, and the Sioux haven't burned the house yet. There might be people holed up inside. If they are, I want you to turn around, return to the herd and get help."

They spurred their mounts into a fast canter, and traveling speedily, they reached the hillside. The horses, sure-footed, climbed the verdant incline, and as they crested the smoke-filled peak, Cassandra peered through the thick haze and down to the valley below. The sight that confronted her wrenched her heart and sent an icy chill up her spine.

"Dear God!" she cried. Looking away from the tragic scene, she met Dru's somber gaze. "Oh, Dru!" she gasped. "Dru!"

Chapter Twenty-five

"Stay here," Dru whispered to Cassandra.

"I don't want to be alone," she murmured. She glanced about fearfully. "What if the Indians are still around?"

"They're gone," Dru replied confidently. "Hon, I've got to go down and bury that family. It's best that you don't come with me. You don't need to see . . . " His voice faded.

"I understand," she whispered. "But you need my help. Two people can work faster than one."

He shook his head. "No, stay here," he said unalterably. With that, he urged his horse forward and started down the gradual slope.

Cassandra, respecting Dru's wishes, remained behind. From her vantage point, she had a clear view of the small homestead surrounded on all sides by rolling hills. She tried not to look at the three bodies in front of the burning home, but against her own volition, her eyes were drawn helplessly to the pathetic sight. At such a distance, the forms were dimunitive in size, but she could make out a man, a woman and an infant. As her eyes came to rest on the dead baby, tears formed, blinding her vision.

Crying openly, Cassandra dismounted and leaned

her head against the sleek neck of Pete's pony. Wiping at her copious tears, she watched as Dru arrived. The shed was untorched, and Cassandra continued to look on as Dru dismounted, walked into the shed, then emerged with a shovel. She pitied him the grievous task that lay ahead.

Carrying the shovel loosely at his side, Dru moved slowly to the bodies. He hoped Cassandra would do as he ordered and stay where she was. On several occasions, he had seen massacred bodies left behind by Indians, and he braced himself for the sight that awaited him.

He stepped to the dead man, and as he had suspected, the Indians had scalped their victim. Dreading viewing the woman and her child, he moved to them hesitantly. The woman's skirts were up about her waist, and her lower torso was nude. She had been raped, then killed and scalped. Bending, Dru pulled down her dress and petticoat.

The infant was lying a few feet away, and Dru stepped to its side and knelt. The child's scalp was still intact, and examining the ugly, blood-clotted gash across the baby's forehead, Dru knew death had been quick and merciful.

He extended his hand and brushed his fingers gently over the infant's lifeless arm. Grief for this child, mingling with thought of his own dead son, tore painfully into Dru's heart.

The campsite was unusually quiet, and the stillness was somewhat eerie. The wranglers, ensconced in their bedrolls, dismissed their customary chatter and lay silently waiting for sleep. They were grateful they hadn't been the ones to come upon the massacred family and were spared such a tragic sight. However, they sympathized with Dru, and out of regard for him, they had been quiet scent during supper and had retired immediately afterward.

As sleep began to overtake the wranglers, Virgil, sitting at the fire beside Cassandra, was deeply immersed in his somber thoughts. He had read from the Bible and had said a prayer over the three nameless graves. Although he grieved for the unfortunate family, it was Dru who was filling his thoughts. Virgil knew his nephew well and was aware that coming upon the massacred baby had revived Dru's memories of his own dead child. He had begun to believe that Dru had learned to put his past behind him, but then he knew from personal experience that time couldn't completely heal all wounds. After all, he himself hadn't fully recovered from losing Johnny.

Meanwhile, as Virgil remained buried in his private reverie, Cassandra sat silently, her gaze centered on Dru. He was sitting beside the chuck wagon, leaning back against one of the wheels. A bottle of whiskey dangled from his hand, and as Cassandra continued to watch, Dru helped himself to a large swallow. Her heart ached for him, for like Virgil, she knew Dru's old wounds had been reopened. She wished he'd turn to her for consolation, but since finding the massacred family, Dru had become withdrawn. She was hurt by his aloofness, his refusal to share his pain with her.

"Virgil," she murmured, revealing her thoughts, "why won't Dru let me help him?"

He smiled kindly. "How can you help him, missy?"

"I could hold him in my arms. If I was grieving, I'd want Dru to hold me."

"That's because you don't run from your emotions. You stand firm and meet 'em head-on. Dru's not like that."

Cassandra heaved a wistful sigh. "I wish I could take away his pain."

Virgil was touched. "Don't worry, missy. By tomorrow, he'll be himself again." He reached over and patted her hand. "It's hard for us to relate to his feelings because we've never lost a child. Also, we didn't see that poor dead baby."

"I saw the baby from a distance, and it was almost more than I could bear. I cried and cried."

"This land shows no mercy to the young," Virgil stated introspectively.

"This land?" she questioned. "Don't you mean the Indians show no mercy?"

"What goes around, comes around. Indian families have been butchered by the whites. I've come across more than my share of murdered Indian babies."

"If only the whites and the Indians could learn to live in peace," she said sadly.

"Maybe someday," Virgil muttered solemnly. "Maybe someday."

Cassandra was about to say more on the subject, but catching sight of Dru standing and leaving the camping area, she asked, "Do you think I should follow him?"

"What do you think?" Virgil questioned.

She looked intensely at the elder Jensen. "I think I can help Dru."

"Missy," he warned gently, "Dru's had a lot to drink, and when a man's drinkin', he can say things that he doesn't really mean. I ought to know. I've done my share of drinkin'. Maybe you should let 'im be and talk to 'im in the mornin'."

Thinking about the life growing in her womb, Cassandra murmured, "I have something important to tell Dru."

She got quickly to her feet, and as she headed in the direction Dru had taken, she hoped her news would lift Dru's sullen mood. Surely learning he was going to be a father again would considerably ease the pain of losing Johnny. Dru was sensitive, considerate and capable of loving deeply. When she told him of her pregnancy, how could he be anything but ecstatic? She knew he loved her, and he'd also love their child.

Making her way carefully through the darkness, she looked about for Dru but couldn't find him. "Dru?" she called softly. "Where are you?"

"Over here," she heard him reply.

Peering into the dark shadows, she spotted the red glow from his lit cheroot. The moon, suddenly peeking out from under a cloud, shone a path to Dru's side. He was standing beneath a tree, and she watched as he tilted the bottle of whiskey to his mouth and gulped a generous amount.

Hurrying to him, she said quickly, "I hope you don't mind that I followed you."

Dru, studying Cassandra in the soft moonlight, didn't answer. His body grew taut as he was unexpectedly struck with how dearly he loved her. God, she was his heart, his soul, his main reason for living! What if they were to have a child, and this untamed land took that child away? Could he suffer that kind of pain a second time? Could he bear to watch Cassandra go through such terrible grief?

Dru turned away from Cassandra's loving gaze and quaffed down a large swallow of whiskey. He was feeling his liquor and his mind was too muddled to make important decisions.

Leery of his continued silence, Cassandra said warily, "Dru, I think . . . no I'm certain that I can help you."

He raised a brow somewhat cynically. "Help me?" Feeling anger rising within him, Dru tried to keep it submerged. He didn't want to say anything to hurt Cassandra. God, she was the last person on Earth that he wanted to hurt! However, the whiskey was in control, and throwing down his cheroot, he uttered sharply, "There's nothing you can do to help. I have to work this out in my own way."

She grasped his arm. "But, Dru, you don't understand! I know losing Johnny was devastating. If you were to have another child, perhaps a son . . ."

"No!" he cut in, flinging off her hand. The murdered baby plus a vision of Johnny flashed across his mind. "No!" he repeated thunderously. "I don't want any more children!"

Paling, Cassandra gasped, "You don't mean that!"

"I mean it," he replied. His tone sounded final.

Unconsciously, Cassandra placed a hand on her stomach as though she could protect her child from its father's rejection. She cringed and fought back tears. Dru didn't want their baby! Anger surfacing, she cried harshly, "Dru, you unfeeling bastard!"

He eyed her quizzically. "There's no reason to call me names. Because I don't want kids doesn't make me unfeeling."

She glared at him scornfully. "You're right. You aren't unfeeling. You're a damned coward!"

With that, she whirled about and started for camp, but placing his bottle on the ground, Dru stepped lively and caught her arm.

Spinning her around and into his embrace, Dru said deeply, "Casey, try to understand my feelings."

Struggling, she spat petulantly, "I understand perfectly well! Because you lost one child, you're too damned scared to try again! Now, let me go!"

Complying, he released her brusquely. He felt woozy, and he wished he hadn't drunk so much whiskey. He was about to tell Cassandra that he'd accompany her to camp, drink some coffee and sober up, but before he could, she turned on her heel and retreated into the darkness.

He didn't give chase, but moved back to the bottle, picked it up and wrenched off the cap. Instead of taking a drink, he merely stared at the bottle blankly. Then, recapping it, he threw it into the nearby shrubbery. He heard it crash into several pieces.

He tried to remenber exactly what he had said to upset Cassandra, but his whiskey-clouded mind refused to cooperate. Well, in the morning, he'd

331

apologize. He was certain that he hadn't said anything unforgivable.

Cassandra, avoiding Virgil, went straight to the chuck wagon and climbed swiftly inside. Going to her pallet, she lay down and stared vacuously up at the white-canopied ceiling. She was too distraught to cry, and she remained dry-eyed. Had Dru really meant what he said about never having children? If she had told him she was pregnant, how would he have reacted?

She knew Dru well enough to know that he was a man of principles and would never shirk his duty. If he knew she was pregnant, he'd still insist on marrying her. He'd accept their child, and, in time, would learn to love it. But, deep down inside, would he ever truly want this child? Was there no room in his heart for their baby? Was his heart filled completely with the memory of his and Anita's child?

Cassandra sat up, and extinguishing the lantern, she undressed in the dark. She slipped into a cotton nightgown, then returned to bed.

Suspicion struck her unawares, causing her to gasp aloud. All this time, had she been mistaken? She had believed that Dru was completely over Anita. Was that why he couldn't let go of his past? Did he adhere tenaciously to his memories of Johnny because they were linked directly to Anita? She could sympathize with his lingering grief for Johnny, but she couldn't cope with his extended grief over losing Anita. The woman had betrayed him! Had run off with his best friend! How could he still love her so desperately? Why couldn't he release her memory and start over again with no inhibitions? Why must he let memories of Anita stand in the way of their own happiness?

Cassandra, now deeply depressed, rolled to her side and tried to block thoughts of Anita and Dru from her mind. If Dru was still in love with his dead wife, then there was nothing she could do about it. How could she possibly compete with a memory?

Reminding herself that worrying changed nothing, Cassandra tried to will herself to fall asleep, but it was a long time before repose took over.

The next morning, Dru was waiting for Cassandra as she climbed down from the wagon. He looked unkempt: his hair was uncombed and his face unshaven.

"Casey," he murmured hesitantly, "can we talk a moment?"

Her expression impassive, she answered tonelessly, "I need to start breakfast."

"The hell with breakfast!" he remarked snappishly. He cringed, for his outburst had sent a pain throbbing at his temples.

"Do you have a hangover?" Cassandra asked, her grin openly spiteful.

He quirked a brow. "I have this feelin' that you're enjoying my suffering immensely."

"It'd be no more than you deserve."

"Casey, about last night," he began.

She waited, but when he said no more, she prodded, "What about last night?"

"My memory is hazy. Did I say something to upset you?"

"Don't you remember?" she asked testily.

"No, not really." He looked embarrassed. "I'm sorry, darlin'. But when I drink to excess, I have a hard time recalling everything I said."

"Then you shouldn't drink to excess," she remarked querulously.

"Casey, please don't preach."

She eyed him sternly. "What do you want from me, Dru?"

"I want to know if I owe you an apology. But, more importantly, do you still love me?"

"You don't owe me an apology," she answered, leaving it at that.

Stepping closer, he placed his hands on her shoulders and gazed down into her face with deep longing. "Do you love me, Casey?"

Love him? She adored him! Would give her life for him! "Yes," she whispered. "I love you, Dru." Referring to her pregnancy, she added, "But I promise you that I'll never be a burden."

"A burden?" he questioned. "Why do you think you could ever be a burden

"Never mind why," she replied firmly. "Just remember what I said."

He grinned disarmingly. "I'm glad that last night I didn't say anything wrong. You can't imagine how worried I've been." His face sobered. "Casey, if I were to lose you . . ."

Suddenly, drawing her into his arms, Dru bent

334

his head and captured her lips in a passionate, love-filled kiss.

Surrendering, Cassandra wrapped her arms about his neck and returned his ardor.

As he released her, she rubbed a hand across her chin. His whiskers had been a little irritating.

Grinning sheepishly, he murmured, "While you're cookin' breakfast, I'll wash up and shave." He favored her with a quick wink. "I love ya, Casey."

Cassandra's emotions were dubious as she watched Dru move away. This morning, if she had mentioned that he should have another child, she wondered if he'd have reacted as negatively as he had last night. She wasn't sure, for she didn't know if Dru's refusal to have children had come from his heart or if it had been the whiskey talking.

Cassandra raised her chin determinedly, and her eyes shone with resolve. She had meant what she had said; she'd never be a burden to Dru. If Dru didn't want their child, then somehow, some way, she'd take care of herself and her baby without any help from Dru Jensen! If he wanted to cling forever to his past and cherish his memories of Anita and Johnny, then as far as she was concerned, he could do just that!

However, she was a survivor, a fighter and a realist, and she had her child's future to consider.

But I'll always love Dru, she thought ruefully. I'll love him until the day I die.

335

Chapter Twenty-six

The final lap to Fort Laramie was covered with no mishaps, and the herd was delivered to the army on schedule.

With the demanding responsibility behind him, Dru's mood became lighthearted and carefree. But despite his high spirits, he couldn't shake the gnawing feeling that something was amiss between him and Cassandra. Although she hadn't said or done anything to give him that impression, he suspected nonetheless that Cassandra was troubled. He was sure it went back to that night when he'd been drinking. If only he could remember what he had said. More than once he had asked Cassandra about the night in question, but she always assured him that he'd said nothing that warranted repeating. Her reserved answer alone gave him reason to suspect otherwise. However, certain that Cassandra intended to remain elusive, Dru decided to put the incident behind him. The future was all that mattered, and he intended to spend his with Cassandra.

Dru didn't try to avoid the inevitable. He knew marriage meant children. Although he was still plagued with fear of losing another child, he was determined to face up to his paranoia. If Cassan-

336

dra were to become pregnant, he'd want the child as much, if not more, than he had wanted Johnny. Somehow, though, he'd have to control his fear and not become an overprotective father. After losing Johnny, he had sworn that he'd never have another child, and coming upon the massacred baby had temporarily reinforced that decision.

Deep down in his heart, Dru knew that he longed for a family, daughters as well as sons. He simply had to find a way to conquer his fear of losing one or more of them. He had considered confessing these feelings to Cassandra, but in Dru's opinion, fear made him less of a man, and he didn't want the woman he loved to know of this weakness. So he was determined to work it out in his own way.

Cassandra left the Fort Laramie hotel and hurried across the courtyard to the traders' store. The fort was surrounded by adobe walls, and heavily fortified blockhouses stood at each corner. A large number of trappers, trading Indians and soldiers filled the busy compound, and Cassandra had to maneuver her way past them.

She was wearing her boy's attire, and the men, mistaking her for a lad, paid her scant attention as she hurried to the traders' store.

Pausing in front of the mercantile, Cassandra glanced through the open door and into the store. There were several customers inside, and she dreaded nudging her way into the crowd to look for the articles she planned to purchase.

She glanced down distastefully at her attire. Even with the threat of Jubal behind her, her boyish clothes had been suitable for the rough trail drive. But now there was no longer a reason for her to wear such unbecoming apparel. She hoped to find a couple of dresses at the mercantile, plus other feminine articles.

Early this morning, Dru had checked her into the hotel, telling her that he'd return at six o'clock to take her to dinner. The wranglers, still watching over the herd, were camped about a half mile from the fort. She knew Dru would be busy all day. First, he had to settle up with the army; then he planned to find the chaplain and set up a time and place for their wedding.

Thoughts of her wedding filled Cassandra with apprehension. She couldn't marry Dru without letting him know that she was with child. She hoped, prayed, that he'd receive the news joyfully, for if he reacted negatively, she would refuse to marry him. Cassandra had her pride, and she was determined that she and her baby would never be Dru's burdensome responsibility.

A large trapper, his arms loaded with merchandise, suddenly filled the open doorway, and Cassandra stepped quickly to the side, giving him ample room to pass. Hoping more customers would leave, she remained standing outside the store. She'd wait and go inside when the place wasn't quite so crowded.

"Cassandra!" a man's voice suddenly called.

Peering into the congested compound, she saw Roy DeLaney coming toward her.

338

"Roy!" she exclaimed warmly.

Taking her hands and squeezing them gently, Roy bent over and kissed her cheek.

"Cassandra, it's so good to see you again."

"I have so much to tell you," she began. "Jubal Thurston is dead."

"Yes, I know," he replied. "I came across his body and his brother's." He didn't dare tell her that he had helped himself to the money still tucked in Jubal's pocket. Fortunately for Roy, except for Dru, he had been the first traveler to come across the bodies.

Cassandra looked puzzled. "How did you know it was Jubal and his brother?"

Roy cursed himself for speaking rashly; then, thinking quickly, he replied, "I didn't know for sure, of course. But with the bandage on the man's face, I assumed it was Jubal." He shrugged tersely. "Naturally, I figured the other one was his brother."

Cassandra nodded. "Yes, of course. The bandage would identify Jubal."

Roy sighed inwardly with relief. He hoped Cassandra would never learn of his dealings with Thurston.

"Jubal told me that he killed Russ," she said quietly.

"Are you sure he wasn't lying?" Roy asked, deciding it was the prudent thing to say.

"A part of me had hoped that it was a vicious lie. But the doctor in Silver Creek sent a telegram to Dru. It was here when we arrived. It said that Russ was dead."

"I'm sorry," Roy murmured. "I rode back toward

Silver Creek," he lied, "but when I didn't meet up with your brother, I figured I'd probably missed him. So I decided to come to the fort. I was hoping to find both of you here."

Cassandra offered no reply, and DeLaney continued, "Who killed the Thurstons?" When Roy's horse had healed, he had headed out to catch up with the Thurstons. From the moment he had found their bodies, his curiosity about their killer had been plaguing him. He'd dismissed Dru as their possible murderer, for slitting a man's throat wasn't Jensen's style.

As simply as possible, Cassandra told Roy about Hawk and the part he had played in her abduction. She also let him know that Hawk had killed Vivian.

"My God!" Roy groaned. "Hawk's certainly not a man to cross."

Steering their discussion onto another course, she asked "Are you still planning to go to San Francisco?"

"Yes, I am. In fact, I've already bought a wagon and supplies. I plan to leave in the morning. I heard that a wagon train pulled out two days ago. I'll travel quickly and catch up to it."

"Where in the world did you get the money to buy a wagon?"

"I won the money in a card game," he fibbed. Actually, the funds had come from Jubal's pocket. He grinned charmingly. "Why are you loitering in front of the mercantile?"

"I plan to do some shopping. I was just waiting for it to become less crowded." Her eyes sparkled pertly. "Last night when Virgil paid the wranglers, I received a cook's wages."

"Good for you!" Roy remarked. "Tell me, how's things between you and Dru?"

"Things are . . . are fine," she mumbled haltingly.

"Do I hear a note of uncertainty?"

"We're getting married tomorrow." Her voice, however, lacked confidence.

"Something is wrong, isn't it? Would you like to tell me about it?"

She shook her head. "It's something I can't talk about. But if things go well, Dru and I will get married. Otherwise . . ."

"Otherwise, what?" he pursued.

Squaring her shoulders and raising her chin determinedly, she replied, "Otherwise, I might accompany you to San Francisco. If I do, I'll pay my way and do my share of work."

He studied her questioningly. "You're more than welcome, but, hon, what will you do in San Francisco? You don't have family there."

"I'll cross that bridge when I come to it. I'll survive, even though I'll be alone."

"You won't be alone," he was quick to reply. "I'll be with you, and I'll take care of you." His eyes probed deeply into hers. Even in her boyish attire, she was enchanting, and Roy was helplessly smitten.

"Roy," she began, "I couldn't possibly . . ."

"I know what you're about to say," he cut in. "But, believe me, when I offered to take care of you, I meant it as a friend. No strings attached."

341

Before she could protest further, Roy glanced inside the store and said briskly, "The crowd has cleared somewhat. Come; I'll shop with you."

He offered her his arm, and she accepted.

The horses had been counted and corralled, and when Dru rode into camp, it was deserted except for Badge. All the wranglers, Virgil included, were visiting the fort's enlisted men's bar.

Dismounting, Dru joined Badge at the fire. Six o'clock was only a couple of hours away, and he knew he should get a room at the hotel, order a bath, dress, then take Cassandra to dinner. But Badge seemed so lonely that he decided to spend some time with him.

Badge, knowing Dru had planned to talk to the chaplain, asked, "When are you and Cassandra getting married?"

"Tomorrow afternoon. We'll be married in the chapel. You and the wranglers are invited."

"I'll be there," Badge answered with a smile. Then, absently, he glanced down at the object he was toying with.

Dru, noticing he had something in his hands, asked, "What's that?"

"It's a locket that belonged to my mother." He slipped the dainty piece of jewelry into his pocket. "I don't know why I even keep it, let alone look at it." Anger suddenly sparked in his gray eyes. "She didn't give a damn about me! So why should I give a damn about her?"

"What happened to your father?" Dru asked.

Badge shrugged. "I don't know. I think he was killed when Ma and I were abducted. Ma never talked to me, so I couldn't ask her about my pa. I was just a babe when Tall Tree kidnapped us, so I don't remember anything about it. When Tall Tree married my mother, I was sold into slavery. I belonged to Crooked Arrow. Once a year, his tribe visited with Tall Tree's. But my mother never acknowledged me. I wouldn't have known who she was if the other kids hadn't enjoyed teasin' me about her. They thought it was funny that my mother ignored me. One summer, when the two tribes were visiting, I slipped up to Tall Tree's tepee. I wasn't bein' nosy, I just wanted to look at my mother."

The boy paused and heaved a wistful sigh. "I guess I was kinda hoping she'd say something to me. When I got close to the tepee, I heard her and Tall Tree arguing."

Badge patted his shirt pocket where the locket lay. "Tall Tree had found her with this locket. I watched as Tall Tree stormed out of the tepee. He headed for the river and I followed him. He threw something into the water, but it was so heavy that it didn't travel very far. As soon as Tall Tree left, I waded into the river and felt along the shallow bottom. I found the locket and decided to keep it."

"When I was at the fort," Dru began, "I told Captain Wilson about the massacred family we came across. He said that Tall Tree and his warriors have been spotted leaving the Black Hills. Quite a few homesteads have been attacked and there's been reports of stolen cattle. Tall Tree is

343

under suspicion, and the captain's waiting for permission from his superiors to go in the Hills and arrest him."

"Tall Tree won't surrender," Badge replied, remembering the warrior's courage and his deep hatred of soldiers. "If the captain and his men try to arrest him, they'll be killed."

"Captain Wilson knows that. He'll have a full company of soldiers with him. Tall Tree's village will be wiped out if the army's met with resistance."

Badge tensed. "What will happen to my mother?"

"If a fight does erupt, and if she isn't accidentally killed during the chaos, she'll be brought back here to the fort. The army will try to find her next of kin."

"That's me," the youngster mumbled with no sign of enthusiasm.

"Before we leave for home, I'll tell the captain to notify us if he finds your mother."

"Then what?" Badge asked, his tone bitter. "What can we do to help her? Furthermore, she won't even want our help."

Dru smiled kindly. "We'll offer it anyhow. That's all we can do."

"Thanks, Dru," he replied sincerely. "I appreciate you offering to help my mother. Even if she doesn't deserve it." Slipping a hand into his pocket, he withdrew the locket.

"May I see it?" Dru asked, reaching out a hand. Badge gave it to him.

The gold locket, resting on a dainty chain, was

exquisite. As Dru studied the expensive piece of jewelry, it took a moment for him to realize that he had seen it before.

His brow broke out in a cold sweat, and his hands trembled slightly as he turned over the locket to read the inscription on the back. The gold surface was badly scratched, making the letters difficult to read.

Leaning closer to the fire, Dru held the piece to the flickering light. Making out the inscription, he murmured raspingly, "Anita, I'll always love you."

Dru's fingers, making a fist, tightened about the locket, and it disappeared inside the palm of his hand. *Anita, I'll always love you*. The inscription thundered through his mind.

Dru's thoughts wandered speedily back in time as he remembered with clarity the day he had purchased the tiny locket. He'd wanted to have his name engraved but there hadn't been room.

Badge, watching, was puzzled by the strange expression on Dru's face. "What's wrong?" he asked.

"This locket!" Dru rasped. "I gave it to Anita as an engagement present!"

The full meaning of his words failed to register with Badge, causing him to look blankly at Dru.

"Don't you understand?" Dru yelled hoarsely. "Your mother is my wife!" Suddenly, Dru felt as though he'd been hit in the stomach with a sledgehammer. He dropped the locket, turned to Badge and grasped his shoulders. "My God! You must be Johnny!"

Stung, Badge drew back and exclaimed, "I'm not Johnny! Your son is dead!"

Badge had heard that Dru's wife and son had been killed by the Sioux. Although he'd never learned the wife's name, he knew the son's name was Johnny.

A great exultation filled Dru's chest to bursting, and excitement raced through his whole being. He rose shakily, his knees weak, trembling. He drew several deep breaths and calmed his emotions. He couldn't let his heart overrule his better judgment. He wanted Badge to be his son; God, how desperately he wished it was so! However, he had to remain sensible. Badge's mother could have found the locket, or perhaps the locket had ended up in the possession of some Sioux woman, and Badge's mother had gotten it in a trade.

He turned to the boy, who was watching him, his eyes wide, glazed with confusion.

"Badge, is Anita your mother's name?"

"I don't know her white name. I only know her Sioux name. She's called Yellow Flower."

"Describe her."

"She's very beautiful. She has blond hair, and I think her eyes are gray like mine."

The description fit Anita, and once again, Dru was filled with hope. Kneeling in front of Badge, he peered closely into the youngster's face. Could this boy be his son? He tried to find a resemblance between himself and Badge. They both had black hair, and the boy's lips were full, sensual, like Dru's. Also, the same as Dru's, his build was tall, and although slender, masculine.

His scrutiny deepening, Dru searched for a resemblance to Anita. Badge's gray eyes and high

346

cheekbones were identical to hers.

Yes, Dru thought, his hopes escalating, this boy could be my son and Anita's. Impossible! his better judgment infringed sensibly, sending Dru's expectations plunging. Anita and Johnny were burned! You saw their bodies, buried them yourself. But they were burned beyond recognition, Dru reminded himself. How do I know for sure that it was them?

Standing, Dru began to pace back and forth, his thoughts racing turbulently.

Remaining seated, Badge watched as Dru paced restlessly. He didn't dare believe that this man was his father. It would be too miraculous, too wonderful, to be true! If he were to let himself believe, then found out he was wrong, the disappointment would be heart-shattering.

Dru, his thoughts similar to Badge's, suddenly stopped pacing and remarked, "There's only one way I can be sure. I have to go into the Black Hills, find Tall Tree's village and see if Yellow Flower is really Anita."

Badge gasped. Tall Tree was at war with the whites! If Dru tried to enter his village, he'd most likely be killed.

Badge started to speak of this danger to Dru, but he knew that it wouldn't alter his decision. Seeking the truth was too important, and the truth lay with Yellow Flower, the wife of Tall Tree.

Chapter Twenty-seven

Virgil's long strides remained abreast of Dru's as they crossed the fort's busy courtyard. The elder Jensen was finding it hard to keep his exultation under control. The news that Badge might be Johnny had not only shocked Virgil, but had pleased him immensely.

Dru had found his uncle at the enlisted men's bar, where he had floored him with the incredible news. Now they were on their way to Captain Wilson's office to ask his help in contacting Tall Tree.

Reaching Wilson's quarters, Dru told the young sentry that he needed to speak to the captain at once. The soldier relayed Jensen's message to his commanding officer, and receiving permission to enter, Dru and Virgil stepped inside. The sentry closed the door behind them.

Captain Wilson, an attractive man with reddish hair and a handlebar mustache, was sitting behind his desk. He gestured toward the two chairs facing him. "Please, sit down."

The Jensens complied, both sitting stiffly, apprehensively, as though they might leap to their feet at any moment.

"What can I do for you, gentlemen?" the captain

inquired, his eyes flitting from one to the other.

As calmly as possible, Dru told Captain Wilson about Stephen, Anita and Johnny, explaining how he and Virgil had come upon their burned wagon and had found three bodies inside, a man's, a woman's and a child's. Dru's story continued to unfold, and he told Wilson about Badge, the boy's abduction and his years with the Sioux. He elaborated in detail, revealing the way he had met Badge and why he had given him a job. His tone was unmistakably tinged with excitement as he explained about the locket that had belonged to Badge's mother, emphasizing that it was the same one that he had given to Anita.

Finishing his explanation, Dru sank back in his chair, and for the first time since he had discovered the locket, his body grew somewhat relaxed. Inwardly, though, he was still tense, and he felt as if his emotions were likely to explode at any minute. Badge might be his son! His son!

"I find your story amazing," the captain remarked congenially. "And for your sake, I hope you learn that Badge is your son." He spread his hands on the desk top. "However, I don't understand how I can help you."

"Earlier," Dru began, "you told me that you're waiting for orders to arrest Tall Tree. When you go after him, my uncle and I want to accompany you."

"I see," the officer replied. "Mr. Jensen, it may be weeks before I receive permission to pursue Tall Tree. He's nomadic, and by then he could be farther into the Hills. It might take weeks or even

349

months before my scouts can locate him again."

"Then give me a map to his village, and Virgil and I will go by ourselves."

"That would be suicidal. You'd both be killed before you could even state your business. If you want my advice, then I suggest very strongly that you wait a few more days and see if my orders come through. If they do, you two are welcome to ride with me. However, I must warn you that Tall Tree won't surrender submissively. A battle will most likely ensue, and there's always the chance that one or both of you could be wounded or even killed."

It was Virgil who responded. "We aren't dissuaded."

All at once, the captain snapped his fingers and sat upright. "How could I have forgotten!" he exclaimed.

"Forgotten what?" Virgil asked.

"There's a man here at the fort who can take you to Tall Tree. He's half Sioux, his mother was Tall Tree's aunt."

"Where is this man?" Dru questioned.

"He's in the stockade," Wilson answered. "He rode into the fort a couple of days ago, drank too much liquor, got violently drunk, and beat up three soldiers. From what I've gathered, though, the soldiers got what they deserved. They were giving him a hard time because he's a half-breed. But that's beside the point. The man's kin to Tall Tree and can get you into his village peacefully. But he might not be able to get you back out with your scalps still intact. If you don't want to wait for my orders to come through, you can probably pay this man to take you to Tall Tree."

"How long does he have to stay in the stockade?" Dru asked.

"If he'll agree to help you, I'll see that he's released in the morning."

"Thanks," Dru replied. "Can we talk to him?"

"Of course," Wilson answered. Standing, he stepped around his desk and went to the door, opened it and told the sentry, "Go to the stockade, get Hawk, and bring him here."

"Hawk!" Virgil exclaimed softly.

"Don't say anything to the captain about Vivian," Dru whispered. "If he knows Hawk killed a white woman, he won't turn him loose."

Virgil concurred and remained silent.

The captain poured a round of port, and the men were finishing their drinks when the sentry returned with Hawk.

The half-breed's brawny frame tensed noticeably as his gaze fell across the Jensens. Their presence didn't surprise him, though, for he naturally assumed they were here to see to it personally that he hanged for killing Mrs. Lance.

Speaking to Wilson, Dru asked, "May we talk to Hawk alone?"

"Yes, of course. I'll be at the officers' club if you need me." He spoke to the sentry. "When the Jensens are finished, take the prisoner back to the stockade."

Hawk waited for Captain Wilson and the soldier to leave before asking Dru, "When does the Federal marshal arrive?"

"Marshal?" Dru questioned.

Lumbering to the captain's private liquor cabinet, Hawk helped himself to a glass of bourbon, drank it neatly, then remarked, "I suppose you two plan to attend my hanging."

Understanding, Dru replied, "We aren't here about Vivian."

Hawk's amazement was evident.

Dru continued, "We want to hire you to take us to Tall Tree's village."

Tensing, Hawk poured himself another drink, quaffing it down quickly. He replaced the empty glass, composed himself, then turned back to the Jensens. His face expressionless, he asked Dru, "What's your business with Tall Tree?"

"My business isn't with Tall Tree but with his wife, Yellow Flower."

Although Hawk's face remained impassive, an unmistakable note of curiosity sparked in his eyes. He made no comment, but merely continued to stare directly at Dru.

"How well do you know Yellow Flower?" Dru asked.

"Well enough," Hawk mumbled.

"Did you know that she's Badge's mother?"

"I knew she had a white son, but my path never crossed with Badge's until he came to work for you."

"Badge has a locket that belonged to Yellow Flower. It's the same locket I gave to my wife."

"So?" Hawk questioned.

"Is Yellow Flower's white name Anita?"

The half-breed shrugged his powerful shoulders.

352

"I don't know."

"Did she ever discuss her past with you?"

"No." A cold smirk suddenly touched Hawk's lips. "You think Yellow Flower is your wife?"

"Yes, she might be."

Hawk laughed tersely. "She won't leave Tall Tree, so why do you want to find her?"

"Because she's Badge's mother."

"Which means?"

"Which means, if she's Anita, then Badge is my son."

Hawk had no sons, but he was nonetheless sensitive to Dru's feelings. However, he kept his emotions concealed behind a stony mask. "How much will you pay me to take you to Tall Tree's village?"

"A hundred dollars," Dru answered.

"We have one minor problem," Hawk revealed, smiling slyly. "I don't know where Tall Tree is camped."

Dru wasn't dissuaded. "There are Sioux camped outside the fort who are here to trade their pelts for supplies. Ask around, I'm sure you can find one who knows where Tall Tree is."

"But I still have another week in the stockade. By then, many of them will be gone."

"If you agree to help us, the captain will obtain your release. You'll be set free in the morning."

"All right, it's a deal," Hawk complied. "In the morning, I'll learn Tall Tree's whereabouts and then we'll leave." His tone became unyielding. "I will take only the two of you. Leave your wranglers behind. I can promise you a safe entry into Tall Tree's village, but chances are good that you'll never leave it alive."

He walked past the Jensens, went to the closed door, turned about and asked Dru, "Did you find Cassandra?"

"Yes, I did. You spared her life, and for that, I'm grateful."

"She is a good woman." He opened the door and told the sentry he was ready to leave.

"Cassandra!" Dru suddenly exclaimed, glancing anxiously at his pocket watch. "I was supposed to take her to dinner over an hour ago."

"You'd better hightail it to the hotel," Virgil suggested. "I'll go to the officers' club and talk to the captain."

Cassandra paced her room apprehensively. Why was Dru so late? It wasn't like him to be so unreliable. She hoped nothing had happened to him.

Passing the dresser, Cassandra paused and studied her reflection. She had found two dresses at the traders' store that fit her perfectly. She had chosen to wear her favorite one, a pink gingham gown. Enchanted by its simplicity, it was designed to be worn off the shoulders, had short puffed sleeves, fit snug at the waist, then expanded outward into long, soft folds.

Wondering if Dru would find her pretty, she scrutinized her reflection thoughtfully. She had used a pink ribbon to draw her short curls back and away from her face. Actually, the hairdo was becoming, and she almost wished short hair were fashionable.

A knock on the door brought her away fr[o]m [the] dresser, and she hurried across the room.

"Dru!" she exclaimed, letting him in. "Why [are] you so late? I was worried!"

"Sorry, darlin'," he apologized, kissing her cheek. "But something important has come up."

Noticing he still had on the same clothes he'd worn this morning, she asked, "Aren't we going to dinner?"

"Of course we are. You're hungry, aren't you?"

"Yes, but . . . but . . ."

"But what?"

"You haven't changed clothes."

He glanced down at his shirt and trousers, which were coated with dust from a day's work. He apologized a second time. "Sorry . . . again."

Concerned, she grasped his arm and asked anxiously, "Dru, is something wrong?"

Suddenly, he swept her into his arms and held her close. "Casey," he whispered huskily, "I love you." He kissed her deeply, passionately; then, taking her hand, led her to the bed and they sat down.

Slowly, he gave her a full account of everything that had happened. Cassandra listened avidly and without interruption. For Dru's sake, she hoped that Badge was his son, but for her own sake, she almost wished it wasn't true. If Badge was Johnny, then Yellow Flower was Anita. If Dru's family was still alive, then she could see no place in his life for her and her unborn child.

Dru rose from the bed, stepped to the window and glanced vacantly outside. "Hawk, Virgil and I the morning. I don't know how long ... I talked to the desk clerk before ...ere, and he said you can keep this ...an settle your bill when I return."

...away from the window and met her gaze. "I'll leave you some money, though, in case I don't make it back."

Cassandra knew Dru's trip was dangerous, and it took all her willpower to keep from begging him not to leave. But she knew that, regardless of her pleas, he'd go into the Black Hills.

"I plan to send the wranglers and Badge back to the ranch," Dru continued. He wished Cassandra would say something, but she hadn't uttered a word since he'd told her what had happened. He cleared his throat nervously and went on, "I talked to the chaplain today. He agreed to marry us tomorrow at three, but now . . ." He couldn't continue.

"But now," Cassandra said sadly, "you can't marry me because you're still married."

"We don't know that for sure," Dru hastened to point out.

Willfully, Cassandra controlled her tears. "Oh, Dru, you know as well as I do that Yellow Flower is Anita!"

"No, I don't know. That's why I have to find Yellow Flower. I've got to learn the truth! I can't go the rest of my life wondering."

"I understand," Cassandra acquiesced, lowering her eyes. Oh, yes! She understood only too well! For ten long years, Dru had clung to his memories of Anita and Johnny, and now his wife and son had miraculously reappeared. She could well imagine how difficult it was for Dru to keep his joy at a minimum while in her presence. He had to be excited — his wife and son alive! And where did that leave her? It leaves me with nothing! she thought bitterly.

Dru was completely unaware of Cassandra's insecurity. He had confidence in their love, thought it could weather any storm. He didn't find Anita a threat to himself and Cassandra. If his wife was still alive, he'd have to find a way to divorce her. He and Cassandra would still get married; they would just have to wait a while.

Returning to Cassandra, Dru sat beside her. He placed a hand under her chin and tilted her face up to his. Seeing a note of sadness in her eyes, he attempted to brighten her mood. "I'll hurry and get a room, take a quick bath, then take you to dinner."

His gaze swept over her appreciatively. "By the way, darlin', you look very beautiful."

"Thank you," she murmured.

His mouth came down on hers, and his kiss was full of passion and need. Linking her arms about his neck, she surrendered breathlessly.

He broke their embrace reluctantly. "I'll be back as quickly as possible," he said, giving her an affectionate wink.

He hastened across the floor, opened the door and stepped into the hall. Pausing outside of Cassandra's room, a frown furrowed Dru's brow. He had expected Cassandra to be overjoyed to learn that Badge might be Johnny. She had to know how much it meant to him and how happy it would make Badge.

Maybe the full extent of what this could mean hasn't fully registered with her, Dru told himself. After all, the news is startling, and it takes time for it to sink in.

Mistaking Cassandra's lack of enthusiasm for shock, Dru was sure that by the time they went to dinner, she'd be completely recovered. Anxious to share this evening with Cassandra, he hurried to the stairway, descended quickly and went to the lobby, where he encountered Roy DeLaney.

Virgil, riding into camp, found Badge at the chuck wagon. He had lowered the backboard, and was sitting on it, his legs dangling over the edge. A few of the wranglers had returned from the fort and were gathered about the fire, talking and joking with one another.

Dismounting, Virgil nodded amicably to his men before ambling over to Badge. Although dusk was giving way to the shadows of night, Virgil could see the boy clearly.

Badge glanced up and met Jensen's intense gaze.

Musing, Virgil studied the youngster's face. Could this boy be his great-nephew? Was this Johnny, the child he had once loved immeasurably?

"You can't tell simply by lookin' at me," Badge murmured, discerning the man's query.

"No, I can't tell for sure," Virgil replied. "But I do see a resemblance to the Jensens, and also to Anita."

Badge grinned disagreeably. "Maybe you just

wanna see it so badly that your eyes are playing tricks on you."

Virgil raised a brow questioningly. "Do I hear a bitter note?"

The boy shrugged. "Maybe."

"Don't you want Dru to be your father?"

"Wantin' doesn't make it so," he mumbled sullenly.

Virgil emitted a heavy sigh. "I understand how you feel."

Badge's temper flared, and he leapt from the backboard. "You don't understand how I feel! And neither does Dru! You're both too wrapped up in your own feelings!"

"Then suppose you tell me what you're feelin'," Virgil suggested gently.

"If I turn out to be Johnny, then I'm suddenly loved, and I have a family. But if I'm not Johnny, then I'm nothing more than a hired hand." His eyes narrowed angrily. "Well, I've lived this long without a family, and I don't need one now!"

Virgil understood Badge's bitterness and was ashamed to admit to himself that the boy's words had a ring of truth to them. He and Dru had been too involved in their own feelings to consider Badge's.

Tears came to the boy's eyes, and wiping them away, he continued harshly, "I can't turn my feelings off and on like you and Dru can!" His next words came out chokingly. "Dru bein' my pa won't make me love him any more than I already do!"

The youngster whirled about and headed away from camp.

"Badge!" Virgil called. "Come back!"

He kept on walking and was soon out of sight.

Virgil started to follow him, but then decided to let the boy have some time alone. He had always known that Badge thought a lot of Dru, but he'd never dreamed that the lad's feelings went so deeply.

Chapter Twenty-eight

After Dru left her room, Cassandra remained sitting on the bed, her thoughts plunging her into a deep depression. She could understand and share in Dru's joy that his son might still be alive. Her depression stemmed from Anita's possible existence. Apparently, Dru had once loved the woman; otherwise, he wouldn't have married her. The fear that he might still love Anita was very real to Cassandra, and she wondered if his elation was due mostly to his son's existence or his wife's.

She rose from the bed, stepped to the window and gazed vacuously down at the fort's courtyard. If Yellow Flower was Anita, did Dru plan to bring her back with him? What if Anita insisted on staying with her Sioux husband? Would Dru agree, or would he try to force her to leave?

Sudden tears stung Cassandra's eyes. Most likely, Anita won't want to stay with Tall Tree, she thought glumly, but will ask Dru to take her back to his ranch.

A knock on Cassandra's door interrupted her solemn reverie. She thought it was too soon for Dru's return, and she wondered who was calling.

Admitting the caller, she was pleasantly surprised to see DeLaney. "Roy, come in," she said warmly.

Entering, he kissed her cheek. "I saw Dru in the lobby, and he told me that his wife and son might still be alive." Regarding Cassandra closely, he could see that she was disturbed.

This unexpected turn of events had bolstered Roy's spirits. If he played his cards wisely, winning Cassandra from Dru should be a piece of cake. It was as simple as using her present vulnerability to his advantage.

Placing his hands on her shoulders, he gazed caringly down into her face. "Hon, how are you holding up?"

DeLaney's concern broke down her defenses. "Oh, Roy!" she cried tearfully. "I'm so afraid that I've lost Dru!"

He took her gently into his arms, and holding her tenderly, he said with calculated deceit, "I understand what you mean. When Dru was telling me about finding the locket, I got the distinct impression that he was overjoyed to learn that his wife might still be alive. Although he was excited about his son, Anita's possible existence seemed to mean more to him."

Actually, Dru had said very little in regard to Anita; he had spoken mostly of Johnny.

Cassandra moved out of Roy's arms, and meeting his gaze, she asked brokenly, "What did Dru say to give you that impression?"

Reminding himself that all's fair in love and war, Roy lied with selfish intent, "He started reminiscing, telling me that Anita had been a beautiful bride and how much he had loved her." Roy arched a brow and said intently, "Hon, I hope you don't

362

repeat this to Dru. He wouldn't like it, and Dru's not a man I'd care to tangle with."

"Of course I won't tell," she assured him. Although Roy's account had wounded her deeply, she nonetheless appreciated his frankness. He was a good friend, and she trusted him.

"Cassandra," Roy began, his tone gentle, as though he were speaking to a child, "you must realize that Anita was Dru's first love, his wife, and the mother of his son. Those are strong and uniting bonds. Although Dru loves you, I don't think he loves you enough to break away from his past. Anita and Johnny are his family, and you're . . . you're . . ."

"I'm just someone who loves him," she finished sadly.

Roy decided that this was a good time to give her false encouragement. "Hon, you can always hope that Yellow Flower isn't Anita."

"She's Anita, all right!" Cassandra remarked firmly. "I just know she is!"

Turning away, Cassandra returned to the bed and sat down. Following, Roy pulled up a hard-backed chair and positioned it facing her.

Sitting, he said strongly, "If you ask me, Dru's a damned fool to go into the Black Hills. The chance of Tall Tree letting him live is very slim. But then I guess a man like Dru is willing to risk his life for the woman he . . . " Purposefully, Roy let his words drift away.

"The woman he loves?" Cassandra asked sharply. "Is that what you were about to say?"

Roy looked embarrassed. "Sorry, hon. I have a

bad habit of opening my mouth when I should keep it shut. I didn't mean to hurt you. Please forgive me for being so callous."

"You aren't callous," she hastened to assure him. Her green eyes took on an angry glint. "Dru Jensen has a monopoly on callousness!"

Moving to the edge of his chair, Roy asked, "Will you take some advice?"

"I'll try," she answered.

"Don't sit around this hotel for weeks waiting for Dru to come back. Don't let him make a fool of you. Come with me to San Francisco."

He could tell that she was considering his advice, and he pressed on, "I have a good friend in San Francisco. We'll leave his address with Captain Wilson, and he can give it to Dru. That way, if Dru decides to find you, he can."

"We both know there's only one reason why Dru would want to find me. If Anita turns him down, I'll be his second choice."

"Are you willing to be his second choice?"

"No!" she remarked proudly. "Regardless of how much I love Dru, I'll never settle for second place!"

Sure now of his victory, Roy smiled inwardly. "Then you'll come with me to San Francisco?" he asked expectantly.

Cassandra knew she couldn't leave with Roy without telling him that she was pregnant. She wondered if he'd retract his invitation.

"Roy," she began, hesitant to discuss her condition, "before I consider accompanying you to San Francisco, there's something you should know. Something so vitally important that it might change your mind about taking me with you."

"Never," he said, meaning it wholeheartedly.

For a long moment, Cassandra gazed down at her lap; then, raising her eyes to his, she said softly, "I'm going to have a baby."

Roy was genuinely surprised, and, at first, was at a loss for words. Then, composing himself, he asked, "Does Dru know?"

"No, I haven't told him. I was going to tell him tonight, but now, considering his excitement over Anita and Johnny, my pregnancy seems unimportant in comparison. Besides, Dru doesn't want our baby. He once told me that he never wants children."

Bounding to his feet, Roy remarked heatedly, "Jensen's an inconsiderate bastard!" Stepping to the bed, and sitting beside Cassandra, he drew her into his arms. "You poor darling. To think you've been going through this all alone with no one to help you." He hugged her tightly, and needing comfort, Cassandra nestled her head on his shoulder.

It was at this moment that Dru, finding the door ajar, stepped undetected into the room. The sight of Cassandra in DeLaney's arms hit him with a powerful, wounding force.

"Cassandra," Roy was murmuring, "I think I fell in love with you the first moment I set eyes on you.

"Roy," Cassandra whispered kindly, "I love you, too."

Dru, his jaw clenched, fury radiating from the depths of his eyes, whirled about and vacated the room. He stormed down the hall and to the stairs.

Meanwhile, Cassandra was pushing gently out of DeLaney's arms. "But Roy, I love you as a friend, and I thought you felt the same way."

"I am your friend," he said quickly. "But I'm also in love with you."

"But I can't return your feelings. I love Dru, and I don't think I'll ever stop loving him."

He smiled tolerantly. "Time has a way of healing wounds. I think someday you'll get over Dru. Then, hopefully, you'll learn to love me."

Roy reached for her hand, but avoiding his touch, she rose quickly and stepped away.

"Roy, considering how you feel about me, I can't possibly go to San Francisco with you."

"Cassandra, as I told you earlier, there'll be no strings attached. I offer my services as a friend, not as a hopeful lover."

He stood and went to her side. "As far as your pregnancy is concerned, it makes no difference. My invitation still holds."

"I . . . I'll have to think about it," she stammered.

"I have a room here," Roy said. "Two doors down on the right. I plan to leave early in the morning, so let me know your decision before then."

"I will," she promised. "Now, I think you'd better leave before Dru arrives."

He agreed, and gave her a chaste kiss on the lips. Anxious to avoid Dru, he left quickly.

Cassandra removed her dress and threw it angrily

366

toward the chair. She missed, and the garment fell on the floor. She didn't care; she was too upset to be concerned over where it landed.

Disrobing completely, she stuffed her undergarments in the dresser drawer, took her dressing gown from the wardrobe and put it on. The elegant garment billowed gracefully about her slim ankles as she paced the room with the restlessness of a caged cat.

She had purchased the sheer dressing gown for her wedding night, but now, certain there would be no wedding, she saw no reason not to wear it.

Her anger grew more intense as she continued her pacing. How dare Dru stand her up! After Roy had left, she had waited eagerly for Dru, hopeful that they could reach an understanding. She loved him with all her heart, and if he loved her even half as much, then there was no obstacle they couldn't overcome. Slowly, though, her eagerness had turned into anger as the hours passed without Dru's arrival.

Grabbing the hard-backed chair, Cassandra dragged it to the open window and sat down. The lamp was within her reach, and she adjusted it down to a low glow.

She had been such a romantic fool to believe that she and Dru could work things out. He didn't love her! He'd even had the gall to thoughtlessly stand her up! His thoughts were so filled with Anita that he'd probably forgotten that he was supposed to take her to dinner.

Forgotten, hah! Cassandra bristled. He didn't forget! He simply doesn't care!

367

Tears threatened, but she forced them back. She wasn't about to cry over Dru! The heartless cad wasn't worth it!

A hard knock on the door startled Cassandra. Tensing, she asked, "Who's there?"

She had neglected to lock the door, and it was suddenly swung open. Dru's tall frame filled the threshold. He stood poised for a moment, then stepped inside and slammed the door behind him.

"Where have you been?" Cassandra demanded testily.

He smiled, and its coldness sent a shiver through Cassandra.

"I've been at the officers' club," he replied calmly. He had gone there immediately after finding Cassandra with DeLaney, and had taken a corner table to himself. Fuming, he had spent the intervening hours drinking heavily.

"I suppose you've been drinking and celebrating!" she spat petulantly. She looked away from his icy stare. "You inconsiderate cad!"

"Cad, am I?" he questioned, moving toward her with deliberate slowness. "Look who's callin' the kettle black."

Her gaze flew to his. "What do you mean?"

He paused mere inches from her chair. The low burning lamp bathed her in a soft, golden light. Her sheer dressing gown defined her feminine curves, and Dru's eyes raked over her hungrily. Against his will, he suddenly envisioned DeLaney's hands fondling Cassandra intimately. The vision was infuriating, and he thrust it from his mind.

"Did you know DeLaney's here?" he asked, baiting her. He despised himself for playing cat and mouse. Why didn't he just come out and tell her he knew about her and Roy?

"Yes, I know he's here," she answered, looking away guiltily. She had nothing to hide, had done nothing wrong, so why was she feeling guilty? It wasn't her fault that Roy loved her. She had never encouraged him.

Her inability to meet his eyes didn't escape Dru. It gave him more reason to believe that she was indeed in love with Roy.

"I suppose you were happy to see him," Dru murmured, watching her closely.

"What exactly are you implying?"

"Well, you must think a lot of him. After all, you once ran away with him."

"I wasn't running away with Roy. I was trying to find Russ."

She was impatient with Dru's subtle innuendos. How dare he come here and treat her as though she'd done something wrong! He was the one who should be explaining himself!

"Damn you, Dru!" she uttered with barely controlled rage. "Why did you leave me sitting in this room for hours waiting for you?" A note of pleading crept into her voice. "What's wrong with you?"

A picture of Cassandra in DeLaney's arms flashed before him, intensifying his fury. "There's nothing wrong with me. Not anymore! I took off my blinders and now I can see clearly."

He'd been a fool to trust Cassandra, to believe she wasn't like Anita! The moment his back was turned, she was two-timing him with DeLaney!

Thinking back, he remembered that when Roy was working on the trail drive, he and Cassandra had been very close and had spent a lot of time together. Dammit! If she had wanted DeLaney, then why had she come on to him? Had she taken him as a second choice? Damn her cheating heart, her lying tongue! Well, if she wanted DeLaney, then she could damned well have him! He was stepping out of her life, for good!

Dru's eyes pierced hers coldly. "Our engagement's off."

His decision hit Cassandra like a physical blow, and she gasped aloud. She came close to revealing her heartache, and she almost leapt to her feet with intentions of throwing the herself in Dru's arms and begging him not to leave her!

But Cassandra's pride emerged and pinned her to the chair. Her chin lifted in a defiant gesture, and she met Dru's icy stare without wavering. Certain that he was leaving her for Anita, she wondered desperately how he could still love the woman. Apparently, Roy had been right. Anita had been Dru's first love, his wife and the mother of his son, and the strong, uniting bonds were too powerful for Dru to break. She thought him a fool for still loving Anita.

"Very well, Dru," she managed to say collectedly. "We're no longer engaged. I release you from your commitment."

He damned her cool, heartless composure. My God, how could he have been so wrong about her?

An angry scowl crossing his face, he uttered between gritted teeth, "The hell with you, Cassandra!" Reaching into his pocket, he withdrew some bills, and pitching them in her lap, he said gruffly, "That's more than enough to get you wherever you want to go."

Her temper flared, and throwing the bills on the floor, she sprang to her feet. "I don't want your money! I don't want anything from you! Get out of my room, and don't come back!"

He started to comply, but, suddenly, noticing how the lamplight was silhouetting her delectable curves, he responded to her tempting beauty.

His hands shot forward and clutched her arms, jerking her against him. "This is no way for us to say goodbye," he said in a harsh whisper. "Considering your passionate nature, I'm sure you won't mind accommodating me one last time."

Outraged, Cassandra attempted to struggle free, but keeping her imprisoned with one arm, Dru used the other to rip away her dressing gown, his brutality tearing the fragile garment in several places. Lifting her into his arms, he carried her to the bed and dropped her roughly.

Frantically she tried to get up, but the threatening tone in Dru's voice dissuaded her. "Don't try it, my deceitful little vixen! I'm gonna have you—one way or another!"

Moving impatiently, Dru pulled off his boots, then began peeling away his clothes.

Watching, Cassandra felt as though she were staring at a stranger. She'd never been exposed to this dark side of Dru's nature, and she was genuinely frightened. Confusion was mingled with her fear. Why was Dru so obviously angry with her?

371

She'd done nothing to arouse his rage. She hadn't broken their engagement, he had! Furthermore, she wasn't the one holding tenaciously to a past love!

Anger swelled within her, taking full control of her faculties and catching Dru unaware, she leapt from the bed.

Nude and unhindered by clothing, Dru moved incredibly fast, and grasping Cassandra's arm, he flung her back onto the bed. He moved over her, his frame hovering inches above hers. Suddenly, his lips captured hers in a brutal kiss.

Cassandra tried vainly to turn away from the mouth bruising hers, but Dru wouldn't relent and set her free. His kiss became a wild, hungry caress, and Cassandra could feel her defenses weakening. As her body began to betray her, a small submissive whimper came from her throat.

Dru, aware of her surrender, smiled cynically against her mouth. The vixen might have a heart as cold as ice, but her body was hotter than the fires of hell!

Parting her lips fully, Cassandra let him possess her mouth. His tongue entered aggressively, meeting hers in love's warfare.

He lowered his hips to hers, and as an explosive sensation swept through her, Cassandra's legs wrapped about his waist.

"Oh, Dru! Dru!" she cried throatily, wanting to feel him deep inside her. "Now! Do it now!"

A cold smirk touched his lips. Was she this wonderfully passionate with DeLaney? Consumed with jealousy, he took her powerfully, penetrating so deeply that she cried out.

His swift invasion had been somewhat painful, but the discomfort was quickly replaced with ecstasy. His maleness now filling her with unspeakable pleasure, Cassandra arched her thighs as a moan of longing escaped her lips.

Glorying in the feel of her moist heat, Dru drove into her rapidly. Cassandra, engulfed in total rapture, met the full force of his passion and responded with untethered abandon.

Dru's forcefulness soon took them to love's electrifying completion; their release left them weak and breathless.

A silent tension hung heavily between the lovers, interrupted only by their labored breathing, which was soft, rapid gasps.

His strength returning, Dru broke their intimate joining, stood, and began putting on his clothes.

Hurt by his cold indifference, Cassandra came dangerously close to crying, but telling herself that Dru wasn't worth it, she controlled her tears.

Sitting up gingerly, Cassandra was about to retrieve her ripped dressing gown when Dru grabbed it off the floor and handed it to her. Standing, she quickly slipped into the garment. It was badly torn and barely covered her.

Sitting on the edge of the bed, she waited uneasily for Dru to say something.

Dressed, Dru turned to Cassandra and studied her with an expression she couldn't discern. Looking deeply into her beautiful green eyes, he saw a note of sadness. Her eyes were misty, and he wondered if she was about to cry.

She appeared vulnerable, helpless, and more

lovely than words could describe. Had he miscon-strued her and Roy's embrace? No, of course not! he thought angrily. He'd overheard their whispered words of love!

However, a gnawing doubt stayed in his mind, driving him to distraction. Ask her, you damned fool! his better sense demanded. Ask her if she loves DeLaney!

"Casey . . ." he began, obviously hesitant.

Cassandra's heart pounded. Calling her Casey was like an endearment. "Yes, Dru?" she asked, waiting breathlessly for his reply.

Throwing away his pride, Dru was about to ask her if she loved DeLaney when a soft knock sounded on her door.

"Cassandra?" they heard Roy call. "Hon, I need to talk to you."

DeLaney's interruption was like a cold splash of water in Dru's face, bringing him back to his senses.

"Not now, Roy," Cassandra called back. "I'll talk to you later."

She waited for Roy's footsteps to fade before turning back to Dru. The unexpected fury in his piercing blue eyes took her by surprise.

"Dru, what's wrong?" she cried. Then, wonder-ing if he was jealous, she bounded from the bed and grasped his arm firmly. "Surely you don't think that Roy and I . . ."

He flung off her hand. "It doesn't matter!"

"Of course it doesn't matter!" she retorted, his curtness infuriating her. "The only thing that mat-ters to you is finding Anita!" Placing her hands on her hips, she demanded furiously, "Get out of my room!"

Afraid his anger might turn physical if he remained, Dru brushed her aside, went to the door, opened it and left.

Slowly, Cassandra crossed the room and closed the door behind him. Then going to the bed, she fell across it.

She waited for the tears that failed to materialize. Her pain was too deeply embedded to be washed away with a flow of tears.

Chapter Twenty-nine

Dru's room was across the hall from Cassandra's, and as he stepped inside, he was surprised to see Virgil waiting for him.

"I asked the desk clerk which room you were in," his uncle explained. "The door was unlocked, so I let myself in. I figured you were probably with Cassandra, and I didn't want to disturb you two, so I decided to wait for you."

"Is anything wrong?" Dru asked.

"I'm not sure," Virgil replied. "I'm kinda worried about Badge."

Dru was immediately concerned. "What do you mean?"

"He wandered away from camp and has been gone since dusk."

"Wandered away from camp?" Dru repeated, baffled.

Quickly Virgil gave Dru a full account of the conversation he'd had with Badge.

"I never dreamed the boy felt that way," Dru remarked, his tone tinged with remorse.

"We've both been so wrapped up in hopin' he's Johnny that we haven't taken time to consider his feelings."

Reflecting on Badge's remarks, Dru said, "Where

did the boy get the idea that I could think of him simply as a hired hand? He's already like a part of our family. I think the world of that kid."

"Don't tell me; tell him," Virgil mumbled.

"I will, just as soon as I find him!"

Moving quickly, Dru gathered his possessions and stuffed them in a carpetbag. Finished, he opened the door and stepped across the threshold. A movement farther down the corridor caught his eye. Turning, he saw Roy DeLaney ushering Cassandra into his room. The door shut soundly behind them.

Dru scowled furiously. It didn't take her long to leave his arms and run into DeLaney's!

His uncle, following him into the hall and toward the stairs, asked, "How did Cassandra take the news that Badge might be Johnny?"

Dru paused in midstride. "It doesn't matter. It's over between us."

Virgil was astounded. "What do you mean, it's over?"

"She's in love with Roy DeLaney."

"Hogwash!" Virgil grumbled. "That gal loves you. I'll get to the bottom of this and straighten everything out."

"No, you won't." Dru's eyes narrowed angrily. "If you wanna keep your teeth, you'll mind your own business!"

"Touchy, ain't you?" Virgil remarked, unintimidated. He knew his nephew would never strike him.

"Just stay out of it!" Dru warned, continuing onward.

Virgil stared at his nephew's departing back. In

the morning, he'd talk to Cassandra and find out how Dru got the ridiculous notion that she was in love with DeLaney.

Losing sight of Dru, he hurried and caught up to him. Familiar with the younger Jensen's temper, Virgil made no further mention of Cassandra.

As the Jensens were leaving the hotel, Roy was handing Cassandra a glass of sherry. "Here; drink this," he said. "You look like you need it."

Cassandra knew she must look dreadful. Her hair was mussed, and she had dressed quickly, haphazardly. She was wearing her boyish attire. She didn't want to wear either of her new dresses. She had bought them with Dru in mind, hoping he'd find her pretty in such feminine apparel.

"Did you and Dru have a tiff?" Roy asked.

"Tiff?" she laughed harshly. "That's putting it mildly." She took a large drink of sherry, hoping it would soothe her raw emotions. "Dru's an inconsiderate, heartless rogue, and I hope I never see him again as long as I live!"

Roy smiled inwardly. "Does this mean it's all over between you two?"

"Absolutely!" she declared.

"Then you're coming with me to San Francisco?"

"Yes, only I don't want to leave in the morning. I'd like to leave now."

"Why the rush?"

"If we wait until morning, I'm liable to run into Dru. I'd like to avoid that possibility."

Roy agreed wholeheartedly. If she and Dru were to see each other, they might patch up their differences.

"All right," DeLaney complied. "Go pack your things. We'll leave right away."

Cassandra finished her drink, handed the glass to Roy, and, telling herself she was doing the right thing, she left to pack her clothes.

By the time Dru and Virgil rode into camp, Badge had returned and was placing his bedroll beside the chuck wagon. The youngster watched avidly as the Jensens dismounted and walked over to him.

Keeping his voice low so he wouldn't disturb the wranglers who were sleeping, Virgil demanded softly, "Boy, where have you been? I was worried about you."

"I just took a walk," Badge mumbled.

"Walk, hell! You've been gone since dusk!"

"It's all right," Dru told his uncle, soothing his ruffled feathers. "I'm sure Badge had a lot to think about and needed time alone." He looked at the boy. "Would you mind takin' another walk? I'd like to talk to you."

Agreeing, Badge fell into stride beside Dru and they strolled away from camp. An uncomfortable silence wedged its way between the two.

When they came upon a small boulder, Dru went to it, leaned back against the rock's smooth surface and lit a cheroot.

Badge, watching, crossed his arms over his chest and waited for Dru to say something.

Studying his young companion, Dru wished he could read the lad's thoughts. Feeling somewhat apprehensive, he began tentatively, "Badge, Virgil told me about the discussion between you two."

Before Dru could say more, Badge interrupted, changing the subject abruptly. "I'm goin' into the Black Hills with you."

Dru shook his head. "No, it's too dangerous. I'm sending you back to my ranch."

The boy's anger flared. "If you won't take me with you, then I'll go by myself!"

"No, you won't!" Dru snapped. "I forbid it!"

"Forbid it?" Badge repeated harshly. "You can't tell me what I can and cannot do! You're my trail boss, not my pa!"

"Don't you want me to be your father?" Dru asked, watching the boy intensely.

Badge shrugged indifferently, the small lift of his shoulders hiding his anxiety. "What difference does it make? We both know it's too farfetched to be true."

"Are you afraid to believe? Afraid of being disappointed?"

"Aren't you?"

Dru took a drag off his cheroot, considered his answer, then replied, "Yes, I'm afraid of being disappointed. But not for the reasons you think."

"You don't know what I think," Badge muttered sullenly.

"Yes, I do. You think if I find out you're Johnny, I'll instantly love you. But if you aren't Johnny, you'll simply be the lad I took under my wing because I felt sorry for him."

"Well, won't you?" he questioned, still sullen.

"Let me ask you this, Badge. If you learn that

I'm not your father, will it change your feelings for me?"

"No, of course not," he was quick to reply. "I already . . . I already." He was too embarrassed to continue.

"You already what?" Dru persisted. "Say it!"

"I already think of you as a father!" he blurted out.

"And why should my feelings for you be any less?" Dru questioned gently. "Don't you realize that I already think of you as a son?"

Badge's eyes were challenging. "Then why will you be disappointed if I'm not Johnny."

"Because I want my son to be alive!" Dru said emotionally. "What kind of man would I be if I didn't?"

Badge understood. He looked at Dru somewhat uncertainly. "But if I'm not Johnny, you'll still . . . ?" His question faded.

"Still think of you as a son?" Dru asked.

The youngster nodded.

"Yes, I will," Dru replied sincerely. Putting out his cheroot, he stepped to Badge and placed his hands on the boy's shoulders. "If you aren't Johnny, then when I return home, I'd like to legally adopt you. Would you mind?"

Badge couldn't conceal his joy, and his face lit up. "No, I wouldn't mind."

"Then it's settled," Dru confirmed. He longed to embrace the boy but wasn't sure if he should. Badge might consider himself too old for a display of physical affection.

Turning, Dru motioned for Badge to follow.

"We'd better get back to camp and get some sleep."

"Wait!" Badge called.

Dru turned back around.

"I'm still goin' into the Black Hills," the boy said stubbornly. "If you won't take me with you, I'll go alone." He set his jaw firmly. "I mean it!"

"Why are you so determined?"

"I want to see Yellow Flower."

"But why?"

"Because she's my mother," Badge answered simply.

Dru wanted to argue the point, but there didn't seem to be any reason to do so. Besides, he could understand Badge wanting to see his mother. Although Yellow Flower was obviously a poor excuse for a mother, she was nonetheless his mother. However, Dru feared for Badge's life.

Reading Dru's thoughts, Badge said confidently. "Tall Tree has no reason to harm me."

"You could be sold back into slavery."

"And you could be killed," he pointed out. "But it's a chance you're willing to take. Well, I'm willing to take my chances, too."

"Do you really want to see Yellow Flower that badly?"

"Yes, I do. Also, if you're my father, I want to be there when you find out."

"All right," Dru conceded reluctantly. "You can come with me. But if anything happens to you, I'll never forgive myself."

The following morning, Dru remained in camp

as Virgil rode to the fort to see Hawk. Dru had told his uncle that he needed to talk with Pete, since they were leaving him in charge of the Bar-J during their absence. Dru's excuse to stay in camp had been partly true; it was important that he meet with Pete. However, Cassandra was his real reason for remaining. He wanted to avoid running into her and DeLaney.

Virgil was gone less than an hour, and upon his return, he let Dru know that he needed to speak to him privately. They walked to the edge of camp, where they couldn't be overheard.

"I saw Hawk," Virgil began. "He learned Tall Tree's whereabouts. He said he'd be here within the hour and for us to be ready to leave. Did you get our supplies packed?"

Dru said that he had.

Hesitantly, Virgil continued, "I stopped at the hotel to see Cassandra." Reaching into his shirt pocket, he offered Dru a handful of bills. "This money belongs to you. Cassandra left it with the desk clerk. She asked him to return it to you, but he gave it to me instead." Virgil raised a brow archly. "Why did you give her this money?"

"I gave it to her so she'd have the funds to go wherever she wanted." A deep frown crossed Dru's brow as he took the bills and stuffed them in his pocket.

His temper blazing, Dru cursed, "Dammit, Virgil! Why did you go to the hotel? I told you to mind your own business! I suppose you and Cassandra had a lengthy talk!"

"I didn't even see her. She's gone."

"Gone? What do you mean?"

"The desk clerk told me that she and DeLaney checked out last night. It seems they're gonna catch up to a wagon train that passed through here a couple of days ago."

Dru didn't understand why the news came as such a surprise. He should've foreseen the pair taking off for San Francisco.

"Well?" Virgil asked testily.

"Well, what?" Dru snapped.

"Aren't you goin' after her?"

"No!" he remarked harshly. "I'm headin' into the Black Hills!"

"Hell, I can go to Tall Tree's village. You get on your horse, get that little gal and bring her back!"

When Dru responded by staring at him as though he'd taken leave of his senses, Virgil grumbled crankily, "I've got eyes, haven't I? I'll know if Yellow Flower is Anita. There's no reason for both of us to see her. Now, stop bein' a stubborn jackass and go after Cassandra!"

"If she wants DeLaney," Dru said, scowling, "then she can damned well have him!"

"Dru, don't be so hardheaded!"

"Hardheaded!" Dru shouted. "You're the one with a thick skull! I already told you, she's in love with DeLaney. I heard her tell him so! Now, if you want her back, you go after her! As you pointed out, it doesn't take both of us to know if Yellow Flower is Anita."

With that, Dru turned on his heel and stalked away. For a moment, Virgil considered following Cassandra. Regardless of Dru's belief that she loved DeLaney, Virgil didn't agree. But realizing only Dru could convince her to come back, he dismissed the idea of pursuing her.

Mumbling under his breath, cursing his nephew's obstinate nature, Virgil headed back into camp.

As the travelers infiltrated the region known as the Black Hills, Dru rode beside Hawk. Virgil and Badge, leading the packhorses, brought up the rear.

Dru, immersed in his turbulent thoughts, had said very little since the onset of the journey. Against his will, a vision of Cassandra with DeLaney kept crossing his mind. The picture was infuriating, and it set his blood boiling. He wondered bitterly how he could have been so wrong about her. He had believed unquestioningly that she truly loved him. A devouring gulf of despair washed over him, drowning his emotions in a bottomless pit of depression.

Hawk's deep voice cut into Dru's somber reverie. "We've been traveling for five, six hours, during which time you haven't uttered more than a couple of words."

"So?" Dru frowned.

"I need to ask you a question. Are you willing to talk?"

"I'm willing. I have a few questions of my own to ask."

Hawk's sudden smile was wintry. "After you, compadre."

"How long has it been since you saw Yellow Flower?"

"It's been close to six years since I last saw Tall Tree and Yellow Flower."

Dru was surprised. "Why so long?"

Hawk shrugged insouciantly. "No special reason. I was living in Mexico and saw no reason to leave."

"Ridin' with the Comancheros?" Dru queried archly.

"Maybe," Hawk said, grinning subtly.

Dru was quiet for a moment before asking, "Is Tall Tree good to Yellow Flower?"

"Good?" Hawk repeated. "Not by white man's standards."

"Why did Yellow Flower disown Badge?"

"To please Tall Tree, I imagine. If Yellow Flower is your wife, then when she left you, she probably took your son to hurt you, not because she wanted him."

"I've always known that," Dru replied. "Anita was a poor mother." He eyed Hawk inquisitively. "How did you know that Anita was leaving me when she was stopped by the Sioux? I never told you that in so many words."

"The wranglers like to talk," Hawk answered. "And I like to listen."

For now, Dru had no more questions. "It's your turn. What do you need to ask me?"

"Why didn't you tell Captain Wilson that I killed Mrs. Lance?"

"Because I needed you to take me to Tall Tree's village," Dru answered candidly.

"I'd never have thought you were the type to overlook murder."

"Well, don't think it now. When this trip is over,

and if our paths should cross again, I'll personally deliver you to the law."

Hawk grinned coldly. "Mrs. Lance plotted against your woman. You should be glad she's dead."

"Hawk, you can't go around being people's judge and executioner."

"Why not?" the half-breed laughed. "I've been doing it for years." He urged his horse forward, taking the lead position.

Dru returned to his dark thoughts.

Sitting beside the small campfire, Cassandra stared past the flickering flames and into her own thoughts. A lachrymose sigh escaped her lips as her inner loneliness penetrated deeply into her heart. How was she to go on without Dru? But I must! I must! she cried inwardly. For my baby's sake, I must go on!

She and Roy had set up camp at dusk, had eaten supper and were now sitting quietly about the fire.

Watching his companion, Roy studied her beautiful, somber face. Knowing her thoughts were on Dru, a pang of jealousy shot through him. However, despite his jealousy, his heart went out to her suffering. He sighed inwardly as he wished Cassandra loved him as much as she apparently loved Dru. He envied Jensen. No woman had ever cared so deeply about him.

He shrugged tersely. Perhaps that was his own fault. At heart, he was a rogue and a philanderer. He had never been serious about a woman until

Cassandra. A small smirk played across his lips. It was just his luck to fall for a woman who was already in love with another man.

Well, he told himself, in time, Cassandra will get over Dru and turn to me. I must be patient and bide my time.

Cassandra, her heart aching, forced back a flood of tears. Imagining her life without Dru was terribly depressing. Her thoughts turned to her unborn child. When he grew old enough to ask about his father, what would she tell him? A worried frown crossed her brow. She couldn't possibly tell her child that his parents had never married, that his father had never wanted him! She couldn't lay such a burden on her child's shoulders!

Her frown deepened considerably. Lord, she was an unmarried woman in the family way. What would people say? She'd be an outcast, and her baby would be branded a bastard!

"What's wrong?" Roy asked, noticing her consternation.

"I was thinking about my baby. I'm worried about what people will say."

"Because you aren't married?" he queried gently.

"Yes. I'll be showing before we reach California. The women on the wagon train will know I'm pregnant. They'll start asking me about the baby's father. Regardless of what I say, they'll put two and two together and know I don't have a husband, never had one. To make matters worse, I'll be traveling with a man. Some of these women are bound for San Francisco, and my reputation will follow me. I'm not worried about myself. I don't care what they say about me, but what will their petty gossip do to my baby?"

Thoughtfully, Roy considered her dilemma, then remarked, "I have a solution."

"You do?" she asked, amazed.

"At the fort, I learned there's a town about a day's ride from here. It's called Backwater. The town's bound to have a reverend. If you agree, we'll go there and get married. It'll put us farther behind the wagon train, but if we travel quickly, we can still catch up to it within a few days."

"Married?" Cassandra murmured, as though the word were foreign.

"Your child needs a father, and you need a husband."

"But, Roy, I'm not in love with you."

"Considering the situation, that, my dear, is a minor point. If you want to save your reputation and your child's, you'll agree to marry me." He grinned wryly, his eyes sparkling with merriment. "After all, I'm not that bad of a catch, am I? I think I have the potential to make a good husband and father."

Smiling, Cassandra replied, "Roy, you'd make a wonderful husband and father." Her smile fading, she added, "But you deserve a wife who can return your love."

"Hon," he began convincingly, "just because you love Dru doesn't mean that someday you won't fall in love with me. Do you honestly believe that a person can only love once in a lifetime?"

"No, I'm sure it's quite possible to love more than once," she answered. Her heart sank, and a rush of remembrance swept through her. Almost literally, she could feel the thrill of Dru's embrace. She knew, irrevocably, that no man could ever mean as much to her as Dru. It might be possible for her to love again, but the way she felt about Dru only came around once in a lifetime. Any other love would be mild in comparison.

Is that the way Dru feels about Anita? she wondered hurtfully. If so, then she could fully relate to his feelings.

Thoughts of Anita revived Cassandra's bitterness, her total rejection at Dru's hands. However, it also reinforced her resolve to survive without him.

Looking at DeLaney, her face showing no emotion, she said matter-of-factly, "All right, Roy. I'll marry you."

He started to rejoice, but she held up a hand and warded off his words.

"Wait! I must be totally honest with you," she began. "I'm marrying you strictly for my baby's benefit. But I'm not completely selfish. I'll try very hard to be a good wife and live up to my part of the bargain. I'm very fond of you, Roy. I know that sometimes love comes after marriage; perhaps in our case, that will be true. But I must remain starkly candid. I don't believe I'll ever truly stop loving Dru. He's in my heart forever. Now, if your offer to marry me still holds, I accept warmly and graciously."

Roy, willing to have Cassandra under any conditions, replied at once, "My offer still holds."

"Very well," she remarked collectedly, as though they had just completed a business deal. "Then it's settled."

"Not quite," Roy murmured somewhat hesitantly.

Cassandra arched a brow quizzically.

"The route to Backwater will take us north and toward the Black Hills."

"So?" she asked, puzzled.

"Heading in that direction increases our chances of being spotted by a marauding band of Sioux."

A shudder coursed through Cassandra as she remembered the day she and Dru had found the massacred family. Sioux! The word itself frightened her.

Seeing her fear, Roy was quick to emphasize, "Hon, I said it merely increases our chances. I didn't say it was a certainty."

Mustering her courage, Cassandra replied with a bravado she was far from feeling, "I've faced danger since the day I left Clarksville. I'm used to it."

"Then we head for Backwater?" he asked expectantly.

"Yes," she answered unwaveringly. "We'll leave first thing in the morning."

Chapter Thirty

Cassandra awoke with a start and sat up on her pallet. She glanced wide-eyed about the wagon. She was certain that a strange sound had awakened her.

The daylight filtering into the wagon told her that it was already past dawn. She reached for her boyish attire, but her arm stopped in mid-movement and dropped back to her side.

She couldn't wear trousers! Not today — for this was her wedding day! The revelation cast a depressing shadow over her, and she had to fight back tears. She longed desperately to give in to her misery and fall back onto her bed and weep until her tears ran dry. But crying wouldn't change anything, and she seriously doubted if it would ease the pain of losing Dru. She had a somber feeling that the hurt would never completely go away.

She told herself to get up, remove her cotton gown, put on one of her dresses, then put forth a smiling face for Roy. He was a kind man and a good friend. He deserved so much more than she could give him, but at least she could give him a smiling bride.

Backwater had been farther than a day's ride, and although they had traveled yesterday at a steady pace, Roy calculated that the town was still three or four hours away.

Well! Cassandra thought, trying unsuccessfully to bolster her spirits. I might as well get up, get dressed and face the day. But she couldn't will herself to move, for she was trapped hopelessly in the web of her own weaving.

A vision of Dru, like a flame leaping up from banked embers, flashed before her, burning mercilessly into her heart.

I can't do it! she suddenly cried inwardly. I can't marry Roy! I love Dru too much! I love him so completely that I can't possibly give myself to another man!

Her mind swirling turbulently, her emotions a wreck, Cassandra felt as though she might go mad.

She drew a deep breath and was trying to calm herself when, all at once, an undefined noise caught her attention. It had come from outside, and she wondered if it was the same sound that had awakened her.

Hoping Roy was all right, she was about to bound to her feet, but she froze in place as the canvas was pushed aside roughly.

Cassandra didn't have time to react before a Sioux warrior leapt lithely inside. He was a terribly threatening figure, and as he grabbed her arm, jerking her against his tightly muscled frame, she paled and came dangerously close to fainting.

Grumbling, he shoved her toward the backboard so powerfully that she lost her balance and toppled over it. She hit the ground face down, the hard fall almost taking away her breath.

She lay still, too frightened to move. As a picture of the massacred family crossed her mind, she wondered fearfully if her fate would be the same as that poor, unfortunate woman's.

Cassandra heard one of the warriors approaching, but she didn't raise herself up. Certain that she was about to be killed, perhaps even raped, she didn't want to look into the eyes of her attacker.

A pair of strong hands wrapped about her arm and drew her abruptly to her feet.

Her eyes were downcast, and when the warrior suddenly released her, she tottered precariously for a moment. Then, retaining her balance, she dared to lift her gaze and meet the warrior's feral eyes.

She was taken aback by the Indian's striking good looks. The man's straight black hair was shoulder-length, and he wore an intricately designed band about his high forehead. His build was blatantly strong, and his muscular legs were covered with tan leggings with long fringes and brass beads. His smooth chest was bare, and strung across it were his bow and quiver.

As she continued to stare at him, unable to tear her eyes away, an inscrutable smile touched his lips.

Cassandra's heart pounded erratically. God, if he intended to kill her, then why was he just standing there smiling?

Suddenly, Cassandra was grabbed from behind by the Indian who had found her. Claiming her as his own, his brawny arms wrapped about her waist. He spun her around and against his hard body.

Cassandra almost surrendered meekly, for she knew fighting was futile. However, submissiveness was not a part of her nature. Her deeply embedded bravery surfaced, taking full control. If she must die, then she'd die fighting, not like some mealy-mouthed coward!

She grew limp, and as she had suspected, the warrior erroneously assumed that she had surrendered. He let down his guard, and taking him by surprise, Cassandra brought up her knee and slammed it into his groin.

Racked with pain, the Indian yelped and released her hastily.

Cassandra, stepping quickly out of his reach, scanned the area, searching for Roy. She found him standing helplessly between two warriors, his face as white as a ghost's. His eyes were pleading with hers to forgive him for failing to keep her safe.

Turning away from his tortured gaze, Cassandra's vision flitted over the Sioux, making a quick count. The marauding band was small: there were only six of them.

The injured warrior, now recovered, suddenly lunged at Cassandra, but she caught sight of him and sidestepped his attack.

Tottering, clutching at thin air, the man yelled viciously.

Cassandra didn't have to understand Sioux to know that he was vowing to kill her.

The other Indians, finding the incident humorous, laughed gustily, their mirth adding fuel to the warrior's wrath.

Cassandra looked on, paling, as the irate warrior slipped his knife from its sheath. She prayed he'd kill her swiftly, mercifully. Sudden sorrow impaled her as she thought about her child, and her heart ached for the baby who would never be born, its life snuffed out while still in its mother's womb. Oh, God, forgive me! she prayed desperately. Forgive me for letting this happen to my baby!

The warrior's approach was deliberately slow, for he wanted to see naked fear on the woman's face before he killed her.

Watching him, Cassandra blocked all thoughts from her mind, raised her chin with intrepid courage and awaited her own death with a dauntlessness that amazed the onlookers.

Inwardly, though, Cassandra was quaking with fear. But she'd be damned if she'd give these wild savages the satisfaction of seeing her break down, scream, and beg for her life.

Unknown to Cassandra, the warrior who had lifted her off the ground was deeply impressed with her defiance. The white woman was not only beautiful, but as fearless as a warrior. Moving swiftly, he stepped forward, blocked his comrade's approach and uttered sharp, demanding commands.

Although the Sioux's words totally escaped Cassandra, she hoped that he had chosen to save her life.

The other warrior, grumbling under his breath, slipped his knife back into his sheath. He whirled about angrily and stalked away.

Cassandra watched numbly as her rescuer came to her and gazed down thoughtfully into her face. Determined to remain brave, she met his piercing eyes without flinching.

The warrior's hand moved slowly to her blond tresses, and he wrapped a silky curl about his finger. He wondered why the woman had cut her hair.

Still impressed with Cassandra's courage and beauty, he said gruffly, "I have made my decision. You will not die."

His English took Cassandra by surprise, causing her to inhale sharply.

He pushed her toward the wagon. "Get dressed."

Disobeying, she demanded, "What about my friend?" She gestured toward Roy. "Please don't kill him!"

Again, the warrior was impressed with Cassandra. She would not plead for her own life, but would plead for a friend's.

"The man will die later," he mumbled bluntly. "No more talk, white woman. Get dressed." His black eyes narrowed dangerously. "Obey me, or I will change my mind and let Stalking Wolf kill you!"

Deciding prudently not to stretch the warrior's patience, she climbed inside the wagon, grabbed Casey's attire and dressed as quickly as possible. Spotting her gun and holster, she took the pistol and slipped it inside her shirt; then, putting on her wide-brimmed hat, she hurried back outside.

The Sioux warrior was waiting for her. He was shocked by her strange attire. "White woman, why do you hide your sex with a man's clothes and short hair?"

"So men like you and your warriors will mistake me for a boy and leave me alone. If you hadn't caught me in my nightgown, you would never have known I was a woman."

"You are not only brave, but very sly." He threw

397

back his head and laughed. It was a deep, humorous laugh.

Then, sobering without warning, he clutched her arm, jerking her to his side. His hand shot out, reached beneath her shirt and removed her pistol. "Do not be too brave and too sly," he said with a menacing smile, "or I will have to kill you."

A cold chill prickled the back of Cassandra's neck, for she sensed, correctly, that the warrior meant what he had said.

Sitting beside Roy, Cassandra watched the Sioux warriors gathered about the small campfire. They were talking in loud voices, and the one called Stalking Wolf was apparently agitated, for he kept waving his arms in angry gestures.

The Indians had tied their captives securely, and then had left them beneath a tall cottonwood a short way from the center of camp.

Cassandra was bone tired, and her whole body ached with fatigue. It had been an exhausting day, for the warriors had traveled nonstop. She and Roy had brought their saddle horses with them, and Cassandra had ridden Lady. Throughout the long, tiring day, she had been thankful for the mare. Lady's smooth gait was easier on Cassandra's delicate condition and lessened her chances of miscarrying.

The same as Roy's, Cassandra's hands were tied behind her, which added to her discomfort. She was also hungry, and needed the privacy afforded by bushes.

"Cassandra?" Roy murmured.

"Yes?" She turned and looked at him. His face was haggard.

"Hon, I'm sorry I let this happen to you."

"Roy, please don't blame yourself."

He smiled pensively, reflectively. "Tonight was supposed to be our wedding night."

"No," she whispered.

He studied her quizzically. "No?"

"I had changed my mind about marrying you."

"But why?" he asked pressingly.

She sighed miserably. "I love Dru too much."

"Cassandra, you're such a romantic fool." He spoke kindly, though.

"Yes, I know," she murmured. A sad smile lifted the corners of her mouth.

"Hon, I have some advice for you, and I want you to listen and take heed. That Sioux warrior who saved you from Stalking Wolf didn't do so benevolently. He wants you for himself. You realize that, don't you?"

"Yes, I realize it."

"Regardless of how much you love Jensen, don't refuse that warrior's advances. Fight him, and he'll kill you. Now, you might be telling yourself that you'd rather die than give yourself to a man other than Dru, but, hon, it's not just your life, but also your baby's."

"Roy, for my child's sake, I intend to stay alive. Dru may have taken my heart, but I still have my common sense. I'll protect my baby's life at any cost."

"Speaking of the damned savage," Roy uttered

399

irritably, "here he comes. He's probably coming for you. Cassandra, just let him have his way and get it over with. That way, you and the baby will remain alive and unharmed."

Apprehension filling her, Cassandra watched warily as the warrior came to her side, knelt, and untied her hands. Grasping her arm he helped her up.

"Come with me," he said flatly.

Submissively she allowed him to usher her away from camp and into the surrounding trees and shrubbery.

Pointing toward a large cluster of bushes, he said, "Go behind there, but do not try to run away. You cannot escape, and if you are foolish enough to try, you will be sorry."

"I'm not a fool!" she remarked. Then, moving quickly, she darted behind the shrubbery.

A few minutes later, she returned to find the warrior standing where she had left him.

Believing he was now going to molest her, she raised her chin proudly and met his watching eyes without wavering.

The Sioux discerned her thoughts, causing a wry smile to curl his lips. "You have much pride, yet I see in your eyes that you would not fight me. Why?"

"I don't fight battles I can't win."

"But you fought Stalking Wolf," he reminded her.

"That was different. He wanted me to grovel at his feet and beg for my life. If I must die, then I'll die with dignity."

His admiration for the beautiful white woman deepened. "What are you called?"

"Cassandra," she answered.

"When you become my wife, I will give you a Sioux name."

"Your wife!" she gasped.

"You will not be a slave. You are brave and have much pride. You will give me sons who will grow into fearless, proud warriors."

"And if I refuse to be a wife to you?"

"I will give you back to Stalking Wolf. He is very angry because I took you from him. When he is finished with you, if you are still alive, I will kill you myself."

She could see in his stoical eyes that he had spoken the truth, and she trembled imperceptibly.

"I will not take you now as my woman. I will wait until we reach my village. First, there will be a great celebration."

"Won't your chief object? Surely he doesn't want you to marry a white woman?"

"I am the chief of my village. I am called Chief Tall Tree."

Cassandra staggered backward as though she'd been struck physically. "Tall Tree!" she exclaimed incredulously.

"You have heard of me?"

"Yes, I have. I've also heard of your white wife, Yellow Flower. What will she say when she learns that you intend to take another white wife?"

"Yellow Flower is dead."

"Dead?" Cassandra cried.

"How do you know about Yellow Flower?" he

demanded.

"I heard about her through her son," Cassandra decided to answer.

"Badger?" he queried.

"Yes. He was rescued by the army. He told me that his mother married a Sioux warrior. He also told me that her name was Yellow Flower, and her Sioux husband was called Tall Tree."

Cassandra wasn't about to let Tall Tree know that she had really heard about Yellow Flower through Dru, and that he and the others were on their way to his village. There was a viciousness in Tall Tree that frightened her, and if she told him the truth, he might decide to search for Dru and his party and ambush them.

The warrior was perusing her skeptically. "Is that all you know about Yellow Flower?"

"Yes, that's all," she answered him.

He believed her. "Come; it is time to return to camp. You will cook something to eat."

He took her arm, and as he began leading her back through the shrubbery, she asked as though it were merely an afterthought, "Tall Tree, what was Yellow Flower's white name?"

"She was called Anita."

Cassandra's heart pounded. Oh, Dru! she cried with inner joy. Badge is your son! Johnny's alive!

Dru had decided to take the first watch and had taken up a position on the edge of a cliff. From this vantage point, he could see for miles.

A small, flickering fire, far in the distance, held

his attention. He suspected that the camp belonged to an itinerant band of Sioux. However, he knew quite a few white men were foolish enough to penetrate the Black Hills looking for gold. Only a small number of these men ever returned.

Dru dismissed the campfire. Sioux or gold-hunters, it made no difference to him. They weren't his concern.

A wolf's woeful howls sounded over the quiet landscape, and Dru spotted the wild beast perched on a high cliff. The animal's cries were soon answered by another's wolf's wailing.

The pair's howling could be heard down below in the distant campfire, and the eerie sounds had awakened Cassandra. Lying on a bed of blankets, her hands tied behind her, she tried to shift into a more comfortable position, but the effort was useless.

Once again, the wild beasts' woebegone intoning cut into the stillness of the night. Cassandra, feeling as dismal as the wolves sounded, tried vainly to will herself to fall back asleep.

Meanwhile Dru, gazing blankly down at the distant campfire, was comparing his own feelings to the wolves' forlorn cries. He decided that he felt lonelier than they sounded. The morose atmosphere was attuned to his mood, and he welcomed the wolves' melancholy music. His emotions were spent, dulled, and he felt empty inside.

The first wolf's howls, although repetitious, were no longer being answered. Dru, knowing it was a male beckoning for a mate, glanced at the lone wolf and said with a bitter smile, "Did she desert you, fella? I know how you feel. Damned if I don't!"

And it hurts like hell, his thoughts added.

Chapter Thirty-one

The second day's journey with the Sioux was even more demanding than the first. As they penetrated farther into the Black Hills, the terrain became steep and treacherous. The trip was exhausting, and by the end of the day, Cassandra was so tired that she could barely move.

Again, Tall Tree ordered her to cook the evening meal, and although she did so without complaining, she was so weary that the chore drained her completely.

Leaving the Indians eating hungrily, Cassandra moved languidly to Roy, who was sitting a short way from the campfire.

Reaching him, she dropped to her knees, then stretched out on a bed of high grass.

Roy longed to take her into his arms, but his hands were tied behind his back. "Are you all right?" he asked, concerned.

"Yes," she whispered feebly. "I'm just tired, and there's a gnawing pain in my back."

"Where exactly does it hurt?"

She moved a hand to the lower part of her back, rubbing the aching area gently. "It hurts right here."

"Damn, I hope you aren't going to lose the

baby," he mumbled.

That a backache could be related to her pregnancy hadn't crossed Cassandra's mind, and Roy's words sent her sitting up with a start.

"Oh, no!" she cried desperately.

Hoping to lighten her fear, Roy said quickly, "Hon, it probably doesn't have anything to do with your condition." He inwardly berated himself for speaking rashly, but he hadn't stopped to consider that Cassandra hadn't associated her backache with a possible miscarriage.

"Roy," she groaned intensely, "I just can't lose my baby! I just can't! I want this baby so much!"

"Cassandra," he began carefully, "maybe it'd be better if you did lose the baby. I mean, what kind of future will it have with the Sioux?"

"Future with the Sioux?" she exclaimed. "I don't intend to give birth in a Sioux village!"

"Surely you don't think you can escape!"

"Dru is on his way to Tall Tree's village. When he finds us there, he'll rescue us."

Roy chuckled thinly. "Hon, your faith in Dru is admirable, but unbelievably childish. In the first place, Tall Tree will probably keep us hidden and Dru will never even know we're there. And in the second place, Dru and the others will most likely be killed."

"They have Hawk to protect them," she pointed out. "He's kin to Tall Tree and has a lot of influence with him."

Roy shrugged tersely. "Well, for the Jensens' and Badge's sakes, I hope what you say is true. However, we're Tall Tree's captives and will remain so until he decides to kill me and marry you."

"Oh, Roy!" she said pressingly. "You mustn't give up hope! There's always a chance that we might escape!"

He grinned tenderly. "Cassandra, you're a survivor and a fighter. Even with the cards stacked against you, you hope to find that ace in the hole. Now, as for myself, when I know the cards are stacked, I fold my hand."

"As long as there's breath in my body, I won't give up hoping!" she remarked. "And I won't let you give up either. We'll get out of this. I don't know how, but we will!"

"Keep right on hoping, sweetheart," he said, a note of bitterness in his voice. "Because that hope will keep you alive, but as for me, I'm a dead man."

Suddenly, Stalking Wolf's harsh voice broke into their conversation. Looking at the fire, they watched as the warrior leapt to his feet, pointed in their direction and yelled furiously. Then, turning back to Tall Tree, the angry brave spoke in a demanding tone.

"What do you suppose is happening?" Cassandra asked.

"I don't know," Roy answered. "But I have a feeling Stalking Wolf is still upset over losing you."

Tall Tree, standing, responded calmly to Stalking Wolf's tirade. The irate warrior was apparently appeased, for a large smile crossed his face.

Continuing to look on, the two captives watched as Tall Tree left the fire and walked over to them.

Eyeing Roy, the chief uttered flatly, "Because I

407

took the woman away from Stalking Wolf, he demands that I give you to him in return. He is right to want payment. You are now Stalking Wolf's prisoner. He craves excitement, so he has decided to burn you at the stake."

"When's the party?" Roy asked, his voice somewhat choked.

"Tonight," Tall Tree replied.

"No!" Cassandra cried. "Tall Tree, please don't let Stalking Wolf do this!"

His eyes narrowing furiously, Tall Tree grumbled, "If you are not quiet, I will gag you!" Wheeling about, he returned to the fire.

"Oh, Roy!" Cassandra moaned brokenly.

"I told you I was a dead man, didn't I?" he remarked, smiling with a bravery he wasn't sure he felt. He hoped he'd die like a man and not turn into a groveling coward. The thought of dying painfully and slowly at the stake was terrifying.

"I wish the savages would just shoot me and get it over with," Roy continued hoarsely, "But hell no! They have to get their sick thrills watching me burn to death!"

Throwing her arms about Roy's neck, and holding him desperately close, Cassandra prayed tearfully, "Oh, God, help us! Help us!"

Dru was taking the first watch and had spotted the distant campfire. Now that he had seen it two nights in a row, he knew the travelers were journeying in the direction of Tall Tree's village. Wondering if it was a band of Tall Tree's warriors, he

408

considered slipping up to their camp to see if Tall Tree was among them. If it was a hunting party, Yellow Flower might be present, for the hunters often took their women with them.

His mind made up, Dru left his post and returned to camp. The others hadn't retired and were still sitting about the fire.

"What's wrong?" Virgil asked, surprised to see Dru.

"Probably nothing," he answered. "But last night I spotted a campfire and tonight I saw it again."

Hawk and Virgil both commented that during their watches they had also seen the fire.

Dru spoke to Hawk. "Do you think it could be a small party of hunters from Tall Tree's village?"

"It could be," he replied.

"If it is, Tall Tree could be with them."

"You want to sneak up to their camp and see?" Hawk asked.

"I was thinkin' about it, but I wouldn't know Tall Tree from any other warrior. I need you to come with me."

Hawk nodded his consent.

"We'll all go," Virgil remarked, standing.

Dru was about to tell his uncle that all of them going wasn't necessary, but Virgil was already heading for the horses.

"Come on, Badge," the elder Jensen said over his shoulder. "You can help me saddle up our ponies."

Bounding to his feet, the boy was quick to oblige.

* * *

Watching the Sioux warriors as they piled kindling around the base of a tree, Cassandra felt as though she were living through a nightmare. This couldn't be happening! It had to be a horrible dream! It was too horrid to be true!

But it is true, she thought distressfully. She inched closer to Roy and placed a hand on his arm. The consoling gesture was feeble, but words had failed her.

"God, I hope I die courageously," Roy groaned.

Cassandra could think of nothing appropriate to say. So, instead, she once again prayed for God's help.

"Cassandra," Roy began quietly, "since I'm going to die in a few minutes, I'd like to die with a clean conscience."

She looked at him questioningly.

"I knew Jubal Thurston," he said heavily. "We fought together during the war." Taking a deep breath, he told her about his dealings with Jubal, giving a full and candid account. Finishing, he said pleadingly, "Please believe me; when Dru found us, I had already decided to take you back to the trail drive. I wasn't going to hand you over to Thurston."

"I believe you," she murmured.

"Then you don't hate me?"

"No, I don't," she answered sincerely. "In fact, I can understand why you got involved with Jubal."

He smiled admirably. "Hon, you're a wonderful lady. However, you're too trusting."

"Why do you say that?"

"Because I have another confession to make."

"There's more?" she asked, surprised.

"I'm afraid so," he answered contritely. "At the hotel, when I ran into Dru in the lobby, he did tell me that his wife and son might be alive, but he didn't carry on about Anita. He said very little in regard to her. He was excited, but his excitement was over Johnny."

Cassandra was confused. "Then why did you tell me that he talked about Anita and told you that she was a beautiful bride and how much he loved her?"

Ashamed, he looked away from her searching gaze. "I wanted you and Dru to break up so that you'd turn to me."

Cassandra was silent for a long moment, then murmured defeatedly, "It doesn't matter. Your lies had more truth to them than you realize. Dru broke our engagement because he hopes to find Anita."

"I don't think so," Roy replied. "I don't know why he left you, but I doubt if it had anything to do with his wife."

Cassandra disagreed. "You're wrong, Roy. There was no other reason for Dru to act the way he did. He's never stopped loving Anita."

Drawing close to the campsite, Dru and the others reined in. Speaking to Badge and Virgil, Dru ordered, "You two stay here with the horses. Hawk and I will slip up to their camp."

Virgil wanted to object, but his nephew's tone had brooked no argument. "All right," he mumbled, acquiescing with strong reservations. He didn't trust Hawk and was seriously contemplating disobeying Dru's wishes.

The riders dismounted, and leaving Virgil and Badge behind, Dru and Hawk moved stealthily toward the distant fire.

Making their way soundlessly through the surrounding vegetation, the two men crept furtively to a full bush that was located close to the camp.

The Indians were chanting, and casting each other a quizzical look, Dru and Hawk wondered why the Indians were celebrating.

Parting the bush's heavy branches, the men spied into the camp, and the sight of the piled kindling answered their unspoken query. The Sioux were about to burn someone at the stake.

Dru's eyes scanned the area, and finding Cassandra and Roy, he gasped incredulously. Then, his shock waning, he cursed DeLaney for letting this happen to Cassandra. To be captured, the two had to be heading north instead of west. He wondered why they had changed direction.

Hawk had followed Dru's gaze, and his body had tensed at the sight of the woman.

Tearing his eyes away from Cassandra, Dru asked quietly, "Is Tall Tree present?"

"He is here," Hawk whispered, nodding in the chief's direction.

The instant Jensen broke their gaze to look at Tall Tree, Hawk drew his holstered gun and jabbed it into Dru's ribs.

"Damn you, Hawk!" Dru cursed in a hushed tone.

412

"Tall Tree is my cousin, and I cannot let you harm him."

"You sorry bastard!" he whispered harshly.

"Don't worry, compadre."

"Don't call me compadre. I'm not your friend."

Ignoring Dru's retort, Hawk said, "I don't think Tall Tree is about to kill your woman. She is too young and too beautiful. The kindling is for DeLaney."

"You don't know that for sure."

Hawk shrugged. "We will wait and see." Keeping his pistol held against Dru's ribs, he returned to watching the action.

Suddenly, Hawk's huge frame stiffened as a shotgun touched the back of his head.

Cocking both barrels, Virgil ordered quietly, "Hand over your gun, or I'll blow your head right off your shoulders."

Grinning coldly, Hawk remarked, "Old man, you move as soundlessly as a Sioux warrior."

"And I'm twice as mean as any of 'em. Now, hand over that gun."

Hawk gave his pistol to Dru. Turning, he saw that Virgil was accompanied by Badge.

Meanwhile, Dru, taking advantage of Hawk's turned back, raised the pistol and brought it down against the half-breed's skull.

As Hawk dropped to the ground, Virgil asked, "Did you hit 'im hard enough to kill 'im?"

"No, but he'll be out for a spell."

Stepping over Hawk, Virgil knelt beside Dru as he motioned for Badge to stay back and under cover.

413

Seeing the kindling, Virgil asked, "Who the hell are they gettin' ready to burn?" The question had barely passed his lips when, suddenly, he saw Cassandra and Roy. "Missy!" he groaned. Quickly, he regarded the Sioux. The two stacking kindling were unarmed. The others, standing off to one side, where carrying rifles.

Virgil spoke quietly. "If we give 'em a chance to throw down their weapons, do you think they'd do it?"

"No," Dru answered. "But there's only six of 'em. I think we can handle it, don't you?"

"I don't see why not," Virgil murmured with a grin.

Dru pointed to the chief. "That's Tall Tree. We want him alive."

"No problem," he uttered confidently.

"Cassandra," Roy whispered, "the Indians who are stacking the kindling left their rifles close to the fire. If I move quickly, I can reach the guns before anyone can stop me."

"But, Roy, you can't possibly shoot all of them before being killed."

"I know," he answered. "But if I have a rifle in my hands they're gonna have to kill me with a bullet. That's a helluva lot better than dying at the stake."

"Roy!" she moaned.

"I don't want to burn to death!" he uttered vehemently. "Now, while no one is watching, untie me!" When she hesitated, he demanded, "Do it!"

414

Complying, Cassandra reached shakily behind Roy and fumbled at the tight knots binding his hands.

"Hurry!" he whispered.

Steadying herself, Cassandra untied his hands, setting him free. She watched, her breath held, as DeLaney leapt to his feet and dashed toward the weapons.

Her eyes flew wildly to the Indians. Stalking Wolf spotted Roy, and as the warrior took aim, Cassandra screamed.

When a gunshot rang out, Cassandra expected to see Roy topple to the ground. It took a moment for her to realize that the shot hadn't come from Stalking Wolf's rifle but from the nearby bushes. Shocked, she watched as the warrior, dropping his gun, clutched at his bleeding chest before falling face down.

As a blasting barrage of gunfire thundered from the shrubbery, Cassandra, moving alertly, lay back and rolled to her side, burying her face in her folded arms.

The warfare ended within moments, and sitting up cautiously, Cassandra's astounded gaze swept fleetingly over the campsite. Stalking Wolf and two other warriors were on the ground, apparently dead. The three remaining Indians, including Tall Tree, had thrown down their weapons and surrendered.

Tall Tree was fuming, for surrending went against his grain. But he and his warriors had been sitting ducks, and to resist would have been suicidal. No, it was best to give up, then

415

wait for a chance to escape. He wondered if the ambushers were soldiers.

DeLaney, avoiding the flying bullets, had dropped to the ground, and he was still down when Cassandra reached him. Kneeling, she asked, "Roy, are you all right? Were you shot?"

"No, I'm fine," he answered.

Grasping his arm, Cassandra was helping him to a sitting position when Dru, Virgil and Badge emerged from the shrubbery.

"Dru!" Cassandra cried, hardly able to believe her own eyes.

As Virgil kept his gun on the warriors, Dru turned to Cassandra. His icy stare chilled her to the bone.

Her knees trembling, she got to her feet as Roy stood up beside her.

Regarding the pair with disdain, Dru asked gruffly, "How in the hell did you two manage to get captured by Tall Tree? You were supposed to be headin' west, not north."

"We changed our course," Roy replied.

"Apparently," Dru grumbled. "Where were you going?"

"Backwater," DeLaney answered.

"Why Backwater?"

Roy responded haltingly, "Well . . . we were planning to . . . to get married." Before he could explain that Cassandra had changed her mind, Dru wheeled about brusquely and walked over to Tall Tree. Grasping his arm, he led him away from his men.

"I hope you can speak English, because I have

some questions for you," Dru told the chief.

Crossing his arms over his chest, Tall Tree mumbled, "I will not answer your questions."

Furious, Dru demanded, "You'll answer me or I'll . . ." He was interrupted by a hand on his arm.

"Dru!" Cassandra said strongly.

He brushed her hand aside. "Go back to your fiancé, and stay the hell away from me!"

"Listen to me!" she said firmly. "Tall Tree told me that Yellow Flower is dead."

She studied his face intensely, looking for a sign of grief. She failed to find even a fleeting glimpse of sorrow. Evidently, she had been wrong about his feelings for Anita. Then why? Why had he broken their engagement, and why had he been so angry with her?

"What else do you know?" Dru asked.

"Yellow Flower's white name was Anita." Her eyes misty, she exclaimed with emotion, "Badge is your son!"

Chapter Thirty-two

Looking for Badge, Dru found the boy standing directly behind him. "Did you hear what Cassandra said?" he asked, grinning.

"I heard," Badge answered. A bright twinkle shone in his eyes.

Virgil was still holding his gun on the Indians, and Dru yelled, "Virgil, Badge is Johnny! Our boy's alive!"

Tears in his eyes, Virgil replied jubilantly, "That's the best news these old ears have ever heard!"

Dru gazed warmly at the boy. "Do you want to be called Badge or Johnny?"

"I don't know," he said uncertainly. "Badge, I guess. I'm kinda used to the name."

Dru nodded. "All right, son." He could barely keep his elation subdued. God, how he longed to embrace the boy! My son! he rejoiced inwardly. My son lives!

Watching quietly, Cassandra felt as though she were on the outside looking in. She wanted to share in Dru's joy, hold him in her arms and tell him she was happy that his son was alive. Considering how close she and Dru had once been, how could they now be so far apart? Why had Dru turned against her? What had she done to anger

418

him so?

Meanwhile, Dru, his feelings close to Cassandra's, wished he could share his joy with the woman he loved. He wanted to draw her into his arms and hold her tightly, but it wasn't his arms that she desired, but Delaney's.

Tall Tree, studying the people before him, turned his gaze to Dru and asked, "Were you Yellow Flower's white husband?"

"Yes, I was," he replied. "When I came across the burned wagon, whose bodies did I find?"

Tall Tree thought for a moment, then decided to cooperate and answer any questions the man might ask.

"I killed the man who was traveling with Yellow Flower," he said. "His body, and the bodies of a Mexican slave woman and her child were thrown inside the wagon and burned. I knew if Yellow Flower was being followed, then whoever was following would think that she and her child were dead."

Tall Tree grinned impudently, adding boastfully, "My plan worked. You found the burned bodies and believed your wife and son had been killed."

The chief's insolent grin set off Dru's explosive temper, and doubling his strong hand into a fist, he sent it smashing into Tall Tree's face. As the warrior stumbled backward, Dru delivered a tremendous blow to the man's stomach.

Tall Tree sank to the ground. Blood was oozing from his split lip, and his stomach hurt as though it had been hit by a sledgehammer.

"Get up, you sorry bastard!" Dru raged, his fists

doubled, ready to strike with the swiftness of a snake.

Handing Roy his shotgun, Virgil hurried to Dru, grasped his arm and pulled him away from Tall Tree.

Breaking free, Dru roared furiously, "Dammit, Virgil! Because of that no-good bastard, we spent over ten years thinking Johnny was dead!"

Dru's anguish was apparent, and Cassandra's heart ached for him.

"Virgil," Dru groaned, "remember the grief and the pain we went through?"

"Yes, I remember," Virgil answered somberly. "But beatin' the hell out of Tall Tree isn't gonna change anything."

"It'll give me satisfaction!" the younger Jensen growled.

"But it won't change anything!" Virgil repeated firmly.

Dru's temper cooled somewhat as he caught sight of Badge walking over to Tall Tree.

Badge waited until the chief got to his feet, then asked, "How long has my mother been dead?"

Suddenly, Dru felt ashamed. He'd been so wrapped up in his anger that he hadn't even thought about Anita.

"By white man's count," Tall Tree told Badge, "Yellow Flower has been dead two years."

"How did she die?" the boy asked.

"There was an outbreak of cholera in my village. Yellow Flower, and many of my people, took sick and died."

Badge, having no more questions, turned and

walked away.

However, Dru wasn't finished. Stepping back to Tall Tree, he asked, "When you abducted Anita and my son, why were you and your warriors so far south?"

"We were visiting with the Cheyenne. We traded them many pelts for horses. Did you think the Cheyenne killed your family?"

Virgil, listening, said crankily, "You left some of your arrows behind. Think Dru and I don't know the difference between a Cheyenne arrow and a Sioux?"

Watching the chief closely, Dru asked, "Was my wife happy living with you?"

Tall Tree decided to answer candidly. "At first she was happy. She liked the way I treated her."

"Treated her?" Dru questioned.

"Yellow Flower did not like for a man to be gentle. She liked to be treated roughly."

"Sounds like Anita," Dru grumbled reflectively.

Tall Tree's nose was still bleeding, so Virgil handed him a handkerchief.

Wiping away the blood, Tall Tree continued, "Yellow Flower's happiness did not last. She grew tired of her Sioux husband and began longing for her white husband. Many times, I thought about sending her back to you. Yellow Flower was a nagging squaw and there were many times when I wished that I had never taken her as my wife. When I married Yellow Flower, my father was still chief. He and the people did not want me to marry Yellow Flower. They were against me taking a white wife. But I stood my ground and married her

421

against their wishes. Later, when Yellow Flower turned into a nagging squaw, I could not send her back to you. If I had, I would have lost face with my father. The people would have laughed and told me that they had been right to oppose the marriage. I could not even take a second wife because she might have told the people that Yellow Flower complained and whined all the time. To keep Yellow Flower happy, I gave her many slaves to do all the work. Still, she complained and cried to return to the white man's life. When Yellow Flower died, I quickly took another wife. She gave me a daughter, then died giving birth to my dead son." He looked quizzically at Dru. "How did you learn that Badger is your son?"

"He has a locket that I gave to Anita."

"Yes," Tall Tree murmured pensively. "I remember the locket. One day, I found her looking at it. I took it away from her and threw it into the river. Badger must have fished it out."

"Why didn't you want Anita to have the locket?"

"Back then, I still loved Yellow Flower. I was jealous because I knew the locket was a gift from her white husband."

"Why did you sell my son into slavery?"

"I did not want Yellow Flower to have anything to remind her of her white husband." Tall Tree shrugged. "She did not seem to care. Yellow Flower loved no one but herself."

Cassandra had been listening raptly, but catching a movement in the shrubbery, she whirled about with alarm.

Hawk, rubbing his bruised head, made his way

out of the thicket and into the clearing. He was woozy, causing his steps to stumble.

"Hawk!" Tall Tree exclaimed, shocked to see his cousin.

The half-breed stumbled again, and worried about him, Cassandra hastened to his side.

The others, watching as she went to Hawk's aid, didn't notice that Stalking Wolf had moved.

The warrior was seriously wounded, and he knew his life was ebbing. As he spotted the woman, a demonic smile crossed his face. Recalling the way she had embarrassed him in front of his comrades, he decided that if he must die, then he'd take the woman with him.

Stalking Wolf's rifle lay within his reach, and grasping it, he rose quickly to his knees and took aim.

Cassandra had almost reached Hawk when he suddenly caught sight of Stalking Wolf. Moving incredibly fast, he shoved her aside. The half-breed's brawny arm knocked her to the ground simultaneously with the rifle's blast.

The bullet, meant for Cassandra, plunged into Hawk's chest. He staggered for a moment; then, falling, he landed beside Cassandra.

In the meantime, DeLaney, cocking Virgil's shotgun, pointed it at Stalking Wolf and fired. The gun's powerful force was fatal, and the Sioux warrior died instantly.

Cassandra got awkwardly to her knees and leaned over Hawk. The man's wound was ghastly, and she was afraid that he was dying.

Dru, hastening over, knelt beside Cassandra.

423

Hawk's eyes were open, and he gazed up at the pair through a blurry haze.

"Oh, Hawk!" Cassandra cried brokenly. "You saved my life! Why? Why?" She'd always had the feeling that the half-breed didn't especially like her.

"You are a good woman," he whispered, and before he could say anything more, his life was over.

Dru murmured surprisingly, "I think Hawk loved you. I didn't know the man was capable of such an emotion."

Then the unexpected sounds of horses sent Cassandra and Dru bounding to their feet.

Captain Wilson, accompanied by two Kiowa scouts and over a dozen soldiers, rode into the camp. Dismounting, the captain stepped to Dru.

"I received my orders to arrest Tall Tree the same day you left," the captain explained. "We're camped close by and heard your gunfire. I decided to bring a few men and investigate." He glanced quickly about the area, and taking note of the dead warriors, he remarked, "Looks like you ran into some trouble, but, apparently, you were able to handle it. But I heard a shot just a moment ago. What happened?"

Dru nodded toward Hawk. "One of the warriors wasn't dead, and he shot Hawk." Dru gestured toward Tall Tree. "You don't have to search any farther. There's your prisoner."

"Tall Tree?" Captain Wilson exclaimed.

"In the flesh," Jensen mumbled.

"Well, I'll be damned!" the officer declared.

Cassandra moved away from the captain and

Dru and took a stance at the edge of camp. She felt terrible about Hawk's death. Although the man had been a murderer, he had saved her life at the cost of his own.

Suddenly she felt a sharp twinge, and bending over she clutched at her stomach. The cramp passed, and drawing a deep breath, she straightened up.

God! she prayed fearfully. Please don't let me lose my baby! Please!

Captain Wilson and his troops took the prisoners back to their own camp. They also took the dead bodies. The captain would deliver the dead warriors and Hawk to the people in Tall Tree's village.

After the soldiers left, Virgil built up the fire and put on a pot of coffee. He kept a watchful eye on Dru and Cassandra and was annoyed at the way they kept purposefully avoiding each other. How in tarnation were they going to make up if they didn't talk?

Noticing Dru and Badge going off by themselves, Virgil decided this was the opportune moment for him to speak to Cassandra. She was sitting with Roy at the edge of camp.

"Missy!" he called. "I need to talk to you."

Cassandra stood up slowly, for the ache in her back had returned. Going to Virgil, she sat beside him.

"You want some coffee?" he asked.

"No, thanks," she declined softly.

He studied her thoughtfully. "Are you feelin' all

425

right?"

"I'm just tired, I guess." She sighed wearily.

"Missy," Virgil began firmly, "where the hell did Dru get the foolish notion that you're in love with DeLaney?"

She was genuinely confused. "I don't know."

"Well, think hard. He told me that he heard you tell DeLaney that you loved him. Did you?"

Concentrating deeply, her thoughts drifted back. Then, remembering, she explained, "When I was waiting for Dru to take me to dinner, Roy came to my hotel room. I was terribly depressed because I thought Dru was still in love with Anita. Roy took me into his arms, and needing his comfort, I rested my head on his shoulder. That's when he told me that he loved me. I had no idea that he felt that way. I told him that I loved him, too; then I made it quite clear that I only loved him as a friend."

Virgil smiled. "I think I've got it all figured out. I bet Dru came to your door, overheard you tellin' DeLaney that you loved 'im, then bein' the hard-headed jackass that he is, he stormed off without waitin' to hear the rest."

"Do you really think so?" she asked intensely.

"Yep, I sure do," he remarked with certainty.

"No wonder he's so angry with me," she murmured more to herself than to Virgil.

"Tell me, missy, where did you get the crazy notion that Dru was still in love with Anita?"

She preferred not to reveal Roy's treachery. "I just had the feeling," she murmured. "But now I know that I was wrong. If Dru was still in love with Anita, then when Tall Tree told him she was

426

dead, he wouldn't have taken her death so calmly."

"Dru got over Anita years ago. In fact, I don't think he was ever all that much in love with her. He was just a young, inexperienced man infatuated with a beautiful woman." He looked meaningfully at Cassandra. "He's not a young, inexperienced man anymore. He's full-grown and mature. When he told you that he loved you and wanted to marry you, he meant it with all his heart."

Cassandra sat silently. Although she'd been listening avidly, the constant pain in her lower back had her deeply worried. God, she hoped she wasn't about to lose her baby!

Virgil reached over and touched her hand. "Dru and Badge walked off together. They probably didn't go far. Give 'em a few more minutes to talk alone, then go to Dru and straighten everything out between you two."

"He won't listen to me," she said dejectedly.

"Then make 'im listen!" he declared.

Cassandra's eyes were downcast, and placing a hand under her chin, Virgil turned her face to his. "Missy," he began gently, "what's wrong with you? It's not like you to give up without a fight. Where's Casey's spunk, eh?"

She smiled, for his words had bolstered her spirits. However, the pain in her back had gone away only to be replaced by a sharp stomach cramp.

Keeping her discomfort from Virgil, Cassandra said, "In a few minutes, I'll do as you say and talk to Dru."

"It'll all work out fine," he told her cheerfully. "Just wait and see. You and Dru will patch up

427

your differences, and then everything will be hunky-dory."

Hunky-dory? she thought, bitterness mingling with her sorrow. I hardly think so! I'm losing my baby, and there's nothing I can do to prevent it!

Dru, watching Badge in the soft moonlight, asked gently, "Son, do you mind tellin' me exactly how you feel?"

He didn't quite understand. "What do you mean?"

"I have this feelin' that you aren't really happy about bein' Johnny."

"I'm happy, Dru. Honest, I am. It's just that . . ."

"Go on," Dru encouraged.

"I don't know what I'm supposed to do."

"Supposed to do?" Jensen repeated archly.

"Am I supposed to suddenly start treatin' you like my father when, in a way, I still think of you as my trail boss?"

"Why don't you just treat me as a friend," Dru smiled. "I'll never again be your trail boss, but, in time, I hope you'll start thinkin' of me as your real father."

"Do you think of me as Johnny?" Badge asked pointedly.

Dru was warmly amused. "Touché, Badge. I guess it's gonna take time for both of us to get used to it."

Moving to the youngster, Dru placed his hands on Badge's shoulder. "But you are my son, and I

428

love you."

Taking Dru by surprise, Badge threw himself into his father's arms. Close to tears, he murmured sincerely, "I love you, too . . . Pa."

Dru was so emotionally touched that it took a moment for him to find his voice. "My son! Thank God, you're alive!"

Stepping back, Badge looked at Dru and remarked somewhat hesitantly, "I guess right now I'd be the happiest person on Earth if I knew I was gonna have Cassandra as a stepmother. What happened between you two? Why was she travelin' with Mr. DeLaney? I thought you two were gonna get married."

"She's in love with another man," Dru replied.

"No, I'm not!" Cassandra's voice suddenly remarked. She had approached the two so quietly that they hadn't heard her.

Badge's eyes flitted back and forth from Cassandra to Dru; then, knowing he should leave them alone, he made a hasty departure.

"You're not only untrustworthy, but you're also fickle," Dru grumbled. "Does DeLaney know you're here?"

The sharp, fleeting cramps had returned, and grimacing imperceptibly, Cassandra replied collectedly, "My whereabouts are of no concern to Roy."

"Of course not!" Dru answered sarcastically. "After all, he's only your fiancé!"

"Dru Jensen, did anyone ever tell you that you're a hardheaded jackass?"

"Virgil makes a point of remindin' me of it ever so often."

"Well, he's right!" Another cramp hit, this one more powerful than the others. Grief for her child tearing into her heart, she cried furiously, "Furthermore, you're an unfeeling cad!"

"Unfeeling?" he questioned gruffly.

"Yes! You're so wrapped up in yourself that you don't even want children! I'm surprised you cared enough to claim Badge!" Cassandra wanted to bite her tongue. Why was she spouting such hateful remarks? She hadn't come here to argue with Dru, she had come to make up with him. But his rejection of their own child had filled her heart with bitterness.

"Where the hell did you get the idea that I don't want children?" he demanded.

"That night when you were drinking, you told me that you never wanted children."

Dru couldn't recall what he had said, but he didn't doubt Cassandra's accusation. "I didn't mean it the way it sounded," he replied calmly. "I suppose the whiskey sharpened my tongue. It's not that I don't want children. I can't rid myself of the fear of losing one or more of them. Even now that I've found Johnny, I'm still afraid."

Dru could hardly believe that he had opened up and confessed his deepest fear. Now that it was all over between them, why had he found it necessary to be so damned honest?

"Why didn't you tell me you felt this way?" she pleaded.

He answered truthfully, "I didn't want you to know that I was weak."

"Weak?" she exclaimed, astounded. "Considering

what you went through with Johnny, your fear of losing a child is only natural." She was about to say more when a penetrating cramp doubled her over.

Dru stepped quickly to her side. "Casey? What's wrong?"

Perspiration started beading up heavily on her brow, and dark spots began darting crazily before her eyes. A loud ringing roared through her ears as, light-headed, she swayed unsteadily into Dru's arms. Then, fainting, she sank into total blackness.

Hurrying, Dru carried her to camp. "Badge!" he yelled. "Saddle my horse!"

Virgil, grabbing a blanket, spread it out beside the fire, and as Dru placed Cassandra on it, he asked urgently, "What happened?"

"She fainted," Dru answered, his face etched with worry. "Captain Wilson mentioned that one of the fort's doctors is ridin' with him. A Major Devlin. As soon as Badge gets my horse saddled, I'll take Cassandra to Wilson's camp."

"Jensen, what in the hell did you do to her?" Roy suddenly demanded angrily. He was on the verge of kneeling beside Cassandra when Virgil stood and shoved him aside.

"DeLaney, keep your mouth shut. This is a bad time to get Dru riled."

"Oh, yeah?" Roy shouted. "Well, someone needs to knock some sense in his head!"

Dru rose slowly. "Do you think you're the man for the job?"

"Stop it!" Virgil ordered, his gaze darting to both of them. "If you've got such a hankerin' to fight, then save it for later! Right now, we got to get Missy to the doctor."

Virgil's words cooled Dru's temper, and as Badge led his horse over, Dru told his uncle, "Hand her up to me."

He mounted quickly, watching as Virgil lifted Cassandra. Handing her to Dru, he said, "We'll saddle our horses and join you at the soldiers' camp."

Virgil slapped his hand against the stallion's flank, and Dru's horse took off with a bolt.

Holding Cassandra securely, Dru headed out of camp. It was a cloudless night, and as he gazed down into Cassandra's pale face, he could see her clearly in the moonlight.

A soft moan escaped her lips as her eyes fluttered open.

Pulling her tightly against his chest, Dru murmured huskily, "Darlin', you're going to be all right. I'm takin' you to the doctor."

Cassandra knew she should let Dru know that she was pregnant and was probably miscarrying, but she couldn't bring herself to tell him.

Chapter Thirty-three

Dru paced nervously beside the covered wagon. The doctor had been inside with Cassandra for only thirty minutes, but to Dru it seemed interminably long.

Roy, standing between Virgil and Badge, watched Jensen as he walked back and forth. He wondered if Cassandra had told Dru that she was pregnant. He frowned irritably, for in his opinion, Dru didn't deserve Cassandra. However, there was no accounting for love. Apparently, Jensen was the man Cassandra wanted. She had made her choice between the two of them, and he might as well be a good sport about it. Furthermore, Cassandra had forgiven him for deceiving her; in return, he'd help her win back Dru.

His mind made up, Roy stepped to Dru and said firmly, "Jensen, we need to talk. Privately."

"You don't have anything to say that I want to hear," Dru mumbled angrily.

"If you don't like what I say, you can always use it as an excuse to punch me in the nose." He gestured toward the distance. "Shall we?"

Speaking to Virgil, Dru said, "If the doctor comes out before I get back, send Badge to find me. DeLaney and I are gonna have a talk."

Roy took off, and Dru followed. Coming upon a clearing at the edge of camp, DeLaney paused.

Eyeing his rival adversely, Dru grumbled, "All right, start talkin', but make it fast."

"Earlier, when I told you that Cassandra and I were going to Backwater to get married, you didn't give me time to tell you that she had changed her mind about marrying me. She told me she couldn't marry me because she's too much in love with you."

"DeLaney, at the hotel, I came to Cassandra's room to take her to dinner. The door was ajar, and I not only saw her in your arms, but I also heard her tell you that she loved you."

Roy smiled. "So that's why you broke your engagement! You thought she was in love with me! Obviously, you didn't eavesdrop long enough to hear what else she had to say. She made a point of letting me know that she merely loved me as a friend. Furthermore, the only reason she was in my arms was because she was upset. She thought you were still in love with Anita."

Dru was surprised. "Why would she think that?"

Roy answered hesitantly. "Well, that's another story, and one in which I admit that I was mostly to blame. However, at the moment, it's not important."

"I don't understand. If Cassandra isn't in love with you, then why did she agree to marry you?"

DeLaney met Dru's puzzled gaze and answered candidly, "Because she's pregnant."

"What?" Jensen gasped.

"She's pregnant with your child," Roy said. "She

agreed to marry me to protect her baby. And although it was the best solution to her problem, when push came to shove, she couldn't go through with it. She's too head-over-heels in love with you." Roy's visage hardened. "And now she's in that wagon losing the baby you never wanted!"

Dru, taking Roy by surprise, whirled about and walked away swiftly. DeLaney watched for a moment, then followed.

Dru reached the wagon just as the doctor stepped outside. Moving to him, Dru asked, "How is she?"

"She's going to be fine," Major Devlin answered.

"And the baby?" Dru murmured unsteadily. "Did . . . did she lose it?"

"Baby!" Virgil exclaimed, astounded.

"No, she didn't lose the child," the doctor was glad to reply. "She was never in immediate danger of miscarrying."

"But she was doubled over with pain!" Dru remarked.

"Miss Stevenson told me that she hasn't eaten a bite in over two days. And before that, she had eaten very little. Her stomach cramps are not surprising."

"But the pains in her back," Roy cut in.

"They are most likely caused by strenuous traveling. I understand that the Sioux didn't stop to let her rest."

"Why did she faint?" Dru asked.

"Exhaustion," the doctor replied. "Miss Stevenson needs at least a week of complete rest, peace and quiet, and nourishing food." His voice became severe. "Considering what that young lady has had to endure, it's a wonder that she didn't miscarry!"

The doctor paused, eyeing Dru somewhat reprovingly. Then, deciding that Jensen wasn't entirely to blame, he continued on a friendlier note, "On our way here, we passed an abandoned trapper's cabin. I suggest that you take her there for a week's rest. Captain Wilson plans to take the dead warriors back to their people, but on our way back to the fort, I'll stop by the cabin and check on Miss Stevenson."

"I know where the cabin is," Dru replied. "I'll take her there in the morning."

"Then it's settled," the doctor remarked.

"May I see her now?" Dru asked.

"Yes, of course. I'll find the cook and have him dish her up a large bowl of stew."

"And I'll make sure she eats every bite," Dru declared before climbing inside the wagon.

Cassandra was lying on a bed of blankets. Dru sat down beside her and took her hand into his. He studied her beautiful face for a moment, then asked, "Why didn't you tell me that you're pregnant?"

She swallowed heavily, answering, "I didn't think you wanted our baby."

"Well, I do want the child," he said intensely. "And I want you, too."

Cassandra smiled timorously. "Dru, you aren't just saying that, are you? I mean, considering . . . ?"

His hand tightened about hers. "Casey, I love you. I swear to God, I love you!" He moved his

436

hand to her stomach. "And I love our baby."

Bending over, he kissed her lips lightly. Then he quickly told her about the discussion he'd had with Roy. Finishing, he murmured deeply, "I was wrong about you and DeLaney. I was so damned wrong!"

"Dru, I'm also to blame. I was mistaken about your feelings for Anita. I was so certain that you still loved her."

"I love only you," he whispered.

Cassandra's heart pounded joyfully. "Oh, Dru, I love you! I love you more than life itself!"

"Double that and that's how much I love you."

She held out her arms, and he went into her embrace, holding her as though he'd never let her go.

"Dru," she murmured emotionally, "I was so afraid that I was losing our baby. But the doctor said there's nothing wrong with me that nourishment and rest won't cure."

Gently, he moved out of her arms. "Honey, when you were riding with Tall Tree, didn't he allow you to eat?"

"Yes, in fact, I even did the cooking. Although I was hungry, starved, I couldn't eat. I was so upset and frightened that I couldn't even chew my food, let alone swallow it. My appetite was sorely lacking even before Tall Tree captured Roy and me. I was so depressed over losing you."

"I'm sorry that I hurt you," he moaned.

"Dru, we're both at fault. Hereafter, we must always tell each other what we're thinking and what we're feeling."

His smile askew, he replied, "It's a deal."

They sealed their bargain with a deep, lingering kiss.

"There's a cabin about five miles from here," Dru told her. "In the morning, I plan to take you there so you can rest for a week. You'll spend the entire week lying in bed and taking care of yourself and our baby."

She smiled saucily. "Sounds heavenly."

"I don't want you riding to the cabin on horseback, so I'll make a travois."

"Dru, surely that isn't necessary."

"It's very necessary," he remarked. His hand returned to her stomach. "You and my child are precious cargo . . . very precious."

"Excuse me," Major Devlin interrupted, stepping inside. He carried a bowl of steaming stew.

Taking the food, Dru handed it to Cassandra and said, "Young lady, you're going to eat every bite."

"Yes, sir!" she answered gaily, sitting up. "I will gladly eat all of it, for not only am I starved, but I'm eating for two."

The next morning, Dru and Badge made a travois and fastened it to Lady. Then Dru carried Cassandra from the wagon and placed her on the Indian-style conveyance.

Virgil, Badge and Roy planned to ride to the cabin with Dru and Cassandra; then Virgil and Badge would escort Roy back to his wagon. The Sioux had taken the team, but they hadn't bothered to steal anything from inside the wagon. Unless someone had come upon the abandonded wagon, Cassandra's things would still be inside. Virgil planned to get them and bring them back to the cabin. Roy's team had been returned to him, and he intended to go through with his original plan to travel to San Francisco.

The journey to the cabin was short, and even with Roy's team and the packhorses, it didn't take long to get there.

Arriving, Dru decided to check the interior's condition and hurried inside.

Roy dismounted and walked over to the travois and knelt beside Cassandra. Until now, he hadn't had a chance to talk alone with her.

"Hon," he began gently, "I'm anxious to get to my wagon, so Virgil, the boy and I plan to head on out. I just wanted to tell you goodbye and wish you happiness." He grinned somewhat tentatively. "I know how much you love Jensen, and I'm happy for you. Really, I am."

"Thank you, Roy." She reached over and squeezed his hand. "Take good care of yourself."

"I will," he replied.

She wanted to tell him to keep in touch, but she couldn't picture Roy DeLaney writing to a lost love. She smiled warmly. "From what I understand, San Francisco is a bachelor's paradise. You'll think you died and went to heaven."

He chuckled softly, leaned over and kissed her brow. "Goodbye, hon." He was getting to his feet as Dru stepped out of the cabin.

"What does it look like?" Virgil asked Dru.

"It's in pretty good shape."

"We're gonna keep on movin'," Virgil remarked. "We should be back in about four days."

Roy took a step toward the horse, but turning around, he went over to Dru and offered him his hand. "Good luck, Jensen."

Dru accepted his handshake. "The same to you, DeLaney."

Obeying the doctors orders and Dru's demands, Cassandra remained in bed. Dru doted on her as though she were an invalid, and even though she enjoyed his constant attention, and relished her needed rest, she soon grew restless. Active by nature, Cassandra was overly anxious for Major Devlin to stop by the cabin and pronounce her completely recovered. She knew Dru wouldn't let her out of bed until the doctor said it was all right.

Virgil and Badge returned on time, delivered Cassandra's belongings, then left the following morning without even telling her that they were leaving. Their curt departure had annoyed her. When she asked Dru where they had gone, he merely told her that they had decided to ride to Fort Laramie. Cassandra had insisted on knowing why they hadn't told her goodbye. Dru's answer hadn't soothed her ruffled feathers, for he had tersely informed her that they hadn't found it necessary.

Cassandra and Dru had been at the cabin six days when the soldiers and Major Devlin arrived. Following a thorough examination, the doctor announced her fully recovered.

Cassandra was elated. Now, she and Dru could return to the fort, get married, then travel to the Bar-J. She could hardly wait to begin her new life. Mrs. Dru Jensen! The title itself was thrilling!

The soldiers and Major Devlin had arrived early in the afternoon, and eager to get back to the fort, they only stayed a couple of hours.

The moment Cassandra heard them riding away, she bounded from bed. Still in her cotton night-gown, she hurried outside. Dru was standing on the edge of the porch, and turning, he took her into his arms.

"Dru, let's leave now!" she exclaimed.

"Leave?" he questioned, releasing her.

"Yes! I'm anxious to get to the fort so we can be married." Her eyes pleaded with his. "Please!"

"We'll leave in the morning," he replied, his tone final.

She pouted attractively. "Oh, Dru, aren't you as eager as I am to get married?"

He laughed heartily. "Casey, I'm probably even more eager."

"How can you say that when you're willing to wait another day?"

"You'll see," he replied evasively.

Then, as if on cue, they heard Virgil's voice calling from a close distance, "Dru? It's us, so don't get trigger happy when we ride up to the cabin!"

Taking Cassandra's arm, Dru led her off the porch and pointed in the direction the troops had taken.

Cassandra, thoroughly confused, watched as Virgil, Badge, and a soldier pulled up to exchange

441

words with Captain Wilson. "Why did Virgil and Badge come back? And why do they have a soldier with them?"

"That's not just any soldier," Dru answered, grinning expansively. "That, my dear, is the fort's chaplain. He's here to marry us."

"Dru!" she cried, flinging herself into his arms. "So that's why Virgil and Badge left so mysteriously. You had this all planned. How do you suppose Virgil managed to convince the chaplain to come so far?"

"Considering how damned unrelenting Virgil can be, the chaplain probably agreed just to shut him up." Dru hugged her tightly. "Don't you think you should hurry and put on one of your dresses? You don't want to get married in your nightgown, do you?"

"Heavens no!" she exclaimed, whirling about and heading toward the cabin. Reaching the porch, she called over her shoulder, "Keep everyone outside for a while because I'm also going to take a bath!"

She darted inside. Never in her life had Cassandra been so happy!

If Cassandra had been married in a church with dozens of guests, she couldn't have been more delighted than she was marrying Dru in the rural cabin with only Virgil and Badge as witnesses. A formal wedding, bridesmaids and a beautiful wedding gown wouldn't have made her one bit happier.

Virgil had remembered to bring champagne and glasses, and following the ceremony, one of the

442

bottles was opened and toasts were made to the bride and groom.

Then, none too discreetly, Virgil hinted that he, Badge and the chaplain should leave and make camp about a mile or so down the road. Cassandra and Dru could meet up with them in the morning for the return trip to the fort.

Agreeing, the chaplain wished the couple happiness; then, as Dru was escorting him to the door, Badge went to Cassandra.

Hesitantly, he said, "Cassandra, I don't guess I should call you Ma since you aren't even old enough to be my mother."

Cassandra, eight years his senior, replied, "All the same, I wish you would."

Badge's joy was evident. "You mean, you don't mind?"

"I'd be honored," she assured him, leaning over and kissing his cheek.

Walking up to them, Virgil said to Cassandra, "Missy, I don't reckon I have to tell you that this is a happy day for me."

She hugged him affectionately. "Virgil, I love you!"

He blushed beneath his full beard. "I love you, too, missy. And from here on out, you better start takin' good care of yourself and my new great-nephew or great-niece."

"I will," she promised.

His gaze swept over her. She was wearing the pink gingham gown with the puffed sleeves. "Missy, you're a beautiful bride. That nephew of mine is a lucky man." Then, nudging Badge with his elbow,

Virgil said hastily, "Come on, boy, let's leave the bride alone with her groom."

As Dru was showing everyone outside, Cassandra rushed into the bedroom, where she quickly removed her clothes and slipped into her sheer dressing gown.

She had just finished the exchange when Dru entered, carrying a bottle of champagne and two glasses. Her gown merely shadowed her desirable curves and his gaze raked over her passionately.

Placing the bottle and glasses on the dresser, he said huskily, "The drinks can wait."

He came to her side, lifted her in his arms and place her gently on the bed. Impatient to make love to his pretty bride, he undressed hastily, letting his discarded clothes fall to the floor in a disorderly heap.

Cassandra's eyes, glazed with love, watched as her husband came into her outstretched arms. "Oh, Dru," she whispered raspingly. "I love you so much."

"I love you, Mrs. Jensen," he murmured before capturing her lips in a long, demanding kiss.

With anxious hands, Dru removed her gown and flung it to the floor. His lips returned to hers, and his passion sent her mind swirling and her heart pounding.

His mouth blazed a feverish path down her slender neck to her soft breasts, kissing one and then the other. Tantalizingly, his lips moved over her stomach and then downward. Responding, Cassandra arched her hips as strong, vivid pleasure coursed through her.

Raising himself up, he stretched out beside her. She molded her body to her husband's, and his lips seared hers in an aggressive, passion-stirring kiss.

Their hands feathered over each other's bodies, glorying in the feel of warm, naked flesh.

Their need rose to fever pitch, and moving over her, Dru entered her deeply, his inserted maleness filling her with ecstasy.

"I love you," she whispered, locking her ankles over his back.

"Casey," he moaned hoarsely. "I love you. . . . You're my life, my reason for existing."

Engulfed in total rapture, they made love wildly, their thrusts demanding and all-consuming. Together, they were transported to a plane of ultimate fulfillment, descending it with breathless satisfaction.

Dru kissed her tenderly; then, leaving the bed, he moved to the dresser, filled the glasses with champagne and returned.

Sitting up, Cassandra leaned back against the sturdy headboard. She had been surprised to find the bed in such amazingly good condition. She wondered who owned this cabin, and if they had really abandoned it. More than likely, the owner had taken a trip and had every intention of returning.

Raising his glass, Dru said softly, "Here's to us, Mrs. Jensen."

She started to take a drink, then murmured dubiously, "Considering my condition, I wonder if I should have champagne. It might not be good for the baby."

"You're right," Dru remarked, taking the glass from her hand and placing it on the floor. "From now on, you get only milk."

She giggled merrily. "Darling, I do hope you don't become so protective that you become a nuisance."

"You're damned right I'm going to be a nuisance. I'm not only going to be an overprotective father, but I'll also be an overprotective husband. So you and any children we have will just have to bear with me."

"Dru, I want lots of children," she declared eagerly.

He quirked a brow. "How many is a lot?"

"Oh, at least a half a dozen. Maybe more."

"Lord!" he groaned. "With that many kids to worry about, I'll be gray-haired before my time."

She smiled pertly. "But just think of all the fun we'll have making them." Leaning over him, she took his glass and placed it on the floor beside hers. Seductively, she whispered, "After all, creating children is half the fun."

He grinned wryly. "I think we already created one."

"Yes, but we mustn't get out of practice. We might forget."

"Fat chance of that!" he retorted, his smile spreading sensually.

Wrapping his arms about her, he raised himself up and drew her beneath him. Gazing down into her green eyes, he murmured, "Darlin', if you want lots of children, then if the good Lord's willin', we'll have them."

446

"Promise?" she asked, smiling happily.

"I promise, and I never break a promise." He kissed the tip of her nose, winked, and said, "I love ya, Casey."

DISCOVER DEANA JAMES!

CAPTIVE ANGEL   (2524, $4.50/$5.50)
Abandoned, penniless, and suddenly responsible for the biggest
tobacco plantation in Colleton County, distraught Caroline Gil-
lard had no time to dissolve into tears. By day the willowy red-
head labored to exhaustion beside her slaves . . . but each night
left her restless with longing for her wayward husband. She'd
make the sea captain regret his betrayal until he begged her to
take him back!

MASQUE OF SAPPHIRE   (2885, $4.50/$5.50)
Judith Talbot-Harrow left England with a heavy heart. She was
going to America to join a father she despised and a sister she
distrusted. She was certainly in no mood to put up with the insulting actions of the arrogant Yankee privateer who boarded her
ship, ransacked her things, then "apologized" with an indecent,
brazen kiss! She vowed that someday he'd pay dearly for the liberties he had taken and the desires he had awakened.

SPEAK ONLY LOVE   (3439, $4.95/$5.95)
Long ago, the shock of her mother's death had robbed Vivian
Marleigh of the power of speech. Now she was being forced to
marry a bitter man with brandy on his breath. But she could not
say what was in her heart. It was up to the viscount to spark the
fires that would melt her icy reserve.

WILD TEXAS HEART   (3205, $4.95/$5.95)
Fan Breckenridge was terrified when the stranger found her near-
naked and shivering beneath the Texas stars. Unable to remember
who she was or what had happened, all she had in the world was
the deed to a patch of land that might yield oil . . . and the fierce
loving of this wildcatter who called himself Irons.

*Available wherever paperbacks are sold, or order direct from the
Publisher. Send cover price plus 50¢ per copy for mailing and
handling to Penguin USA, P.O. Box 999, c/o Dept. 17109,
Bergenfiled, NJ 07621. Residents of New York and Tennessee
must include sales tax. DO NOT SEND CASH.*